# TWO SHIPS

# TWO SHIPS

JAMES H. REDWOOD

# 1 6 3 2

The rock lay on the steep hillside overlooking the green valley. Grainy and covered in gray moss, it had remained in this place for more than ten thousand years. It was hard and largely immune to the rain that lashed at it from time to time. It had traveled nearly three fourths of the way around the earth's surface since its original formation some two hundred million years ago in the Mesozoic era.

The sides of the rock were lined with elongated, narrow seams that laid together like wrinkled bed sheets. These were layers of sedimentary deposit that had melted into one another under the tremendous forces that formed it. They had been pushed together and raised vertically, folding on top of themselves as they were squeezed with the strength of shifting tectonic plates. Molded, pressed, and heat treated in the earth itself, a roughly oval-shaped boulder of over two hundred pounds per square foot of dense granite emerged. This intense pressure pushed a bulging vein of quartz to the surface of the rock. It ran along the side and sparkled when the sun hit it.

At the base of the rock, in what had once been a muddy tropical coastline, were three fossilized footprints, frozen in time. They looked markedly like those of a chicken, except so large that the chicken would have been six feet tall. These were made by a type of Dromaeosaur known as Ornithomimus. A precursor to birds, it had colorful feathers and a toothy beak. It stretched out to over three meters and ran with long-legged strides.

In the early Jurassic Period, the Ornithomimus stepped into the mud next to the rock. It took three small steps as it tilted its head, listening for the sounds of the tiny rodents it hunted. On its next step, it completed a one-legged hop up onto the rock. This made the track deeper, and more clearly imprinted in the mud. The footprints remained undisturbed, and the mud fossilized into stone. The footprints and the rock traveled together on the shifting surface of the earth for sixty million years.

On this green and forested hillside overlooking the valley, nearly all of the Mesozoic rocks had been eroded by the massive glaciers that had frozen their way down from the Northern Canada Plateau. This repeating process pulverized them into the soil. The rock and its companion footprints slipped beneath the surface of the earth and were only exposed by the last glaciation period, a mere ten thousand years earlier. As the hillside of shale, limestone, and sandstone eroded into brown soil over thousands of years, the rock and the footprints had drifted to the limit of what the slope of the hill would contain. Someday, the one remaining Mesozoic rock in this region would come tumbling down. There was no way to know if that would happen this year or in a thousand years. Eventually, and as always, gravity would win.

The valley below the rock was shielded by trees. Maple, oak, ash, and chestnut spread their branches outward like an umbrella, protecting the rich ecosystem that thrived below. A wetland of streams and ponds stretched out across the valley floor, constructed with branches and trunks felled by the teeth of the many thousands of beavers that lived there. Three feet long and nearing seventy pounds as adults, their teeth were built for chewing, and their fur was waterproof. It was used to make a felt cloth that was ideal for constructing hats and clothing in a damp European climate.

The demand for that fur would continue to grow over the next one hundred and twenty years. The supply for the initial demand was soon trapped out of Europe. A new source would be sought. As information about where to find the beaver spread, adventurers and wealth seekers set forth to find their fortune in the green valleys of the New World.

# Chapter 1

# PIOTR NOWAK

The vomiting finally stopped after three days. He was thankful for that. His stomach had begun to empty its meager contents about five hours after leaving Saint-Malo. Now, on the third day of the journey to the New World, Piotr Nowak was certain that he could not throw up anymore. He looked back at the deck of the ship moving against the horizon of the deep blue ocean and felt a surge of nausea hit again. His sandy brown hair was near shoulder length and flopped over his ears. Blessed with markedly straight and healthy teeth, he had used them to eat and drink his fill the night before the departure. The crewmen who brought him into the dockside pub the previous evening consumed robustly and sang songs of bravery at sea. They had been working nonstop for three weeks to prepare the ship, oiling hinges, patching damaged areas, stitching cloth sails, and loading and packing the contents needed to make a voyage across the Atlantic. They had slept on the ship or in the public houses lining the dock front.

He turned and held his head over the railing of the foredeck for what felt like the hundredth time, but nothing would come out. Just silent retching, and a bile taste from the back of his throat.

Flagger, the first mate, looked at him. "Just keep working, boy; this will pass within the day."

He knew that Flagger would say this, as he had been saying it for three days. Dutifully, he went back to his work. He was charged with checking every beaver trap in the hold for functionality. He had never seen

5

a beaver trap prior to this journey. It occurred to him that he had never actually seen a beaver, either. Flagger had been his guide as they worked their way through the pile of traps, four hundred in all, fixing loose springs, tightening loose parts, oiling stuck hinges, and testing them on a thick stick of hard French oak found on the dockside before departure.

"These here are all good," Flagger grunted in his Basque-accented French, and he tossed the last trap into a box piled with traps. "Put them with the other goods and bring up another pile of bad ones."

They had separated the traps based on the eyeball test at the beginning.

Piotr looked up from his retching with a "Yes sir," as he turned to gather the box of traps and go below deck. Flagger was old, scarred, wiry, and had the thickest, heaviest beard that Piotr had ever seen. He carried a large Indian kukri knife with a leather-wrapped wooden handle he had obtained in a trade many years ago. His long gray-and-black beard was often holding bits of food and obscured his mouth. This sometimes made his speech seem as if it mysteriously emanated from the air around him when he spoke, which was infrequently. His red knit hat partially covered his mass of long, grey, curly hair, and it kept him warm on deck in the cold North Sea. Piotr had seen him move enough cargo with his large hands to know that he was uncommonly spry for an elder statesman among the crew of the *St. Longinus*, the ship they sailed.

Piotr did not have to use the title "sir" with Flagger, but he did so out of respect. Since his arrival to the *St. Longinus's* crew some three weeks earlier, Flagger had made a point of looking out for him. For more than a year before, Piotr had learned what it was like to be on his own.

He carried the heavy wooden box down to the hold, carefully maneuvering the steps as the ship swayed on wind and waves. His arms and back strained through his linsey-woolsey shirt, but he was agile with youth. Not large in stature, he had always been strong. Around him, the ship was alive with the movement of sailors working. Men moved in all directions and somehow stayed out of each other's way. He had been yelled at and cursed the first few days at sea for walking into the paths of other men as they worked in unison to operate the ship. To Piotr, they looked like they were all on the stage of a theatre in a grand dance, moving together and apart but in time with the rocking of the ship. He had seen a play, once, when he was seven years old.

Despite his illness, he liked the spray of the salty sea water and the smell of the air when on the deck or foredeck. He was not so keen on the smells below deck. The sleeping quarters reeked of body odor, leather, and tobacco. The hold and the galley smelled of wet wool, copper, sweat, and sea salt. He did appreciate the constantly bubbling stew pot over a small, contained cooking station in the galley. That stew, known as burgoo, was the primary food source for the crew.

Eggard, the Danish ship's cook, was constantly working to feed the crew and maintain the supplies. His broken French did not allow him to understand the insults from the sailors about his stew, nor did they understand his curses and insults in Norwegian. This was fortunate for the crew, as Eggard was the most immense person Piotr had ever seen. Not only tall, at least a head taller than Piotr's father had been, he was also thickly built. Eggard was fond of wearing a dirty white linen tied over his completely bald head, and he would frequently wipe his massive hands on it, leaving it stained with dirt and grease. Eggard also constantly wore a brown leather tool belt that he had made from the remnants of a saddle. Loops were fitted so he could carry multiple kitchen tools and a butcher's blade, as well as a long-handled English-style axe that served as a hammer on one side. His great height made the axe look like a regular-sized hatchet on his large frame. Piotr was frequently assigned to help him in the galley as a cook's assistant. Eggard was a good teacher. They used seawater to scrub the pots and cooking utensils, which Piotr became proficient at gathering with a bucket tied to a rope.

Their wooden sailing vessel was a small, square-rigged, two-masted caravel originally designed for warfare. It was not large for a wooden sailing ship and moved by sail power only, no oars or human power. It was not fast or particularly beautiful, but it was highly maneuverable. It was difficult to sink and had survived the journey from France to the coast of Newfoundland on fishing voyages. Originally constructed in Portugal for fighting and trading off of the African coast—made of French oak that hardened like iron—it was old but strong. Launched in the same year as Piotr's birth, the *St. Longinus* had plenty of wear and tear. Docking accidents and splintered bullet marks had caused the need for repairs on multiple occasions. The caravel design was made famous by Columbus's ships, the *Niña* and the *Pinta*, which had sailed in 1492.

Originally designed for a crew of seventy-nine officers and sailing men, it now held a skeleton crew of thirty-one souls made up of trading company officers, sailors, traders, and one seasick cabin boy.

Flagger taught Piotr about the ship. He explained that it wasn't overly large at 129 feet long, with a moderately deep draw that prevented it from accessing the more shallow docking areas. The original cannons, sixteen of them, had been removed for more cargo room. It now held only a single cannon on each side, and two .75 caliber matchlock long guns, one on the bow and one on the stern. This minimal armament was defensive at best. It was spacious for its size and floated like a cork bobbing in a pond. The hold was modified in every way for more storage room for fur. The interior below deck had been stripped, opening the space for storage of the heavy wrapped bales of fur. It could carry back 100,000 pounds of cargo on its return journey.

On the trip west from Saint-Malo, it was filled with goods in the hope that the Native Americans would trade with the crew for beaver fur. Metal knives, hatchets, pots, pans, blankets, trinkets, bolts of cloth, and leather skins were all tied down in bundles or wooden boxes. A stash of matchlock muskets and pistols were stacked in the hold as well, not for defense but for trade. Barrels of gunpowder and boxes of cotton patches, horsehair wicks, and lead shot were stowed. Additional barrels of fresh water, beer, and a mixture of grain alcohol, limes, and water were stacked in the galley. Piotr had been a part of the loading of the ship, using his strength impressively. Enough so that the grown men in the crew had noticed and appreciated his effort.

"He is not as big as a man," Gerard Paquet had joked, "but he is strong like a man!" Gerard was one of the five Paquet brothers who had signed onto the trip.

Anton Paquet responded, "Some men are bigger than others!" This drew a bawling laughter from his four brothers, Abel, Abraham, Gerard, and Mason.

All of them balding, bearded, sweating and dirty from the work, it was easy to see that they were brothers. They were short with broad shoulders and muscular, tanned arms. Mason was the tallest by far, and he was of average height. They looked like they were built for hard labor. Experienced seamen and fishermen by trade, they sought their wealth with beaver fur. While fishing would never make a man rich, their father had told them, he would not go hungry. They had been fishermen for most of their lives; now they wanted to be rich.

Their loyalty to the ship and each other was evident from the start of the voyage. They had signed up for this expedition together, making a pact with each other as brothers do. Bickering and challenging each other to manlier feats of daring, they constantly harassed each other, sometimes not so good-naturedly. While they went at each other, pity the man who attacked one of them, for if you came for one, you got all.

"Piotr!" Flagger said his name with the heavy French accent on the second syllable. "Pete-air, drop the traps here. It's time you made the captain's supper. Get on with you."

Piotr nodded and diligently made his way to the captain's quarters. He was grateful to Captain Linville for the opportunity to work on the ship, and he truly wanted to succeed and please the captain. His stomach's current condition, however, did not make preparing food easy. He peeked into the small window at the side of the door and quietly knocked. Captain Linville waved for him to come in as he was bent over and staring at the maps spread out on his mahogany desk.

"Captain, it is time for supper. Can I bring you a meal from the galley?" Piotr asked.

Linville looked up from his work as he pushed the sleeves of his white cotton shirt up his forearms and responded with a nod. He used a magnifying glass in one hand for reading, as his eyesight had dimmed. He was narrow in build with thin features and a sharp nose, and Piotr thought he looked somewhat aristocratic. He was always dressed in finer clothing, with jackets tailored to fit and ornate black leather boots for riding or walking. Piotr opened the door and stepped halfway into the room.

"Stew bowl is sufficient; bring me beer, as well."

Piotr nodded and turned to go.

"You have done an effective job these first few days, Piotr. I appreciate your willingness to work through your illness. It will pass. You won't get sick again...until we get to land!" As he said that last word, he pointed with his finger at a spot on the map and tapped it a few times.

"Land sick, sir?" Piotr asked hesitantly.

"Aye, and it is sometimes worse than the seasickness. It's as if your body can't decide where to settle. But this too shall pass. We will need every man able bodied and prepared upon arrival, even the young ones."

He gave a small smile as he said this. Piotr nodded in agreement and began to close the door as he turned to get the stew and beer.

"Also, have Flagger and Thames come to my quarters with this meal. We need to discuss a few things. They can bring their own food."

"Aye, sir," Piotr responded quickly.

Flagger was no worry to Piotr, but he was nervous to talk to Thames. The black-haired Frenchman was tall and powerfully built. He was named after the river in England, and the crew all pronounced it the English way with a short *e* sound in place of the long *a*. Clad in tan buckskin and fur, he wore a French-style hatchet with an upturned blade on his belt and a long knife with a handle carved from a moose antler. His buckskin shirt had string loops for tying on small, bone-carved powder charges. He had been to the St. Lawrence River twice before on expeditions, and he had encountered native tribesmen in the New World. The Paquet brothers and other crew members said he came back with blood on his knife and hatchet. They said he was a crack shot with a musket and could hit an apple at fifty yards. Piotr saw that he carried a brace of ornate snaphance pistols that he wore when on shore. They said he was a marksman of the highest orders with these, as well. He was the ship's pelletier, the chief fur trader and tracker. His job was to fill the boat with beaver pelts, and he had no time for an inexperienced cabin boy.

When Piotr had first arrived on the dockside, dressed in nothing more than a ragged cotton shirt and torn pants, he found the captain, walked up, and asked in broken French for a job on the ship. Thames had advised Captain Linville not to bring Piotr on board.

"There will be no room for a boy who can't pull his weight. And what happens when we have to fight? Then what? He will simply get in the way or be killed!"

Linville had brought Piotr on anyway.

Now he found Thames and Flagger standing together below deck, going over the traps and trade goods.

"Sirs, Flagger and Mr. Thames, Captain would like you to come to his quarters to talk. I will bring your stew and beer."

"I am not a sir," said Thames dryly. "Just call me Thames, boy."

"Yessir, uh, Thames," Piotr replied. He quickly went to the galley to get the stew and beer.

When Piotr had delivered the three bowls of stew and glasses of beer, he was waved away by Captain Linville. With a few precious moments to himself, Piotr left, got his own bowl of stew and beer from Eggard, and went to the corner of the ship's hold to eat it.

In the captain's quarters, Linville sat down around the smallish oak desk with Thames and Flagger. "Gentlemen, we are moving on schedule so far, with six or seven weeks to go, pending the wind. Praise be to God the weather holds." Linville spoke between bites of stew. "What do you have to report on the crew?"

"It's a good crew, I think," Flagger responded, scratching his heavily bearded chin. "The brothers Paquet are rowdy, but they get the work done. I have watched Piotr and he is as good a shipmate as any man. He outworks most of them and is strong as a bull, for a youth."

Thames grunted. "He will be a liability on land. My recommendation is to leave him on the ship when we arrive. Let him stay aboard. We will not have time to look out for him if we run into trouble. And we don't want him talking with natives when we are trying to make our deals. Leave him on board to man the galley and keep the ship afloat."

"You weren't on the dock when we first met him," Linville said with a small grin. "I thought he was coming up to me to beg for a coin. He walked right up to me with nothing but ragged clothes, a cloth bag, and that vicious-looking club he was carrying. He set his shoulders back, held his head up, and asked if there was a job on the ship. His French is awful, and he is obviously running from something." He waved his hand. "But so is half the crew." He looked Thames in the eye when he said this.

"What club?" Thames responded, meeting his gaze.

"You have not seen it?" Flagger asked. "It's a war club. I saw some like it when we fought against the Swedes in Rheinland a year or so back. Polack infantry uses them. They're homemade out of hickory wood. Hard as stone, but lightweight. They smash the armor, and the bones under it break. Why a fifteen-year-old boy has one, I guess I don't know."

The men sat silently pondering that last point. They did not know, but they respected Piotr's right not to tell them. And they had more important things to look after.

Piotr sat down wearily in the corner of the hold and finished his beer. The salty stew did not taste very good, but it was filling. It was made of water, ground oatmeal, and salted beef fat. Sometimes Eggard would add molasses or a vegetable he had available. Piotr enjoyed the mug of beer, though. It was frothy, a little bitter, with a mint flavor. It had been brewed from the trimmings of a spruce tree. He gratefully realized he could eat and drink, and keep it down, for the first time at sea.

His eyes wandered through the dimly lit hold, coming to rest on the stacks of muskets in the far corner. More than a hundred fifty in all. They were bundled and tied down with ropes to prevent them from sliding out of place with the waves. He wondered if he should try to touch them. He had never fired a musket or gun of any sort, but he knew the smell of burnt gunpowder and the loud, explosive sound.

He felt his eyes grow heavy with the gentle rocking of the ship and the food that stayed in his belly. In just a minute, his breathing slowed and his eyes closed. He fell into the weary state between awake and asleep. His mind drifted to the image of the smoke and flames roaring from the barrels of muskets and small cannons. He had seen and heard this from the wrong side of the barrel.

His closed eyelids flicked back and forth as he recalled the sound of musket balls whistling past his head and men screaming. He remembered the balls hitting the wooden shields as well as thumping into the dirt and mud, and the smacking sound when a musket ball hit flesh, followed by a cry or a scream. In his daydream, he still saw the cannon balls bounce and skitter off of the ground as they ripped into the men of his town. The cannon balls moved so fast that he could not get his body to react, even though he could see them traveling in the air. They splintered barricades and trees, as well as limbs and rib cages. They removed hands and feet on contact. Men didn't cry out when struck by a cannon ball. They didn't have enough time.

He had turned in fear to run from the screaming roar of withering gunfire, but his father had reached back with his gloved, armored hand, grabbing his collar. "HOLD FAST!" his father had shouted. "NOW MOVE TOGETHER! WITH ME!" The men stopped in their tracks and turned to face his father.

"We move to the left below the ridgeline and turn and face the enemy. They will surely charge us soon. SHIELDS! PIKEMEN, AS WE MOVE!"

The group of dazed Polish villagers dressed as infantry all followed him. Those with wooden shields and long pikes held them up, shuffling forward as sporadic musket fire ripped at them from their right flank.

In his daydream, Piotr had reached his hand out toward the muskets in the hold of the ship. As he startled awake, he pulled his hand away from the musket barrels as if they were hot, like the small stove in the galley. He opened his eyes, expecting to see the smoke and fire and drifting clouds of haze, and the red mist exhaled by men as they lay dying on the ground in the field.

None of that was there.

Just the hold of the ship, dimly lit below deck, gently swaying with the movement of the sea. He realized he had quit breathing and he inhaled sharply. He roused himself with a rub of his eyes, stood up, and turned back to the captain's quarters to collect their dishes.

*Chapter 2*

# THE ST. LONGINUS

L inville stood on the foredeck and trained his eyes east back toward the southern tip of Ireland. After a moment, he held his spyglass to his right eye and nodded his head in agreement with his own decision.

He had decided on a northerly route. When sailing west from France and Britain to the New World, the wind was rarely at your back. He set his route to make the trip west as fast as possible. The northern route allowed for easier navigation of the nor'easterly currents of warm water moving up and over from the coast of the New World. The possibility of a significant storm, more common in northern waters, left them with more difficult options for avoidance, but he believed that the wind and the tide provided a faster route. He gambled that it was worth the risk.

He noticed Piotr watching him and gestured to the boy, offering him a look through the glass.

"Have you used a glass like this before?"

"I have seen them, but I have never looked in one, sir."

"Well, have a look then. Tell me what you see." He handed the long tube to Piotr and pointed him in an easterly direction. "Focus on the horizon, and you can see the last glimpse of the Irish coastline on the left. This will be the last land we see for a few weeks."

Piotr looked through the long tube and saw a lot of water. He could not seem to locate anything else. As he scanned across the watery horizon, he finally saw the vague outline of land poking out from the left side of his circle of view. His face revealed how startling the difference was between the eye and the spyglass. He stared with his naked eye again. He saw nothing but water. He put the glass back to his eye and could once again make out the faint shape of land.

"How can this work?" he asked while looking through the lens.

Linville's smile creased his narrow cheeks. "In the tube, two pieces of curved glass. It bends the light to your eye, so everything looks closer."

"That seems almost like a miracle."

Linville turned his gaze to the west and the open sea. "Wait till you use it to see land looking to the west. That will be the real miracle."

Piotr was not concerned about leaving land to the east. So much of what he left behind on land, in that direction, was now dangerous to him.

Over the next few days at sea, Piotr worked, observed, and learned the basics of how a sailing vessel operated. He learned to tie the knots needed for different purposes. He learned to follow the commands for different sail configurations and the reasons for using them. He learned to walk on the ship with the movement of the waves. In the third week of the journey, he learned that storms and high seas on a sailing ship can be terrifying.

The first storm that came to them was a large one. They had watched it approaching for hours with the spyglass. Piotr had been a part of the shouted commands from Linville, given to prepare the ship for the impending storm. Every hatch, window, door, or opening was sealed. Square sails were reconfigured and lateen, or angled, sails were put up. Linville had the ship tacking to the north to try and get around the storm as much as possible. Piotr didn't know, but Linville had already avoided a couple of storms. This one was too large.

A red sun had risen that morning in the east, and Linville could see the storm coming on the distant horizon through his spyglass. His command was to sail the *St. Longinus* right through it. Still, he worked a path to the north, in the hopes of getting to the outer edge of it and limiting their exposure to the larger waves. About six hours out, though, he could see they would be in the heavy part of it. He was anxious, but confident in his ship.

"The ship is riding well. I believe we can sail through it," he told Flagger and Thames, looking out from the foredeck. He handed Flagger his spyglass to have a look.

"I don't see a way around it anyway, Captain. It's too big," Flagger said while squinting with one eye down the spyglass into the distant sky. Thames remained silent, but he stared into the distant clouds as the wind picked up, blowing his black hair around a bit.

The captain ordered sails taken down to a minimum and turned the ship into the waves. They would get blown off course, but he figured they could recover their route after the storm had passed. There was no land for hundreds of miles in any direction. The yellow evening sun began to sink below the horizon as Flagger and Perdo, their small Italian helmsman, worked to bring the ship around in the increasing winds. Linville grimaced as the first stinging rain hit his cheeks and began to pelt the deck. He knew that he and the crew would be battling the waves throughout the night.

Thames, Piotr, the Paquet brothers, and the rest of the crew were sent below deck. Piotr stayed in the hold and watched the men around him. He saw that they laughed and joked, but their mannerisms revealed some tension. These men had experienced many storms at sea and knew that survival was a likelihood. Every sailor also knew that sometimes, the sea turned against you.

As the storm grew, the boat rocked and shifted upon the waves. The men joked and ate their burgoo and hardtack bread, drank the spruce beer, sang songs, and told stories. The stories were about the girls they left behind, their dear sweet mum left at home, or their bastard fathers who had forced them to go to work. The stories they told were often bawdy, and each became more extravagant than the previous one, all with laughter and an apparent lack of outward concern about the raging waves and wind. Piotr, with his understanding of French still developing, listened and learned.

When the ship would move and twist suddenly on the waves, causing her to strain with groans and squeaks from the hull, their eyes would flick and dart around the walls of the hold. Silence would prevail for a moment, as they waited to see if the next wave was *the* wave. The wave that would take the ship under. For a crew shut up in the hold of a sailing ship, long storms at sea could be maddening.

Stories were told and passed about like a jug of liquor from sailor to sailor, and Eggard was finally called upon to tell a tale. He sat in the shadowy hold with the crew and untied his dirty white linen, wiping his bald head with it. Having seen each man fed, he was now ready to speak. He told a story of his home where the Schilde River meets the sea.

He stood to his full height, his face still hidden in the shadows of the dimly lit hold. His hands moved while he spoke in his Norse-accented French to the crew.

"When I first went to sea as a boy, in a storm like this, my father told me of Nehelenia, Goddess of the North Sea."

He paused, looking around the hold swaying with the waves in the dim light, letting the weight of his story settle in.

"She is beautiful to look upon. She has long, flowing black hair. Black as deep water on a night with no moon. She keeps tabs on sailors and watches out for them in difficult situations. Sometimes she helps to save their lives. But she can also be deadly...for sometimes, when she looks upon the face of a sailor, she falls in love and wants him to stay with her forever."

Many of the men in the crew knew of this story—the Nordic people had been crossing the ocean for longer than anyone—and their stories were well-known legends among seafaring folk. Still, they listened with rapt attention.

"If the time is right, they say that a sailor can see her face in the depths on a dark night. If you should look into the water and see her, do not look into her eyes. If you do, she may decide to take you down and hug you close to her bosom. Because while you stare at her beauty in the dark, she stares back at you. And if she wants what she sees, her black hair grows and swells and ripples upward under the boat, like fingers in the waves. It pulls the ship over and downward into her dark embrace, never to return to the surface."

The men were silent in the hold; only the creaking of the ship could be heard. Even the Paquet brothers stopped joking.

"A few years back now, I saw her face, staring up from the cold dark water during a storm." He cupped his hands like he was holding the face of a child. "But she left our ship to pass. Because," he paused, looking around the room, "like all women, she will take men only on her own time, and it is not up to you, the poor sailor, to decide when that time is."

The men of the *St. Longinus* sat in silent contemplation of his words.

Abraham Paquet broke the silence. "Was she beautiful, Eggard? Was Nehelenia beautiful when you looked upon her face?"

He nodded. "Aye, she was...the most beautiful face I have ever seen... but...I was lucky." Eggard looked around the room at the eyes of the men.

"I was lucky, because when I saw her face," he stepped out of the shadows leering, and his massive bald head gleamed in the lamplight, "she saw mine too!"

Laughter erupted from the group, and they slapped each other on the back, giggling at the story.

Mason Paquet shouted, "With a face like that, we shall all be safe for a long, long time!"

"Cheers, Eggard! Well done!" voices shouted from the hold. Cups were raised and a toast was made for Eggard and his story.

After a bit, Gerard Paquet looked over at Piotr sitting quietly and invited him to the conversation. "Pete-air! Tell us about where you are from!

Tell us about your women and where you grew up. What is your story?"

The eyes of the sailing men all turned toward him in the candlelit hold. They all looked and waited. Piotr paused in the middle of raising a cup to his lips and looked back. He was never comfortable as the center of attention, and he was still working to think in French.

"My French is not good enough to tell you all a story, Gerard."

"Nonsense," Gerard said, between bites of burgoo, "just spit out what you have…we will make up the rest!"

He laughed out loud as he said it. His brothers and the crew joined in with laughter and encouragement.

"It will probably make it more interesting anyway, no?"

The hold grew silent after a moment, waiting for Piotr to start. He felt the eyes upon him and he knew he was stuck. He decided to start with the truth.

"I grew up in a place called Tylice, in the southern hills," he started, and was interrupted quickly.

"Stand up!" someone shouted from the darkness of the hold.

Piotr tentatively rose to his feet in the corner and started again.

"In a village called Zlotoryja. It means gold town. The German word for it is Goldberg. My village is outside the city walls. Near the border with Rheinland. We have gold mines and copper mines that keep the king rich and the townsfolk fed."

He stumbled forward in French.

"My father was, how do you say, smithie? A blacksmith. I started working in his shop at age six. I have learned the basics for smithing. I can make some simple tools, given a fire, a forge, iron, and a hammer."

"Ah, mon ami, this is why you are so strong, eh," said Abel Paquet.

"I can work the bellows and pound with the sledge. I am a good assistant, my father says."

The entire ship rocked hard to its side and the door to the hold flew open. Rain and wind howled in briefly. Flagger and Perdo stumbled down the dimly lit steps, slamming the door behind them. Wiping the rain from his soaking wet brow and beard, Flagger tiredly said, "Four men to the aft deck with Captain Linville. He has sent us down for rest and food."

Thames stood up and said, "I will go. Anton and Abraham, you are with me. Piotr, you as well. It is time you learn to be a sailor, as well as a blacksmith assistant."

No one in the crew dared to question Thames, and Piotr was certainly not going to be the first. He placed his clay bowl and wooden spoon in the galley and started toward the steps.

Eggard reached out and touched his arm, speaking in his poor French. "Hang on, up there. The deck in a storm like this is very difficult." Piotr nodded, understanding.

"Piotr, you may need a knife. Ropes get tangled in storms." Eggard extended his other hand from under the counter, and in it was a knife with a five-inch blade in a leather sheath. The blade's full tang metal handle was wrapped with a leather strip to give it better purchase. "Put it on your belt," Eggard directed.

Piotr looked down, realizing he had no belt. He looked back at Eggard, his eyebrows arching.

"Your pocket then. Keep it handy, you may need it."

Piotr slipped it in his pants pocket inside the sheath. He looked back as he turned toward the stairs and said, "Thank you, Eggard."

He stumbled a bit as he went up the stairs as the ship rocked and shifted. He stood, waiting with uncertainty, for the other men. Anton and Thames started up the steps, and Abraham opened the hatch to pounding rain and howling wind.

As he stepped out onto the deck, Piotr thought, *I am blind.*

The rain was sideways and it was pitch black out. Even the dim candlelight of the hold was brighter than this. After a moment, his eyes began to adjust to the darkness. He squinted and staggered toward the aft deck to find Captain Linville standing behind the wheeled helm, holding it steady with a wide-legged stance. One hand shielded his eyes from the sideways spray of rain as he stared into the darkness of the storm, and one hand gripped tightly to the helm's wheel. Piotr, Thames, Anton, and Abraham all made their way, lurching on the moving deck and huddled around the captain.

"What are your orders, Captain?" shouted Abraham above the loud wind and rain.

"The yawl boat is off its block."

Though they were only a few feet away, Linville shouted in the faces of the men above the din of the weather. Piotr looked out across the deck, but the blackness of the storm and the sideways rain stinging his eyes made it difficult to see more than a few feet.

"Abraham, with me, at the helm. Anton, I need you as lookout on the foredeck. Signal me for large waves. Thames and Piotr, get the yawl secured."

Thames waved "come on," and they made their way down the deck as it rocked and swayed violently. Piotr watched Thames walk. He crouched with bent knees to take the waves on as the deck shifted in multiple directions. This was different from the normal waves. He could feel the deck sliding and rocking below his feet. The ship groaned under the twisting pressure of swirling currents underneath the hull, and the wind and rain pounded the deck and its passengers, making everything slippery and more difficult. Piotr was surprised by how cold the rain was, and he shivered a bit as he followed behind Thames.

The yawl boat was a wooden rowboat with a single mast in the center that could hold a small, square sail. This was a way to get to shore for the crew when the ship was at anchor. It was secured to the starboard deck in a wooden block fitted with a slot that allowed the shallow V-shaped hull of the yawl to rest in place. It was tied down at the corners by ropes on modified cleats. The aft rope had snapped, and the yawl was sliding out of its holding slot as the waves buffeted the ship. The front ropes were holding at the yawl's port notch, but the starboard notch had slipped free when the rope went slack. If it came out with the deck moving like this, Piotr thought, the heavy wooden boat would careen across the deck, smashing everything in its way.

Thames shouted at the side of his face above the wind, "We have to get it back onto its block. Grab the back with me and lift!"

Piotr squatted next to the square back of the yawl and wrapped his arms around the hull as best he could, his fingers searching for a hand-hold. Thames shouted from the other side of the boat, "ONE, TWO, THREE…" Piotr surged with all his might as he and Thames raised and slid the boat back toward the wooden block.

"It's not in. Again!" Not offering a countdown this time, Thames started to push the hull toward the slot, so Piotr joined in. The yawl shuddered and slid down into the slot.

"I will hold it; you get the ropes tied off!"

Piotr staggered to the front of the yawl on the pitching deck and pulled the soaking wet rope up. There was just enough give in the rope to force it into the notch on the starboard side. He secured it and made his way back to the rear rope as the deck moved. He picked up the two frayed ends and showed them to Thames. "This rope is broken!"

"I see that!" Thames yelled over the storm, rain dripping down his face. "Thread it through and tie it off. Do it proper! It has to hold." The deck continued to sway and pitch in the storm.

Piotr threaded the longer half of the broken rope through the notches and pulled the two ends toward each other. There was not enough slack to tie the ends together. He reached down and untied the rope from the cleat, giving himself enough slack. He pulled his new knife from his pocket and cut the frayed ends, then tied the two broken ropes together using a fisherman's knot as Flagger had taught him. When Piotr finished, Thames let go of the stern and pulled on the two ends with his powerful arms, testing the knot.

"Good knot. Put it to the cleat."

Piotr tied it to the cleat and it held.

Thames watched carefully and gave an approving look. "You have learned quickly."

At the bow of the *St. Longinus*, Anton Paquet waved his arms suddenly, gesturing wildly toward the port side, and screamed at the top of his lungs, "HARD TO PORT!" Linville and Abraham leaned on the wheel at the helm and turned the boat fractionally, but not enough.

The large wave slammed into the boat, quartering into the port side and the bow, causing it to lurch and spin sideways on the water's surface, even while tilting vertically as it rose up the face of the wave. Anton was slammed back into the railing of the fore deck and went down. Abraham and Linville were both thrown back, rolling across the deck.

The yawl slid backward in the block and the front cleat snapped off the surface of the deck with a pinging sound, sending the front of the shore boat out of the block again. Piotr was knocked to the deck on his left shoulder and was pinned between the railing and the sliding yawl.

At first he did not realize that he couldn't move. His entire side was wedged between the lower side of the yawl and the railing. As the bow of the *St. Longinus* slid upward on the wave, the tension between the yawl and railing increased, pinning him against the rail. He grunted as he scrambled to find purchase with his legs, to push against the boat and free himself. Seawater from the crest of the giant wave came crashing over the bow onto the deck, raining down and submerging the deck a foot deep.

The *St. Longinus* groaned under the heavy pressure. Piotr had no idea that Thames had been bowled off his feet and tossed into the gap between the starboard railing and the aft deck. He, too, was stuck there while the ship slowly climbed the wave. Piotr now realized he couldn't move, and he pushed with all his strength against the side of the yawl, but the added gravity increased the weight so he could not budge it. As he lay sideways, awkwardly twisted against the rail, seawater rolled down the deck and poured over his face and mouth. He sputtered and attempted to gasp for air but caught only water. He looked out into the wetness pouring over his head for what was a few seconds, but felt like hours. He began to wonder if he would die here, stuck on his side against the rail.

Finally, the ship crested the wave and the nose leveled for a moment, then began to tilt as the ship rode down on the back side of the large wave. Water sheared off the deck as Abraham scrambled to his feet and assisted Linville in getting to the wheel. As the ship gathered speed on the monster wave, Abraham now sprinted to Anton, helping him to his feet. Thames untangled his limbs and ran to Piotr, attempting to shove the yawl back toward the block to free him. Abraham raced to the yawl and pulled on the front of it, moving it slightly.

Piotr, sputtering and coughing but happy to no longer be submerged, was able to shift to a seated position with his back against the rail and push with both his feet on the side of the yawl as well. The boat slid back into its resting place in the block.

Abraham screamed into the roaring wind, "The cleat in front broke loose; I will get tools to repair it. Hold it here!"

Thames latched onto the stern of the yawl, and Piotr staggered to the bow and grabbed a firm hold. Thames smiled as they stared at each other across the length of the boat. It was the first time Piotr had ever seen him smile. Strangely, he realized Thames had strong white teeth.

Thames threw his head back while hugging the stern of the yawl and shouted, "SONOFABITCH!"

Then he laughed harder while holding the yawl in his powerful grasp and shouted, "I thought you were crushed like a grape!"

Piotr noticed Thames's cheek was red and bruised and a small drop of blood was forming from a tiny cut on his earlobe. Piotr smiled and belly laughed for the first time in nearly a year. The absurdity of it all, and the maniacal laughter of Thames, struck him as funny, and he began to shake with shock and relief. Thames looked down at the ropes and kept chuckling as he strained to hold the boat in place.

"Why are you laughing?" Piotr yelled out at Thames through the wind while laughing at himself.

"Look." Thames gestured with his eyes and face at the rear tie down rope. Piotr craned his head around the yawl to see what he meant.

"Your knot held. You might have been taken through the railing and out to sea if it had broken!"

He looked at the knot in the rope. It had not come loose at all.

Abraham returned with Gerard and Mason in tow. Working quickly, they pulled and stretched the rope and, with two men holding it, reattached the cleat to the deck, tying the rope around it and securing the yawl once and for all against the wind and the rain. Thames let go of the stern and bent over with his hands on his knees, inhaling deep breaths in the heavy rain.

He turned toward Piotr and asked, "Are you injured?"

Piotr checked himself over from head to toe. He shook his head in mild disbelief.

"Go below deck. We will handle things up here. Get some rest," Abraham advised.

Thames nodded and grinned through the pounding rain, his black, soaking wet hair hanging in his eyes.

Abraham smiled. "You will be a good sailor someday when this is all said and done, Piotr. If you survive!"

As he carefully made his way across the wet moving deck, Piotr smiled through the cold rainwater dripping on his face. His knot had held, and he was not lost to Nehelenia and the black waves.

*Chapter 3*

# THE RENDER

S he traced her fingertips over the patterns in the red brick wall while sitting on the bench outside the priory. The bricks were similar to the ones used to build the massive gothic church St. Petri Dom in her hometown of Bremen. *Brick Renaissance*, she thought. That was the term they had taught her in the Catholic school. It was a style of architecture. She felt like that was a long time ago and far, far away right now. But it was only a year ago and a few hours of sailing across the North Sea.

She remembered that the redbud trees had started to bloom early last spring, the same deep red color as the brick. Now, waiting here on the bench with her single leather-bound suitcase of belongings and her practical, wood-soled shoes, she touched the bricks and wondered what the future would hold. She, Jana Mueller, would soon be bound for the New World.

She took a letter from her pocket that had worn and deeply creased folds in it. She unfolded it and looked at the script spaced perfectly on the line, as if copied by monks with decades of experience. Her mother had wonderful handwriting. Her eyes traveled over the familiar text that she had memorized.

Only a little over a year earlier, she had never traveled beyond the fields surrounding Bremen in the Holstein region, on a river near the coast of the North Sea. She had grown up in a small village outside the city that had converted from Roman Catholic to Lutheran.

Being a northern town, when the Swedish army came ashore in Prussia and began to march across the north of Europe, her village was in their path. The Lutherans in her village rejoiced, and the Swedish army grew in size as German Lutherans joined the fight. Finally, the town leadership had said, we have a protector for our city.

Just as all armies, it needed to be fed, housed, and supplied. As neighboring towns and cities gave their food stores and housed soldiers, so did Bremen and its surrounding villages. Armies are mostly made of young men, with training, a capacity for violence, and long waits between battles. Incidents of hostility between the locals and the invading army happened, and Jana's family was not exempted.

Her father was a window maker, a Fenstermacher, and was busy working in his shop when the soldiers came. Jana worked most every day in her father's shop and had shown a talent for detailed wood carving. She remembered the smell of his shop. The smoke of burnt hardwoods and horsehair glue. That was what she smelled when the knock came at the door. Five soldiers in blue uniforms demanded her father's service immediately. He would have to go with them, they said, and fix their problem. He assured Jana and her mother it would be all right, nothing would happen, he would be back soon.

He did not come back.

Her travels began at that moment.

She whispered the words in the letter aloud once again to calm her nerves.

*My Dearest Little One,*

*I am so sorry to write this, but I know you understand. You have been so brave. What I have done is only to protect you, and your father would have wanted it, as well. I hope you are safe and well. I will come as soon as I find your father, or find out what happened to him.*

*The world has become treacherous. This army is growing as more and more people are coming. There will be a fight soon and I fear all of us will be caught in it. Catholics and Protestants fighting. Over nothing. It makes no sense. Just last night, our neighbors were assaulted in their fields by the villagers of the next town over. Poor Mr. Hofmann was beaten and stabbed by people he used to trade with! We are being divided, and it will not end well.*

*I am so proud of you. You have become a beautiful and kind young woman. At least you are safe in Ireland and away from this terrible war. Please keep up your studies dutifully. I know this was not your plan for the future, but sometimes God's plan is all we have to follow. I miss you deeply. I continue to inquire daily with the Swedish officers about your father, but they have done nothing. I will come as soon as I can to join you.*

*Love,*
*Mother*

The soldiers had taken an eyeful of Jana when they took her father away, and her mother knew that she would not be safe. When two Swedish officers came back by the shop, inquiring about her father's disappearance and asking how she and her daughter were getting along, her mother put them off and took action. She devised a plan to hide Jana. After a week, they walked to a nearby town, a Catholic town, and asked for help from the priest. He forged documents and secured Jana's admission to a priory in Youghal, Ireland, in just two short months.

She had left her mother in tears, sailing across the sea to Ireland. Now, a year later, she was a postulant, the second stage of training to be a Catholic nun. In another year, she would make her first Profession. As she sat on this bench, waiting for a ship to take her across another sea to the New World, she wondered at how fast everything had changed. She had written back to her mother every two weeks since arriving in Ireland. She had not gotten a response.

Jana was waiting for a ship named *The Render*, a barque cargo ship with an English name. It was coming from Saint-Malo to Youghal on the southern coast of Ireland. Commissioned by the Burgundy Trading Company in France, *The Render*'s purpose was to pick up four passengers there for their journey across the sea.

Built in Spain, she was a three-masted vessel with a shallow draft and good speed for her size. Their ultimate destination was Quebec City. There, they were to deliver a shipload of supplies and then return with a hull stuffed full of beaver fur. The final cargo pickup, before crossing the northern Atlantic to the New World, was at St. John's monastery on the south Irish coast. The "cargo" consisted of Catholic missionaries: two priests and their companions, an elderly French nun from Paris, and a young woman who had begun her committed novitiate to the sisterhood less than one year earlier.

Their contracts were signed by Cardinal Richilieu himself. A leader in the Catholic church and a direct advisor to the Pope, he was also the church's representative as the principal investor in the Burgundy Trading Company. The company, formed by the church and royalty from Paris and Rome, provided the capital necessary for the start of the journey, in exchange for profits, of course. His representation of the church in this venture allowed for the bending of rules in obtaining their charter. They were able to locate and supply a ship, a captain, and a crew in a remarkably quick time period. The parties in this expedition sought to take advantage of the burgeoning market for beaver fur that had developed in Paris.

The meeting with ship's captain, Gilbert Laurent, and Father Renier Archembeau took place in Cardinal Richilieu's office in Paris. He stood behind his richly carved walnut desk and issued a series of directives that were not to be questioned. Exploration and exploitation of the riches of the New World were going to be profitable for men willing to risk their necks, and for the church as well.

In addition, it would be part of the church's mission to spread the word of God to the savages. Conversion and the saving of souls were imperative in the light of the recent wars with heretical Lutheran deniers in the north. As such, Richilieu would send Archembeau and some assistants to help the aged priest. A young priest, for sure, and a nun or two. They could do the day-to-day labor, keeping Archembeau from working himself to death, and leaving him free to guide the building of the church in the New World.

Gilbert Laurent was selected to captain the ship. Cardinal Richilieu's men at the Burgundy Trading Company found him, gave him the offer of a lifetime, found a ship for him, and expedited the charter through the local bureaucrats. He was allowed to join as an investor in the expedition, and in a mere three months they were at sea, traveling westward. While the church was losing its power in the north, Paris remained Catholic, and the church was the supreme power among competing local governments and the royalty.

Father Renier Archembeau was not as excited or appreciative at the decision of the church to involve him in this venture. He believed this assignment was a disparagement. However, he was not able to question the dictates of the cardinal. When the ornate wooden door slammed shut behind them as he and Captain Gilbert Laurent exited the cardinal's office, he knew that Cardinal Richilieu was never going to alter his decision.

Archembeau had made his way back to the Irish coastal monastery in a pique of discontent. A man his age should not be sent out on such a wild adventure! He was content with his position as the headmaster of a monastery. Now, that would all be lost. It mattered not, because in a few weeks they were at sea, heading west to the New World.

Under Captain Laurent's guidance, *The Render* had found smooth sailing and light seas during their six-week journey across the Atlantic, only encountering light rain until the coast of Newfoundland. The storm there was a heavy northeaster and arrived in full force. This caused the captain to make a decision to run for cover in the Gulf of St. Lawrence and attempt to hide behind whatever land he could find. Maybe he was being overly cautious, Captain Laurent thought, but better to wait it out than suffer catastrophic damage.

The land he found in the gulf was called Les Iles de la Madelaine, a small group of islands in the southern center of the Gulf of St. Lawrence, consisting of two land masses, a long sandbar peninsula, and a smaller island just north of the main two. He slipped *The Render* into the opening of the channel between the two main bodies of land and dropped anchor in hopes of avoiding damage to his heavily loaded ship, using the land mass as a buffer to the waves and wind.

As the storm pounded the deck and chopped up the waves, the captain listened intently to the sounds of the ship from his dimly lit quarters below the aft deck. He sat with Raul Montreaux, his first mate. Montreaux was not young anymore at forty-two years old. He was a solidly built, square-jawed man. His salt and pepper beard were the only signs that revealed his age. He still had the kind eyes and vigor of a young man. He was reliable, and never needed reminding of his duty.

Captain Laurent had come to value his counsel during their crossing of the Atlantic. Montreaux was fond of wearing the black, long-tailed duster jacket he had obtained for his years of naval service for the city of Paris on the river Seine, though it looked out of place on the deck of a cargo ship. The insignia of the city's river sailors, a barge with a snake wrapping around it, was stitched in gold-colored thread on the breast pocket.

The Catholic missionaries were sitting at his small desk in the captain's quarters with tea, while the storm blew outside. Captain Laurent stood, silently worried about his choice in anchoring, and Raul Montreaux sat quietly, listening to the conversation. The missionaries were blissfully unaware of the risk the captain was taking, and they chatted incessantly about how they would go about building the church in the New World, as directed.

Pascal Demari was a very young, newly ordained priest who had been chosen by Cardinal Richilieu to assist Father Archembeau specifically because of his youth. Having committed to the priesthood at fifteen, he was still barely twenty-one years old. His curly hair and stout, cherubic frame was offset by the fiery strength in his eyes. He was the fourth son of an Italian merchant and a wealthy Parisian woman of Nordic heritage, leaving him with red hair and a larger frame. He was a true believer in the faith and, tasked with bringing it to the savages in the New World, he was determined to complete his mission.

It was obvious to Captain Gilbert Laurent that his compatriot, Father Renier Archembeau, was less enthusiastic. Nearly completely bald, with rotted teeth and a hooked, bulbous nose, Archembeau was well past middle age. He wore the same red cloak for warmth that he had worn when he had first met him in the cardinal's office. He lacked the physical strength of youth and was clearly not interested in roaming about the forest looking for native souls to convert. His vision of missionary work with native populations involved staying near the fort in Quebec City. Building the church in the New World, as he saw it, would involve the construction of an actual church in Quebec City, and bringing the native population into it to be saved. The savages would contribute their labor in exchange for their souls' eternal life. It was a more than fair trade-off.

Father Demari attempted to counsel the elder priest. "When we arrive in Quebec and have secured our lodging and belongings, the first thing we must do is find a guide."

Archembeau disagreed.

"We will assess the situation upon arrival, Pascal, we will proceed once we know where we stand. The letters from Quebec City are not indicative of a place from which we are to begin our work. We will need to see what resources we are afforded and build from there. Once we have established what the territory governor will give us, we can make decisions about going forward. I am not going to run into the forest with a poorly vetted guide to sleep in the wet and the cold. Remember our orders, from Cardinal Richelieu himself, were to build. Build the church in the New World! Build it, that is what we will do. Captain Laurent, we are so close to Quebec. When do you see us venturing forth to finish our journey?"

Captain Laurent did not respond immediately, as he was listening to the storm and not the conversation.

After a long pause, he said, "We will be here till this storm ends; we cannot dock at Quebec City to offload in these winds anyway. In a few hours, we will be on our way, and a day or so after that, we will arrive in port. Please, gentlemen, enjoy the tea. I am going back out to check the quality of our position."

He walked on the creaky floor and turned toward the door, then stopped suddenly. He sensed a movement in the hull that should not be. "Raul, are we moving?"

He snapped his head, tilting his ear, because the sound he had feared slipped into his senses, over the loud hammering of the wind, rain, and roiling ocean waves.

It was the sound of the aft anchor chain snapping against the hull, quickly followed by the rudder scraping on the sand of the sea floor. *The Render* suddenly lurched and staggered, tilting hard to its starboard side. A long, grinding groan shuddered through the railings and floor of the ship. Captain Laurent caught himself on the wall with a quickly outstretched hand. Raul shifted in his seat and locked his eyes on the captain. The two priests looked at each other in shock and surprise, falling backward to the floor as the ship vibrated and ground to a lurching stop, increasing its sideways and slightly nose-up position on the sandy shore of Les Îles-de-la-Madeleine.

Captain Laurent and his first mate instantly knew he had made a grievous error in judgment.

The anchor had shifted in the soft sand of the sea floor. The current in the channel had rotated the ship laterally, and it had shifted onto the sandbar that extended out from the main landmass. She was aground.

As his mind raced through all of the possible outcomes, Laurent immediately hoped that the ship could recover with the tide. Higher tides could loosen the grip on the rudder and the ship might plane back to level and sail forward with little or no damage. They were so close to their destination. A mere day and a half of sailing would get them there. When the storm cleared, they would be able to see the mainland of the New World. He shook his head in disbelief and worry.

"Get the longboats ready! We have gone aground in the night!" he shouted to the crew. He was hopeful to see this from the water level in the daylight. "When dawn breaks, we lower a longboat to see what can be done."

Dawn came with a bright yellow sun rising over the edge of the Atlantic and the coast of Newfoundland. Captain Laurent looked wearily to the sky and said to no one in particular, "At least the rain has stopped."

After a night of little sleep, the longboat was lowered with ropes by the hands of the anxious crew, as the deck of the ship was now sitting twenty degrees tilted to starboard. Laurent and his longboat crew made their way around the ship in the shallow water and his heart sank. With a long face, he realized that the hull had burrowed into the sandbar and was embedded. This created a suctioning effect that would not free the boat, especially while loaded down with cargo. He closed his eyes and shook his head in regret and fear, and with the realization of what they would have to do. He gathered the crew and the four concerned passengers on the tilted deck and gave his commands.

"The ship is aground, and we cannot get her free without the strength of another ship. We will offload all that we can, to lighten the ship. We will use the longboats to hide it on the Island. We will take what we can and row to the mainland, follow it north to the St. Lawrence River, and make our way to Quebec City."

The experienced sailors of *The Render* had already surmised the situation and knew what was coming. They listened resolutely.

Father Archembeau, on the other hand, listened with disbelief. "You are going to row us the rest of the way! In these!"

He yelled these accusatory words as he pointed at the longboats, two of them, each one twenty-two feet long, wide and heavy, and painted with whitewash. They were stable and held four oarlocks. They were wide enough for two rows of seats side by side and could hold ten passengers and a coxswain in the bow. A small sail could be rigged off of a removable mast in the center seat for added speed.

*Or some cargo, and less people,* Captain Laurent thought, looking at the boats.

"Well, Father, you may want to stay here, on the island, until we get back with a boat to pick you up. As you see fit." Laurent spoke directly. There was no sense in hiding their predicament.

The nun and her young companion both turned their heads and looked at Father Archembeau with purposeful, wide-eyed stares. They did not fancy their choices. Being left on the island with little or no shelter, not to mention a hungry crew of stranded, desperate sailors, or facing the open sea of the Gulf of St. Lawrence in a longboat.

Sister Mary Therese O'Boyle had experienced much adversity in her life. Barely five feet tall, her long hair had gone completely gray with old age. She knew when to be bold. Her young charge Jana had shown her that she was tougher than she looked. Despite her rather thin appearance, Jana had more than carried her weight at the priory in Youghal. Helping to build the convent, she had been devout and resolute since arriving.

Sister Mary Therese stepped up to Captain Laurent. "You will take the four of us with you. We are still your passengers, and you are contracted to get us to Quebec City. Sailing ships or longboats, it matters not to me, as long as we arrive."

Captain Laurent eyed the small, aged nun with a weary gaze, then nodded his head. It was decided, then.

"Let's get this ship unloaded, men. Everything to the island. Montreaux, take two men and scout the best location nearest the shore to store the cargo. We will drop down to the longboats and row it in from there. Sister, any help you can give to help set up camp will be appreciated." His eyes flicked toward Archembeau.

"We will do our resolute best, Captain." Sister Mary Therese was not about to shrink in the face of duty. She understood that Archembeau could be difficult.

Two days later, most of the cargo was on shore. Some of the reserve sails were repurposed into makeshift tents for the men staying on the island. Fresh water in barrels were left available, while other men had been sent to scout for a water source on the island. The sailing men debated in quiet conversations about whether it was best to go with the longboat or stay on the island. Standing on a rise just past the sandbar, they could see the clouds and fog gathering on the mainland. The water of the Gulf of St. Lawrence was cold and could easily take a longboat under. If the longboats did not make it to Quebec City and with no help coming, those on the island would be left to starve, in time. The sailors knew that none of these options were good. The debate went back and forth among the crew.

Sister Mary Therese took over the setting up of camp. This freed up the sailors to do the heavy work of unloading and moving cargo, organizing the fires and construction of the tents, and guiding the placement of supplies, including the barrels of fresh water. She directed the gathering of firewood, tools, cooking utensils from the galley, and every detail that she could think of. Jana more than pitched in, helping in every part of the camp construction.

Sitting on a log, Archembeau had protested in his tiredness, "We are not staying here, Sister. We are leaving as soon as possible." He gestured toward the longboats now pulled up the beach and stowed.

Mary Therese eyed him coldly. "These men have done their best to see to our needs and our safety. We owe them the kindness of helping them to find comfort in this place. Whether we stay here or not, some of them will be here, possibly for several days or weeks."

Archembeau knew this, of course, but had allowed his exhaustion and stress to get the better of him. He rose, adjusted his red cloak, and apologized with a slight bow.

"You are right, of course, you are right." He waved his hand at her while he spoke. "I thank you for reminding me. I am simply tired. But, we will carry on."

"I will help you, brother," Father Demari smiled, "you need not be overwhelmed. We shall overcome."

Finally, after a long night and second day, the camp was set up and fortified as best they could, and the time had come for the longboats to leave. Captain Laurent addressed the entire camp by firelight late in the evening, as the red sun set and gave way to the nighttime. He stood between the tents.

"The longboats sail at dawn. We will take eleven in the first boat, ten crew and a cox. Our four representatives of the church will be on this boat. Montreaux will be the coxswain. So that makes six men for four oars. The second boat will have cargo in it and four oars. Six crew, and a cox to pilot. So twelve of you will be going." He gestured toward the sailors.

Archembeau rose from the log he was sitting on. "Captain, are you not at the helm of one of these boats? Surely you will be coming with us?"

"The captain does not leave his ship. My ship sits here." He pointed directly toward the hull of *The Render*, firmly wedged into the sands of

Les Iles de la Madelaine. "So, I stay here." He pointed to the sandy dirt where they stood. "Montreaux is a good man, he will get you to Quebec City. Then he will send a boat back for us, to bring us along as well. The people there want this shipment of goods and will come for us as soon as possible. The territory governor will see to it."

The crew shuffled their feet and stood wearily but listening. The decision to be on the boats was at hand.

"We will draw sticks for it." Montreaux brought out an oaken bucket with small sticks in it. "Anyone with a red mark on their stick is on the boat. If there is no mark, you will stay on this island, gentlemen." He held the bucket in his dirty hands and gave a square-jawed smile.

The forty-four sailors stuck their hands in and took their chances. Moans of disappointment, hoots and shouts of success, all came forth as they reached into the bucket and drew their stick. Some were excited to be on the longboat. Some were excited not to be on the longboat.

After the drawing, the camp quieted down. Men began to shuffle about to find the best place to bed down near a fire. Jana thought that at least the night was not overly cold. There was a chill, to be sure, but not freezing. She did not like to be cold all the time. She made a space on a blanket for her and Sister Mary, between wooden boxes of supplies and under the cover of the sailcloth tent. She surmised that the body heat of the two women in this smaller space would be sufficient for that night. Together they said a short prayer for the safety of the men and boats.

Captain Laurent signaled for Raul Montreaux to follow him. They made their way a few steps away from the fire and the group.

"Armaments?"

Raul had expected this question and had been giving it thought. He nodded and said, "Well...we have eight matchlock muskets with powder and ball for ten shots each. We have four snaphance pistols, also with ammunition for ten shots each. We have a blunderbuss. All are now loaded. The blunderbuss is loaded with pellets and rocks." He handed two pistols to Captain Laurent as he spoke.

Laurent tucked one into his belt and thought for a moment. "Keep the blunderbuss, two pistols, and four of the rifles here at the encampment. Put two rifles in each longboat with the cox. There are some small axes and knives in the crate branded with the crown's mark, these were to be used to trade with the natives. Make sure each man has a knife, at least."

"Aye, Captain."

"Keep two of the pistols in your belt. You never know how men will behave in extreme situations."

Gilbert Laurent shook his head in weariness and disgust. Their circumstances weighed heavily.

"We are safe here, on this island, for the time being," he whispered. "As long as you and the other boat make it to Quebec City and send for us! You have your work cut out for you. If the maps are correct, you have a two-hundred-mile sail in front of you. I doubt that the maps tell the full story, though. Head west and follow the shoreline. Stay on the north side of the river as you row west, closer to French ground as need be."

"Aye, Captain."

Montreaux was an experienced seaman. He already knew the maps and he knew the dangers of what lay ahead. A thousand things could go wrong. But the longboats were well made and sturdy. Weather was key. A storm bringing big waves before they got into the river could easily swamp the boats.

Captain Laurent was in a horrible position. If the cargo load did not arrive in Quebec City, he would lose his charter and be held liable by the Company. He faced financial ruin. That is, if he survived at all, and returned to France. Still, Raul admired him for making the best decision the situation would allow. Laurent had made a mistake. He was now correcting it as best as he could.

Captain Laurent sighed heavily, patted him on the shoulder, and turned toward the tents. At forty-seven, he felt very old.

"Get the best sleep that you can tonight, Raul. You will need it come morning."

In the dim moonlight, amid the creaking insects and the rustling of people trying to find a comfortable sleeping spot on the ground, Raul Montreaux, first mate for the cargo ship *The Render*, watched his captain walk back toward camp. His shoulders were slumped and his head hung down.

St. Lawrence River

NEW FOUND LAND

LES ILES DE LA MADELEINE

QUEBEC CITY

Old Willow Cove

PRINCE EDWARD ISLAND

## Chapter 4

# NEW FOUND LAND

Learning the work of a sailor was a task that Piotr grew to enjoy. In the seven weeks that he had been at sea, he found that a sailing life was an improvement over the hunger and homelessness of the ragamuffin existence he had been thrown into. He never minded the struggle of learning. He was able to learn from his mistakes. He had begun to enjoy the camaraderie of the crew, and he even found some of his daily chores to be pleasurable on board the *St. Longinus*.

He climbed the rope ladder daily for his shift as lookout in the crow's nest. Captain Linville had told him that his youthful eyes would be valuable up here. The best part, however, was that he got to take the spyglass up with him. He found a small leather satchel in Linville's quarters and tied a short length of rope to it so that he could easily carry the telescope up the ladder in the rocking waves. He looped the rope around his shoulders and hung the satchel next to his hip for easy access.

This morning, he climbed to the top as the mast gently rocked on calm seas and bright sunshine. It was cold, but he enjoyed the feeling of the cool wind. It blew off his smell and made him feel clean. He carefully took the spyglass out of his pouch and extended it. He looked to the west, as the morning sun was low on the horizon and still blinding.

At first glance, he saw nothing but a lot of water. But he had learned to look closer. He began to watch the waves, not only their size, but how they moved. He watched the birds and how they flew just above the surface. They glided fast downwind and flapped hard flying into the wind.

He saw the color of the water as it changed: the dark blue and black of the deep ocean; the green, gray and light blue in shallower waters. One morning, he had even seen a red and purple sea, as a large mass of algae had crossed their path. His first view of whales had caused him to stare in open-mouthed disbelief. They had sailed within a hundred yards of a pod of humpback whales resting on the surface just a week earlier. Their sounds, and the spray of their breath spouting above the surface, were mystifying. He had not known any animal could be of such size.

His job in the crow's nest was to look for other ships. He had seen just a few. He would shout down their directional location and stand and point toward them. None of them had changed their course. Captain Linville had always pulled his own spyglass and stared at them for some time.

This was a time of war, after all, and all of Europe was fighting someone. The captain believed that all approaching ships were hostile, until they demonstrated that they were not. Also, he had few defenses. His single cannon on each side would only buy them enough time to escape.

Piotr knew his scanning of the sea was important, and he tried his best to see everything. So it did not alarm him today when he looked to the west through the spyglass and saw the vague and distant tip of a sailing mast poking up over the edge of the horizon.

"Flag to the west!" he shouted down to the deck.

"To the west," came the echoing call from Perdo, at the helm.

Linville looked up at the crow's nest and marked where Piotr was pointing. He pulled his own glass and stared for a full minute to confirm what he heard. As Piotr kept looking, he realized there were two separate masts, one behind the other, bobbing up and down, but not in unison. Two flags. He shouted down again, "Two ships to the west!" and Perdo echoed his call again.

Linville stared through his spyglass for a moment more, then raised his eyes to the crow's nest. "Keep on them, we need to know what they are."

Piotr followed the ships closely as they dipped below the horizon and popped up again. He surmised that they were sailing due east toward the *St. Longinus*, which was sailing due west. He saw the movement of one of the masts, rocking in the waves, and finally saw a glimpse of the colors of the flag. It was white with a red cross angled sideways in the waves.

"I see a flag!" he shouted down to the deck. "White background, red cross." The deck crew echoed his report.

Piotr did not know it, but he was staring at the mast of an English warship, the deadliest thing on the sea in 1632. Easily capable of reducing the *St. Longinus* to bits, and there were two of them.

Flagger had moved to the helm with Captain Linville.

"English."

He spit over the railing, his voice deep with concern.

Linville turned his head eastward for a moment, and back again toward the western horizon where Piotr was still pointing, checking.

"We have the sun. We have the wind. We can hide from their view for another few minutes or so. As long as the sun is low enough. They are staring straight into it, as they look east." He looked at Flagger directly and said, "We run fast. As fast as we can."

Then he turned and gestured to Perdo. "South by southwest, keep the sun at our backs. FULL SAILS!"

"South southwest, aye!" Perdo confirmed as he turned the ship.

Piotr watched from above while the crew scrambled in synchronicity. In moments, all of the sails were full and the *St. Longinus* began to surge a bit faster.

Standing in the crow's nest, Piotr felt the ship catch the wind. The spray increased, and he could feel the hull sliding forward as it picked up speed. He had never moved so fast in his life. The wind on his face streamed past now, and he stood tall with his hands out, balancing on the narrow planks. The speed caused a rush of excitement to surge in his blood.

Linville looked up and realized that Piotr was enjoying the speed. "The ferocity of youth." He gestured with a small smile. Flagger and Perdo looked up as well.

"That's because he doesn't know what an English warship will do to us, if they can," Flagger said.

"And that's probably all right for now," Captain Linville said. "Piotr," he cupped his hands and shouted to the crow's nest, "keep us informed if they change course in any way, understand?"

"Aye!" Piotr responded.

"Let's see if they spot us," Captain Linville whispered.

The *St. Longinus* sailed on this course long enough for Piotr to see the two ships shrinking in the distance. As he stared through the glass, they appeared to be maintaining their course to the east.

From the deck Captain Linville shouted, "What say you!"

"They hold their course!"

Thames joined Flagger and Perdo at the helm.

"English ships?" Thames said with deep disgust in his voice. "If there are two, there could be more."

Linville nodded, then took out a pipe and began to clean the bowl with a small metal pick. "My concern as well, Mr. Thames."

He knocked the bowl against the rail, dumping its charred contents into the sea. He dug the bowl into a small leather tobacco pouch pulled from his pocket, filling it to the brim. He then tapped this down with his finger and poked a few air holes in it with the pick, while continuing to consult with his crew. "What say you, gentlemen?"

Flagger said, "Newfoundland and Labrador are close now. With the wind, we could be on it in a day or so. We can come around it from the southern channel into the Gulf of blessed St. Lawrence. Then we continue west and north, onward to the river, and west to Quebec City. I have not entered the gulf through the southern channel. Maybe it will bring good luck to see some new lands."

"Maybe so, old friend. I have not either, but I have sailed out through the southern channel."

Thames agreed. "As long as we get there, I suppose. No sense in running into an English fleet."

The three of them paused and turned simultaneously to Perdo.

"I just steer the boat," the small helmsman said with his Italian accent.

They smiled at that.

Piotr stood in the crow's nest the next day at mid-morning. His shift would soon be over, but he did not mind the waiting. Frequent gazes through the looking glass had found no other ships, whales, or anything except water. He continued looking, though. He had been taught in his father's work-shop to be dutiful. He held the glass up for a final look to the west before heading down the rope ladder, pausing mid-squint. There was something different in the water. In the circular lens, he could see a dark mist rising above the water. He panned the glass left and right. It was darkening and was spanning the horizon to the west.

He realized suddenly that this was what land looked like from the water when you were still a long way away.

"LAND!" he shouted down to the deck, pointing due west.

Perdo and Flagger were at the helm. Linville and Thames were somewhere below deck.

"Land!" Shouts and hoots began to ring out from the deck.

The door to the hatch opened and everyone began to pour out onto the deck, gathering at the railing, searching for a spot to see.

It was not visible with the naked eye, even for Piotr. *But it will be in a few minutes*, he thought. He stared westward, switching back and forth between the glass and his eyes.

After a few minutes, someone at the bow shouted "Land ho!" pointing due west.

More shouts rang out as more crew members could make it out. Abel Paquet looked up at Piotr and shouted, "How close, Piotr?"

"Close!" Piotr had never been around a crew that found land after weeks at sea.

"We will make for the southern coast when we get within the clear view with the naked eye. Keep us at least a mile out," Linville ordered, as he walked to the helm.

"Aye, Captain, one mile," Perdo repeated.

The day passed slowly for Piotr. He was excited by the sight of land, as was the rest of the crew. Finally, in the early evening, the order came to turn due south. The coast of Newfoundland was now easily visible, rising up from the sea as a dark mass on the ocean's surface. The *St. Longinus* made her way south toward the gap between the large island and the mainland.

As he helped tie down a sail with Abel Paquet, Piotr asked, "Abel, how long till we get to Quebec City?"

"We are still a hundred or a hundred and twenty, maybe one hundred forty leagues at least," Abel estimated. "Perhaps four days more at sea. It will take a few days to offload and Thames will do his bidding on shore. We will see from there. I expect many days in port. Many days to load the ship with beaver fur, once we have secured it. Maybe six or seven months, we will return to Saint-Malo, unloading the fur as fast as possible. Then we will get paid."

He had a wolfish grin with the last sentence.

Piotr nodded. He did not really understand, though, and in his youthful ignorance, he ruefully remembered that he had not thought about the return journey. He had come to the *St. Longinus* in desperation. He did not want to go back to Saint-Malo, or northern France, or anywhere east of there. People were looking for him, and if they found him, they would collect the price on his head.

"Abel, how far is a league, anyway?" he asked.

Abel laughed at the question, smiled, and said, "You are so serious, I forget that you are still just a boy. A league is three and a half miles at sea. This land you see here," he gestured with his head over the starboard railing while tying down the rope, "is Newfoundland. It is an island."

He picked up his end of the sail cloth and positioned it while talking.

"It's more than that, though. It's a doorway, really. The doorway to the New World. We have to go around it, and then sail up to the river of Saint Lawrence. Then still farther west to Quebec City. That is our port." He paused to see the reaction his words would bring.

Piotr's face revealed curiosity, not concern.

Like a lot of the crew, Abel wondered what it was that had caused the boy to run away to the New World and grow so tough. He discarded the thought, though. He supposed that Piotr would tell him if he wanted him to know.

As night fell, they came to the southern coast of Newfoundland. Piotr gazed at the tall cliffs on the shore in the moonlight. Even from this far out at sea, he could tell they were well above the shoreline. They moved through the channel, and he saw the western shore of Newfoundland in the distance as Eggard yelled at him to come to the galley and eat.

Near midnight, Flagger and Anton were at the helm as Perdo and Linville were asleep. Mason Paquet was in the crow's nest when he spotted something in the night sky on the horizon that he couldn't believe. He looked at it for a long time before saying anything, but clearly, there was a light on the surface of the Gulf of St. Lawrence. It looked like a fire, flickering and changing shape. He wasn't certain at first, so he held his tongue initially, but the ship was moving closer to it.

"Fire, on the horizon, southwest!" he shouted down to the deck. The deck crew echoed it back to Flagger and Anton.

They were as puzzled and curious as everyone by this information. Flagger moved to the foredeck to get a better view. He looked through his glass, which was not as useful in the moonlight. He saw the tops of flames through the movement of the boat, and trees and debris on the shoreline. Something was on fire. He made his way back to the helm with Anton, where he pulled out a map from his pouch and held the lantern above it. It must be Les Iles de la Madelaine. His mind calculated; they were about three leagues away from the island, having sailed north along the western coast of Newfoundland to avoid any rocky peninsulas and outcroppings as they turned northwest in the night. Yet he could still see this fire, which meant it was a big fire. Not a campfire.

"Wake up Linville," he advised Anton Paquet.

## Chapter 5

# A SIGNAL FIRE

Something on Les Iles de la Madelaine was burning. At least a part of it. As they drew closer in the night the flames became more apparent. Captain Linville had been here before. When he was on his first voyage across the sea some thirty years ago, the fishing boat he was on stopped at the island. They had fished for cod off the western coast of Newfoundland and had been successful. The cod were salted, and then they made for North Africa in the Mediterranean Sea, where they traded the salted fish for molasses and sugar, and then returned to port in Saint-Malo to sell their rich cargo. Their catch had been so large that they had run out of barrels, and the ship's captain had come to Les Iles de la Madelaine. They had spent five days salting fish, while the coopers on board the fishing boat had gone ashore and harvested white oak on the island to make more barrels.

He remembered the elongated circular shape of the chain of islands. They were connected by a long sandbar on the north shore that would wash away at times. The *St. Longinus* could not get near that sandbar due to the shallow water. There was no way to go ashore at night. The amount of available beach was uncertain, and rocky cliffs covered the rest of the island. He had no interest in putting the *St. Longinus* at risk. The taller cliffs along the shore prevented their view from being clear enough to tell what was going on, even with a spyglass, but the fire was burning bright enough to be seen from some distance. It would take a couple of hours to circumnavigate to the opposite shore.

"Gentlemen," he told the deck crew, "it is too dangerous to attempt at night. We can wait here, offshore, for daylight. We can get a better look then."

Thames thoroughly disagreed. "Why stop at all, Captain? It is just a fire in the middle of nowhere. Lightning struck a tree and caused a section of the island to burn. So what. Why should we risk our ship, and more, to even see? Let us continue on our way to Quebec City."

"And when we arrive and report, the territory governor will ask why we did not stop and investigate. Maritime law requires that we help stranded souls at sea."

Thames said, "At sea, Captain. This is not at sea. Anyway, it is dark, the middle of the night, and there is no safe way to approach the island. This is all true. We can simply report what we saw, so he can send a boat to investigate if he wishes."

"I agree that we are within our rights to continue onward." Linville paused and held his pipe near his mouth. "If you were on that island, Mr. Thames, and you lit a signal fire, you would want someone to answer it."

Piotr looked out over the railing at the light emanating from the fire. It was a spot of light in the otherwise black horizon. He wasn't sure what to think, but Captain Linville seemed to think he had a duty to investigate.

"I would at that, Captain. I am simply suggesting that it is not a requirement at this time. We are duty bound to report it, not stop for it," Thames responded.

"I appreciate your candor, Mr. Thames." He puffed on his pipe and blew out a small cloud of blue smoke while reflecting on the situation. "We will wait a few hours till sunrise. We will sail around to get a better look. And then we will see what we need to do." He looked at Flagger and Perdo. "Let's stay well offshore till dawn. Then we will have a better look."

Thames offered no visible reaction. He simply accepted the decision and went about his business.

Piotr awoke to the sound of Linville's orders outside the door of the captain's quarters. He was ordering the yawl boat lowered for departure.

Piotr blearily struggled into his shoes and shirt and ran out onto the deck to see what was happening. The sun was bright and blinding in a low eastern sky as he opened the door from his small bedroll in the captain's quarters. He shaded his eyes as he looked out over the railing. They had circled the islands during the night, and now rested at anchor in the channel between the main bodies. Looking to the shoreline, he saw a beachy arm of sand sticking out to the northeast.

"Get the yawl ready!" Perdo yelled from the helm.

Piotr quickly went to the helm and joined with the men freeing the yawl from its hold. He checked to see if the knot he tied was still in place. It was.

With some heavy lifting and pushing, they had the yawl roped and ready to be lowered over the side. Captain Linville addressed the men standing on the deck while he was strapping on his belt with a cutlass and a snaphance pistol tied down in it.

"Landing crew will be six men with me. Armed. Thames, Abel, Anton, Gerard, Mason, and Jean Claude. Flagger, you have the helm."

The men he called all disappeared back to their billets to find armaments, and whatever else they were bringing. Soon they reappeared and began climbing into the yawl, suspended in the air over the side. When they were all aboard, Linville gave a nod.

"Together now!" Piotr heard the order, and he strained on the rope to lower the yawl. It quickly began to tilt as it was being lowered.

"Keep both sides even, Piotr, watch the other ropes!" Flagger shouted at him.

He kept his eye on the other ropes. In a minute or so, the yawl was gently resting on the water with its crew aboard. They pushed away for the short row onto the beach of Les Iles de la Madelaine. Piotr stood at the rail with Flagger and watched them approaching the beach.

A pillar of smoke rose from beyond the beach; the yawl tracked straight for it. He saw them reach the shore and ride a wave up well onto the brown, sandy beach. Two men jumped out in the surf, pulling and pushing the boat higher still. All of them then got out and one tied the boat off to a tree branch sticking up from the sand. They huddled and checked their gear, then started inland up the dunes. As they crested the last dune, heading for the center of the land mass, one of them turned and waved.

"Get your glass out and see if you can spy them," Flagger said.

Looking through the telescope, Piotr watched them walk through the dunes into the leafy branches and undergrowth. Soon they were out of sight. Piotr kept checking periodically for signs of movement, but he could see nothing beyond the leafy screen.

Flagger began pacing with his hands behind his back. After several anxious minutes, Piotr saw movement in the branches. Two men came out of the dunes and trees, made straight for the yawl, and began pushing it out to the water. Soon the two of them were rowing back to the ship in the surf. Through the looking glass, Piotr saw that it was Mason and Gerard Paquet. They plowed through the small waves. As the yawl got closer, they shouted up from the waves, "Captain Linville wants four more men, Eggard needs to come. Bring digging tools."

The entire remaining crew was on deck at this point. Flagger looked at Eggard and he disappeared behind the hold door, emerging with three shovels and a flat spade. He handed them to Piotr. "Get them bundled together with some twine. Lower them down."

Piotr quickly found some twine in the galley and lashed the shovels and spade. As he lowered the tools down to the yawl, Eggard appeared next to him on the rail. He tossed a knotted rope over the railing, with knots every two feet or so. Eggard climbed over the railing and, gripping the rope in his meaty hands, walked down the side of the *St. Longinus* to the waiting yawl. He did this with surprising ease, despite his great size and not being a young man.

Standing in the hull of the yawl, Eggard looked up and waved at Piotr. "You're next."

Piotr was startled and stepped backward half a step. "Me?"

Soon hands were picking him up from behind and he was being lifted over the rail. He grabbed at the knotted rope and twisted to get his feet on the hull. He scrambled about for a moment, trying to get a proper foothold. He was strong for his size, but this was so much harder than Eggard had made it look.

"Lean back, let the rope take your weight," he heard someone say.

Piotr got his feet onto the side of the ship and leaned back.

"Feet and hands work together now."

He took a tentative step down to the yawl and moved one over the other to the next knot down. It was working. He took another step, then another; in a few more he was just above the railing of the yawl. He stepped backward till his toe found the yawl gunnel, and he dropped down into the boat. He moved carefully to the back seat, as the yawl rocked and shifted on the small waves.

Gerard and Mason, wearing the traditional blue and gray cotton and wool buttoned shirts of naval men, each grabbed an oar to row them back.

"Let's go," Eggard said without any decorum.

The men pushed off from the side of the *St. Longinus* and Mason and Gerard started the row back to shore. Piotr reached his hand over to touch the dark blue water of the Gulf of Saint Lawrence. It was very cold, but it felt good to the touch.

"What are we going to see, Gerard?" Eggard asked. "Why the shovels?"

Gerard looked at Eggard for a moment, then at Piotr.

"We have bodies to bury."

Piotr's eyes widened but he did not flinch. He had buried dead bodies before, even the bodies of people he loved, and people who loved him.

He wondered how many were on the island. The fire from the night before had been large. Large enough to get the captain to stop the ship to see what was happening. He now wondered if the fire was a distress signal, just as the captain and Thames had been discussing on the deck.

They approached the rocky beach and the boat picked up speed. They rode the last large wave into the beach.

Mason smiled a ragged-toothed grin at Piotr and said, "We will beach it. You take that side, jump in when I do, grab the side and start running it up onto the sand. Keep the speed up, strong one!"

Piotr gathered himself and crouched in the back of the yawl as Eggard took the oar for him. He saw Mason move his feet to the bench and crouch, so Piotr did the same. As they sped into the shallow water and were almost to the beach, Mason jumped over the gunnel into the water, so Piotr jumped as well.

He landed in knee-deep water and felt the shock of the cold on his legs and feet. The leather and soles of his shoes hit the sandy beach, and he grabbed the gunnel of the yawl and started dragging it as fast as he could, his legs pumping in the soft sand and water. They raised the oars and beached the boat effectively, running it up high enough on the sand to be free of the tide.

"Well done, gentlemen," Gerard said, as he kicked his legs over the side of the yawl down to the sand.

"Like he has done it a hundred times! I should not be surprised." Mason clapped Piotr on the back and laughed.

The men exited the boat one by one and began to shuffle forward on the sandy, rocky beach toward the forested cliff beyond the dunes. Mason handed a shovel to Piotr with a grunt. Piotr looked over the tool while they walked. The short-handled shovel was only five feet long, six inches shorter than Piotr was tall. The blade was spade-shaped and slightly curved with a sharp point. Piotr thought the rust spots were shallow and would rub off in the dirt with some use, especially in these rocky shores. He looked up toward the still-dark smoke pillar coming up from beyond the trees, as they approached the end of the beach. He noticed how it was rising nearly straight up, so there must be very little wind past the beach.

Then, suddenly, the smoke trail began to tilt sideways, and he felt himself listing to the right. He tried to right himself and over-corrected, now listing hard to the left. Eggard, behind him in line and not carrying a tool, reached out with his left hand, grabbed his shirt and angled him back to square.

"Easy."

"I, uh, difficult, walking…" Piotr attempted to respond, but the swirling in his stomach caused him to look away quickly.

He stumbled on for a few steps before he remembered Linville's warning. Land sick. He breathed in deeply over and over again to try and calm his stomach. As they walked, he found it better to be going forward. Faster was better than slower. Any sense of forward direction was better than attempting to be still.

"How long does this last?" he gasped, as he felt a surge of bile roiling in his stomach.

Eggard smiled ruefully at him, his large bald head and leathery skin wrinkling up at the corner of his eyes.

"Just keep walking. It will pass soon enough."

Piotr trudged onward with the occasional sway. The walk was not too far, though, and soon enough they were in view of the fire. Linville, Thames, Abel, Anton, and Jean Claude were standing near the fire. It was way too big for a campfire, and had mostly burned out. Piotr looked around; the diameter of fire damage was nearly twenty feet. Something in the center had burned nearly completely and was still smoking; a few small, crackling flames were left. Looking farther, he saw the bodies in the grass and scrub brush nearby. He started counting them as they approached and got to eleven, as they stopped to speak with the rest of the crew from the *St. Longinus*.

The men were somber, speaking in quiet, hushed tones. Piotr was sickened by land sickness, and the stench of the dead bodies in the grass did not make it better. He looked with bewilderment at Captain Linville, wondering what they were going to do in this macabre landscape.

"We have graves to dig, gentlemen," Linville said. "And from what I can tell, most of these were Frenchmen. It's hard to say for some of them. Eggard, let's bury them over there, nearer the beach." He pointed to the southwest.

"Aye," Eggard responded, looking down. "Come on then."

Eggard stuck his shovel in the sandy, rocky dirt, and pushed it in with his booted right foot. Piotr followed, as well as the others, and they began to dig in silence. Abel, Anton, and Jean Claude joined them in time, and they began to dig a shallow pit wide enough to lay the bodies side by side. Piotr wondered what had happened here, but no one was yet talking, so he dug in silence. After several minutes, Eggard stepped away and handed his shovel off to Abel. Piotr just kept digging and listened.

"What went on here?" Mason finally asked.

Jean Claude looked at the bodies. "Most of these men were shot. Some of them multiple times. Some were stabbed, and one poor bastard has an ax sticking out of his neck." Jean Claude spoke in a whisper, still digging.

"Could it have been savages?" Abel said.

"Savages? Savages would not burn the camp. They would have taken everything they could carry, then snuck away," Gerard said.

"Whatever happened," Anton said, "we got here before the fire was even done burning. Whoever did it, they could still be here, and can't be that far away. We better be careful and keep watch."

"Why would they burn the camp and all of their stuff?" Gerard said. "If it was an attack by savages, they wouldn't burn it. This was likely the English. Piotr saw those warships a couple of days ago."

Jean Claude said, "Maybe they were here first. Had their fun, killed these men, and then sailed on back to jolly old."

They dug in silence for several more minutes. The sandy soil was easy to break through, except for the occasional rock of significance. The shovels changed hands as men grew more tired. Piotr could feel the strain of the effort creeping his heart rate up, and he began to sweat, even on the cool, cloudy spring day. He got down into the hole and turned the shovel over and chopped down to square off the edges of the grave. It was still mostly quiet amongst the men of the *St. Longinus*, while they completed the task.

Linville walked over while they were digging.

"This hole is deep enough, gentlemen. Gather them up for interment."

Piotr clambered up out of the hole with a helping hand from Anton. The men all stuffed their shovels into the ground and shuffled toward the campfire and the scattered bodies.

As they came upon the first, Eggard pointed at the dead sailor's boots.

"Get his feet," he whispered.

Piotr looked down at the body. The young man was twisted up onto his right side, the blood having stilled in his limbs, his gray sailing shirt stained red around his chest. Eggard and he heaved together. Carrying a person is awkward, even in the best of circumstances. The man's shirt was stuck to the ground as they raised him up by hands and feet, causing his waist and center torso to scrape the ground. As they pulled, the shirt fell open, revealing the ragged chest wound from a musket ball.

Piotr, straining with the literal dead weight, traced his memory back to the wounds like this he had seen before. No one recovers from such a wound. Rib bone splinters, and the ball breaks apart, sending chunks of lead into the chest cavity, piercing the vital organs. Within a few minutes, maybe quicker, this young man had died. Piotr knew other men who had died in the same way.

Piotr and Eggard carried the young man's body to the grave site and gently laid it in. Eggard straightened him out as best he could, but his stiff arms could not be folded across his chest. They stood for a moment staring down at the dead sailor in silence. The sun shone overhead now, the daytime heat still cool, even at noon. More sailors from the *St. Longinus* came, carrying the dead to the mass grave.

"Let's keep going," Eggard said, as he left to get another body.

The grass was beginning to lie down under the trampling and movement. It was becoming a green, brown, and red trail. Piotr had walked a path like this just a year earlier. The images of men dead or dying, a muddy trail, blood-stained uniforms, and blood-soaked patches on the grass all came rushing back to his mind. He stopped where he stood, looking off into the horizon.

Eggard was watching him. He was patient. After half a minute, he nudged Piotr. "You all right?"

Piotr blinked and looked at him.

"Chodz'my," he responded in Polish, accidentally. "Let's go," he quickly added in French and shook his head to clear it. They made their way back to retrieve another body.

After all of them were retrieved and put into the hole, the men gathered around the grave site. Captain Linville, Thames, and the others who had hats removed them. They stood quietly in the afternoon sun. A cool breeze washed across the island and the grave site, keeping the bugs and smell down. Linville pulled a rosary from his breast pocket. He whispered a prayer to himself briefly, then addressed the gathering of sailors and fur traders.

"Our Father, who art in heaven, hallowed be thy name. Thy kingdom come, thy will be done, on earth as it is in heaven."

He paused and looked around at the group.

"Sometimes we do not know the purpose for thy will, Lord. Sometimes we wonder why you let such things occur. These men were countrymen to me and many on our ship. They were not soldiers. And yet...thy will be done. They have come to their end and final resting place.

"Give us this day our daily bread. And forgive our debts, as we forgive our debtors. Lead us not into temptation, but deliver us from evil. For thine is the kingdom, the power, and the glory."

"Amen," the group responded.

Gerard and Mason had prepared a marker on a slab of wood from one of the boxes, using the coals as chalk. They placed it at the top. Piotr could not read it in French.

He leaned over to Eggard, as they gathered the shovels and began to fill the dirt into the grave. "What does it say?"

"Eleven Frenchmen, killed here. Found by the men of the fur trading ship *St. Longinus*. April 17, 1632," Eggard replied. He added, "True enough, I suppose."

As the first shovels of sandy dirt were being pushed back into the grave, Thames stepped forward. "Wait a moment."

He carefully stepped down into the grave and took a long careful step over the frozen and bent limbs of the dead. He reached down and his hand found the handle of the small ax in the collarbone of a young sailor in a gray, blood-spattered shirt. He tugged once, but it did not budge. He gripped it tighter and pulled harder. Then, with a squish it came free of the collar and breastbone into his hand. He held it up and looked it over, standing among the bodies. He kept it in his hand while he climbed up out of the hole in an easy movement, and stood next to Eggard and Piotr. All the men waited.

"This is a soldier's field ax. The English use them. The paintings on it are from the Miami savages of Ohio." Thames pronounced it the Algonquin way, O-he-yo.

"I traded with them last year when they came to the fort at Quebec City. They spoke of many furs in their lands south and west of Quebec City, south of Erie."

Piotr looked the ax over while Thames held it in the air. He could see the red and purple painted markings, but the handle was smooth and sanded by someone who knew how to make tools. Thames bent over and wiped it in the grass to clean the blood and bone from the small but sturdy ax head.

"You don't have an ax, Piotr, you take it." He handed it to him.

Piotr took it and looked it over, examining the ax head. It was well forged and had a rather long handle; the blade was not nicked from smashing through the collarbone of that poor French sailor. It was not rusted or stained. The handle quality was what he noticed next. It had sawtooth marks and had been sanded smooth. It was made of fire-hardened hickory. No grooves or patterns were cut into the handle. This was made by someone making a lot of these handles at once with high function and low beauty in mind.

The paint markings appeared amateurish, done with a little finger dipped in paint. He had no idea what the swirling symbols meant. He set it in the grass and picked up his shovel, as all the men went back to filling the grave.

After the grave was filled, Thames quietly walked over, next to Linville, and said, "I found a blood trail leading away to the northeast from the burn site. We should have a look."

Linville nodded. "It is probably more dead sailors. Go, take a couple of men with you, just in case."

Thames nodded back and turned toward Piotr. "Piotr, with me. And Anton."

Linville gave orders to salvage anything in the campsite that could be useful, and the men began to rifle through the various pieces of cargo spread out on the ground. Piotr picked up the ax and followed Thames and Anton. Thames noticed that he had no belt to slide the small ax into. He walked over to a crate that had been busted open, reached in and pulled the wooden lid off, nails and all. He pulled out a black leather belt for use around a soldier's shoulder, with loops added to hold knives, axes, lead and powder horns. He looked Piotr over, then pulled his knife out and quickly cut the belt about a foot shorter, handing it to the boy.

"This will do."

Piotr took the belt and looped it around his waist. His cotton pants, worn out with small holes in the knees, had three loops for a belt, and it fit well enough. He pulled Eggard's knife from his pocket and punched a hole where the belt would latch, fed the cut end through, and secured it at his hips. He then slid the knife scabbard onto the belt so it hung in the front on his right hip. He slipped the ax handle into a loop at the back of his right hip and it fit.

"Keep the blade facing backward, so your swinging hand does not hit it accidentally, when you walk. Always wear an ax farther back on your hip for the same reason," Thames advised.

Piotr pulled it out and flipped it around into the correct position.

"Let us go see what we can find." Thames turned and walked off north and west of the camp, musket cradled comfortably in his left arm.

Piotr noted his ease with the weapon while they walked. Anton was armed with a short cutlass that he always had at his belt and a shorter skinning knife that he kept on the opposite side.

Fifty yards from camp, Thames gestured to the grass. Blood splatters showed red against the green grass and grayish brown soil. Every few steps as they walked, they saw more speckled marks. Someone had run this way after an injury and was leaking blood significantly. The afternoon sun made it easy to see; in a few hours, this trail would be lost till the next day. Thames picked up the pace and they started a rapid walk. Piotr quickly realized he was not used to covering ground at such a pace after several weeks aboard the *St. Longinus*. He kept up, however; Anton and Thames seemed to have no difficulty.

After moving more than a mile from the camp, Thames pointed out that the blood splatters were getting harder to find, and farther apart. They could lose the trail soon. As they walked, Thames pointed out the occasional additional clue: a heel imprint here, broken and crushed grass blades, a stick broken and pushed down into the mud. All in line with the blood trail. Piotr began to look for such detail too.

They came upon a small, shallow creek bed of smooth, rocky stones and slow flowing, clear water. Thames pointed out that some of the stones were flipped over, leaving a dull side upward. The other stones were shiny side up. The bleeding person had crossed through the creek bed here.

They waded through easily enough. A few yards past the creek bed, in a plot of waist-high grass, was a flat circle of grass that had been crushed flat. There was blood in the center of it. The person had laid down here for some time. The grass was still trampled in the direction following the creek bed to the northwest. They walked on for fifty or so more yards and found little to no sign.

Thames was hesitant to go back. They had time before darkness, and could run back if necessary, but there was no indication of where the trail led next. He crouched down in a squat and gestured for Anton and Piotr to do the same. They huddled together.

Thames whispered, "Apparently, our injured person was able to bind his wound while resting in the tall grass, because the blood trail has disappeared."

"There is no one else around, I don't think," Anton said. "Let us go upstream a little bit farther and see. If we find nothing, we go back."

Thames nodded. They moved out slowly. Thames gestured for them to spread out and walk parallel to the stream.

Piotr was the first to hear a sound. A small rustle in the leaves and grass. He thought this could be anything, but he heard it again, a second time. He held his hand up in the air; Thames and Anton stopped in mid-step. A third time, there was rustling in the grass. Piotr was certain it came from behind a stand of short, scruffy fir trees only steps away from the north shore of the stream. Anton heard it as well. He pulled his cutlass from his belt with his right hand and crept silently toward the group of small evergreens, slowly parting their branches to peer underneath.

Anton looked down into the face of an older man, dirty and pale. He looked dead. Suddenly, the blue eyes opened and looked directly at Anton.

"Who are you?" came the soft whispered voice of the injured man.

Anton's eyes widened in surprise. "I am Anton Paquet, of the brothers Paquet. Who are you and what are you doing here on this island lying under a tree?"

"Gilbert Laurent. Captain of the cargo ship *Render*. Marooned, stranded on this island for four days. We were set upon by marauders in the night two days ago, they shot some of my men. I fled in confusion and ran here, where I lay." He looked up as Piotr stuck his head in between the branches. His face and clothes were dirty, and his beard was covered in debris from the dirt and plants.

"You are injured?" Thames circled the stand of evergreens from the opposite side and knelt down near Captain Laurent.

"I have been shot." Laurent paused for a long moment. His eyes then swelled with painful tears. "I never thought I would see another Frenchman again." His voice cracked with relief and pain. His face grimaced as he said it, both from the joy at being found, and the knowledge that he was still in grave danger, probably dying.

Thames slid his bladder canteen off and pulled the stopper out, guiding the water to the lips of the injured man.

"We will take you back with us, eh. Do not give up." He gestured to Anton and Piotr. "Make a travois. Cut some pine branches to fill it. We will drag him out of here, with us."

Piotr and Anton quickly found some young spruce trees and he put his long-handled field ax to use, cutting two green branches of about eight feet in length to build the sides of the A-framed travois. Anton found a crossing piece at the top and they lashed the two green poles to it with small, flexible green branches from the fir trees. Piotr cut several progressively longer bows and they laid them across the poles, lashing them as they went. In a few minutes, they had it completed. They dragged it by carrying the cross piece with one on each side, near to where Thames knelt.

"I will hold the branches up; get under there and slide him toward the travois." Piotr knelt down and crawled under the branches. He slid his arms under the shoulders of Captain Laurent and eased him upward. Soft groans escaped his lips as the pain of movement hit him. Piotr found his footing and, as gently as he could, slid him out from under the pine branches. Anton quickly got his feet and they eased him onto the frame, with his head up toward the narrowly angled top part. Piotr took the left side of the handle and Anton took the right. Together, they raised him up so that his head was above his feet and only the back tip of the poles would drag on the ground, leaving a trail of two marks in the dirt. Thames looked at them and turned to start the journey back to the burnt campsite and the *St. Longinus.*

They came back to camp on the same path they had followed out, Piotr and Anton dragging Captain Laurent through the grass and over the creek with Thames's help. They found Eggard in the makeshift sail cloth tent, directing the traffic of men busy with the process of finding anything of value.

Eggard looked at them and signaled Linville to come over.

"Where are you injured?" Linville asked after Anton and Piotr quietly lifted the travois up onto the crates and wooden boxes that had been stacked next to Eggard.

"Shot in the chest," Laurent answered weakly, wheezing as he spoke. Eggard peeled back his layers of outer coat and undershirt, turning his head sideways and back to get the most light.

"He says he is the captain of a ship, stranded here for some four days now—the one that all of these men came from," Thames explained.

"Roll him to his right a bit so I can find if the ball exited."

Captain Linville pulled his knife from his scabbard. He pulled the outer coat off of the groaning Captain Laurent and cut away at the bloody white shirt. As they rolled him to his side, he found what he was looking for: a round, smallish exit hole on the back of the ribs on his left side. The ball had hit him in the front left side and bounced along the rib cage, exiting out his back. The round hole meant that it was more or less intact coming out. If it had broken up upon contact with the rib cage, it would have sent bits of lead into his left lung and there would be several small exit wounds. The man would have died in a few minutes.

"How long ago?" Linville asked his counterpart from *The Render*, not stopping his work.

"Two nights ago," wheezed Laurent.

"Gather him some stew and more water to drink when we are done here. We will cauterize the wound and move him back to the ship." Eggard turned to address the task.

Linville looked about at the men standing nearby. "Who has whisky?" Gerard Paquet produced a small metal flask from his shirt pocket. "I will need some black powder as well." Eggard nodded and reached into his sack, pulling out a powder horn.

"Your ribs are broken on the left side, but putrefaction has not yet set into the wound. We have to seal the holes, so you will stop leaking." Laurent nodded, his eyes closed with the pain. Linville grabbed a leather strap discarded from one of the boxes. He held it to Laurent's mouth; Laurent clamped his teeth down on it.

"Hold him still, gentlemen."

The men gathered closer, putting their hands on a foot or shoulder, holding Laurent from squirming. Linville poured a cupful of whisky and, with Laurent still lying on his right side, quickly poured the contents into the wound. Laurent's eyes widened in pain, and he shuddered and jerked in the hands of the men helping to hold him. A second cupful into the exit wound caused several small grunts to escape through clenched teeth. Linville took the powder horn and poured a small amount into the entry and exit wounds, careful to not move Laurent or spill any powder. He went to the fire and pulled out two small sticks with red-hot tips, glowing from the flame. He handed one to Eggard and nodded for him to light the powder simultaneously.

"Hold still."

They lit the powder on the front and back of his torso at the same time. Black smoke and a short, yellow flame flared from the wounds, escaping into the air in the tent. Laurent screamed into the leather strap between his teeth, grunting and squirming in the hands of the crewmen. Then his eyes rolled back in his head, and he mercifully passed out, head sagging toward the table awkwardly while being held on his right side.

Linville looked over the two wounds. The flesh melded together, with black stains from the powder on the surface of the skin. "Well," Linville shrugged and held his bloody hands up, "we have done all that we can. If he wakes, see that he is fed and given water. Get him back to the ship and give him a clean shirt."

The men nodded, Anton and Eggard picked up Captain Laurent and moved him to the travois.

Laurent groaned, and sitting up slightly as he lay on the travois, he gestured to Linville. "My ship is aground! There is no point in going back..." He then lay back and sagged into the pine boughs of the travois.

"Rest easy, rest easy, Captain," Anton Paquet soothed him.

Linville turned and looked at Captain Laurent lying on the travois. Then he looked out to sea at the *St. Longinus*, anchored in the cove, offshore of the beach. "What is he talking about? There is no ship run aground. We sailed around the island before we anchored. No ship is on the rocks or the shore. Thames, is there a ship we have not seen?"

Thames shook his head. "Ours is the only ship near this place, as far as I can tell."

"We could scout across to the northern shore then, have a look about. He and those men, what is left of these supplies, it all got here some way." Linville looked to Thames.

Thames was not interested. There were no beaver pelts on Les Iles de la Madelaine. "This will take a full day, Captain. It is not as close as you might think, to the northern shore. There is no other boat, sir. If there was, it is gone now, somehow...or, he is simply out of his head with the pain. He said he was captain of a cargo ship, when we found him in the woods. A cargo ship that could sail all the way from France would be large. There is nothing here."

Linville paused in considerate thought, the lines on his face creased. He was a dutiful man. They had come here when they saw the fire, after all. "You're right. That fire was not a signal, but it was a sign, telling us of the bad things that happened to these men, and poor Captain Laurent." He pointed back toward the grave site, then at Captain Laurent, as Eggard and Anton were dragging him on the travois to the beach. "Let us get on our way. We have furs to gather." He stood face-to-face with Thames and clapped him on the shoulder.

The men gathered on the beach with what belongings they had been able to gather in hand. Most everything had burned or been hauled away by the invading marauders. Whoever they were, they had taken everything they could and tried to burn the rest. But even scattered bits had value in a place where there were very few manufactured goods of any sort. This new world was filled with a vast wealth of natural resources. It was sorely lacking in the everyday manmade objects obtainable in Europe.

Eggard held a canvas sack as the yawl pushed off for a return trip to the *St. Longinus*, Captain Laurent aboard it. He walked back toward the group. There were enough people and found goods to necessitate three trips back and forth, so he expected to be standing on the beach for some time. Holding the bag up, he gestured at Piotr to follow. They walked down the beach, away from the group.

"I saw it when we landed, there is a great beach for foraging, just down from here. A beach is good when the tide comes all the way up onto the shore at high tide, and then retreats and exposes a big area, at low tide. Right here, see? It does that."

He started off down the beach into wet, rock-strewn sand. Puddles of water still remained, many only an inch or so deep. Piotr followed as Eggard strode purposefully into what looked like a wasteland of rocks, mud, sand, bits of seaweed, and occasional driftwood.

"Here. And here." Eggard pointed with his long knife at the sand. Piotr saw nothing, until Eggard gestured him to kneel down in the mud and look closer. He brushed a bit of seaweed over, and there was a half-moon-shaped shell in a half-inch of water.

"Scallop. Good to eat plain, and in the burgoo." Eggard picked it up and it clapped its shell shut, squirting water out as it sealed itself. Eggard put it in the canvas bag.

Piotr picked up the other one he had pointed at, and Eggard smiled. "Yes."

Piotr put it in the bag.

"No smaller, though, hand size at least." Eggard held up his wide palms to demonstrate, and Piotr thought his giant hands were twice as big as his own.

"Look out along the beach, find more."

As Piotr gazed across the sand, the scallops began to reveal themselves with tiny clapping motions as they burrowed down a little deeper when the men walked near. He realized that what originally appeared to be a muddy wasteland was filled with food.

Eggard stooped down and grabbed a small gray and black shell with very small white dots in rows. "Cockles, too." He threw the smaller shell into the bag.

Piotr soon became adept at finding the small, shallow indentations in the sand where the scallops lived. There were hundreds, even thousands, on this section of the beach alone. Still, he only took the larger ones, as instructed. He felt a little sorry for them as they really couldn't escape his search.

"See this hole?" Eggard beckoned him over, pointing at a small pencil-sized hole in the sand. "That will be a clam, or a razor clam. Possibly big enough to eat."

Piotr looked about the beach. He saw dozens of those small holes now. Eggard shoved his hand into the sand around the hole and pulled up a pile of sand. It was, indeed, a brown and white clam shell, slightly larger than the scallop shell, and clamped shut. "That will do." Eggard scooped it into the canvas.

In a few minutes, they had harvested a sack full of edible shelled clams, cockles, and scallops. They made their way back toward the launching point to join the rest of the crew waiting to go. A few of the men had started a small fire with driftwood and were heating up a teapot. Eggard pulled a scallop out of the sack and drew his knife.

"Look, stick your knife in this spot and," he inserted the knife about an inch and twisted it expertly, "opens right up." He pried it the rest of the way with his hand and quickly cut the scallop meat away from the shell.

"Get the meat here, like this." He showed Piotr how to remove it.

Eggard then reached down and grabbed a loose stick, then pierced the round, white bite of meat in the center.

"Open a few more, and we will grill them right here while we wait." Piotr took one from the sack and completed the task, awkwardly but successfully. In a few minutes they had several on the stick, grilling over the small fire, with a pot of tea boiling.

After they had cooked, Eggard passed the stick around to the men on the beach, each taking a grilled scallop or two, chewing and swallowing them with noisy slurps. The teapot was passed from person to person to wash down the succulent treat, a few of them pulling out metal cups from pouches or pockets. Piotr bit into a scallop and enjoyed the tasty meat.

Linville stood in the group of men with the late day sun dropping and red in the sky, with Thames, the Paquet brothers, Mason and Gerard. The breeze on the beach was pleasant, and the hot tea fortified them. They all watched, chewed, and sipped as the yawl reached the side of the *St. Longinus* and began to unload its haul of Captain Laurent and the scattered supplies.

"Gentlemen, let us make sail tonight for Quebec City, with all due haste," Linville said.

"We can be there in a few short days. Then," Thames concurred, "the real work begins."

*Chapter 6*

# THE LONGBOATS

They stamped out their meager campfire on the beach at the shore of the big island and made a quick breakfast of hard-tack biscuits and dried beef, softened in sea water. First Mate Raul Montreaux tried to keep a positive outlook on their situation. He was in charge of this expedition, in any case.

The crew pushed the longboats back into the water of the gulf, and the passengers clambered aboard. Soon they were through the incoming tide and rowing smoothly out to sea. Crossing some of the open waters of the gulf was in his plan. The two longboats had left the beach on Les Iles de le Madelaine the morning before, rowing around the southern point of the island on calm seas, and making their way across the Gulf of St. Lawrence, before stopping to camp on this barrier island's beach for the night.

He had spent his life on the sea. The days of his youth had been filled with time in small rowboats, fishing and clamming in the waters of the North Sea. He knew the ocean better than he knew his own brother, left back in Saint-Malo. He had worked on it since he could remember, and so had his father before him.

Their departure in the early morning, on a light breeze with mild waves and a clear blue sky, was the best he could have hoped for. They rowed smoothly on the calm water and the longboats handled well. Maybe they could make it in three days, he thought, if the weather held.

After crossing this stretch of open water, his intent was to skirt the shoreline all the way north to the entry point of the St. Lawrence River. Keeping within sight of the shoreline was a longer route than rowing directly across the gulf, but he did not have the manpower to make the two-hundred-mile distance straight away. He worried about what or who might see them from the shore, but if one of the longboats got into trouble, they had a better chance of getting to land alive. By mid-morning they had covered most of the distance across open water and would soon be within sight of the western shore of the gulf. Raul focused on the waves carefully as the crew rowed steadily and the small sail they had raised for added speed remained full.

As if from nowhere, he felt the hot breath of a musket ball whiz past his head and the bow of the longboat from behind, and then heard a sizzle and then the crack of a musket barrel a long moment later. He turned his head in open-mouthed shock. In an instant, he began to calculate the distance to the large warship bearing down on them.

The ball splashed down after crossing their bow a mere twenty yards in front of them. *A warning shot?*

As hard as it was to comprehend the sight of the massive ship behind them, what surprised him to his very core was the flag. Flying right off the bow, a yellow cross and a small blue rectangular sigil in the corner on a white background. Every seaman and soldier in Europe knew the flag of Gustavus Adolphus, the Swedish king. His mind raced with questions. *How and why is a Swedish ship here on the shores of the New World, and why are they shooting at us?*

"Row! Double-time!" he shouted to the boat off of his port bow and to the men in his own longboat.

No time to figure it out now, just flee, his brain screamed. The small sail they had erected on the temporary mast was full, but the longboats could move much faster when all the oars were working at maximum speed. The sailors looked up in confusion from the rifle shot, but doubled their effort, and the two longboats were quickly racing on the surface of the waves. Montreaux's eyes flicked left and right rapidly as his mind began tracking through options. There were not many.

The longboats were loaded with cargo and passengers, and he knew they could not outrun them for long. The warship behind him was huge. At first glance, it seemed easily the biggest ship he had ever seen. It was nearly a thousand yards behind them, but he could see the many cannon barrels and that it was four decks tall. They had fired a long gun from the bow and were certainly reloading now. There was no chance of fighting, only to flee. It was probably staffed with two hundred and fifty trained men, and it was moving shockingly fast for such a massive ship. He quickly made a decision, hoping to save their lives.

Father Archembeau looked over his shoulder and his eyes widened in fear. He taped Pascal on the shoulder and gestured with his head. They both looked with disbelief at the huge warship bearing down on them from the east.

"Why chase us?" he asked no one in particular.

Raul, looking over his shoulder at the ship, shook his head apprehensively. Raul's main concern was not getting sunk or shot by cannon and musket fire. He had no idea why a Swedish ship from the military might of Gustavus Adolphus would chase them, let alone be here, on the edge of the New World. He had seen only English and French ships in his trips to Quebec City. The English ships he had seen had all been from a distance, not necessarily hostile, but usually.

"Mr. Montreaux, what do we do?" Father Demari asked.

"We run, as fast as possible, to the shoreline southwest from here. I had hoped to camp there tonight, but about twenty leagues farther along. There are barrier islands off the coast of it, and we can get in behind them and possibly sail upriver. A ship so large will not be able to follow us!"

He angled the rudder and moved closer to the other longboat. When he was within shouting distance, he yelled out his plan. The second boat followed as he angled the rudder more and the bow came over as the longboat was skirting over the top of the waves.

Jana looked out over the water and shouted, "There is land. There, ahead, there is a peninsula," as she pointed.

Montreaux looked out but could not see it yet, but he was encouraged by the thought of it. He looked back and saw that the warship was closing. They were gaining. It looked even larger as it closed.

A puff of smoke burst forth from the long gun on the bow of the warship, and Montreaux ducked instinctively, and shouted, "Incoming!"

The .75 caliber musket ball zipped past the starboard side of the boat. The cracking report from the muzzle arrived just as it splashed down with a plunk between the two longboats. The French sailors on the other longboat looked at Raul, eyes widening in fear, but they kept rowing.

"Row boys, row hard!" Montreaux shouted.

Jana looked back over her shoulder, and beyond the warship chasing them. She had always had good eyes. She saw movement behind the warship, and there in the distance, following but not keeping pace, was a smaller ship.

"Mr. Montreaux, there is another ship." She pointed.

Raul snapped his head around to see this new threat.

There it was, in the distance, following behind but losing distance, as the warship was at full sail.

"Is that *The Render*? *The Render* is following it!" Father Demari shouted.

More questions raced through Montreaux's mind. How? They must have freed it from the sandbar, using the weight of the enormous warship. What of Captain Laurent and the men? Did they take them from the island? Were they on *The Render* now?

The peninsula was visible on the horizon, a blue and gray line pointing out into the horizon, rising up from the water line. He stared at it, trying to figure the distance needed to get to shelter. The men at the oars were panting and sweating with exertion now, sweat soaking through their shirts despite the cool wind, as they fixated on their task of following smooth, long, fast stroke after stroke.

"Keep at it, lads, land is there!" He pointed ahead toward the peninsula sticking out into the bay.

He looked back over his shoulder to check the distance to the warship. His eyes widened with dismay and fear to see the gap had narrowed even more. The immense ship was faster than they could row.

"Can we make it, Mr. Montreaux?" Father Archembeau asked, nodding back toward the trailing warship. His face was creased with lines of stress and his voice cracked with fear.

"Maybe. Probably. We have to get as close as possible. If it shallows out enough, they will be forced to slow and even stop. If we can, we get around the barrier island and work up the river, if we can find a way in. They will be within cannon range in minutes. Then...."

"Will they not have to get alongside us for cannon fire?" Father Demari pointed out.

"Not that ship. Look at the third deck."

Demari and Archembeau craned their heads to see it.

"See the shuttered hatches on the bow...they will open...out will come those long-barreled 16-pounders. They have more range. Not big enough to sink another ship, but big enough to cut a mast, or smash a rudder. They are meant to cripple whatever that beast is chasing."

"Surely, we are not that important of a target? Why even bother with a couple of rowboats?" Father Archembeau asked again.

"I do not know, Father, but they have *The Render*. They probably have our crew. I can only guess that the crew has told them who and where we are. They want us captured or sunk so we don't tell anyone in Quebec City what we saw here."

Two hatches on the bow of the massive warship's third deck opened, and a long-barreled cannon poked out toward the longboats, followed by a second barrel, side by side.

"Keep rowing, men! No matter what, by God, keep rowing!" bellowed Montreaux.

A blast of smoke shot forth from the barrel of the first cannon. A ball whizzed through the air with a booming crack and splashed down in a geyser of water fifty yards short of them.

The crew and passengers of longboats shivered in fear and cowered, awaiting the next blast. Moans echoed from the passengers; the rowers were fixated on their task.

The second cannon shot smoke out, and the thunderous boom arrived moments after the ball smashed the water ten yards to the front and right of the starboard bow. A towering geyser of water grew up from the waves and rained down on the crew and passengers as they rowed past.

"They will have our distance marked on the next shot," Guillaume said, panting heavily with exertion, while rowing. "We have to make a move!"

"We have to make it to cover," Montreaux shouted.

A puff of smoke burst from the long gun on the bow of the warship. A musket ball cracked through the air, smashing a chip off of the bow of the other longboat, ricocheting with a whine out over the water.

Montreaux shouted to the other boat, "Five hard strokes then to port, toward land!"

"Aye!" the other boat's coxswain responded, shaken.

Montreaux counted out the five strokes. "One, two, three..." A blast of smoke from the front of the approaching warship as it launched another cannonball drowned out the next number in his count.

To Jana, the sound of the cannon was a thunder that she felt as it reverberated in her bones. The cannonball zipped past the stern, just behind Raul Montreaux's head, and slammed into the longboat next to them. Her keen eyes watched as it exploded upwards into the air. It splintered the hull into a thousand pieces as it rose up out of the water. The two men in the bow were thrown into the air more than ten feet and smashed down into the water in front of where the longboat had been. The men in the stern and the coxswain were gone. Jana stared at the wreckage in fear. She spotted the blast of smoke from the second cannon firing, but just before the sound and ball arrived, water began to rain down filled with splinters of wood, bone, and tissue on the passengers of the remaining longboat in a mist of red droplets.

The spinning of the cannonballs was so fast against the air, they buzzed as they flew. The booming sound of the gunpowder exploding, and the crack of the projectiles breaking the speed of sound, traveled slower than the balls themselves, arriving a fraction of a second later. Montreaux saw Jana's open-mouthed warning scream but didn't hear it. The sound was blocked out by the sizzle and loud boom of the next shot.

The ball smashed into the water where the other longboat had been, sending more water skyward. Montreaux reacted quickly, turning the rudder, and shouting out orders. "Stop!"

The exhausted rowers responded admirably, working together as a unit under stress.

"Jana, throw the rope at your feet," Montreaux commanded with desperation.

She looked down to see the coiled rope, and gathered it up as quickly as she could, tossing it to the nearest man in the water. He weakly grabbed it in both hands as it landed in the water near him.

"Pull him in!" Montreaux shouted.

Jana began to pull, and Father Demari and Sister Mary also grabbed the rope, putting their strength into it. Fueled by adrenaline and fear, they quickly pulled the man to the side of the boat. He grabbed the hull and Demari pulled him up onto his lap, soaking wet.

Sister Mary Therese immediately began looking him over for injuries. Other than cold and shock, he appeared to be all right. Jana gathered the rope and threw it out again as fast as she could, standing upright to do it. The remaining sailor in the water weakly swam a couple of strokes to get it in his hands. Once he obtained a handhold, they pulled him in as fast as they could. Montreaux looked back at the warship, waiting for the next blast of smoke. It came.

The long gunner tried to take out the men at the oars.

At this range, the gunner was still arcing the shot—from a moving deck to a target bobbing on the waves. His skill was such that he might pull it off. He cocked the hammer on the long matchlock rifle, its lit fuse ready to set off the powder charge in the pan that would ignite into the powder in the magazine, exploding and expelling the .75 caliber ball at a little over five hundred meters per second. He lined up his sights and squeezed the trigger smoothly.

The large-caliber long gun blasted out white and grey smoke, and the ball zipped toward them, arcing downward and just over Guillaume's shoulder, striking the water between Jana and the man still in the water. The water sprayed up on her face and arms as the ball skipped on the waves, a foot from her pulling hands. She moaned in fear but kept pulling the rope as fast as possible. He finally was close enough to grab the hull and began pulling himself up with Demari and Jana's help.

As he fell into the boat, Montreaux shouted, "ROW!"

Guillaume and the others began to move again. The warship behind them was now less than two hundred yards away. If it got broadside to them, they were doomed, Montreaux thought. A broadside cannon blast from all of the cannons on that ship would swamp them, even if they were not blown into dust.

"The point is right there! They can't come this close to land."

He pointed emphatically at the peninsula just a hundred yards ahead. Small trees and scrub bushes lined the narrow, rocky piece of land jutting out. It was high enough above that water line that it might offer them some cover, at least briefly.

"Get around the peninsula and we have a chance!"

The single longboat began to pick up speed once again. The oar men found their rhythm. As they got closer to the point, Montreaux was hoping the warship would slow, not wanting to ground itself in pursuit. The cannon fire had stopped, though, and he wondered why. Within a minute of hard rowing they were at the point of land and moving into shallow water nearer the rocky shore of the peninsula.

"It's turning," Jana said with a surprisingly calm voice.

Montreaux looked over his shoulder to see the massive warship indeed slowing and turning to angle itself sideways to the target. *Us.*

They had but seconds to round the point and head up the river channel, into shallow waters. As Guillaume and the sailors stroked desperately fast, Jana looked back over Montreaux's shoulder and saw the hatches on the side of the warship starting to open. One after the other, three deck levels began to open the small doors and the cannon barrels were pushed out.

The rocky shore of the peninsula was just within reach, and Raul Montreaux leaned on the rudder to angle the longboat.

"Row, don't stop!"

He turned the longboat as sharply as the boat would allow, getting the peninsula between them and their pursuer. The warship was no more than a hundred and fifty yards behind them and dared not come closer to land. It would not be able to turn as sharply and would have to curve around the point. This would increase the distance between them, giving them time to find a cove or channel to duck into, he hoped. The longboat completed the turn and they moved along the shoreline now, southward, away from the open water of the gulf. *These men are nearing the limit of exhaustion*, Montreaux thought, when the fusillade blast from the warship hit them.

The cannonballs, thirty-two of them, came forth like thunder and lightning from the hand of Odin.

Jana saw the fire and smoke erupt from the side of the warship. The cannonballs screamed in the air as they flew out of the barrels. The roar of the cannon hit just as they smashed into the shore of the peninsula, and sent exploding dirt, rocks and wood into the air. Some of the cannonballs plowed into the trees, but the majority bounced off the rocks, spraying dirt and debris everywhere. The balls sizzled as they skimmed over the heads of the desperate longboat crew. Jana could see them, and she felt a sting on her neck and arms as bits of rocks and wood were blasted through the air. The water beyond the longboat sprayed upward as the remaining cannonballs skipped across the surface, before losing enough energy to splash down into the sea.

The giant warship rocked sideways with the recoil from the broadside, and the entire ship was quickly enveloped in smoke from the massive blast. Montreaux saw an opening. They were obscured from view for a few precious moments. He saw an entry to a cove, just beyond the peninsula that guarded it.

He shook his head to clear the ringing in his ears and steered the longboat into the cove opening, behind trees and vegetation. Looking back over his shoulder, he could just see the bow of the warship as it drifted through the cloud of smoke from the broadside.

"To the tree! At the end of the cove!" he urged his exhausted crew.

The longboat rowed across the cove as fast as the crewmen could make it. A large willow tree stood at the shore. Its long, leaf-covered branches hung down like a great green umbrella, their tips brushing the water of the cove. The roots of the tree secured that rocky bank of shoreline, and water from the hillside beyond the cove had fed the massive tree for decades. Montreaux steered the longboat right toward the tree. Archembeau and Demari parted the hanging branches open like a heavy green curtain. The longboat slipped into the dark stillness under the large tree.

Shaking with exhaustion, fear, and adrenaline, covered in bits of mud, vegetation, rocks and sand, bleeding from multiple scratches and small wounds, the desperate longboat crew pulled in their oars and slid the boat up against the steep edge of the shoreline, right up next to the trunk of the massive tree that now hid them with its curtain of branches.

Montreaux reached into the pocket of his long-tailed duster jacket and pulled out his spyglass. He poked it out between the hanging willow leaves, looking out at the massive ship that had now drifted beyond the huge cloud of black and grey smoke floating above the water. A name was painted on the stern in gold letters. *Wasa.*

He whispered it aloud.

Hidden in the shadows of the tree, the former passengers of *The Render* waited in their longboat. The only sounds were the heavy breathing of the oarsmen, the water lapping the shore, and wind gently rustling the green leafy branches of the great willow.

## Chapter 7

# QUEBEC CITY

The deck of the *St. Longinus* was covered by the feet of its crew, as all hands stood in the sunshine of mid-morning. It was a glorious spring day, with bright sun and a gentle breeze from the southwest. As the ship sailed westward in the center of the river, the men looked over the railing at the approaching dock of the small city. The tree cover and forest were so thick with green leaves that, from five hundred yards away, you would not know that Quebec City was there at all. As they got closer, Piotr could see a glimpse of the dock and people working on the shoreline.

Construction of log buildings and a wooden wall of tree trunks was well underway by groups of workers. Men dressed in buckskin and patterned linsey-woolsey shirts worked in the sun, banging freshly made nails into place with mallets and hammers. Women in blue cotton dresses and red tartan wool scarves and throws were working on the dock and on the street. Cooking pots boiled and steamed in several locations. A clothes-washing stand with a large wooden table and a huge metal tub of wet clothing was bubbling in heated river water over an open fire. Clothing, hung on lines strung up from tree to tree, decorated the dirt path that served as a street.

Flagger, pointing at the structures lining the street running north away from the dock, said, "The tent city has grown to considerable size."

Piotr looked up above the dock at a muddy dirt path going up the slope away from the river and the dock. At least thirty tents of many varieties lined the path two and three rows deep along the main thorough-fare. People were moving in and out of tents and walking into the woods beyond. Up the slope, he saw the tops of more and more tents hidden in trees beyond the pathway. Houses, of a structure he had never seen before, were visible through the spring leaves. Long, single story, covered in bark and moss, with smoke drifting upward from holes in the rooftops. Birds flitted about the shoreline and flew in and above the tents, making a racket of chirps and whistles. This was a city, of sorts, a city of oilcloth and wood.

Running parallel to the shore and starting at the dockside, a wooden wall of logs guarded the front of single-story log buildings, their roofs visible just beyond the palisade. A gate of split trunks guarded the entry-way beyond the unfinished wall. A single two-story building dominated the rooflines, and a French Catholic flag from Paris flew at full mast off of a post from the top corner of the building, sticking out like a yardarm on a ship. There was a blue rectangle at each corner with a white sigil of a crown surrounded by gold trim, and a picture of a more elaborate crown in the center. Piotr could not quite see the finer details, but it made him think that building must be of some importance.

Linville shouted out orders for docking, and Perdo turned the ship into the center of the river, to make the arc necessary for docking port-side. Piotr jumped to, following the orders of retrieving and tying down sails, and the deck of the *St. Longinus* burst into action as the crew readied the ship for port. The boat would be facing east when it came to rest. A cargo ship was already tied off at the end of the dock, so the *St. Longinus* would be using the rest of the unfinished dock.

Piotr watched as Perdo followed the shouted instructions of Abel and Gerard Paquet, who had climbed out onto the rigging hanging from the bow mast and the stern, respectively. *Here*, they directed Perdo, as the ship angled itself slowly toward the dock, using the current and momen-tum to finish the last hundred feet of a journey that started nearly three thousand miles ago.

Captain Linville watched over all of it with a practiced eye. The ship came to a slow stop as it eased up to the edge of the dock. At Flagger's direction, Piotr helped to send ropes down to tie off the cleats, and the crew hung coils of rope down, to protect the side of the boat from banging into the dock while at rest.

The rope ladder was thrown down to the deck some twelve feet below, and Linville, Thames, Gerard and Anton Paquet all descended to the wooden planking of the dock one after the other.

Linville gave orders as he climbed down the rope ladder. "Everyone stays, until we meet with the territory governor, or whoever is in charge."

They made their way across the dock toward the gated entrance to the wall.

People emerged from the tents and walked down the path toward the dock. The crew were lining the port side of the deck, hanging over the railing. Several women approached the boat first, some native women and some French or European looking, thought Piotr. They began to call out to the sailors of the *St. Longinus*, suggesting to the men that they should come down off the boat. As one stout woman got closer, Piotr saw that she had a missing front tooth and her hair was a mass of tangles. It was pulled back to reveal a tanned, deeply lined forehead, and rosy cheeks. She had a thin blue tattoo extending from the corner of her mouth and swirling down to her chin on the left side of her face.

She looked up at him from the deck below and shouted, "You, young one, come down and see me awhile, I will make your first night in the New World one you will not forget!"

Flagger and the other men laughed as Piotr looked at her, not knowing what to say. Her lack of a front tooth slurred her speech.

"Leave him be, Marta, you old hag!" Flagger shouted down from the foredeck. People on the dock and on the deck of the ship began to hoot and shout at the spectacle.

"Flagger, is that you?" She shielded her eyes from the mid-morning sun. "You must be a grouchy old man by now...it is good to see your face again, what part of it can be found behind that mess of hair." Marta spat out her words, spraying saliva with each syllable.

"It is me! And I missed you too!" Flagger shouted back.

The people on the dock now began to ease up to the boat, holding bottles of liquor, clothing, necklaces made of shells or animal teeth, and anything else a sailor might find valuable. The men of the *St. Longinus* leaned over the railing and tossed down their own trinkets and clothing in trade. At least a dozen successful exchanges occurred in the first few minutes.

"Keep the corks in those bottles, gentlemen, until offload is completed," Flagger warned as several bottles of whisky made their way up to the hands of the crew.

Thames came walking back down the path and stopped at the dock, waving his arm to Flagger with a *come-on* gesture.

Flagger shouted, "That's it, boys, time to get going. Start with the tents." Immediately the crew left the railing and scrambled in multiple directions to begin emptying the *St. Longinus*.

"Piotr," Flagger gestured, "go with Thames."

Piotr crawled over the side railing to the rope ladder and worked his way down, knife and ax on his hip. He hit the dock with a jump off the bottom rope rung and stood up on the wobbly dock.

Thames was waving him over.

Piotr turned and followed. They made their way up the muddy path into the tent city of Quebec. Piotr's eyes were wide open as he looked about. He breathed in the air. The New World felt a lot like the old one. Brown dirt, blue sky.

While Piotr and Thames were searching out the tent camp location, Captain Linville, Gerard and Anton met with Johan Easterly, the short, fat, bald governor of the Quebec Territory. His heavy jowls around his tight collar jiggled as he leaned forward across his ornate oaken desk and poured whisky into small glasses set up in a row. Clad in a fashionable blue and yellow coat with long tails that he had recently obtained from a ship arriving with goods from Paris, he gleefully attempted to make the newcomers feel relaxed.

"We welcome you gentlemen to Quebec City and the New World. May your venture be successful in every way!" He raised the glass as Gerard and Anton joined him. The men tossed back the shots of liquor, then tapped their empty glasses twice on the wooden desk.

"And to you, Governor, our supporter and leader in this wilderness," Linville responded, before quickly drinking his whisky with a full swallow and a steady eye.

"So, do tell, Captain, what is your plan?" Easterly opened the conversation.

"We will spend the summer and the first part of autumn trapping and securing pelts with our native guides. Load the ship before fall ends, and get back to Saint-Malo before the ice comes down from the north."

"You will need to dock your ship for some time then? You have a small crew, no? We can watch it for you, here in Quebec, for a small fee of course."

Linville was expecting this proposition. He knew that Easterly would want to make as much money as he could from this endeavor, as he likely did on every ship that came to Quebec City. In his preparation for the journey, Linville had looked into Easterly's past with some friends working for the exchange in Saint-Malo. The exchange was the trade market for all goods arriving at the dock.

Linville had found out that Easterly had fought to retrieve the city back from the English, after it was taken by two brothers and their small group of bandits in 1628. The French government in Paris had made a treaty with the English, giving the city back to the French. Easterly was appointed territorial governor thanks to his service in the fight, and his family connections in Paris. In Easterly's view, these ships coming in from

France owed him for this freedom. A small percentage of their earnings seemed appropriate for protection from locals and savages.

"I suppose you would want a portion of the ship's profits; however, we will not be staying in Quebec. We will be sailing up the river, all the way to the first of the great lakes, and then beyond till we can go no farther." Linville offered this plan with the knowledge that it was impossible. His hull ran too deep to get through the river to the body of the great lake.

"Come now, do not be foolish, Captain! Unless you are running a Viking longship, you cannot possibly make it upriver all the way to On-tario." Easterly said On-tar-i-o in the native fashion, with tiny pauses at the syllable breaks and rhyming the *tar* syllable with *far*. "I know I do not look like a woodsman or a soldier, Captain, but I spent my share of time fighting to take this fort back from the English."

"I do not believe we will be in need of your services, Governor. We will sail up as far as we can, and simply anchor in the river." Linville was working to keep this as cheap as possible.

"And how long do you think that your ship will go unmolested in this place? Savages are not the only dangerous people in this New World. The English have men roaming the woods, as well as French. They incite the native population into attacking every kind of target. Then the English take the goods. What will they do with your heavy, loaded ship come autumn? They will board her in the night, kill your crew and strip it bare, or sail it back to London town, that is what, Captain. You will come back to an empty river."

Easterly presented a good argument with his royal accent, and Linville admired his oratory skill.

"So, Governor, if we left it here under your protection, what would you charge?"

Easterly paused and thought about it for a moment, looking upward and turning his head to his left, his fat jowl bulging over his collar.

"I can see that you have a direct way about you, Captain, always a good trait. Five percent of the value of your ship's holdings upon your departure seems a fair amount."

Captain Linville paused with intent for a long moment, then said, "Well, I guess you have to start building a bridge somewhere. I appreciate the generosity of your offer. If five percent is your final offer, I simply sail upriver and leave more men on the boat guarding it. I have guns, Governor, and the will to use them. We will protect our ship."

Easterly painted a dour picture.

"It will take you longer to fill your hold if more men are protecting your boat, sir. You will not get out before the winter ice. Winter here is cold; the river freezes from shore to shore as early as October, in some years. Snow falls several feet deep. This is not like France. You could get stuck here till the thaw, in April or May of next year."

"So be it, sir, we can wait. I am not a slave to creditors like all of the other ships' captains you see, Governor. This is my ship. I own it. I can wait till next spring if need be. I am an adventurer, here to seek wealth, not give it away. My men all signed on for a piece of the success of the venture. If we fail, we all fail. If we succeed, we all succeed, together."

Linville fashioned his position with integrity, and that is harder to overcome when you are building yours on half-truths. Despite his oratory skill, Easterly was doing just that.

"I offer you this then, Captain. What is each sailor's share? Two percent perhaps? Make me an equal partner in this adventure. I will see that your ship is protected and give your crew the freedom to pursue the riches this land can offer."

"One half. One half of a percent is a sailor's share," Linville answered truthfully. "Do you know what beaver hats are selling for in Paris, sir? Sixteen French livres for a single hat. Two pelts are needed to make a hat. I intend to provide for this market."

Inwardly, Easterly was awed. Sixteen French livres! A small fortune for a hat. He quickly calculated what he thought half a percent would be, based on his look at the ship from the second story of his log-built office. The total was larger than what he could have imagined. He paused as if in reflection but was stunned at the potential for profit.

"I think we may have common ground after all, Captain. I will do it for a sailor's share. One half percent." Easterly paused, tapping his fleshy fingertips at his temple. "In addition, I think I can save you and your men some time. I have some canoes from our livery to use as you go west. We have several dugouts and a few birchbark as well. The dugout canoes are heavy, but they are wide and can carry a heavy load without sinking. The birchbark canoes are light and fast. I traded for them with a Huron fellow, for blankets and iron pots and such. They can travel in just a few inches of water and are easy for portage. What say you?"

"A sailor's share. And the canoes will be valuable to our venture. We will return then, come autumn. So be it."

"The dugout canoes are sunk at the southern shore at the mouth of the Cuyahoga River, the Huron name for it. The birchbarks are stacked nearby in the brush just off the shore. We used them, coming down from the Ottawa lands, last fall. They have sticks, with red strips of cloth tied to the end, sticking up several feet out of the water. Their wood doesn't rot when stored this way. A handshake, sir, is as good as a signed contract in this land."

Easterly stood up behind his desk, leaning forward and extending his right hand.

"Indeed." Linville joined him in pressing their palms together, and their deal was struck.

As they stood, Linville added, "We will need to purchase a few pack horses, and cross the river to the southern shore. Is there a stable to purchase from?"

"There is one. Lucien Greely owns it. Be careful dealing with this man. He is ill-tempered and greedy. He also owns the ferry that crosses the river a couple of days walk down the riverside trail. He can take you across to the southern shore, for a small fee, of course."

"Mr. Greely it is, then," Linville responded.

"You will not confuse him for someone else, though, he is a big man. Tall and heavy. He is building a business empire of sorts here in the New World. Which means a stable and a ferry. He is not easily dealt with, but he does sell good horses. They look like they could use a good meal, but they are healthy enough. I am sure you can work it out with him." Easterly damned him with faint praise. "To be fair, Captain, he is a difficult man. You should know that he and his men were part of the army of men I led to recover this fort from the English. He fought bravely, and I owe him for that. Also, his men are loyal to him. When they are sober, they are good fighting men."

"I understand, Governor. I thank you for your candor," Linville said.

"Another toast, then, to our adventure!"

Easterly poured the whisky and raised his glass, as the others followed suit.

"May you have all of the good luck you need, gentlemen!" They downed their glasses as one, and everyone double tapped the desk together.

Gerard and Anton had been sitting back on some comfortable chairs in the rather ornate office here at the edge of the wilderness. They looked at the giant fossil bones on display on Easterly's wall. A spine, a shoulder blade, and part of a ribcage from an ancient animal. On a table next to it was a muddy track that had frozen in time, a massive footprint from some unknown creature. It covered nearly half the table.

Gerard asked, "Governor, sir, what are these creatures that you have here? Where did you get them?"

"The ancients, as I call them, were found west of here. A Huron chief gave me this footprint. It had broken off of a rock face and fallen down a cliff. The other footprints were destroyed, he said, but this one survived. But this is not all; I have this one, on the wall, and also this…"

Easterly dug into a wooden box under the table and pulled out a smaller box. Opening the lid, he pulled out an object wrapped in a cloth, about the size of a cannonball. He gently unwrapped it. It looked like the head of a bird with an unusually long skull and beak, but the beak was filled with tiny, needle-sharp teeth. He held it up for the others to see.

Anton and Gerard had never seen anything like this and were curious. Easterly obliged them.

"This was found southwest of here, hundreds of miles away—truthfully, I am not sure where. The Huron obtained it in a trade agreement with a tribe from the south. They traded it to me for some metal knives. Think about this, gentlemen, a chicken's skull is about this big" he held up two fingers together in the air "A skull of this size, almost as long as my forearm, must have been five or six feet tall. And, it had teeth." He held the skull up so that it was about how tall it would have been, and walked it around the room at shoulder height, as if the rest of the great bird were still present.

"Are there more of them, these bones? In the wilderness?" Anton asked.

"There are, and if you should find one, bring it back to me. I will pay you for it. I am hoping to bring back all of these and more to Paris. There is talk of a museum to be opened. A place of natural history, where these types of things can be saved and shown to visitors who come through."

He continued to walk about the room, holding the skull up, as if he were dancing with a giant chicken.

"When I bring back this and other treasures, it will set me up with the socialites, you know." He smiled at the absurdity of it.

"Well, if we see one…" Gerard left the sentence hanging.

Anton finished it for him. "We'll bring it, don't you doubt us."

While Linville and Easterly were making their deal, Thames and Piotr scouted about the tent city. Piotr peered into the myriad tents and shelters as he walked along the muddy path. He saw bedrolls and blankets, candles, small boxes and chests, and all the personal belongings of people living in a temporary habitation. There were small colored glass bottles of unknown liquids, used tin plates and wooden spoons strewn about, as well as bottles of liquor, half gone. People sleeping and awake, smoking or sitting near the many campfires, many half-dressed and preparing for the day. Women stirred pots of steaming broth, tending to the food and the fires. All of this reminded Piotr of the tents he had slept in with his father and village men in the farmer's field before the battle, ten days' walk from the house he grew up in. He had wandered about that tent city as well, watching the people prepare for war.

This was different in some ways, though. A lot fewer people, and a lot fewer men in uniforms. The clothing choice here was mostly buckskin and fur. Some people had gray woven shirts of wool and cotton, with colored patterns sewn in; many of the native men were dressed simply in shirts, loincloths, and what he thought were deer hide shoes, but no pants. Painted symbols were on nearly every tent or lodgepole. Many of the lodges had trinkets, beads, feathers, and strips of cloth hanging about. Several had woven fishing nets laying on the ground. The entirety of the city smelled of stewing meat, fish, and spring mud. He was grateful for the change in smell, to have gotten away from the wet wool, copper, and body odor smells of the hold in the *St. Longinus*.

"Let us take this clearing over here," Thames said as they moved through the tent city eastward along the north shore of the river.

Piotr followed him a good hundred yards past the tents to a flatter, open spot, covered with grasses and small bushes, and guarded by trees growing along the river and behind it. A lot of fist-sized rocks were strewn about, extending up from the shore of the river.

"This is above the flood line, if the river comes up. See the sticks and debris above the shoreline? That is where the river rises when it rains. You must make your camp above this, always, unless you want to lose your belongings to the water. We will set up a couple of tents here and here."

He paced out the area, pointing out the dimensions.

"Gather rocks from the shoreline, fist-sized or bigger, and make a pile over here. We will use them for the fire, and to help anchor the tents."

"Aye," Piotr responded as a proper sailor would. He started out on the shoreline tossing the rocks into a pile.

After he threw a few more rocks, he spoke. "I am sixteen now, you know. Today is April eleven, I think. It is the day of my birth."

Thames looked up and smiled at such a long and revealing sentence.

"Your French continues to improve. Happy birthday then, you have survived to the age of manhood." Thames bowed slightly. "Make your way back to the ship when you are done, eh? We will need to offload."

"Aye."

Thames walked back toward the tent city to the ship, so quietly that his footsteps made no sound. Piotr gathered stone after stone and tossed them, underhanded, overhanded, two-handed, until a pile began to grow. After a bit, he stood up to stretch his back and looked around as the sun slid over the tops of the newly leafed trees and shone down upon him in the now late morning. He breathed in deeply and smelled the river and the damp green of the forest in the air. Birds flew overhead, and the sky was blue with hardly a cloud. His eyes traveled across the tops of the tall trees and down the river, back toward the tent city and then out to the seemingly endless forest extending on both sides of the river, as far as he could see. He had never been anywhere that felt so large.

"A person could get lost here," he said aloud to no one.

The next two days were filled with backbreaking labor. Piotr became very good at scrambling up and down the rope ladder, on and off the ship. He did it over and over again as the crew unloaded the necessary cargo for their venture. Tents, boxes of trade goods, including the muskets, and everything that could possibly be needed was placed on the dock, and then carried by hand to the location that Thames had selected.

Flagger and Thames oversaw it all, with Linville and Eggard setting up the camp. The crew worked efficiently, and Piotr was grateful for the lack of rain. The dock was wobbly and slippery enough without it, and the mud on the path to the camp was difficult while carrying heavy loads. As the tents were raised and campfires lit on the first evening, Piotr saw the purpose of the stones he had gathered. They used them to hold down the edges of tent walls, to add support to the tent poles, and to line the shallow fire pits they dug. He was given a short-handled wooden spade and told to dig a shallow trench around the tents, to help the rainwater run off as it ran down the hill toward the river. He dug the trench and sweated in the late afternoon sun.

In the early evening of the second day in the New World, Eggard gestured Piotr over to the campfire, with a pot of bubbling burgoo cooking over it. "Walk with me along the river. Hold these, we may have use for them." He handed Piotr a couple of stones big enough to throw.

They made the trek slowly, as Eggard was looking for something. Through the brush and reeds growing in shallow pools along the river, they moved quietly. Eggard pointed out plants that could be valuable as they moved.

"Bullrush. See it here," he said as he pulled some of the plants from the bank. "Grows on riverbanks, you can eat it." He took the plants, roots and all, and placed them into his canvas sack, for use later. After another few steps, Eggard paused and reached down to pull the leaves off of a plant growing up from the rocky slope. "Sage. It is good for flavoring. Use the leaves."

He again gathered several into his sack.

As they walked along, Piotr winced on a few of his steps. Eggard noticed it too, but said nothing. Piotr's toes were hitting the ends of his shoes when he walked. He had outgrown them. Somehow, he had grown taller while on the ship, and his feet had expanded. He stopped and took them off, tying the laces together and slinging them over his shoulder, going barefoot in the rocky soil.

Eggard pointed out his obvious problem. "You will need proper shoes to do the work this summer. It is many, many miles to walk."

Piotr thought about that as he walked, stepping on rocks and sticks occasionally. Maybe so, but he was certain Thames was going to have him stay with the ship. He would not be sent out to search for the beaver fur.

Eggard paused in front of him and slowly dropped down into a crouch. He put his left hand up to signal Piotr to do the same. Eggard reached into his sack and pulled out a rock that was mostly round and fit easily into his ham-sized fist. He gestured for Piotr to move up next to him.

"See them?" He pointed. Twenty-five yards or so ahead, walking through the cattails and reeds, just above the edge of the river were the heads of birds. Piotr thought that they must be at least three feet tall, if he could see their heads. He wondered why they walked in a perfect line, like troops on the march.

"Turkey. Wait for them to move up the hill a little bit," Eggard whispered. "Take the nearest one."

Piotr felt the edges of the palm-sized rock in his hand. He rotated it around to find the best grip for throwing it. The birds kept walking slowly in a straight line and cleared the cover along the water. One by one, they started to make their way up the hill, staying in a line, pecking occasionally at the ground as they looked around. Slowly, Eggard rose up from his crouched position, easing his left foot forward silently in the grass. Piotr copied his movements and brought his right hand up toward his ear. Suddenly, Eggard let fly with a hard throw toward the second to last bird in the line, striking it cleanly at the base of the neck. A small burst of feathers puffed into the air as the startled birds jumped and flapped their wings. Piotr threw his stone as well, missing short and right. The birds squawked and cawed as they took flight, moving up the slope into the trees with furious flapping. The bird Eggard's stone had struck thrashed on the ground. Eggard leapt forward, covering the distance so quickly that Piotr was shocked and rushed after him to keep up.

After quickly scrambling up the slope, Eggard grabbed the wounded turkey by its long neck in both his hands. Wringing it caused all of the struggles to cease. The birds on the slope squawked as they scattered into the trees and disappeared into the forest.

"You have to move quickly. Sometimes they are just stunned and they will jump up and fly away. They do not fly far, you can see, but once they know where you are, you cannot catch up to them."

"I missed," Piotr admitted more to himself than to Eggard.

"You have to throw with great intent," Eggard replied.

"How did you learn to do this? The clams on the beach, the plants to gather, hunting these birds. You have so much knowledge," Piotr said with wonder in his voice.

"A savage taught me this. The plants, and how to hunt small game with stones, anyway. The beach...I learned that as a kid. We had to know it, we needed it for food. That seems a long time ago, now, though."

He pulled a knife from his belt and opened the bird from throat to anus with a single pull of the blade, scooping the contents of its body cavity out onto the ground.

"Keep your knife sharp, and field dressing is not such a hard job. Make sure you clean out the throat as well. It's hell on your hands when you have a dull knife." Eggard handed the still-draining bird carcass to Piotr and knelt to the ground, wiping the blood off his hands onto the grass. "Pluck it as we walk back."

Piotr was surprised by how heavy the bird was, even after being field dressed. He began to pull the feathers loose as they made their way back to camp. His feet found the occasional stone or pointy stick. He watched the ground to plan his steps and avoid stepping on sticks and rocks.

After a few minutes of silent walking, except for plucking, Piotr asked, "You said a savage. You have been here before?"

Eggard looked down at him with a sideways smile and a raised eyebrow and said, "Quiet people have big ears." He strode on without saying anything for a few steps.

Piotr thought that maybe he was not going to tell him about it, but then Eggard spoke again, his wrinkled brow revealing that he had to work at remembering what it was he had to say.

"I came here fishing off the coast as a boy, even younger than you are now. Then, fifteen years ago or so, I came here to Quebec City with a trade ship to supply the city, as the French were just building it. I met an Ojibwe woman and stayed for two years—northwest of here, about a hundred miles or so. We lived with a group of people, mostly with other French traders that had taken up with Indian women, and some other natives that had nowhere else to live, in a village by a lake they called Gift Lake. The place was called Kikono in her tongue."

Piotr listened intently. Other than Eggard's tale about Nehelenia during the storm, it was the most he had ever spoken in the few months he had known him.

"What was her name?"

Eggard raised his large head up and turned his face to the sun for a moment, then closed his eyes and stopped walking.

"Estas. Her name was Estas. It means cold snow; she was born in winter."

"It was a good place, back then?"

"It was the best place, the best time of my life. But...she became ill, and after a while, she died." Eggard's voice thickened with emotion. "And I had no other reason to stay on, in the village. So, I came back. I walked back to Quebec City in the spring and got on a boat. I went back, all the way back, to my hometown on the Schilde."

Eggard kept looking up at the tops of the trees, but Piotr still saw the pain in his face. They walked on in silence for a long while, following the shoreline back to the camp.

"I thought about never returning here, to this beautiful place," Eggard said at last. "But here I am. Back in the forest again." He looked around at the woods and river, earth and sky, inhaling the scent of it deeply.

As they neared the camp, Piotr pulled out the last remaining feathers from the turkey and handed it to him.

Eggard looked it over, and declared, "It will make a fit enough meal on an open fire. I will show you how to roast a turkey on a stick. We will have more than just stew tonight!"

They made their way to the central fire between the two tents, and Eggard rigged up a spit for roasting. Soon, the burgoo and wild turkey were smoking and bubbling over the fire. They ate and toasted their successful journey to the New World.

## Chapter 8

# THE ONION, THE ARM, AND THE WORM

After their evening meal of roast turkey and stew, the men were gathering in groups to talk, smoke pipes of tobacco, and pass some of the jugs of liquor they had traded for. Piotr was told to clean the dishes, so he was, with sand at the edge of the river. Scrubbing off the big chunks, anyway. Behind him stood Thames, Eggard, Flagger, and Captain Linville. They were pouring from a bottle into their tin cups. He was eavesdropping bits and pieces of their conversation while working.

Thames smoked on a long-stemmed clay pipe and said, "Well, let us gather our strength tonight, for tomorrow we head upriver for the Huron camp. They will have knowledge of the beaver ponds. Three or four days upriver should get us there."

Linville nodded in agreement.

"The men will want to celebrate our journey. I will watch the *St. Longinus* tonight. I am sure they will want to go to Marta's public house. Let them have their fun. We made it across the sea, and no one died."

He raised his metal cup to them in salute. Thames, Flagger, and Eggard shared the cheer, and they all clinked their cups together before gulping down the mouthful of whisky.

Linville asked, "Flagger, did you and Perdo have any trouble obtaining the horses from the stableman? The governor had said he could be difficult."

"No trouble, Captain. The man you refer to is Lucien something-or-other. He was not there. His man sold us the horses. They are stabled until morning. We can pick them up then."

"Very well. Easterly seemed concerned, but it is done then."

Flagger said, "I bought a mule, too. And a two-wheeled cart for it to pull. It is a strong beast."

Eggard said, "I will join you on the ship, Captain. I want to gather up some other things to take, anyway. In my old age, I do not need the fun as much as I used to."

Linville thought about it for a moment, then advised Flagger and Thames, "Be watchful of our crew in that establishment. A lot of the locals will be happy to fleece them of whatever is in their pockets." Linville picked up his brace of pistols and he and Eggard started off.

Eggard turned and called back as they left, "Get the boy some proper footwear. He has outgrown his schoolboy shoes!"

Piotr looked up from the bank of the river with wet sleeves when he heard this. Flagger and Thames were both looking at him with grins on their faces. *Maybe it is the whisky*, thought Piotr.

Thames stepped up onto a large rock and shouted for the crew. "Gather round here, gentlemen. Tonight you may enjoy your beer and whisky. Captain's orders!"

The crew gave a collective cheer.

"Tomorrow we set to work filling up the ship's hold. Flagger and I will be heading over to Marta's public house. If you should care to join us, I am sure that there are plenty of whores and thieves inside, willing to take your coins, should you be so foolish. Her beer tastes like cow piss, and that grain liquor she sells is strong enough to remove barnacles from the hull."

As the Paquet brothers lined up next to each other and jostled each other with elbows and shoves, Abel piped up, "Oh, just like home!"

"I am sure many of you grew up in a whorehouse, or worse...just be watchful is all I am saying. We do not want to start out with legal issues before we have even stepped foot into the wilderness. Please do not start any trouble with the locals."

"Yes, Father," a voice shouted from the tent.

The men laughed as working people do when they get to have fun, finally, after long weeks of work. Many started out for the tent city.

"Come on, then," Flagger said to Piotr.

Marta's public house was a long unfinished three-walled cabin in the center of the tent city with a dirt floor. The three walls were of rough unhewn logs, filled with chunks of moss and irregular wedges of wood to keep out the wind and the rain. A long roof covered the walls, with a wide stone chimney at the end that smoke consistently rejected. Instead, much of it collected in the rafters and corners of the room in small clouds, then sought its exit in the roof's many nooks and crannies. The rafters were covered in lichens that had turned green, yellow, and gray and above that, Piotr could see the mahogany shingles, stained to a fine red by the stubborn smoke. A couple of irregular openings were cut out from the walls and propped open with sticks, to serve as windows.

Instead of a fourth wall with a door, the unfinished end of the cabin had a tent made from oilcloth attached to it. This extended the building another fifteen feet. On the back wall next to the fireplace was a door that operated with leather hinges nailed in place. The earthen floor was packed hard and smooth from years of feet pushing it down. A few roughly hewn tables, held together by wobbly legs, were scattered about. Moderately planed stools, uneven chairs, and small stumps of wood served as seating. On one wall was a long wooden countertop serving as a public bar of sorts. The surface had been worn smooth by years of use. A few locals were already inside when they arrived, occupying a table near the fireplace.

Flagger led the group of sailors in through the open tent entrance.

Piotr smelled woodsmoke and a sickly sweet odor he had not smelled before. He noticed some other local residents as well. Three white and gray passenger pigeons sat in the rafters and two young pigs that had wandered in from the yard through the open tent snuffled about for bits of dropped food.

"Marta, I am home!" Flagger announced as he walked in.

Marta was bent over tending the fire, her more than ample derriere sticking up as she poked the fire with a stick. She stood straight up, and then patted down her frizzy hair before turning around.

"You mangy bastard, I knew you were here a day before your boat arrived, just by the smell. I thought you were staying forever in your beloved Paris!" Marta shouted from across the room as she walked toward the tall man.

Flagger opened his arms and hugged her fully, and for a second her eyes teared up. Piotr watched this with his mouth agape in surprise. Flagger had never shown much of any emotion, happy or sad.

After greeting each other, Marta waved at the rest of the crew. "Come on in, lads, make yourselves home. I have beer tonight, real beer from barley and hops. Made it over in the fort's kitchen and brought a few barrels to my house."

Two serving girls were quickly bringing out clay mugs and pitchers of beer as the men of the *St. Longinus* found chairs and places to stand. It was as cheerful a place as Piotr had seen in some time, and he thanked the girl as she handed him a clay mug and filled it with a pitcher. Thames and Flagger sat, and Flagger pulled out a stool and slapped it, gesturing that Piotr should join them. Marta also joined them at the small table.

Flagger said, "You are well, then, Marta? The tent city outside the walls has grown since I was here last. More and more people come."

"They do; most of them leave into the forest. Some of them return. They are all the same, mostly, just looking for their fortune."

Marta explained the changes since Flagger had last been in Quebec City.

"We are starting to grow into a town, now that the troubles are over." She was referring to the takeover by the English brothers a few years back. "We have a baker, and a candle maker. We even had a blacksmith for a while, till his wife up and killed him. She fled into the forest, and never returned to face her punishment. I cannot say as I blame her; Easterly would have hung her."

Piotr caught himself staring at the tattoo on her chin when she spoke. It was hard to look away.

Thames asked, "Whisky, Marta? Do you have your infamous whisky?"

"Not a drop left. The trade bottles floating about in the tents is the end of last season's crop of barley."

She paused, then continued ruefully. "To my horror, I knocked the onion off the stove when I tried to clean it, and it split open across the top. With the blacksmith dead, I have no one to fix it."

"That is bad luck," Flagger sympathized.

"I don't understand, what does an onion have to do with whisky?" Piotr asked.

"He is a real thinker, this young man," Marta said to Flagger and Thames.

"He is always listening," said Thames. "The onion is the copper tub that is over the mash. It collects the essence of the mash as it boils."

"Copper? Oh. I could fix it," Piotr stated matter-of-factly.

Flagger, Thames and Marta all turned toward him, surprised.

"You did say your dad was a blacksmith," Thames said.

Piotr's father was not really a blacksmith, but he was a smith. He was a gold and copper smith: a trade that required similar knowledge, and an even finer touch. Piotr had not offered that up before, on the boat, or to anyone. It was his father's skills that had started his journey to leave his home, and to end up here, three thousand miles away in the New World, in a cabin by a river, next to thousands of miles of forest. If not for his father's reputation for great skill, the Duke of Brettenberg would never have come to his shop and would never have asked for the favor that led to Piotr fleeing his home.

Keeping that secret had seemed important to Piotr in Saint-Malo, and on the boat. But here, in the forest of the New World? The old world was a long way away. And he probably could fix it, he thought. He had made pipes, large utensils, wire, and a few other basic items from copper. He did not have the artist touch like his father, so his work was basic, but it had been functional.

"If you have tools and a forge, and some copper to use as a patch, I might be able to fix it. Can I see it?" Piotr asked.

"Young man, if you really can fix it, I will be indebted to you," Marta exclaimed.

They went out the back of the public house to the whisky shed, sitting just outside the palisade wall. Lighting a lantern, Marta showed them the onion. It was a bulbous copper bowl that sat atop the brick oven that boiled the mash. It was split open along the side where it had banged when dropped.

Attached to the onion was the arm, and attached to the arm was the worm. The arm was a simple copper tube, narrowing from a larger opening at the onion to a narrow drip tube connecting to the worm. The worm was a tube of copper that spiraled down to drip out the essence of the mash into a container such as a cask or a jug.

Now Piotr understood.

He climbed up onto the side of the oven and reached over the top, lifting the cracked onion off and twisting off the attached arm, gently setting the arm on the top of the unlit oven.

"Can you show me the blacksmith shop?"

They made their way to the blacksmith's cabin. Marta lit some of the lanterns. Inside, it was covered in soot and dust, but Piotr could see the tools he would need, and the forge. He peered into the forge holding a lantern from the wall for light. It appeared to be in working order.

"Let's get it lit," he said.

He set the onion down on a workbench and gathered some twigs from the stack in the corner and some hardwood pieces as well. There were strips of cotton cloth in a basket. Using the lantern flame, he lit a cloth strip on a dry stick and began nursing the forge to life, adding light to the room.

"Well, gentlemen, as exciting as this is," Thames said, "I do have beer to drink. I also do not want to leave those Paquet brothers alone in your saloon for too long, Marta. They may have torn the place down by now."

Thames bid his adieu and headed back to his beer.

"Do you have what you need?" Flagger inquired.

"I have tools, an anvil...I will need some piece of copper to melt down, as a patch."

Flagger looked at Marta. "Do you have such a piece?"

Marta pushed up her sleeve, revealing a wide, handmade Indian bracelet that covered half her forearm. It was punched with holes in a decorative pattern and was tied onto her arm with a deer hide lace.

"Will this do?" She took it off and handed it to Piotr.

He looked it over. It looked like copper, roughly forged and probably not the purest, but it was copper.

"It's from Saguenay, they trade for copper up there," Marta explained as Flagger looked at the jewelry with a raised eyebrow.

"That will do. I have to melt this down, you understand?"

"I do. Let me keep the lace, though. I may have use for that," she said. Piotr unthreaded the deer hide string and handed it back to her. She held it close to her cheek for a second, then put it in her dress pocket. "If you fix this, what can I get for you in exchange, Piotr?"

Piotr thought about it, but before he could answer, Flagger said, "This young man can use some shoes, Marta. We are about to walk through the woods for half a year, in all kinds of mud, through beaver ponds and the like."

Marta shuffled over and bent down to look at his shoes with the lantern for light.

"Let me get a look at you." She stared at his legs and feet, in his now too-short pants, and his too-small shoes. "I am thinking you need some proper leggings as well. I will see what I have in my back room."

"Do you need help with this, Piotr? Are you really able to do it?" Flagger asked, speaking confidentially.

"I do not need help. It is a proper smithy's workshop. I will be working at it for an hour or two."

"We leave you to it, then," Flagger said, and they headed back to Marta's public house.

Piotr looked about the shop after they left. He found a bucket of coal and added a few pieces to heat up the forge. Then he picked up the onion and examined the gash in the metal. After a bit, a plan began to form in his head. His father had taught him to make joints and seams with copper. He was hopeful he could snip the edges and make a joint out of the copper bracelet that would fit into the gash, then braze it with the remains melted onto it. This should seal it up and allow it to work, even though it would not look very artful. First, though, he would pound it out flat. He set to work with the small ball peen hammer, the tongs, and the anvil. He liked this anvil. It had a prominent point for shaping curves.

Flagger joined Thames, having returned to Marta's house. They sat near the back of the room by the fireplace, sipping their beer. Five members of the local tent city made their way into the public house. At first they gathered together near the opening, but in a few minutes, they started to talk with the crew. Soon a game was afoot. The leader of the local crew, a tall, heavyset, lantern-jawed man with a sparse beard and a tremendous overbite, asked one of the busy servant girls to bring them the passglass. His sallow face creased in a twisted smile when she filled it with beer and brought another pitcher to their table, for the refill. And of course, Thames pointed out to Flagger, the Paquet brothers were soon joining them for the game.

Passglass was a drinking game. The passglass was a tall beer glass that had lines marking out the amount of liquid evenly. A number was chosen via a single die. The drinker had to drink beer down to that corresponding line on the glass. The glass was then passed to the next player. The Paquet brothers took great joy in rolling a six and forcing the others to drink a near-full glass of beer in a single pour, slapping each other on the back when they failed or succeeded. Soon, money was being laid down between the two groups when a roll of six was had. If the drinker foundered during the draining of the glass, they lost the bet. Flagger and Thames watched from the back of the room.

As the evening passed into night, more locals arrived at the public house and the servant girls were practically running from table to table with pitchers of beer. Marta removed the top of a barrel and started dipping clay pitchers in and lining them up on the counter, rather than try to pour them out, one by one. The atmosphere had become loud as drunken people shouted to each other from across the room. Other games of dice were being played at various tables. Men, and some local women, were now standing at the bar counter, as there were not enough chairs. The Paquet brothers were petting the pigs, and Anton and Abel lifted one up on a chair, placing a bowl of beer in front of its face. The pig sniffed the beer, knocked over the bowl, and began lapping up the spill from the table.

The lantern-jaw leader of the local group of men stood up and drank a full glass of beer from the passglass, to cheers and jeers. Wiping his chin on his sleeve, he shouted across the bar. "Enough beer, Marta, bring us a jug of your whisky!"

"There is no more whisky, Lucien," Marta shouted back. "It is all gone."

"Now Marta, this is not possible. I donated enough barley for more than a dozen jugs! And I am not the only one," he pointed to some of the local tent city dwellers that had followed him in, "many of these men gave our crop to make the whisky. We all agreed to an even share. You keep half and we keep half. Where is our half?" He grew louder, and talking at other tables subsided as people turned to look at the commotion.

"Again, Lucien? Are we going to go around again? You know why there is no whisky, yet you make a point of it in front of everybody. Why is that, Lucien? Why do you want to point out my mistakes?" Marta spat out her words, and her face began to flush.

Lucien's face was spiteful. He grew louder.

"Because you are not giving your share! We gave ours, but no whisky in return. You are a double crosser, and a liar! You sold some of the jugs this past winter. Where is our share from that?"

His accusation rang out across a silent room.

Reflexively, he dropped his hand to the hatchet in his belt.

Marta's face changed from flushed to rage. She reached under the counter and her hand found a butcher's chopping knife.

"You know that I broke the onion. You know that the blacksmith is not here to fix it. Yet you accuse me and call me a liar. You put your hand to a weapon in my house!" Her eyes widened and her chin thrust out as she said it.

Flagger and Thames, watching from their seats at the back corner table, could see her hand go to the butcher's knife. They looked at each other, then jumped up from their seats. Flagger moved toward Marta behind the bar counter, and Thames moved through the crowd toward Lucien. Thames was a strong man, but he recognized that Lucien was a few inches and many pounds bigger than he was, as he approached.

Marta stared at Lucien, not noticing Flagger coming toward her slowly. She shouted at him, "You have no care about barley, you are just mad because I wouldn't lay with you to consummate the deal, you fat bastard!"

Lucien pulled his hatchet from his belt and raised it as he stepped toward Marta behind the bar. Simultaneously, Marta pulled the butcher's knife from under the counter when Flagger grabbed her from behind in a bear hug, holding her arms to her sides. Thames's left hand grabbed the right wrist of Lucien, and his right hand brought his long knife up in one motion. The knife went to the throat of the big man, under his long, sallow jawline, and he froze in his steps. Eyes locked together, Thames whispered, "If your other hand goes to your knife, I will open your throat."

"You son of a bitch..." Lucien growled as he raised his left hand away from the knife at his belt.

The rest of patrons jumped to their feet, squaring off into two groups: one local, the rest the crew of the *St. Longinus*. The Paquet brothers backed from their table and squared off with Lucien's companions.

In the blacksmith shop, Piotr had snipped the copper bracelet and fitted it into the cracked area, then melted down the remaining bits and used it as a weld to seal the crack in the onion. Brazing it the best he could, he put out the forge.

"It does not look great, but it should work now."

He said the words aloud to himself, as no one else was in the shop. He rubbed it with a cloth from the workbench and held it up against the light of a lantern, checking the seam. He got up and doused the lanterns, taking the onion with him as he walked out the doorway of the blacksmith's cabin.

Heading back to Marta's house in the dark, he could see the light through the open wood windows and glimpses of all the people inside. It seemed more crowded than before.

He pushed open the back door with his hip and walked in, raising the repaired onion over his head and said to the silent room, "I fixed it!"

Everyone in the room turned as one except Thames, and looked at Piotr, holding the shiny copper pot over his head in the air, like it was a sacrifice. Eyes began to look about at the other faces. Without ever looking away from Lucien, it was Thames who smiled first. Finally laughter burst forth from the Paquets and grew in other corners of the room. Marta, still held in a bear hug by Flagger, burst out laughing. The tension in the room broke, and people began to step back and laugh aloud.

Mason Paquet came from across the room toward Piotr and wrapped his arm around him in a hug.

"Mon ami, you fixed more than you know!"

Thames, still not looking away, lowered his knife away from the throat of the larger man, and stepped back carefully, out of striking range, before finally releasing his wrist with his left hand.

As the room relaxed and people began to speak freely, Lucien Greely looked at Thames, his hatchet still in his right hand, now hanging at his side.

"I will not forget that, woodsman."

"Nor I," Thames said back.

Flagger called out to the crew of the *St. Longinus*, advising them to drink up as the end of the night was at hand. They began to drift out, saying goodbyes to the residents of the pub as they left. The Paquets stopped to hug the pigs, bending to one knee and kissing them on the forehead.

Anton said, "Goodbye, piggie my friend, I am sure we will never see you again, as you will likely be grilled and stewed by the time we return." The Paquet brothers laughed in their drunken silliness.

Piotr was still holding the copper onion. Marta gestured him over. Flagger and Thames came to look at the onion as well. Marta held it up against the lantern to see his handiwork.

"The crack looks sealed up. I think this should work. Let us see if it fits onto the oven."

She led them all back to the whisky shed, carrying a lantern. Piotr carried the onion and crawled up onto the oven, placing it over the hole and connecting the arm back where it belonged, gently tapping it into place with his hand.

"There you go, Marta. It will work now," Piotr said as he climbed back down.

"Thank you, Piotr. You have saved me some trouble from these angry fools, as well as what is left of last year's barley. Some of it is still good for mash, I hope." Marta was truly grateful, and her puffy face creased in a gap-toothed smile. "I have some moccasins and buckskin pants for you in the house. A couple of pairs; they should fit you. I soaked them in linseed oil, so they should keep your feet dry!"

Thames and Flagger gave him an approving look, and Piotr smiled in appreciation of the exchange.

"My feet and I thank you, Marta," he said in his best French.

*Chapter 9*

# THE DARKNESS
# IN THE FOREST

*I* *am frozen*, Raul Montreaux thought, as the long, vine-like leaves of the great willow tree rustled in the breeze. The occupants of the longboat sat in silence. In shock and fear, Montreaux's brain had locked up to preserve some sanity. All of the passengers looked to him to lead, and he wanted to tell them what to do next. But he did not know.

After a moment, he peered over his shoulder through the hanging leaves of the willow. What he was looking for finally came into shape.

From the back of the longboat, he could see through the branches a little. He reached out and parted them just enough to get a clear view of the cove. He blinked a few times to confirm what he was seeing. *The Render* was sailing into the cove. He could see men on the deck with muskets, moving slowly, pointing the guns at the shoreline. They were hunting.

He whispered, "*The Render*...they are looking for us. It runs too deep to get close to the shore, we have to stay hidden."

Archembeau, his mind blurry, and bleeding from a scratch across the bridge of his prominent nose, looked at him in confusion.

"How is *The Render* here?"

"It is not our crew; it is the foreigners from the huge warship that tried to kill us. They have taken our ship, and they are using it to hunt us," Montreaux whispered to all of the passengers. "If we are seen, they will kill us."

A rustling in the leaves made a sound from the shoreline. Montreaux pulled one of his snaphance pistols from his belt and pointed it in the direction of the sound. The leaves and branches on the shoreline side of the willow were parted, and the beautiful face of a young woman with dark skin, brown eyes, and black hair appeared.

In perfect French, she said, "Follow me."

She disappeared behind the branches as they closed like a heavy curtain.

For a second, Montreaux wondered if what he just saw was real. "My eyes are playing tricks," he said aloud.

"No trick," Guillaume said, "but we have to move."

He reached out to the shore and grabbed branches and roots, pulling the boat up to the base of the willow along the shore's edge.

"Get going." He looked at Jana and nodded.

Jana clambered out of the boat as quietly as she could, stepping onto the shore of the New World under the branches. She reached back for Sister Mary Therese and helped her out. The others in the longboat quickly followed, scrambling quietly out onto the land.

"Tie it here, to the tree," whispered Montreaux.

He led the group out from under the willow into the forest.

The Indian woman who had spoken in French was standing in the undergrowth beneath the canopy of trees, with a tall, thin man. His head was shaved on the left side, and his long black hair was tied back. His trade shirt was painted with red and blue designs and his left ear was pierced, displaying a loop of bone with a feather and small teeth hanging from it. He wore leggings above his moccasins up to his knees, but only a breech-cloth instead of pants. The woman wore a buckskin native dress, and her hair was pulled back revealing her startlingly beautiful face. As his eyes adjusted to the dim light under the canopy of trees, Montreaux saw that the two were not alone. Three more Indian men stood some twenty feet behind them, dressed similarly, and all of them looked like they could fight.

The Indian man and woman walked toward Montreaux and squatted down into a crouch, inviting him to talk. Hidden from the men on the ship by the trees, Montreaux felt a little safer. He crouched down with them.

In a whisper that was barely audible, the man spoke into the ear of the woman. She translated to French for him.

"Why do you hide from the people on the boat?"

Montreaux attempted to explain. "We flee because they are chasing us. They want to kill us so we don't tell anyone what they did. The ship in the cove is our ship, they have stolen it. We are Frenchmen, and they are Swedes, I believe."

She turned to the man and explained in many words. Many more than he had used. They questioned each other for a while. Montreaux made eye contact with Guillaume. He wanted him to be prepared if this went bad.

"We are going to Quebec City," he offered.

The man spoke through the woman again.

"He says your people fight with each other. We too are being hunted. Iroquois are in the woods. Mohawk and Seneca. They have been tracking us for three days. They are not far, coming from the east. They will find us if we do not keep moving. You must hide until the night, then leave on your boat. If you do not leave by tonight, the Iroquois will find you."

"Why do you help us?" Montreaux inquired.

The Indian man whispered to the woman, telling her what to tell him. "We had stopped to rest, here at this place, when you came. We heard the great ship fire its cannon at you. So did the Iroquois. The Iroquois are our enemy, you understand. Enemy of the Abenaki, our people. They kill and steal from us, they kidnap our women and children. We have led them away from our village. Then we doubled back and put them off our trail. Then the ships fired upon you and you came in here. Now the Iroquois will come from the east. They will find our trail again. They will come here, here where we stand, on this night. They are many, we are few. But we cannot allow them to find our village. When they come, we must lead them away again."

"We led them back to you. For this, I am sorry," Montreaux said. "We would like to leave, and make our way to Quebec City, but we cannot get out of the cove past the ship while they hunt us. How far is it to walk to Quebec City?"

"Two weeks' walk." The woman responded directly.

Montreaux crouched quietly. He looked around at the crew of his longboat. Father Archembeau and Sister Mary Therese were too old for such a journey. They had no knowledge of the path or what lay between here and Quebec City. They had the longboat, and the longboat was their only way.

He rose from the council with the Indians, and checked through the branches to see if *The Render* had moved. It was now at anchor in the cove. He turned to the priests, the nuns, Guillaume, and the rest of the crew as they huddled around.

"We are out of the frying pan and into the fire, I am afraid. *The Render* is now at anchor in the cove. They think we are here." Montreaux paused, exhaling heavily. "Worse yet, there is a band of Indians scouting through the area, Iroquois, and they are not peaceful, as these fine people are. These are Abenaki and they fear the Iroquois."

Montreaux exhaled again, tiredly.

"And, we are two weeks' walk, at least, to Quebec City. I am open to suggestions."

The group of survivors huddled together in dismay over their predicament.

Finally, Father Demari spoke. "We have to wait till nightfall then, and row past the ship. There is no other way, we are too infirm to walk that far." He looked around at the group of survivors.

Guillaume said, "We could row to it in the night and take it by force. If these Abenaki were to help us, maybe we could take the ship back."

Father Archembeau snorted in disgust and rubbed his forehead, his scratched nose still bleeding. "We are no fighting force. You will be killed if you attempt such a thing. Then the rest of us will be stuck here in this... dark wilderness." He shook his head. His skin was clammy and he was sweating. The events of the last three days had exhausted him beyond his capacity to recover and he was feeling ill. "I remind you, Mr. Montreaux, of your duty to see that we get to Quebec City safely. Your ship," he panted, pointing to the anchored ship in the cove beyond the branches of the willow tree, "the ship that was run aground by your captain, your ship that those...Lutherans...now possess, and hunt us with, your ship was bought and paid for by the church! For the express purpose of getting us to the New World!" His voice grew louder and louder as he spoke.

Montreaux's reply was cold. "I need not be reminded of my duty, and you will keep your voice to a whisper." Montreaux paused, gathering the patience needed for this exchange. "Father Archembeau, I sailed with Captain Laurent and many of the crew for more than ten years. These men were my friends, and they are likely dead or imprisoned now. You are not, you are still alive."

Jana and Sister Mary had been listening quietly. Jana nodded toward the Abenaki. "Mr. Montreaux, what are their names?"

Montreaux flushed. "I, I never asked..."

He turned to go back to the Abenaki, and Jana and Sister Mary joined him.

Sister Mary Therese took the hand of the Abenaki woman and spoke in French. "We thank you for helping us. My name is Mary Therese, this is Jana and Mr. Montreaux." She allowed them time to acknowledge. "What are your names?"

The Abenaki woman placed her open hand on her chest. "I am Malian. This is my husband, Nanibosad." She touched his chest in the same way.

The man, Nanibosad, whispered to Malian. She translated quickly. "What do you plan to do?"

Montreaux paused for a moment, looking back at the water. They had only one path. "We will wait for nightfall and try to slip past the ship, out into the main water, then row straight through to Quebec City."

"You have some time until darkness, and your people are tired and hungry. Come, join us," said Malian.

Malian and Nanibosad invited them back to join their men in the undergrowth. Nanibosad waved to invite all of the group of wayward travelers from the longboat. They gathered in the undergrowth below the canopy of tall trees, thirty yards or so behind the willow, where a freshwater creek flowed down to feed the roots of the great tree. They sat on the ground and tried to regain their composure.

The Abenaki passed out pemmican, a trail food made from dried deer and bison meat, tallow, and berries. The fresh water, food, and rest helped them to recover their strength. Sister Mary Therese and Jana expressed their thanks in French and told stories from where they had come, which a few of the Abenaki warriors understood, at least in part.

Montreaux returned to the water's edge frequently, peering out from under the branches of the willow, watching *The Render* and her new crew of Swedish pirateers. As the sun started its downward journey in the sky, they sat at anchor in the cove, several men still on deck with muskets pointing over the side railing. The muzzles of those muskets moved as they scanned the shoreline. After a bit, Malian and Nanibosad brought him a bit of pemmican to chew on. He received it gratefully, and swigged water from his refilled bladder canteen.

"The boat does not move?" she asked while Nanibosad stood by.

"They know we are here," he whispered. "They are waiting for us to try and leave. They have no shore boats left, so they cannot leave the ship to find us. But, they can wait, and when we leave, they will have us. I thank you and your husband again, for your kindness."

Nanibosad whispered to Malian, so that she could interpret.

"We will be leaving together...I mean, at the same time...as you. The Iroquois will be near soon. We will need to leave a trail that leads them away. The sun will be down soon. You should have your people ready."

"In my land, it is unusual to find someone that will help you when it does not help them. Your actions are more Christian than many of my people ever show."

Malian translated for Nanibosad, then she said, "We know of this Christian that you speak of. We have traded with Frenchmen from Quebec City. I learned to speak French from them when they stayed in our village. They spoke of Jesus Christ." She paused, brushing her hair away from her eyes. "We also met white people from England. When I was a girl, we lived far south of here then. Our elders moved our village away from them when they came to shore, they said they looked sick and that they would all die, as they knew nothing. Our elders did not want to be involved."

She paused for a moment to recollect.

"My father disagreed and said we should find out about the new people because we might learn from them. He took me with him to talk to them. An old woman from their village gave me this." She fished into the bag of items she carried on her hip, attached with a length of deer hide cord around her shoulder. She pulled out a small wooden crucifix and rosary beads and showed it to Montreaux.

Montreaux looked on in surprise and smiled as he held it up to the soft evening light that filtered through the willow's branches. "Rosary beads and a crucifix. Carved from a mahogany tree." He looked it over carefully before handing it back to her. "This is very precious. Perhaps it is a good omen."

He felt a spark of hope rekindle.

"That is what the old woman said when she gave it to me. Precious." Malian smiled as she looked at it in her hand.

As she was putting it away, Nanibosad nudged her.

"My husband wants you to answer a question." Malian looked back and forth between the faces of the two men. Montreaux nodded in agreement.

"How many of you are there, in your land? How many people are there?"

Montreaux paused, thinking about how to explain it, then directed his gaze upward into the trees. "Like all the leaves in the forest. Many. Too many to count."

"Do they all want to come here?"

Both husband and wife looked directly at Montreaux's face. Montreaux inferred their meaning. "I do not know. There is fighting all of the time now, many wars, many battles. There are many people that cannot live the way that they want to live. Many of those may feel it is better to come across the sea to start a new life."

"Many," Nanibosad said, in French, with a dire expression on his face, as he looked through the trees at the now-setting sun.

Perhaps it was the fading light as the forest began to grow dark that caused the archer to miss the mark, but the arrow that hit Nanibosad arrived with a hissing whisper and thumped into his sternum.

He fell backward to the ground with an audible grunt, then looked up at Malian and said, "Run."

The Mohawk and Seneca warriors of the Iroquois Confederacy of Tribes sprang their trap with lethal precision.

Malian didn't follow Nanibosad's command. She grabbed him by the arm and pulled him to his feet. The whoops and screams of the Iroquois warriors were mixed with the rustling of forest leaves as they charged at the group of Abenaki and strangers from their hiding places in the undergrowth.

The Abenaki responded first, jumping behind trees and shrubs, drawing bows, knives, clubs, and tomahawks. Guillaume and the oarsmen quickly followed, standing and pulling knives from their belts. Jana quickly grabbed Sister Mary Therese, pulling her to cover in a rhododendron bush. Father Demari and Father Archembeau were the last to react; sitting on a log, they both looked about quizzically.

The scream of a Mohawk warrior turned Montreaux's attention, as the man sprang from behind trees some twenty-five yards away, charging at him. Montreaux saw the tomahawk and knife in his hands. He pulled his snaphance pistol with his right hand and cocked it with his left. He drew a bead on the man's chest as he came running. Squeezing the trigger started the watch spring mechanism that cycled and sent a spark into the pan of powder. His powder was dry, and it ignited, causing the powder in the chamber to ignite as well, sending off the .50 caliber ball with an explosive bang of white and grey smoke that spat forth from the muzzle and then rose upward toward the canopy of leaves. The ball struck the charging man in the middle of his chest, dropping him in mid-stride. He grunted and fell face first to the ground at Montreaux's feet with a gaping, bloody wound blown out of his back.

Montreaux drew his remaining pistol with his left hand as he holstered the first one. He pulled his knife from its sheath with his right hand and stepped toward the coming attackers.

On *The Render*, the Swedish naval fighting men heard the sounds in the forest and quickly rushed to the bow, drawing a bead on the trees with their matchlock muskets; they began searching for targets. As they heard screams and shouting, they began to fire shots at the sounds. Explosive bangs and clouds of smoke came from the cove. Musket balls sizzled and ricocheted through the branches of the great willow tree as the Iroquois, the Abenaki, and the longboat survivors fought.

Guillaume roared as he engaged with a charging warrior, coming up from a crouch to meet the force of the man's charge. The two smashed together, spinning in tangled limbs to the ground, clawing and scrambling for position. The warrior went for his throat with his knife, and Guillaume twisted his head away just in time, clamping his teeth down on his wrist. This freed his right hand, and he drove his knife into the side of the warrior to the hilt. The warrior screamed and twisted away. Guillaume pulled his knife free as they separated, blood spilling from the wound.

He spat out the chunk of flesh from the warrior's arm, stood up, and screamed, "Get to the boat!"

Jana grabbed Sister Mary Therese by the hand and crouched low as they ran thirty yards toward the willow. Arrows whispered past her ear. The Abenaki warriors and the two of the oarsmen were in full contact fights with axes and knives with screaming Iroquois warriors. The other oarsmen were already on the ground, not moving.

Father Demari pushed Father Archembeau onto the ground and, with the whites of his eyes showing, whispered, "Follow me!"

They moved through the underbrush, crawling on their hands and knees toward the boat. Demari took the lead, moving as rapidly as he could, and Archembeau stayed on his heels. More shots began to zip through the tree branches, coming from *The Render*, as the Swedish snipers began to zero in on the sound location in the trees.

Almost to the willow, Father Demari felt a sharp pain in his scalp as a Seneca warrior grabbed him by his red hair, pulling his head back. Father Archembeau bumped into his butt with his head when he stopped and looked up, recoiling in horror as the warrior raised his tomahawk to smash in Pascal's head. A musket ball from *The Render* tore through the branches of the willow and the warrior's shoulder, smashing through the collarbone, spraying blood and bits of bone onto the two men. The warrior collapsed on top of Pascal Demari groaning, who quickly spun him off and discarded him.

Guillaume made it to them and grabbed Archembeau by his red cape, dragging him to his feet and shoving him under the branches of the willow into the longboat. Father Demari followed, collapsing into the boat. Guillaume quickly untied the rope.

"Get on an oar!"

The priests did as they were told.

Montreaux stepped around Malian and Nanibosad, guarding them. "Get in the longboat!" he commanded.

Nanibosad rose achingly to his feet, the arrow sticking out from his chest, and he drew his knife. He looked Malian in the eyes and calmly nodded. "Go to the boat," he told her in perfect French.

Standing to his full height, several inches taller than Montreaux, he reached up to his sternum, grabbed the shaft of the arrow and broke it off just above the entry to his chest. He grunted and took a last look at Malian. Then he turned and ran into the fray of Abenaki, Iroquois, and oarsmen, swinging his tomahawk and chopping down a Mohawk warrior at the temple.

Jana and Sister Mary Therese stood up and ran the last few feet toward the willow as gunshots from *The Render* continued to tear through the trees and whoops and screams from the Iroquois sounded through the woods. They jumped into the boat, Jana getting to an oar and Sister Mary Therese scrambling to the bow.

As the sun finished its journey to the horizon, the Swedish naval men on *The Render* soon found out why the Mohawk and Seneca warriors had chosen to be so loud in their attack. Swimming through the cove in a single horizontal line in the dark water, thirty Iroquois warriors used the anchor chain at the stern to climb on to the ship. The sailors had all gathered to the bow, facing the great willow, in hopes of having a target to shoot. They were not paying attention to what was behind them.

Climbing the anchor chain, the first few Iroquois warriors reached the stern and dropped over the railing, fanning out across the deck in near silence. The smoke from firing muskets drifted back, obscuring the deck even more in the gathering darkness. Soon they had more than a dozen of their warriors on the deck. They advanced from behind the sailors and slaughtered them with efficiency. Arrows came first, through the back of heads or directly into necks, as they could not miss at this range, even in the fading light. Tomahawks and knives came second, as half of the Swedish crew died before the other half knew what was happening. Yelling screams and war whoops, they descended upon the remaining men with fury.

As the light faded completely, the forest grew dark, so dark that it was impossible to see more than a few feet. Three of the oarsmen staggered back, wounded but mobile, and made it to the longboat. Montreaux could no longer see far enough into the underbrush to see the Abenaki and Iroquois only yards away. Then he heard the screams and fighting coming from *The Render*. His mind raced to process what he was hearing.

*The Render* was under attack as well.

He looked down at Malian, who crouched, peering into the darkness, trying to get a glimpse of Nanibosad and the other Abenaki in the undergrowth. "We must go now," he whispered.

She looked up at his face with tears coming down her cheeks. He sheathed his knife and took her by the arm to guide her back to the boat. She pulled her arm away and reached into the underbrush. She stood holding the stone tomahawk of the Seneca warrior who had been shot in the shoulder while trying to kill Father Demari. The warrior was still lying on the ground, moaning. She smashed the tomahawk down onto his head, splitting his skull.

She jerked the weapon free from the warrior's forehead, looked at Montreaux, then turned and walked into the darkness where Nanibosad had gone, the stone weapon still in her right hand and dripping with blood and brain matter.

Montreaux crouched down for a second longer, blinking at the savage vision of Malian walking away into the darkness. Then he scanned the underbrush and trees for any signs of the other crewmen, but without light, he could see nothing. He crept back through the hanging branches of the willow and clambered into the stern of the longboat, pushing away from the shore.

The wounded crewmen that had made it back were in the boat. One of them had slumped over and was pressed against the bow. Sister Mary Therese was attempting to attend to him, and still remain silent. The two priests, Guillaume, and Jana began to row, and the longboat slipped out from under the willow's leaves into the dark water of the cove.

Guiding from the stern, Montreaux heard the screams of fighting and war whoops coming from the deck of *The Render*. He realized that the long-boat could not be seen in the darkness. He whispered in his lowest voice, "Slowly and silently, we will go around near the shore, lest they see us."

The priests and Jana nodded as they rowed, keeping the oars quiet as possible.

Guillaume stole a look over his shoulder at *The Render*. The musket fire had stopped, but screams and shouting continued. In just a glance from the waterline view, even in the darkness, he saw men grappling and fighting; it appeared that there were many more Iroquois on the deck than Swedish sailors. They drifted in near silence, moving through the cove near the shore. In just a few seconds, they would be past the ship and could row hard out to sea. Guillaume and Montreaux kept their eyes on the deck of *The Render* as they slipped past, to see if they were noticed.

Jana thought she felt her oar bump something in the water. She looked out at the end of it, while slowly retrieving the oar above the water, only to see the blackness of the moonless night. Her eyes widened when she saw a hand grab the gunwale. In a movement so quick she did not have time to make a sound, a powerful warrior pulled himself up out of the dark water, leaned into the longboat and wrapped his arms around her, pulling her to his wet body. He then lunged backward, snatching her off of the rear thwart and pulling her down into the cold black water of the cove.

She screamed when she hit the water, but the sound was swallowed by the waves as she was dragged downward. The Seneca warrior who had grabbed her pulled her into deeper water and kicked away from the long-boat. Jana was shocked by the sudden surprise of the attack and coldness of the water. For a moment, she simply went limp as she was dragged away from the boat.

The attack had been so fast that the rest of the longboat survivors could not process what had just happened. Montreaux blinked in surprise, staring into the water where Jana had disappeared. Sister Mary stared at the empty seat where Jana had been, knowing that she could not scream, and was unable to move. She and Montreaux looked at each in confusion for a few seconds, then Montreaux dove from the stern into the cove.

Hitting the water and swimming under the waves, he reached for her in desperation. He had learned to be a powerful swimmer as a youth growing up on the sea, but he couldn't see past his hands in the dark water. He took a few strokes away from the boat but could find nothing with his grasps. With saltwater stinging in his eyes, he surfaced to look back and could vaguely make out the shape of the longboat drifting away from him and the hulking mass of *The Render* near the center of the cove. A splash came from behind him, closer to the shore. Then a muffled, gargled scream. He swam toward the sound and could feel the vibrating movement in the water. His reaching hand touched something smooth and realized it was a person. His reach turned into a grab, and he latched onto the knee of the Seneca, causing him to break his sidestroke.

As the warrior attempted to kick at Montreaux, Jana recovered from her shock. She twisted in his grasp and freed her left hand, clawing his face. He snarled in pain and punched at her head with his fist. Montreaux closed now and grabbed him around the torso. The warrior let go of Jana to turn to this threat.

Jana now twisted all the way around in the water, kicking her knee into the warrior's groin. He threw his head back, grunting in pain. Seeing his face exposed through the splashing saltwater, Montreaux punched it as hard as he could.

Desperate to escape, the warrior kicked Montreaux in the chest, getting a purchase and pushing himself away and out of reach. Bleeding from the scratches, aching from the punch and the knee to his ball sack, he rolled to his back, floating in the water and shouted for help in his native Seneca tongue, "Dasgyenownos! (Help me!)"

Montreaux and Jana were treading water when the warrior screamed. A splash came from near *The Render*, then another, and another. The Iroquois were diving off of the ship and swimming toward them.

The longboat had continued to drift away, and Montreaux could hear the splashes as the Indians swam toward them and the groaning man. They would never make it back to the longboat in time, he knew. If they tried, they would give their position away to the Iroquois in the water.

"GO, NOW!" he yelled as loud and commanding as he could.

He grabbed Jana by the shoulder and swam up face to face with her, looking her in the eyes as more splashes came from near *The Render*. The sound of kicking and splashing in the water grew louder as they began to move closer.

Treading water, she looked at the longboat now moving farther and farther away. When she looked back at Montreaux, he shook his head.

Careful not to splash, the two of them swam away to the far shore.

## Chapter 10

# THE PATH

"D o not forget this." Captain Linville pulled the long war club out from under the boxes that had served as Piotr's bed on the voyage from Saint-Malo and held it up in the dusty sunlight filtering in through the doorway.

"I will not soon forget your arrival at the docks in Saint-Malo...I thought you were a street urchin begging for a coin. Now here we are, just a few months later, and you are more grown man than boy, Piotr." Linville looked at him proudly.

Piotr took the club and held it in his own hands. The hickory wood of the handle felt familiar. His father had helped him build it when he was just seven years old.

"I could no sooner forget this than I could forget my shoes."

Piotr looked down at the moccasins he had received from Marta in exchange for fixing the onion. They were water resistant and sturdy, with the hide and lacings extending up to the top of his shin. They were the most comfortable shoes he had ever worn. The sole was made from multiple layers of thick hardened deer hide that molded to the bottom of his foot as he walked. The laces were cording made from sinew, twisted together to be tough and durable. His buckskin jacket, worn over a linsey-woolsey work shirt, and two new pairs of gray cotton pants were from Marta as well. The pants were still short of his ankles, as they had been made for her younger nephew, but they fit at the waist and did not have holes in them. With his belt, knife, ax, clothes and club, he felt he was properly outfitted for the journey, but he knew little about where they were going.

He trusted these men, though. He had been homeless, penniless, and hungry when they had given him a chance. A choice to live, with a risk, when he had no others. Piotr had never been afforded any time for the anxiety of youth. Like most of the children he grew up with, life was too hard to have much time for worry. He had more immediate problems, like working for food, rather than an existential crisis, like fitting in with his peers. His fate, as he thought of it, had simply put him here. He chose to move forward. To find his way through. This was why he did not cry at night, when his dreams took him back to the battlefield in Lutzen, or to his childhood home, or to his father, or his mother. He had been taught by his parents that life is difficult. That there would be loss and struggle. He had been asked by his father, how will you overcome it? How will you respond?

He had responded by doing the best he could and trying to learn and grow. He was already hardened by the world and these men appreciated him for it, because they were themselves hard men. He would stand with them. Squeezing the handle of the club his father helped him build brought all of these thoughts back to him.

"So, that is the thing you spoke of, eh?" Thames's wide-shouldered frame filled the doorway to the captain's quarters. "May I see it?"

Piotr spun the club in his hands, and handed it to him, handle first.

Thames looked it over carefully. "It is not as heavy as it looks." He hefted it in both hands and looked down the shaft in the sunlight. "These metal studs, how did you get them into the wood? They do not look like you pounded them in. This hickory is hard as rock, anyway."

Piotr said, "My father and I did it. It is a tradition for the boys in my village. When I was seven, on my birthday, we went to the blacksmith shop and gathered these bits of iron. Then we went to the forest and looked for a young tree, a hardwood. We found this small hickory tree. We brought the iron pieces with us and pounded them into the tree in this pattern. When I was twelve, again on my birthday, we went back to the same tree. The tree grows and absorbs them. Only the heads stick out. They will never come out, and they make the impact harder when you hit something."

Thames nodded. "Why this leather wrap?"

"It is soaked in brine and dried, so it hardens. When the edge of a blade hits the shaft, it prevents it from biting deep into the wood. Then the handle will not be weakened."

Thames ran his hand over the leather and the metal studs, and down to the slightly flared and grooved handle. "The handle is like this so it will not slip out of your grasp when your hands get wet, correct? It seems your people put a lot of thought into making this."

Piotr thought about that for a bit while Thames examined the club. "People in my village have been making them for years. It is how we, mmm how do you say…get equal. I mean even…the common folk cannot afford armor. So, we make a weapon that smashes armor, and anyone can make it. Most of the men in my village have one, or something like it. Also pikes. On long poles."

Thames held the club up in the sunlight shafting through the window and said, "So when the armor is mounted on a horse and swinging a sword…you stab it with a pike, and smash it with a club? But what about a gun? Clubs and pikes can stop a man in armor, but not a lead ball. Have you ever shot a gun, Piotr?"

Piotr hesitated. He had never shot a musket of any kind. The blacksmith, the gunsmith and the gold and copper smith were different people with somewhat similar skills when he grew up. His family had no access to a weapon of such expense. Piotr shook his head and looked at the floor. Both of these men could see the untold part of the story, though.

Thames asked, "You have been shot at, though?"

Linville looked at him; his brow began to furrow and he stood up. "You can tell us, son." Yet Piotr remained silent.

Finally, Thames grew impatient. "Captain, I need to know what we have here. You wanted to bring him along when he showed up on the dock. So here we are. We are leaving to go into the woods to find our fortune. Today." His voice grew stern. "I want to know what we have, because we cannot go about protecting him when we are out there." He pointed through the window of the captain's quarters into the trees across the river. "Out there, anything can happen. And every man knows this. But he is not quite a man yet. Does he understand this? Do you?"

Linville rose to the bait. He stood up, an older man, but still formidable. While looking at Thames, he asked, "Piotr, do you understand the risk of what we are about to do?"

Piotr hesitated no longer. "Yes. I have been shot at." He gathered his thoughts. "And, I understand what we are doing out in the woods. I accept that I could die in the forest. But as you have said in the past, Captain, all of us die."

Both men were silent, so he continued.

"My father was killed at the Battle of Lutzen a little more than a year ago last spring. I was there, on the battlefield, with him. When we were told to go to war, he was the man the village elders assigned as a leader in battle. Like a lot of men, he had been a mercenary, well before I was born. So, yes, I know what it sounds like when a musket ball zips past your head, and when it hits the man standing next to you."

He walked over and took the club from Thames's hands, holding it up in a dusty stream of light from the window. "I know what it sounds like when a man breathes his last breath. I know what a musket ball does to a man when it hits."

The words and the familiar feel of the handle stirred his memory. The swirling, smoky images from the center of a battle came whispering back into his mind's eye. The memory of the sound of the mounted knight's horse appeared first. It had fallen after being stabbed with a pike; the rider had hit the ground rolling, knocking the wind out of him. The breadmaker from his village charged in with an axe, but the armored soldier had come up to one knee, drawing his longsword in one motion and swinging it, slicing the breadmaker's neck and torso. The sword had stuck there, in the ribcage, and the armored rider stood up to pull it free. Piotr had instinctively rushed in, swinging the club overhead and crushed the man's helm into his face, knocking him to the ground. The breadmaker from his village died with the longsword stuck in his ribcage. The soldier slumped to the ground, half his face and helm caved in from Piotr's blow, one eye staring blankly through an eye hole, open, but unseeing.

"I know what it is, to be in a battle. I know what it sounds like when the mounted men in armor charge. When the ground shakes, and when they smash into the men of your town. The men and the horses scream. Cannon and musket rain shot down on you. I do know. Maybe more than what you might think."

Thames and Linville were hard men. Like most people, they had experienced war, and they knew the lasting effects of battle on the mind.

Thames nodded. "I see that you do, Piotr." He paused, then added, "You said...was. Regarding your father."

Piotr's thoughts now flooded his mind, and his face flushed with the pain of it. "He died that day in a field of newly sprouted wheat, lying in the mud. I was looking into his eyes when they closed. He told me to help my mother."

He stopped talking after this. He sat down in the chair next to Linville's desk, resting the head of the club on the ground, his right hand draped over the knob, like a cane. His eyes moistened, but no tears came forth. Linville reached out and put his hand on his shoulder.

"You have seen more than many, and at a young age, Piotr. I am sorry for your loss."

Thames said, "As am I, Piotr... You have been on the wrong side of the barrel of a gun, but have you fired one?

"No, I never have. I do not even know how it works. We never hunted. I spent all of my time in a school room or working in my father's shop."

Thames said, "Now I know...perhaps on the journey, when we get a chance, I will teach you how to shoot. You have learned to speak French by listening, I am sure you can learn to fire a musket. You will need to know how, anyway, when we are in the wilderness."

Piotr nodded. "I guess I am going then, not staying on the ship?"

Thames said, "Aye, you are going. You have proven yourself. But stay vigilant! It is a dangerous place, sometimes."

Piotr smiled a little. His mind raced with the thoughts of what he would need to pack.

At mid-morning, Piotr and the rest of the men that were going into the woods were loaded and ready. Piotr thought he must have looked fairly ridiculous with the large, wood framed basket strapped on his back. It contained his bedroll, some food, all of his clothing, an extra knife given to him by Linville, extra moccasins and clothes from Marta, coils of a thin, strong rope made from spun hemp that he had taken from the ship's hold, dozens of sinew cording strips, an extra bag of black powder, patches, dozens of lead shot for the muskets, a wooden bowl, and a spoon.

The pack was heavy enough that he wrapped a strip of cloth around outside of it and looped it over his forehead, adding his neck strength to the load. It gave some relief to his lower back muscles. He still carried his small ax and the knife Eggard had given him on his belt. He tied strips of sinew cording into loops and found that his hickory club fit nicely onto the back of the basket. He tied it so that it was vertical, letting the thickness of the barrel hold it in place. It also allowed him to get it out fairly quickly, if he should need it.

The contents of the ship were being packed onto a dozen horses and one strong-looking mule that Flagger had purchased. Some of the muskets were bundled and wrapped in two layers, cotton on the inside and oilcloth on the outside, then tied on in packs to the frames built for holding them. The horses were not for riding, he discovered. They were for carrying. The men would all be walking and carrying their own packs. In addition, Eggard had a two-wheeled cart pulled by the mule, a long flat bed piled with trade goods and beaver traps. A tarp covered the items completely and was tied down at the corners.

Piotr wondered how a cart would be able to make this journey, with mud and logs and rocks underfoot. Linville advised him he would soon find out.

"Piotr, you will be at the rear of the column. Do not fall far behind. Keep aware of your surroundings. You and Eggard hitch the mule up for the cart."

Like everyone else, Linville had a pack on his back. Piotr noted that he also wore two long snaphance pistols on his belt with his knife.

"Aye, Captain," he responded.

Piotr looked over at Thames and Flagger. The taller, thickly bearded Flagger carried the wooden framed pack on his slightly hunched shoulders, moving easily despite the weight. He had replaced his red cap with a gray tricorn hat that was old and damaged, but he said it kept the rain out of his ears.

Thames's muscular frame took the weight of his wooden basket backpack without difficulty. Both men also carried long-barreled match-lock muskets in their hands. Thames's black hair hung to his shoulders. His blue kerchief was tied around his neck for sweat and bugs. Both men wore brown buckskin shirts with a sash of cloth that served as a bandolier of sorts across their chests. Dangling down from them were a dozen or so small pouches of leather, filled with black powder and a patch and a ball. These loads were ready for use. In addition, a pouch of shot and patches and a powder horn were also tied onto the sashes, hanging above their right hips. With their knives and axes on their belts, they looked formidable.

Looking at the other men in the mid-morning sun, Piotr thought the Paquet brothers were walking packs with legs. All of their packs were enormous and filled to the maximum. They were all short and bearded, but broad-shouldered and strong. They looked like potatoes with two short legs. They joked nonstop with each other and everyone around them, while busily loading and preparing their gear. He marveled at their strength, as they shouldered their large packs with relative ease. His own pack felt very heavy.

Despite the baggage on the horses, the cart, and the men, they carried only half of what was in the ship's hold. Thames and Linville had explained that once a camp was established in the valley, they would make trade agreements with the Indians. They would trade off what they carried, and make return trips to the ship, with bales of pelts, returning to camp with more trade goods for exchange.

Goodbyes were said to the men staying with the *St. Longinus*. Linville left them with orders and watch schedules. Perdo, the pilot, would stay with the ship. Captain Laurent from *The Render*, still wounded and recovering, had become a de facto member of the crew. He would stay with the ship, living on its deck as a watchman. The two captains said their goodbyes. Captain Laurent, still hunched over and sickly from his wounds, said, "I thank you, again, Captain Linville. You saved my life. I will look after the ship while you are gone."

With a warm smile, Linville said, "Remember to look after yourself as well. You are still healing. These men are good men. They will do the labor of keeping her ready."

"Aye, your crew is among the best I have seen. You have been generous with your resources on my behalf. And I, well, my wounds are healing. But I am...lost. Still lost."

Linville looked him over. "You are alive, so there is hope."

Laurent nodded and they shook hands. Linville climbed over the railing and joined the line of men and animals. With the few men left on the ship standing and waving on the deck, the line of men and horses, a mule with a cart, and a nearly grown young man walked away from Quebec City and into the forest.

Piotr had studied the maps with Linville and Thames in his office and had a general idea of what directions they were heading. Walking westward on the trail, they would use the ferry service of Lucien Greely to cross. Then they would travel westward on the hilly trail on the south side of the great lake until they could meet with the Huron, also known as the Wendat, in a few days' time. Thames would broker a deal with the Huron to obtain fur in exchange for trade goods. They would go to where Easterly had sunk his canoes in the river near the second great lake, beyond the falls. They would head south, downriver into the green valley below the great inland seas. The Frenchmen called the first of these massive inland seas La Mer Douce. The Huron and other tribes called the land of the green valley Oh-he-oh.

Previous French traders had named the massive lake after the tribe they found on its shoreline. Linville and Thames had a mind for going south of the lake the Huron called Erie, because this was unexplored and unhunted land. Other trappers had gone north, upstream, to use the current of the rivers and streams when they returned with furs.

Thames and Linville were taking a different approach. Using the rivers to move south to unexplored land would give them an edge. Thames led them along the north shoreline. Mule, as Eggard began to call him, would stop when the cart got stuck, so Piotr was always having to push on the back of the cart. As the afternoon sun rose to the center of the sky, Piotr spoke to Eggard. "I see the forest has undergrowth of ferns and bushes, but not a lot of small trees?"

Eggard, his dirty, greyish white linen cap tied to his bald head, said, "Look at the trees, much bigger than back in Saint-Malo or along the Schilde in Daneland. This is an old forest. These trees have never been cut down. This has always been a forest."

He looked up and pointed at the canopy.

"The leaves are tightly woven together at the top of the trees, only a little light gets in, down to the ground. So not so much grows on the floor of the forest. Where we live, much of the forest has been cut down, and in some places, regrown; in other places, grass takes over. Here, the trees are winning."

They walked, mile after mile, mostly in silence with just the occasional horse snorting and rattle of their packs and straps. As they crested some hills leading down to the water, they came across trees growing on the hillside that were so large, Piotr could only stare in amazement. These giants were more than seventy feet high and ten feet in diameter at the base. They grew incredibly straight, up into the sky, with branches thicker than a full-sized oak. Eggard opened his sack and began to gather some of their nuts off the ground as he led the mule.

He said, "Chestnut trees, they drop these." He held one up. "We roast them," he said, handing it to Piotr.

Piotr examined the spiky green sphere. It looked like a large burr that would stick to your clothing. "You can eat this?"

"They are sweet and tender. Like meat. The inside, they open up when cooked. If we have a fire tonight, I will cook some. Also, deer like them, so you can use them as a lure."

Eggard could find food anywhere, Piotr thought.

After hours of walking, with the cart frequently getting stuck on a rock or a log, Piotr was grateful when they stopped to rest. Having grown used to the constant chattering and joking on the ship, Piotr was surprised at the silence of the men. They did not gather together; mostly they stayed spread out, looking into the undergrowth, watching the forest. They rested and sipped water from their bladder canteens, they ate dried meat strips or chewed pemmican they had purchased before leaving. Even the Paquet brothers were silent on the trail.

"Eggard," he asked, "why are the men so quiet?"

Eggard brushed the dirt off his hands and said, in a low voice, "Every savage within half a mile knows we are here, simply from the noise of our horses. Talking aloud will let everyone for miles know we are here."

Piotr took his cue and stopped asking questions. Taking off his pack and setting it on the ground, he spent the resting time sitting on the back of the cart, looking out at the trees. Eggard unhooked Mule and walked him over to a nearby stream, flowing fast with runoff water, and he drank deeply. He gestured over to Piotr to come and refill his bladder canteen.

Bending down in the knee-deep water to refill it, he heard a ripple of disturbance at the front of the column. He heard men talking in a language he did not know. Eggard moved Mule back to the cart and hitched him up again. As they moved up the line, Piotr saw Thames standing on the path in front of the column of men and horses. Two Indian men were standing on the path. Piotr wasn't sure what was happening. He wondered if they were trying to block their way.

Eggard stepped up to him and leaned down and whispered, "Huron. But I am not sure if they are the same Huron we are going to see. Different."

Eggard's giant hand went to the ax on his belt. He pulled it up and loosened it a bit in the loop that held it, keeping his hand on the ax head. His head snapped up and he looked to the north, into the undergrowth of forest below the trees. Piotr followed his gaze.

He saw leaves, ferns, some rhododendron and nothing else. Until one of them moved. As he scanned into the depth of green and brown forest under the canopy of leaves, he saw them. At least a dozen men. All were completely silent, and blending into cover, behind trees, bushes, and downed logs. They were being watched.

As he looked closer in the shadows of the tall trees, he could see that many were shaved on one or both sides of their heads. Some were painted with symbols on their face or body and adorned with some necklaces of bone or small stones.

Eggard leaned over and quietly spoke into Piotr's ear. "Get your hand on the bridle. When it's time to move, keep him moving."

Eggard reached back to Piotr's pack on the ground and put it on the cart, pulling the war club out of its cordage and handing it to Piotr. He then stepped around the column of men and started walking toward the front of the line.

Piotr peered down the line of men and horses, leaning out to see what was happening in the front. He kept his left hand on the bridle of the mule, and his right held the club at his side. He looked back out into the woods and none of the men had moved. They were still and watchful. He was not able to see all the way down to the front of the column with the men and horses in front of him.

Suddenly, the hair on his forearms and the back of his neck tingled and stood up. He looked out to the forest, but the Huron men still had not moved. He smelled animal fat, as if it were cooking on a smoky campfire. It dawned on him, then, and he spun around.

Two Huron warriors were standing a few feet behind the cart, looking into the contents under the tarp. He let go of the bridle and turned to face them. One was tall, nearly as tall as Eggard, and very thin. His head was shaved on both sides, and he stood shirtless with purple dots painted across his narrow chest. The other one was shorter, only as tall as Piotr. His hair was pulled back into a bun and a porcupine quill was pushed into it for decoration. He held a bow in his left hand. Both men had knives at their hips, and the tall one held a tomahawk in his right hand, by his side. He realized that their skin was shiny over their shoulders and on their arms. It was animal fat they had rubbed on. That was what he smelled.

Both men froze in place when he turned. They did not smile, step back, or turn away. They just stood in place, ten feet away, looking at him and the cart. After a moment, the shorter one stepped toward the cart, and reached his hand toward the oilcloth cover. Piotr instinctively and protectively stepped toward them, bringing the club up to a two-handed grip. The shorter man stopped in place, turning his head and looking quizzically at Piotr. Piotr understood that they intended to take what they wanted off the cart. He could not let that happen. He took another step toward them with the war club in hand, moving into range.

Suddenly the taller man moved, his hand with the tomahawk extending out toward Piotr. Piotr instinctively blocked the weapon away with a click as the stone head smacked off the metal studs of his club. The shorter man moved in so fast that Piotr had no time to react as he had extended to block the first motion. The back of the shorter man's hand smacked against Piotr's face, not hard enough to hurt him but hard enough to make a loud sound. Piotr's head snapped back in surprise, and he swung the club back to ward off this attack. The shorter man had already jumped back and away, and the two Huron warriors then turned and ran back into the forest shadows.

Whoops and yips suddenly exploded from all of the Huron watching them. The Huron on the hillside stood and shouted for a few seconds, making their presence felt, then turned and ran into the forest on an unseen trail, whooping as they went.

Stunned by what had occurred, Piotr stood guard over the cart, brandishing his war club at no one.

Eggard and Flagger were quickly at his side, all looking out into the forest, as the Huron men made a show of whooping and screaming.

"What just happened?" Flagger said.

"He hit me on the face, the one with the long hair. The tall one distracted me and the shorter one hit me on the side of my face."

Flagger and Eggard smiled. Eggard said, "He counted coup on you!"

Piotr looked at the two of them, confused. "What does that mean?"

"It is brave to kill another warrior, but it is considered much braver if you touch another warrior without having to kill him," Eggard explained.

"And it is considered braver still if they touch the face of the enemy.

The greater the enemy, the greater the coup. They think you are a great warrior!" Flagger added.

Piotr rubbed the red mark on his cheek where the knuckles of the shorter Huron had smacked him. It had not really hurt, but the shock of it rattled him. He looked back up into the forest; the Huron were already gone.

"I thought they were on our side," he said.

Flagger chuckled. "The Huron are not on our side, they are just opportunistic. Same as us...they want the muskets we carry for trade. The metal knives, axes, and cooking pots. They have been fighting with the Iroquois. If they could kill us and take them, they would, without hesitation. But they do not want to die trying. They are smart. Devious. Smarter than us in the ways of the wilderness, that is for sure. They live here, and we are encroaching on their home, taking their resources."

Piotr thought about this for a minute. "Are all the savage like them? Smarter than us, here in the forest?"

Shaking his head, Flagger said, "Yes."

"And they all want our stuff," Eggard said, gesturing at the wagon and the packs on the horses.

Thames's command to get moving again rallied the men, and they began to head down the trail throughout the remainder of the day. Piotr moved branches and rocks from the wagon's path. As he walked, he thought about what had happened. If the shorter Huron fellow had wanted to kill him, he would be dead now. If he had held a knife, rather than an open hand, he would be lying on his back on the trail with his throat laid open.

As the sun began to sink toward the horizon, the trail edged along a small cliff face of rock to the north and the river to the south. Thames signaled for the column to stop, and the men began to make camp for the night.

Eggard waved at him to help him set up near the edge of the cliff, using the cliff face to reflect the heat of the fire that he began to build with twigs and branches. Piotr gratefully shed the basket from his back, fishing out his tartan blanket as a bedroll. Eggard sent Piotr to gather some pine boughs with his ax.

When he returned in a few minutes, Eggard asked him, "You were lost in thought for most of the walk."

"Yes."

"It is not a good way to walk in the wilderness. Here, you have to be aware, all the time. Stop stepping on sticks and moving rocks when you walk. Move quietly. All the time. You give away your position with each noise. I know the cart is loud and the horses, too. Do not add to the noise."

Piotr nodded. "I have much to learn."

Eggard smiled. "Yes." He looked down the trail for a few seconds, toward old rotting logs closer to the edge of the river. "Come on."

Piotr followed him to the river. Eggard crouched by a plant.

"These yellow petals on these tiny flowers...wood sorrel. It grows on the ground in low, wet country, around rotting wood. It is good to eat in your food, and these seed pods are good to chew, they will help to quench a thirst."

He handed Piotr his bag of collectibles. Piotr began gathering the small yellow flower petals and a few of the seed pods. He put a seed pod in his mouth and found it to be tasty and surprisingly juicy, like a minty lemon.

Eggard sprinkled some of the wood sorrel into the oats and river water he heated over the fire. Piotr took the small bowl and ate it with relish. He was very hungry. After eating and drinking another bowl of river water, he spread his tartan bedroll onto the pine boughs and lay down with his eyes open, still thinking about the events of the day.

The next thing he knew, Flagger was shaking him. "Get up. We are moving."

He looked around, blurry from sleep, and saw that Eggard had the fire stamped out. The red sun was up but still not above the tree line. Another bowl of oats and water awaited him next to his bedroll. He shook his head to clear it and saw that the line of men and horses were forming to leave. He grabbed the bowl of oats, wood sorrel, and river water, and ate the whole thing in a single bite. Wiping the bowl clean with his hand, and wiping that off on some grass, he then jumped up and gathered his bedroll and belongings back into the basket.

Throwing on his moccasins, Piotr quickly jogged down into the river, splashing water onto his face and hands and scrubbing them clean. He stuck his head down into the water, drinking deeply, like an animal from the forest. The water was fast moving, clean, and crisp. His brown wet hair fell to his shoulders when he stood up, dripping coldly down his back and chest.

Eggard waved him up to the cart. "Tie them pine boughs in a bundle on top of the cart. We can use those again." He threw Piotr some sinew cordage. Piotr caught it with one hand, bending to gather up the bows and tie them into a bundle.

They moved on, walking throughout the morning. As the sun rose to the middle of the sky, the call came to stop. Eggard pointed at the sky above the tree line. "Smoke up ahead."

Piotr craned his head around the horses and men as the column stopped. Thames and Linville had walked ahead, down the trail. Piotr could see a small cabin with a chimney smoking lightly at the bottom of the hill. The cabin had been built up on log stilts so that it wouldn't flood when the river rose. It had a front porch of sorts, and the roof covered a very large man sitting on the porch waiting for them. Piotr could tell, even from this far vantage point, it was the big man from Marta's public house.

Piotr ran to Flagger. "That man on the porch is the big man, the man that Thames held a knife to, in Marta's place."

Flagger gazed down the hill, narrowing his eyes and said, "I believe you are right. Your eyes are young. Come on."

They set out at a jog, Flagger armed with a musket and Piotr with just his belt ax and knife. Four of the Paquet brothers saw what was happening and followed as well, Abel and Gerard both with muskets in hand, while Anton and Abraham were armed only with the knives and hatchets at their belts. They stopped about twenty yards away from the porch where Lucien Greely sat, as Thames and Linville continued on.

As Thames approached the steps up to the porch, he said, "You and I will have business again."

Greely stood up, tall and thick, but moving with surprising ease. Four men came out of the front door onto the porch and stood behind him. Three had muskets, and one a blunderbuss. Piotr could see that the horsehair wicks were lit on their guns.

"Why am I not surprised? I suppose you own the ferry…" Thames said, taking half a step back away from the porch.

"I do own it, yes. And I run it for those that need ferrying. I suppose you all need a good bit of ferrying." Lucien gloated with his position of authority.

Captain Linville straightened up. "I think you and I have not met, good sir. I am Captain James Linville of the trading ship *St. Longinus*. We do need use of your ferry, as we intend to cross the river. Is your ferry available?" Linville gave a sweeping gesture to the trees and river completely empty of traffic.

"Do you see anybody else out here in this godforsaken wilderness?"

Lucien came down the porch steps. He pointed at Thames and stepped out onto the path, his large mass blocking their way. "You and I have an unfinished matter, mister."

The men on the porch, with wicks primed, stepped down off the porch and spread out onto the path behind Lucien.

Thames unshouldered his matchlock, handing it to Linville. "I suppose you're right. So, how do you intend we go about it? Knives? Axes?" Thames removed his bandelier of charges and pouches of lead and shot, handing them to Linville.

Lucien smiled cruelly, rolling up the sleeves of the white cotton shirt he wore under black vest. Piotr saw that his forearms were thick and veiny.

"I intend to beat you to death. With my bare hands. You put a knife to my throat but did not use it. That was a mistake for which you will pay. The man has not been born that can tear my meat house down!"

With that he sprang forward in a surprisingly fast two steps and swung his right hand at Thames's temple.

Thames was no fool and was waiting on it. Jumping to the side and avoiding the punch, he was about to strike, but Lucien was quick on his feet, spinning to his left and striking out again, catching Thames in the shoulder, knocking him backward a few stumbling steps.

Thames was taken aback by his power. He had never fought anyone who could hit hard enough to move his whole body with middling contact to the shoulder.

The two men circled warily, looking for an opportunity. Lucien was experienced as a fighter and moved fluidly for a man so large. Thames feinted with a right hand, and Lucien stepped inside of the feint, throwing a devastating left hook. Thames ducked it with no other option, and connected with a right-hand uppercut to the point of Lucien's chin, snapping his head back, then followed with a hard left to the ribs. It felt like hitting a bag of wet sand.

Lucien was unmoved and unfazed. He grabbed Thames in his meaty hands by his buckskin shirt and spat in his eyes, blinding him momentarily, then head butted his forehead. Thames's head snapped back, his forehead splitting open with a gash. Desperate, Thames threw his arms upward, breaking the hold on his shirt, and stomped down on the toes of Lucien's left foot, smashing the big one with his heel.

Lucien recoiled onto his right foot, grunting in pain. Thames seized the opportunity. Stepping around his right foot and placing his heel just behind Lucien's heel, he drove forward with his arms and elbows up, toppling the large man backward to the ground. Lucien landed on his back and instantly tried to roll over to stand up, but Thames was quick as a cat, and latched onto his back. After a struggle, Thames got his arms around his neck from under his right shoulder, forcing his hand in the air.

Thames sunk his arm deep into the chokehold, holding on for dear life as they lay on their left sides. Lucien tried to roll, but Thames was able to spread his legs and prevent the larger man from flipping him.

Lucien kicked at his legs and swore at him in a choking voice, "Damn your blood, you son of a bitch! I will kill you!"

This was the moment Thames was looking for. He finished the chokehold, getting his left arm across the windpipe of the large man and squeezing it tight toward his own chest, causing Lucien's choked curse to change to a sputter and cough.

Flagger bumped Piotr on the side, as Lucien's men were yelling and engrossed in the fight. He stepped in front of Piotr to shield their view and pushed him into the undergrowth along the trail. Piotr ducked down low, looking to see if he had been noticed. With no obvious sign, he slipped out into the shadows of the tall trees, quietly stepping and circling around the cabin. He came out on the other side behind Lucien's men. Lucien, choking and red in the face, began to lose the struggle.

Bleeding down his forehead and across the bridge of his nose from the gash, Thames yelled in Lucien's ear "Enough? Yield now, so that we may end this while you live!"

Lucien coughed and struggled for a few seconds more, but Thames's hold was deep and not going to be broken. He stopped struggling and raised his hands in surrender.

Thames kicked the ground and rolled them both so that Lucien was face down on the ground. Thames was on top of him with his arm still at his throat. Then he released his hold and jumped away, lest the big man change his mind. Lucien coughed and sputtered, then took in some wheezing breaths, on all fours.

The four men, seeing their leader on the ground gasping for air, all raised their weapons to their shoulders. The man with the blunderbuss was closest, so Piotr pulled the knife Eggard had given him on the ship the night of the storm. He grabbed the man by the forehead with his right hand, pulling his head back, placing the flat of the blade to his throat, under his bearded chin, the same way that Thames had in the public house. Piotr could smell his rancid breath and see that what teeth he had were rotted and stained. The man's eyes rocked back and forth as he realized what had happened. His brothers shouldered their muskets, aiming them at the Frenchmen.

"You men better hold right there lest your man gets his throat cut," Linville pointed out to the other three.

The three men with muskets turned to see Piotr with his knife at their partner's throat.

"Let him go... I will kill you if you cut him," the tall man next to him on the path said, as he stepped back and turned his musket toward Piotr.

"You stop there or I will open him up," Piotr responded, looking him dead in the eye. They stared at each other in a standoff.

After a long moment, Lucien Greely gasped, "Stop... Stop."

Raising his hands, he struggled to one knee, gathering his breath still. After a few heavy breaths he stood up, half a head taller than Thames.

"He beat me. He was lucky...but he beat me." He coughed and wheezed, spitting out a mouthful of phlegm. "Get the ferry ready, take these men and their animals across the river."

The other three men looked at Lucien in disbelief. They had never known him to be bested, and certainly never to give in. They stood their ground.

"Get a move on."

Lucien staggered down the path to the river. His men looked at each other, shaking their heads, then lowered their muskets and followed him. They began to untether the large raft serving as a ferry and ready the wooden gangplank for the horses.

"Take them across. All of'em," Lucien commanded, and walked his weary bulk up the steps of the porch, slumping down in the wooden chair. The men and horses made their way down to the river and began boarding the ferry.

A few trips across with the men once holding muskets on them now pulling on the rope, and the group was across, save for Thames, Linville, Piotr, Eggard, and the two-wheeled cart with Mule.

After everything was loaded for the last trip, Linville walked onto the porch where Lucien slumped over in an old chair and said, "What is owed for this crossing, sir?"

"One livre per crossing with the boat full. You are the fourth crossing, so four livres," Lucien said wearily.

Linville pulled out a few coins from his coat pocket and offered them up. Lucien swiped them from his hand with a meaty snatch.

Looking up from the chair with a still-sweaty brow, and mopping his thinning black hair over his forehead, Lucien said, "Do not come back this way again. Next time I see him," he pointed at Thames standing by the river, a trickle of blood still fresh on his forehead, "I will kill him."

Linville said, "Your anger is misplaced, but I hear your words."

Backing down the steps, Linville turned and headed down the path.

"And that little bastard what pulled the knife, him too." Lucien spat venomously at his back as he walked away.

The man who had held the blunderbuss, with the rancid breath and rotting teeth, stood on the porch next to Lucien.

"Twice these bastards put a blade to our throats. Well, they made a mistake. When they come back with their precious beaver pelts, we are going to show them. They should've used those knives."

Lucien Greely wiped his sleeve across his spittle-flecked mouth, leaned over, and whispered, "You know the cannon at the fort, the mounted one... Find out where Easterly is keeping it. We are going to need it when these sons of bitches come back."

# Chapter 11

# A CLEAN SHIRT

*I am frozen,* Raul Montreaux thought for the second time that night, shivering from exposure to the cold seawater and the night air. Jana, still soaking wet, shivered next to him as they hid behind bushes and leaves near the cove. For nearly an hour they had stayed there. He could hear the Iroquois leaving *The Render* and coming ashore with anything they could carry, including the matchlock muskets of the Swedish seamen. Each one a valued treasure, to be sure.

In the darkness, the longboat had slipped away, rowing nearly silently with the survivors on board. Montreaux reached out to the shivering Jana and pulled her close to share body heat. She was grateful for it, and in the cold night they both wondered if they would see civilization again.

It was so dark, they dared not move out of the undergrowth into the forest. They had no idea where they were going and could not see past the length of their arms. They would simply have to stay put till the sun was up and they could see. He was hopeful the Iroquois would move on, but he could still hear them, talking and laughing on the rocky shore of the cove.

He was so tired he could barely keep his eyes open. He had no idea that he was suffering from shock. Jana knew he needed rest. He had led the group through all of this madness. Face to face, she reached with her fingers and tapped herself on the nose, then signaled by opening her eyelids with her fingertips. She pointed to his bearded face and closed her eyelids with her fingertips. Montreaux understood and laid his head back in the dirt, and in just a minute, relaxed into a needed sleep. Jana forced herself to stay awake, listening to the voices only fifty or so yards away.

Finally, after what seemed like most of the night, the Iroquois left the beach, the whole group jogging off in a single file line into the dark forest. She relaxed, somewhat, laying her head back on Montreaux's chest. She did not close her eyes, however, and she listened. She listened for the sound of steps crunching on the leaves or voices drawing near. But none ever came. For this miracle, she was thankful to God.

Jana had not been raised as a Catholic, but she had committed to the faith when her mother helped her to flee to the monastery. Like all school children, her school days were spent in a religious school, and the Lutheran school she had grown up in had far more in common with the Catholic schools in neighboring towns than it did differences.

Lying on the ground in the dark, cold and wet, next to a man she barely knew, she easily could have given in to her fears. But she was stronger than that. Her innate resilience, her will, would not be broken. She kept her head and waited. In the quiet darkness, she whispered the prayer for protection that Sister Mary had taught her. She whispered it so softly that even Montreaux would have had a hard time hearing it, were he awake.

"Lord, we ask you to cover us and keep us free from evil. Cover us and surround us, keep us safe with your wall of protection, encircled in your arms. Make us strong and fearless for the road ahead. Help us to be alert to your spirit, to walk the path ahead in the wisdom of your words, to hear your voice of truth. We rest in your care, and we use your power to strengthen us. Amen."

Her eyes closed, but she stayed awake, listening to the night.

In a few hours, the early red rays of the predawn sun began to streak over the sky. Jana touched Montreaux on the cheek and his eyes opened immediately, looking up with confusion. After a moment, the wild look left his eyes and he looked around the forest undergrowth. He sat up, leaves and debris in his hair.

Still not sure about what to do, he asked, "You stayed up all night?"

"Yes."

"The Iroquois? They have gone?"

"Yes."

He rubbed his face and eyes. "We are lucky, then."

Jana gave a small nod. She was not sure it was luck, but they were alive.

Montreaux stood up and looked around. They were in the old growth forest along the cove. The remnant of *The Render* floated at anchor with a red sun rising behind it.

Montreaux sat down on the log next to her, rubbing his fingers through his salt-and-pepper hair to brush out the leaves. "Let us take stock of our situation," he said. "I have two pistols, one with a charge in it that is wet. It may dry out as the day goes on. The other is empty. I have a knife and I have a bladder canteen. We have no food." He looked down at his boots, black leather and cobbled with metal ringlets for the laces. "Your shoes? Jana, can you walk?"

Jana's black shoes were made of canvas and about as practical as could be. "I can. If you are taking account of supplies, I took this off of the Indian in the water." She held up a short-bladed stone knife with a hide-wrapped handle. The blade was grayish-black flint and had an incredibly sharp edge.

Montreaux looked it over and shook his head. "He was lucky he let go when he did."

Jana looked the knife over carefully, then looked out at the cove. Their ship drifted on a single anchor line. "I am wondering, can we get back on the ship? Sail it up to Quebec City?"

"We would never be able to operate it with just the two of us."

"What about food, gunpowder, clothes? There may be things we need on it."

"Most of it was offloaded when we were stuck on that island. But there may be some more things we can use. The only way to get on it is to climb up that anchor chain. I am not sure that I can do that." He brushed some leaves off his shoulders and turned his head to look at her. "But, maybe you could, though, if I boost you up? It is another swim in the cold water, but…" He left it hanging.

Jana was cold and bone tired, but there was nothing more to it. "I'll go if you will."

Montreaux roused himself upright and shook off the aches and pains of sleeping on the ground. He put his hands on his knees for a few deep breaths, then started toward the water, stepping over and around the rocks on the shore. Jana followed along. She was so tired. The cold water would wake her up, she thought.

Montreaux sat down on the edge of the water line and took off his heavy boots. Then walked into the cold sea water of the cove, looking back at Jana. As the water reached just below his groin, he paused and shook his head. He wondered about his own sanity at this point. Stoically, he dove forward into the cold blue water.

Jana followed him in, and they made their way to the anchor chain, a hundred yards out. *The Render* was slowly twisting with the current around the single anchor line at the stern. Montreaux grabbed it with two hands, pulling himself close to it.

"Climb up my back." He sputtered in the water.

Jana climbed over him, first kneeling then stepping on his shoulders, reaching up as high as she could on the line. Finally she had to take her own weight on her arms; the soaking, freezing chain was cold in her hands. The heaviness of her wet dress was pulling her down, so she had no choice but to squeeze her legs around the chain, locking her ankles over it to hold her weight.

"Can you inchworm up?" Montreaux asked from the water. He was marveling at the thought of how so many of the Iroquois got onto the deck of the ship using this chain.

Jana coiled her legs toward her hands and then stretched out again, making a foot of progress. The strain was severe, and she suddenly didn't feel cold. She kept going, making a little progress at a time. Her heart rate soared in her chest, and she gasped with the effort. Her wet hair hung down, dripping, but after three more coiled lunges up the chain, she got her hands on the bottom edge of wood at the starboard railing where the anchor chain extended down. She pulled and clawed till she got a grip on the post of the railing, letting go of the anchor chain with her ankles, and scrambled for a foothold on the side of the ship. Her right toe found a wooden edge and she pushed herself up the railing, getting her hands on the top, and pulling herself over onto the deck in a crashing heap.

Exhausted, she lay panting for a moment. Montreaux, treading in the cold water, stared upward, raising a hand to shield his eyes from the morning sun. "Are you all right?" he called.

She stood up, wearily, and looked over the rail, waving down at him. "I will find a rope or something to toss down."

"There is a knotted rope under the bench at the helm!" he shouted.

"What is the helm?" she turned to the deck and said to no one.

She staggered across the deck and looked around, then realized that the deck was a horror. She froze in her tracks, putting her hand to her mouth.

The Swedish sailors were frozen in death. Some of them were pinned to the ship with arrows. Many had their throats cut, or heads split open, staring with open eyes in death. One poor man was tied to the forward mast on his knees, his hands above his head, with his feet tied behind him. His stomach was laid open, and his small intestine was pulled out and wrapped around the mast half a dozen times. It was a ship of dead men.

She tried to look away, but pools of drying blood and buzzing flies were everywhere, like spilled red paint. Her exhaustion from staying awake all night and climbing up the anchor chain, and the shock from the events of the last two days, suddenly began to catch up with her. She felt light-headed and nauseous, and the deck began to spin. Staggering to the railing, she leaned her head over and began to retch as silently as she could. Nothing would come up, as her stomach was empty. Montreaux looked up from the cold water, not understanding what was happening.

"Jana, are you all right?" he called up anxiously.

She steadied herself at the rail and put one hand up to him in a half wave, then resolutely began to look for a rope or something to toss down. She spied what could be a helm, she thought, and there was a cabinet. In it, she found a knotted rope. She tied one end around the central mast and tossed the other over the side, where Montreaux waited in the cold water.

The rope grew taut and scraped against the railing. Soon a left hand, followed by a right hand grabbed the railing and Montreaux pulled himself over onto the deck. Soaking wet and gasping heavily from his climb, he lay on the deck for a bit, breathing and gathering his strength. "Well done," he managed to sputter.

He sat up and looked around at the gruesome scene. He stared in disgust for a moment, inhaling sharply. "They did not find the captain's quarters, the door is still closed."

He walked over to it. The door was locked, as Captain Laurent was prone to do when not in his quarters. Raul Montreaux leaned back and smashed the door open with a kick. Bits of lock and door jamb scattered across the deck. He strode into the small room and began to rifle through the shelves, looking for anything useful. In the cupboard behind the desk, some hardtack biscuits and jerked meat were in a small canvas bag. He tossed it to Jana. She caught it, slinging it over her shoulder by the leather string.

Jana opened the narrow closet, finding a white cotton shirt hanging on a peg and took it, examining it for fit.

Montreaux then found a locker under the small cot that Laurent used as a bed. He pulled it out and used his knife to pry open the lock. Lifting the lid, he found two more snaphance pistols, a couple of powder horns, and a small bag of patch and lead shot. He checked to see; the pistols were not loaded. In the narrow closet, there were a couple of pairs of pants, a wide black belt, some boots, and two coats, one a heavier overcoat. There were also two unused candles and some leather shoelaces.

Looking around for a second, he threw everything except the heavy coat, a pair of pants, and the belt into a pile on the cot, then folded and rolled the blanket around all of it, tying the roll of supplies together with the shoelaces.

He showed Jana the pants and the belt. "You should change into these. It will be warmer for the journey. Take this coat as well." He handed her the overcoat, which was several sizes too large, but was warm like a blanket. It would serve her as a bedroll, if nothing else.

Leaving her in the quarters to change, Montreaux went below deck. In the galley he found some loose oats lying on the shelving. Enough for one meal, at least. He found a leather bag and scraped them into it. There was some coiled rope, and some more hardtack biscuits, all of which he stuffed into a small iron cooking pot and then put it all into the leather bag. He found nothing else of any value. He climbed the stairs back up to the deck. Jana emerged from the captain's quarters, hair pulled back and brushed, a new oversized white cotton men's shirt and blue pants on, with a wide black leather belt and an overcoat. She pulled on the black leather boots and looked like a proper sailing man of the early 17th century, at least from a distance.

"I found this as well," Montreaux said as he tossed her the leather bag. She looked through it, rifling with her hand.

He looked out over the rail and said, "Well, we can jump over and swim to shore again. Or...we can pull up the anchor and let the tide beach her." He said it with recrimination. For once *The Render* was beached on this rocky shore, she would never come off again. "We avoid a cold swim, again, if you and I can lift the anchor together. It is very heavy. What do you think?" He looked Jana in the face, seeking her opinion.

"I would rather avoid the cold water again. We have things to carry now, and everything will have to dry out."

"Let's see if we can even move it."

He and Jana moved to the stern where the anchor rope hung over the side. The tension on the rope was strong, and the anchor itself was heavy; this job was usually done by three men. Montreaux and a skinny girl had little chance of pulling it all the way up, he thought. But they really didn't have to pull it all the way up. If they could loosen it a little, they could tie it off and let it drift free. The current would drag the ship over to the shore, and they could climb down on the knotted rope. At least that was the idea.

Montreaux grabbed the rope in two hands and gave it an experimental tug…the tension was tight. He squatted over the rope and grabbed it with a firmer grip, to use his legs in the pulling. Jana took off the overcoat and tossed it aside, then got behind him on the rope and did the same.

"Pull!" he shouted.

They heaved together and the strain was severe. It was like trying to move a boulder. They kept pulling. Montreaux was about to give up when he felt a slight give from the anchor through the rope. Montreaux was able to go hand over hand and draw in a foot of rope. Jana did the same, pulling with him.

"Again!" he said, after a deep breath. Jana pulled with her arms and pushed with her legs. Suddenly, the anchor pulled free of the mud on the bottom of the cove and Montreaux pulled in some more slack. As he went hand over hand, so did Jana, and rope began to coil on the deck. When they had twenty feet or so, Montreaux, sweating and straining mightily, locked his legs against the gunnel and gestured with his bearded chin at a cleat on the side of the rear mast.

"Tie it off there, Jana," he grunted. She let go of the line and quickly wrapped the loose coils around the cleat a few times. Montreaux let the rope go, falling off to one side of it. The remaining slack zipped back down into the water.

The anchor now hung, suspended in the water, above the bottom.

Immediately, Montreaux could feel *The Render* begin to rotate, as the current pushed the bow around the focal point of the anchor's weight at the stern. Eyes darting back and forth, Montreaux rolled to his feet, panting heavily, and stumbled to the wheel. He couldn't see the approaching shoreline from the helm and was looking at the trees to try and get a bearing on how to control the crash into the shore.

"Go to the bow, tell me where to beach her," he shouted at Jana.

She started toward the bow, then recoiled at the sight of the dead Swedish sailors. With a sideways glance at Montreaux, she picked her way through the grotesque bodies with limbs lying akimbo, and eyes staring blankly into death. Stepping lightly around the pools of blood, she moved around the bodies until she got to the bow. A dead Swedish sailor lay over the railing in her way. Grabbing him by the lapels of his uniform, she rolled him to the side. Bugs swarmed up from the dead man's wounds, buzzing around her face. In disgust, she swiped them away and looked out over the railing with her hands waving.

The ship was spinning on the current, and with no real forward motion from the sails, Montreaux had almost no control of it. He spun the boat's wheel left and right as Jana pointed toward where they wanted to be. The boat slowly began to drift in the generally correct direction. He could feel it picking up speed as the small waves of the cove got it moving into the shore.

Jana began pointing back in the other direction; he had overcorrected, and he spun the wheel back trying to right it. The waves moved the boat sideways to the shore as it picked up some momentum. They were going to hit the shore hard.

"Hang on!" he shouted.

She braced herself against the railing as the hull spun into the current and hit the rocky beach. The entire ship rocked suddenly to starboard, and all forward motion slammed to a halt. Montreaux heard the rocks grinding on the bottom of the hull. This was the last journey for *The Render.*

Jana lost her grip on the rail and fell sideways into the bodies lying on the deck. Several dead sailors flopped and rolled with limbs splaying out, landing on her and around her, covering her in dead men.

Montreaux had the benefit of gripping on the wheel and had maintained his feet during the beaching. He sprinted forward to pull her free of the tangled, gory mess. He pulled one of the bodies off by the seat of his bloody pants. Jana came up, sputtering, and pushing her way out of the mass of limbs.

"Oh dear God! Get them off of me!" she shouted as she tried to stand up, wiping away at the gore covering her face and arms. Her face and her white cotton shirt now covered in red blood and tissue.

"Oh, I did not …" Montreaux began as she wiped at the goo on her face and in her hair. "Perhaps we can find another shirt."

He had reached out to her, but there was no place where he could touch her that was not covered in gore.

"Ugh…" She wiped her hands on her shirt and got up, walking away from the dead bodies toward the stern, shaking her head and rubbing the backs of her hands on her eyes. Once clear of the mess of tangled arms and legs, she stood on the deck. A tremble started through her as her exhaustion and shock over the last few days began to overtake her.

Montreaux dug through the leather bag and pulled out the other shirt he had found. He opened the door to the captain's quarters and tossed it onto the small table, then gestured her in. "Take your time."

Jana emerged after a few minutes. She had used the first shirt as a rag and was still wiping the blood from her hands and face. Montreaux bundled the supplies with rope and set them by the railing to lower down.

"Ladies first." He gestured to the knotted rope. "You get down first, and I will lower everything down to you."

Jana grabbed the rope and he fed it out as she walked down the side of the ship to the knee-deep surf and beach below. He tied the supplies up in a rope and lowered the whole thing down to her, and she carried it up the beach. He followed suit, climbing over the railing to slide down the rope. He stopped, hanging there on the rail, and had a long, final look back at the deck. Then he shook his head and made his way down to the sand.

Once they were unloaded, Montreaux suggested they make camp and rest and recover. Jana agreed. They walked about half a mile inland, away from the ship, eastward. Montreaux had no map, but he had a good sense of direction, and he knew he had to head north and west to get to Quebec City. He could always follow the coastline, if need be, but it was a long way. He was hoping for a trail that was marked and could lead them. Now it was midday, and the heat of the spring day felt good on their shoulders. Finding a small stream next to a stand of maple trees, they made camp. Montreaux got a fire going, and they boiled some of the biscuits and salted meat. After a half an hour or so, they were able to use the wooden spoons to eat a meal for the first time in nearly three days.

"I am starving. It has been so long since we ate, my stomach thinks my throat's been slit," Montreaux said, while stirring the stew.

Jana blanched at the comment, thinking of the dead bodies that had just swarmed her on the boat.

"Sorry, a figure of speech," Montreaux said.

They ate their meal in silence from sheer tiredness.

Jana sat down and spread out the overcoat. "Mr. Montreaux, I can no longer keep my eyes open."

She lay down in the shade of the maple trees, and in a few minutes was sound asleep.

Montreaux let the fire burn down and leaned back against a log. In a few minutes, his head was sagging on his chest, and his breathing became deep. He felt his eyes close and tried to fight it, but he too could not stay awake.

He startled awake a couple of hours later, looking about from his seated position on the ground. He saw Jana, asleep in the overcoat, now pulled over her and lying on her side. He also saw feet, in moccasins, and the brown skin of two legs.

He jumped to his feet, still half asleep, the fight or flight reaction pouring adrenaline into his veins. He stumbled a step backward, tripping over the log he had been leaning against. Blearily, he looked about while wiping at his eyes, and saw three Indians squatting next to his fire warming themselves. Another was seated cross-legged, opposite of the fire from Montreaux, humming quietly and rocking back and forth. His vision cleared, and it took him a second to realize that the person crouching near him was Malian.

"We did not mean to disturb you."

Hearing her remarkable French accent finished waking him up.

He gathered himself and sat down on the log. "I thought you all were dead. When they attacked, I had to get my people to the boat…"

Malian looked at him with her calm brown eyes. "Why do you apologize? You did not attack us. The Iroquois did. They are the cause of our troubles…you have done nothing wrong."

"Yes, but, in the confusion, when you walked back into the forest, I thought you all…" Montreaux attempted to explain, but his voice trailed off.

"We hid in the forest and waited for the Iroquois to leave. We saw the smoke from your fire. Why did you not leave with the others?" Malian asked.

"We tried, but a warrior came up from in the water. Grabbed Jana off the boat. I dove in after them. We fought him, and he gave up. But the other Iroquois heard us and came, they were too close to us and the longboat. So I told my people to go, row away," Montreaux explained. The small campfire crackled, and they sat in silence for a moment.

The man sitting by the fire and humming to himself spoke in a voice cracking with pain, his face pointed down and his long hair covering it. Montreaux leaned closer to him as he raised his head up. It was Nanibosad.

"You live?" asked Montreaux.

"I am dead, but they will live," Nanibosad said.

Montreaux saw the wound on his chest from the arrow. Blood had leaked through a poultice forming a large red stain. He was humming and rocking from the pain. The broken shaft of the arrow was still sticking out of his chest, poking through the hole in his shirt. When he reached up to tug at his shirt, Montreaux saw that he had another poultice on his left hand, covering a wound there as well.

"When you were wounded, your first thought was of your people, keeping them safe. You are a courageous man," Montreaux said.

Nanibosad's face showed the stress of pain. His eyes were sunken, but he was not panicking.

*This is good*, thought Montreaux. He had seen men wounded many times in his life; some could have lived if they had simply kept their wits. But they would see their wounds, and they would speak of going home, to their families, then they would ask for their mothers. Soon after, they would die.

He noticed the other two Abenaki squatting by the fire looking at the small pot and realized he had been remiss.

"Food. I have food. Are you hungry? I have some left." He dug through the leather bag, taking out the last of the hardtack and biscuits, placing them in the stew pot to soften in the water. It was the last of their food, but he owed these people for their kindness from yesterday. "It will be ready in a few minutes; it just needs to soften."

"Your kindness is appreciated," Malian said.

Montreaux now took a moment to look her over. There were bloodstains on her sleeve, and on the front of her doeskin dress. She did not appear to be injured. It was not her blood. The stone tomahawk that she had used to smash in the skull of the wounded Iroquois was pushed into the tie string at her waist. Despite all of the difficulties of the last two days, she was still remarkably composed.

"As was yours," Montreaux said. "I do not have any medicine, but some of this food may help."

"I have put on a poultice made from forest lettuce." Malian pulled a few leaves of the plant from the bag she carried. "It will be time to change it soon. It helps to lessen the pain."

She got up and started scouting around the camp area, looking for something. She found it, picking up a wide flat rock about the size of a dinner plate. She put it down and started pumicing the leaves with a piece of wood from her bag. When she got them mashed up, she put the rock next to the fire, to heat them up.

"Monsieur Montreaux, what will you do now?" she asked.

"We need to make our way to Quebec City. Hopefully, to meet up with those that survived on the longboat."

"Is your woman injured...Jana?"

"No, she is tired from...she is not my woman. Not in that sense. She was a passenger on my ship, bound for the New World. I was the first mate, the second in command. Her safety is my responsibility."

"It is two weeks' journey, maybe more." Malian looked around at their lack of supplies and their miserable condition. "We will walk there, I suppose, at this point."

"You will not make it. You will be on the trail with almost no food. And you will be walking through the Iroquois lands."

Malian scraped up the now warm, mushy lettuce into a cloth and held it over Nanibosad's open mouth. She squeezed it so that the dark juice drained down into his mouth. He swallowed it all, turning his head and grimacing at the bitter taste. After a little bit, he stopped rocking and carefully laid himself back on the ground, closing his eyes in sleep.

"Mr. Montreaux, you should come to our village and stay. It is a day's walk. Rest and recover before you go. You can help carry Nani, if need be."

She put her hand to Nanibosad's forehead, feeling for heat. She was direct and to the point.

"The elders will want to talk to you. Maybe they will help you, even send someone with you. As a guide. If you are captured by the Iroquois, you will be tortured, as a test of your strength. They would like to test a Frenchman. They will keep her as a slave. Or sell her off to another tribe."

Montreaux contemplated this. He had no reason to distrust these remarkable strangers he had met. They had already shown kindness and respect. A guide would increase their chances considerably. They had no other options, anyway. They were in a strange land, with no understanding of it.

"Your offer is generous."

Malian spoke to the two warriors in the Abenaki tongue. They exchanged glances with each other and worried looks at Nanibosad.

Montreaux gestured to the pot of meat and biscuits, "Please, eat."

He speared a piece of salted meat with his knife and handed it to the nearest Abenaki man.

The smoke from the fire drifted up into the leafy canopy of trees. Raul Montreaux looked at Jana sleeping on the ground. He now knew she was a strong person. She would have to be.

## Chapter 12

# THE WENDAT TRAIL

O ver the next five days, Piotr made a more conscious effort to pay attention to his surroundings. He learned how to walk quietly in the forest. Twice he had seen men watching from the forest as they walked by. He had reached out to tap Eggard on the shoulder as he walked in front of him, but before he could touch him, Eggard whispered, "I see them. Just keep walking."

They never approached. They just watched from the trees.

As they walked, the river began to widen. For a day, they walked along a marshy area next to the river's edge, and for the first time in the New World, Piotr noted that they were not under the cover of the tree canopy. As they covered the miles, the river narrowed again, and they returned to the shadow of the canopy. Finally, on the seventh day, they came upon the inland sea that fed the river that ran to the ocean.

Standing on the rocky shoreline, Piotr looked out across the water. He saw no land, just waves. As if he were standing on the rocky shore at Saint-Malo, and this was the ocean, he thought. Except this was freshwater, clean and drinkable. With the sun rising over the shoreline of green trees, blue water, and brown sand and rocks, its beauty was such that it felt like he was looking at an impossible, uncountable wealth. There had been no shortage of freshwater in his youth, but clean water was of value. Cities in Europe were always dealing with dirty water from the runoff of sewage and human waste in the streets. He asked Thames about it, sitting by the fire, as they camped that night.

171

"What do they call this place? It is so big. I have never seen so much freshwater in one place."

Thames put down his bowl and wiped his mouth with the back of his sleeve. "They call it Ontario." He enunciated the syllables in the way of the Huron. "It is the same word for the Iroquois. The size of it is amazing, eh, but Piotr, there are four more of these inland seas just west and north of here." Thames pointed out in the northwesterly direction. "It will take us most of a week to get to the next one. They call it Erie."

Piotr tried to process the idea that a lake would require nearly a week's walking to get to the other side. "Everything is larger here...the trees, the rivers, the lakes. This place has so much abundance. It feels like a holy place, a blessed place."

Thames smiled. "Sometimes, I look up at the sky at night, and I think... how lucky are we? To be here, to see this sky, these trees, to breathe this air. It is open...untouched. The French countryside is cut up into fields, divided with stone walls, towns and villages, and cities. People everywhere, all fighting each other...every bit of land is owned by someone." Thames paused. "You know, the Huron say that this lake, this is the small one."

Piotr's eyes widened. *Bigger than this.*

"When we get past the great falls, we will go west a little way to the Huron encampment. It is on the shore of the next inland sea, Erie. They have moved it farther away from Quebec City since I was here last. The Huron on the trail were telling me this, when you got smacked in the face." Thames smiled a bit. "This is where we will find the canoes that Easterly says are sunk. Just off the shore, marked with sticks, where the crooked river meets it."

Thames then asked, "Eggard and Flagger said you are beginning to understand the ways of the woodsman, of walking quietly. What have you noticed when you walk about the forest? The animals? The plants?"

Piotr thought for a moment. "The trees are so tall, compared to home. Even the birds...the flocks in the sky are so large. They fly over like a storm cloud; the sun is blocked out. The forest feels like it goes on forever."

Thames smiled. His forehead gash from the fight with Lucien Gree-ly was now just a wound, healing with some mild discoloration around the cut. Soon it would scar.

"It almost does...Huron have told me about traveling westward. They say that there is the Great River to the west, that all of the others feed into. West of there is a prairie with only a few trees, here and there. It is so large, it takes weeks to walk across. Then mountains lie beyond that, much, much higher than the ones south of us now."

Thames's blue eyes glowed with excitement when he spoke of those distant mountains. The idea of going to them clearly sparked in his mind.

This confirmed to Piotr what he had thought before, when he was standing alone beside the river in Quebec City. A person could get lost in a place so large, and no one would ever know where to look. Maybe he should get lost out here, and never go back. He gazed deeper into the forest. It would not be so hard.

"It is a big place, Piotr. Bigger than most people will ever know. But it is not empty. There are tribes from here to the far mountains beyond the plains. I have heard that some traders are going to find their way west in search of beaver pelts, and more will come. It will not be that long until a Frenchman finds himself standing on those far mountains. If he keeps himself alive."

"Do you want to be one of those men, Thames? To go to those far mountains?"

Thames considered, cocking his head as he contemplated. "I have given it some thought...but now...we have to find the beaver. We have a ship to fill."

Piotr nodded. *We...* He realized he was now part of this group. He had changed from an outsider, observing, to a member who belonged and contributed. He felt the air in his chest swell as he breathed in.

Thames added, "In order to do that, we will also need to feed ourselves. It will not take long to run out of supplies. When the men go
hungry, they complain. When men are starving, they fight. First with each
other, then with whoever is in charge. So, Piotr, you will need to learn to
hunt, and therefore, you need to learn to shoot. Let's do that now."

Thames walked back down the column to Eggard's cart. Setting his
own weapon on the cart, he unwrapped the oilcloth and the blankets
around one of the packed matchlocks and pulled a musket free of the
group. He carefully wrapped it back up, retying the bundle. Holding the
weapon up to the light of the sun, he examined it carefully, working the
trigger mechanism and the hammer gently. The long black iron barrel and
fishtail shape of the buttstock were the same as Piotr had seen before. At
least he was familiar with that.

"Come on."

They walked over to the small fire the Paquet brothers had started
to warm their teapot, and Thames pulled out a long wick from his pouch,
threading it into the trigger mechanism so that it would light the powder
in the pan. He showed Piotr all of this, with the excess wick forming a
loop, waiting to slowly burn down and be used.

"What are these made of?" Piotr asked, pointing to the wick.

"Horsehair and wax; burns slowly, not a lot of smoke. But it definitely puts off a peculiar odor. Kind of like stockfish. Learn the smell of
it, and you will know if someone is near with a musket. Watch."

Thames pulled one of the dangling small, cylindrical pouches loose
from the bandolier wrapped around his chest and shoulder. Inside it was
seventy-five grains of black gunpowder, the perfect amount for a charge.
He stood the musket on its butt plate and poured the charge down the
barrel as he let the pouch dangle from his mouth. He reached into the
leather bag at his hip, pulling out a .58 caliber musket ball and a cotton
patch. Placing the ball over the patch at the mouth of the muzzle, he
pulled the ramrod out and pushed it down into the barrel.

Piotr noted that it was not loose fitting, it had to be shoved down with the rod. He watched carefully, memorizing the steps.

Then Thames cradled the musket in his arms. Opening the pan, he took the pouch from his mouth, opened the tiny lid, and filled the pan with the last pinch of gunpowder still in the bottom, then closed the pan lid. He looked at Piotr. "Get an ember from the fire."

Piotr pulled out a small stick that was glowing red on the end and handed it to Thames.

He used it to light the horsehair wick, blowing gently on it to get the wick lit. It burned very slowly. Like a candle wick, but just as an ember, no flame. He handed the stick back to Piotr, who tossed it to the fire.

"See that the barrel is always pointed away, down range toward where I am going to shoot. I have seen men shoot themselves in the face, trying to light a wick and accidentally lighting the powder in the pan. Once the wick is lit, you can keep it lit by blowing on it once in a while. Then you can shoot multiple times without having to relight the wick. In battle, there is no time for fussing with the wick."

Piotr nodded, watching and concentrating on learning.

Careful to keep the hammer in the locked back position, Thames gestured him over to take the weapon. Piotr was nervous and a bit shaky as he took the gun to his shoulder. He was surprised by the weight. The barrel was heavy and it felt very unbalanced. He had a hard time keeping it steady. Thames pushed the butt plate hard into his right shoulder and moved his left hand so that it was down the barrel a couple of inches, giving him better control of it.

"Lean into it." He moved Piotr's chest and shoulders forward, putting his weight more toward his front leg. "Now, look down the barrel, and put the bead on that stump over there."

Piotr looked down the long barrel and saw the stump. The bead on the end of the barrel was swaying around and was hard to steady.

Thames guided his right hand up to the hammer. Placing his thumb on it, he said, "Ease this back till it locks into place."

Piotr did so, and the hammer clicked as it locked.

"Keep the bead on the target and then squeeze the trigger."

Piotr concentrated and finally steadied the wobbling barrel, then squeezed. The hammer came down, bringing the burning wick to the pan, igniting the powder through the small hole in the closed pan lid. A flash erupted from the pan just in front of his right hand, sending some stinging flame back toward his skin. A split second passed, and the pan ignited the charge in the barrel. With a loud explosion, flame and smoke erupted from the mouth of the barrel, obscuring Piotr's view of the stump. The kickback from the charge pushed his chest and shoulders back, causing the barrel to jump upward and point skyward.

Thames reached out to him, putting a steadying hand on the musket. Piotr recovered from his surprise at the recoil and the smoke, and cradled the long weapon to his chest. He squinted, trying to look down range at the stump, but the thick gray smoke from the barrel obscured his vision.

"Always down range. The barrel. Always down range... Now, ease the wick back to the locked position, Piotr. Sometimes there can be powder left in the pan or in the barrel that will ignite."

Piotr looked down at the heavy musket in his hands and eased the wick back into the non-firing position.

"Let us go see what you hit," Thames said with a smile. They walked the twenty-five yards to the stump. There, on the side, was a long, ragged tear in the old bark, where the ball had slashed a trench in the wood.

"That is pretty good for the first time. Now, you load it." Thames pulled a charging pouch from his chest and handed it to Piotr.

Piotr looked at it for a moment. "Back there?" He pointed toward where they had stood.

"Yes, do it again," Thames said.

They repeated this process each day after making camp. Piotr would demonstrate each step of the loading of the matchlock, firing, and sometimes hitting the target, sometimes not. He did not understand that Thames was using his gunshot to signal to the Huron that they were getting closer; he simply thought he was being taught to shoot the musket. He improved with practice and could load and fire it in about a minute by the end of a week, hitting his target most of the time.

They came to the great falls Thames had mentioned. Piotr stared with raw amazement at their size and the amount of water cascading over them. It had rained on them the entirety of the day as they walked the trail, and Piotr had never seen water move so fast as it did in the river above the falls. He understood why they had crossed to the southern side, days earlier. The mist rose from the water below the falls like a great veil, and the green water swirled and rippled in a huge pool before ripping downstream at an incredible rate.

They camped above the falls that night. Piotr sat on the shore in the moonlight wondering about the fish and water creatures. How could they survive in such fast-moving water? He walked down near the shoreline and threw a stick into the river. The current grabbed it in the blink of an eye and sent it spinning toward the edge of the falls where it disappeared. He imagined it smashing into the rocks below. To be in the river above the falls was certain death.

Finally, eleven days of hard walking later, they came to the second inland sea. The Huron name for it was Erie. They followed along its shore throughout the next few days, finally coming to the river that Easterly had told them about. Piotr stood with Captain Linville and Flagger on the shoreline where the river fed into the inland sea.

"This river, it flows north?" Piotr asked.

"The tribes call it the crooked river. The Cuyahoga. It flows south and north, at the same time." Linville smiled. "Seems impossible, I know, but this is what the Huron men have told us. It is not on our maps where it begins. It flows south from wherever it originates, but then it turns to the north and flows into the lake, as you see."

Flagger said, "Thames says the Huron village is just down the way." He pointed westward along the shore. "We will be there in half an hour or so."

"Yes, but first we will cross down where it is shallow. There is a big rock in the middle of the river, sticking up. When we cross there, we should find the dugouts and the birch-barks on the other side that Easterly indicated," Linville said.

The column made its way down the path and crossed in the thigh-deep water south of the boulder in the middle of the wide river. After an hour or so of hunting about, they found the swampy inlet that held the promised sticks with the red wool rags tied to them. Linville advised they would rest here for a day and sent out hunting parties with men to find game for food, as supplies were already running low.

Linville looked out at the inlet of cattails and muddy shore. "Piotr, swim out to those sticks with the red rags tied to them and pull up the dugout boats."

Piotr stripped down to just his buckskin breeches. He realized he had gotten stronger as they were walking miles each day. Pushing the cart when it was stuck behind Mule had developed his chest and shoulders. Several weeks of eating regular food had helped as well. Even trail food was better than the frequent periods of starvation he had known before arriving at the *St. Longinus*.

He thought about it for a second, then he pulled his breeches off as well. Naked, he picked his way through the muddy, rocky shoreline, through the cattails growing up in clumps from the shallow water and swam out into the swampy bay. The water was still cold, even in the shallows. The sticks with red cloth ribbons were eight or nine feet long, and they poked up a few feet above the waterline. He had not really understood what they had meant when they said the word dugout before, but he had been taught to listen and wait to see if his question was answered. It turned out that dugout canoes were simply long tree trunks, hollowed out with axes and mattocks.

When he got to the first ribbon, he began searching around with his feet in the muddy water. His foot bumped something hard. He dove under and found what felt like a log, and when he pulled up on it, it began to float upward to the surface. When the dugout came to the surface, he turned it and pushed it toward the shore. He found seven more of them, until there were no more red rags left. He also found one log and pulled at it, but it was just a log.

To his surprise, the dugout canoes looked new. They had been preserved in the cold water. As they floated to the surface, he shoved them toward the shore. Flagger, Gerard, and Abel Paquet gathered them up, pulling them onto the bank.

Piotr made his way back to shore with muddy feet but having had a cold bath. Abel helped him out, grasping him by the forearm and giving a pull. Piotr stood in the cool morning, dripping wet, but drying in the sun and breeze.

Abel inhaled deeply through his nose. "I was beginning to wonder what I smelled on the trail...but it's gone now...and you're clean as a whistle, sharp as a thistle."

Flagger looked dolefully at Abel. "That is an English saying, you twat."

Gerard chimed in, "After that cold morning dip, it's as thin as a thistle."

"Good thing there were no turtles, a snapper might have taken a bite at that skinny worm," said Anton.

"It better have sharp eyes, the snapper. In these temperatures, the worm goes back inside to hide!" Gerard said, laughing. Abel joined him.

Piotr shook his long hair out, pushing it back from his face, laughing at his own predicament. Cold and wet, and getting insulted. He looked at Flagger for help.

Flagger said, "You better get dressed soon, or they will be at it all day."

Thames, Mason and Abraham Paquet scouted about the area, searching for the birch-bark canoes that Easterly had spoken about. They found them standing vertically, in a stand of white birch trees. They carried them back to camp, holding them over their heads with little difficulty, as they were light and shorter than the long dugouts.

In the evening, they set up camp along the river. Piotr could see smoke from campfires rising just a mile or so down the trail. A lot of campfires. He asked Flagger about it as he gathered wood.

"The smoke down the trail, those campfires, savage? Huron?" he asked.

"Yes, we have come to their southern village, on the water. It is big. Several hundred people live here. Maybe more. Half of them are fighting age warriors."

Piotr stepped back and thought about the size of the village. Especially a village with that many fighting men.

"They could wipe us out, if they wanted," he said.

"They do not want to. They want our trade goods. They want iron pots, guns, and all the other things we can bring them. They need them, in fact. They are constantly at war with their neighboring tribes, especially the Iroquois... You know, the Iroquois are trading with the Dutch. They are being supplied with muskets and powder. The Huron are simply trying to survive."

"Seems that is the same as back home," Piotr said, as Flagger walked away.

After the camp was set up for the night, Linville and Thames called the men to gather. Linville spoke to the crew.

"Tomorrow, we will walk to the Huron village. We will be giving them ten of the muskets, some powder, and shot. With a promise of more. No one is to speak with the Huron, except Thames or myself. Keep your eyes off of their women, keep your mind on the task at hand. Every man will carry a loaded musket."

Thames added, "I will lead the talks with their chief, we will see what they have in willingness to trade. Keep a sharp hand on the horses and stay alert. Tonight, we will no doubt be watched closely by their scouts. Keep your wits and do not be provoked."

Piotr was assigned the first watch duties and found himself anxiously pacing and looking into the darkness. When his watch was finished, he slept fitfully, anxious about what the next day would bring.

He was grateful for the tea that Eggard boiled in the morning, and he drank it quickly. He dutifully got Mule hooked up and had the cart ready before Eggard was even done with breakfast.

"Piotr, they will not attack us today," Eggard said.

"How do you know?"

"They will want to see what we have, and what we can trade with them. They may kill us tomorrow, so be more alert then."

Eggard smiled and sat back against a tree trunk, sipping his tea.

They got underway and covered the mile or so to the Huron encampment. Looking down the line of men and horses, Piotr saw canoes rowing along the shore of the lake, as men were fishing with spears. He then saw the palisade wall of the Huron: logs stacked and sharpened at the top, encircling the central lodgings. South of the wall, he could see women and men working in the fields, tending to the soil. Above the wall were the rooftops of the longhouses Flagger had spoken off. They looked like they had brown bark and thatched roofs, similar to what he had seen in Quebec City. All of them had holes with gray and white smoke drifting up lazily toward the sky. He estimated some of them were over seventy feet long.

There was an entrance at the portion of the wall facing sideways and open to the grassy field in front of it. The wall wrapped around like an incorrect circle, where one end misses the other. Women and children were walking in and out. The women wore deerskin dresses and shells and feathers on strings around their necks. Camp dogs and children played with sticks. Many of the women carried baskets and tools for working in the fields next to the palisade wall. It looked to Piotr like a peaceful place with families and crops. Not so different from small farming communities in Rheinland or Złotoryja.

They were not alarmed by the approach of a group of white men and horses.

"Eggard, why are they not concerned about us coming into their village?"

"They knew we were coming for miles. They have been watching us from the forest since we left Quebec City. Even when we could not see them, they watched."

The two Huron men who had been looking into the cart, and who had smacked Piotr across the face, came walking out of the gate entrance and started down the path toward the column. The tall thin man and his shorter, stockier companion walked purposefully toward Thames and Linville at the head of the line of horses and men. Soon they were talking and exchanging gestures.

Piotr could not hear what was being said, but after a minute or so Thames and Captain Linville said something to Flagger, then walked inside the palisade gate with the Huron men.

Flagger came back to the column and waved at Piotr. "Get ten matchlocks from the cart. Fifteen balls each, patch, wick, and powder for each, as well. Bring them up here to the front."

Piotr reached under the oilcloth tarp and started to pull out the lead balls, the powder, patch and horsehair wicks. Eggard saw him and tossed him a canvas sack. "Put it all in here. The powder and lead alone will weigh a ton when you carry it."

Piotr loaded the sack and began pulling out the muskets one by one, lining them up along the edge of the cart. They were very utilitarian by comparison to the snaphance pistols carried by Linville and Thames. There were no ornate metal workings or finely tuned wheel systems, made in the same way that a watchmaker would make the gearing of a fine watch. There was just iron and wood, as straightforward as could be made. But they shot where they were pointed, Piotr knew. His practice had gotten him to consistently hit a chest-sized target at forty yards. He and Thames had dug a few of the balls out of the stumps he shot, even when they were just fragments. They could all be melted together and used again.

Piotr began lugging the weapons and equipment to the front of the column. Eggard pitched in, grabbing several muskets and the small cask of powder.

"That should make it right. Let's hope they bring us a lot of pelts," Eggard said.

Thames and Linville walked back out as they set down the last of the muskets in a row on the grass. Following them were the two warriors that Piotr was familiar with and an elderly Huron man, nearly white hair, and missing many teeth. Behind them came a few dozen women and men. They all gathered around as Thames picked up the first matchlock musket.

"Our gift to you, Houdanaset, chief of the Wendat," Thames said, using the ancient name for the Huron tribe. He handed the long muzzle loader to the elderly man. He took it and fiddled with the hammer a bit, moving it one click to the locked position.

After looking it over, he turned to the gathering of people and began calling out the names of men in the village.

"Enyeto, Hahnee, Hirut, and Ahanu. Come up. Askewheatou, Keme, Nootau, Wematin, Awan." He called out nine names, all of them young warriors. Each man came up and took a musket off the grass, holding it as if it were their first born.

Houdanaset raised the musket in his hands over his head. "Chogan."

The short, muscular Huron warrior who had hit Piotr on the face, his hair still pulled back in a bun with a quill holding it, walked out of the crowd of villagers and took the musket from the chief.

The chief smiled, handing him the rifle, and said, "Use it for the good of the people, my son."

183

He turned to the village people and a piercing war cry erupted from his throat. "Aye, aye, aye, aye, aye!"

His cry excited the growing crowd of Huron villagers, and it was followed by return war cries, whoops, and cheers.

Speaking in French, Chief Houdanaset addressed the Frenchmen and the gathered tribe. "The People are few, now. When I was a boy, maybe fifteen years, there were many Wendat. We used to dominate the Mohawk, Seneca, the Oneida, Onondaga, and the Cayuga. So they band-ed together and became the Iroquois, because they could not defeat us." He used his hands to emphasize his point, nodding and looking out at the faces of the gathered villagers.

"All of the clans of the Wendat were bound together, as one people. The Bear Clan, the Rock Clan, the Cord Clan, the One House Lodge, and us, the Deer Clan. We were undefeatable...but...the English came. The Dutch came, and the Frenchmen. The Iroqouis traded with the Dutch and grew stronger. The Huron traded too, but we became ill. Our women and children began to die. So many died when I was still a boy, we could not even care for the dead. We left them on the ground, and we moved away, to get away from the sickness. For a long time, we hid and did not trade, but the Iroqouis overtook our hunting lands. Now, we few Wendat are what is left of the people. With these muskets we will be strong again, just as the Iroquois are strong."

The Huron people watching nodded, and several of the men shout-ed out war cries in agreement.

"We will find the beaver you seek, and we will bring the pelts back. You will trade with us for more muskets. This will help to make our future better, and we will not leave our children's bodies on the ground where they lay ever again. We can defend our village, and we can live our own way, here in the forest. As Wendat people always have."

He sat down on a log. Linville and Thames smiled and shook his hand in the Huron way, gripping forearms. Piotr listened, impressed by his oratory skills.

The chief, speaking to Linville and Thames, asked them, "Where will you camp so that we may find you?"

Thames said, "We follow the river south, then will take one of the streams to the west, into the great green valley. Many beavers are there, and we will find them. We will come back in the fall. We will trade with you then, for more muskets. We have more, at Quebec City, on our ship."

"Some of the tribes to the south have not seen white men. They may attack you and steal your belongings."

"We thank you for your forewarning," Linville said.

"You all will stay here, with the People, tonight."

Captain Linville refused his offer but did not want to offend him. "We have so much work to do before winter. You are generous to offer your camp. We have to continue our journey, before winter comes"

The elderly chief smiled back. "It is the way of things, to have much work to do before winter. We, the People, have work to do as well. We have to learn to shoot the muskets. You all will stay tonight and teach our warriors to do this."

Linville and Thames looked at each other. It was an offer that could not be refused. Linville was not interested in staying; they still had most of a day to keep the men moving south.

Linville leaned over toward Thames and said, "What do you think?"

"It would be offensive to turn down their hospitality," Thames said.

Linville paused and considered. He pursed his lips and inhaled sharply. "You stay, then. You teach them to shoot and leave in the morning. Keep one man with you. Somebody who can run, if need be, fast."

Thames's eyes widened. He did not like the idea of separating from the group, but it did not appear it was a choice.

"All right," he said carefully, "Piotr can stay with me. He needs the shooting practice anyway, and he looks like he could run all day."

He had picked Piotr for the reasons he said, but also because he knew that Linville liked the young man.

"You can easily track us tomorrow, heading south down the river. We will have the canoes, and the horses on the trail. The two of you will be able to move faster than the column. You and Piotr should catch up in a day or so. We will head south till the Cuyahoga bends. We will take the nearest tributary and head south and west, into the heart of the valley."

Linville stood and shook Thames's hand.

Thames told the chief their plan. Linville started back toward the column, looked down the row at Piotr, and waved him over to tell him the good news.

## Chapter 13

# WHEAT TOAST, EGGS, AND BACON

H is hands were claws now. The knuckles were swollen and misshapen. Father Demari passed him a bladder canteen of freshwater to sip, and he could not hold it. He fumbled with it and finally gave up, pinching it between his two hands like he was wearing oven mitts. His fingers would simply not flex. They had molded to a curved shape around the oar and would not go back to straight. His lower back and thighs ached in a deep, searing burn. Fatigue had begun to take him about twenty minutes after they rowed out of that violent cove in the middle of the night. They had rowed for thirty hours more.

Rowing all night and sleeping sitting up on a wooden bench was not restful and allowed for no recovery for his back and thighs. Renier Archembeau, leader of the church in the New World, could not get out of the longboat that this crew of wounded men and a nun had rowed through the gulf of St. Lawrence. But he had to get up, and out, he thought. They were here, they had made it. He brushed a stiff finger at the cut on his nose. The boat was tied off and the others were climbing out onto the wobbly dock. He could not make his legs straighten up to stand. He turned and tried to pull himself up onto the dock, but his hands could not grasp the wooden planks. His throat was dry, and his mind was so blurry with exhaustion that he could not summon up the words to ask for help.

Hands reached down and grasped him. He moaned as his legs straightened. They pulled him out onto the dock and he slowly stood up, vertical for the first time in two days. He was dizzy and light-headed, but he stood. For a moment. As he began to slump, Father Demari got under one shoulder and Guillaume the other. There was shouting and cries for assistance. He felt himself being carried, and for a little while, his eyes rolled back in his head and his head flopped backward. His jaw went slack, and he passed out while being carried.

That was yesterday.

Today he found himself in a bed in the house of Johan Easterly, governor of the Territory of Quebec. He awoke to a glass of wine next to the bed. He held it with two hands and drank it. In a few minutes he found the strength to stand up, and as he rose from under the covers, it occurred to him that he was in someone's night shirt. He must have been cleaned as well. Flashes of memory of the last few hours of the longboat began to creep into his imagination. He remembered very little.

He looked around for his clothes; there was a cotton shirt and pants on the chair back next to him. Socks and leather shoes as well. He started to put them on, fumbling with the buttons. He got the shirt on, unbuttoned, and dropped the pants to the floor. When he bent down to pick up the pants, the bridge of his nose hurt. He touched it with his thumb, remembering how the cut got there.

A knock on the door, and a voice said, "Monsieur Archembeau? Are you awake? Are you moving in there? No matter, I am coming in."

The door opened and Sister Mary Therese O'Boyle came in at a brisk pace, as if she was not exhausted from their travels.

"You are awake, oh, and half-dressed I see." She turned her head and shielded her eyes.

"Well, you barged in before I could..." he started to say, his voice raspy from his dry throat.

She turned toward him and began helping him with the pants. He wanted to protest but his hands just would not work properly, and he did not think he would be able to do it alone. She brushed his hands away.

"Oh, let me help! I have dressed hundreds of men, Father." She pulled his pants up and buttoned his fly. "I have put the pants on so many men, you would think my profession was not of the cloth, but of the bed sheets." Sister Mary was not a person who took no for an answer. He stood, allowing the humiliation of needing to be dressed.

She buttoned his shirt from the bottom to the top, the collar much too large for his skinny neck. She pushed him back on the bed to a seated position and knelt down and put on his socks and shoes.

"My red overcoat? Did it come in with me?" he asked.

"It was crusted with dirt, sweat, and salt. We gave all of your clothes to the Indian women running the laundry service. You passed out after we got off the longboat. Are you steady on your feet? Let us get something to eat!"

He rose and tentatively began putting one foot in front of the other. His legs ached, but he maintained his balance.

He followed her out the door to find that they were in a log home with multiple rooms and a central hallway. This building was not only the house of Johan Easterly, it was the headquarters for the Territory of Quebec. Easterly had added onto the building over the years, simply building on more rooms to the central hallway, extending it farther each time. It all led back to the main room by the front gate of the palisade. Here was the kitchen and dining room, all in one place. It faced the river, and the roof stood taller then the palisade wall.

Sitting in the dining room, as it were, at a rough-hewn table, were his compatriot Father Pascal Demari, Guillaume, and a short, plump man he took to be Johan Easterly, governor of the territory. They were eating a breakfast of toasted bread and butter, thick cut bacon, and fried eggs. Archembeau staggered in and groaned as he pulled himself toward the table. His back and legs were treating him unfavorably, at best.

Father Demari stood up, more than a little sore himself, and gave a short bow.

"Welcome back, Father Archembeau. It is good to see you on your feet."

Guilliaume added, "Yes, it is good to see you, monsieur. I am happy that you are awake. Do you remember much of the journey?"

"I'm afraid I only remember little flashes in time. It rained, I remember that, and there were waves. We just kept rowing."

"We kept rowing. You kept rowing. You did not give up, even though you were in a terrible state. The wounded men in our longboat have you to thank for their lives, as well as all of us."

Archembeau was surprised and slightly taken aback by these words from Guillaume. He had simply done his best to survive. He was truly surprised he had so much will to live left in him, at his age.

"I...I thank you, Guillaume. Your kindness is generous. I simply kept up as best I could."

Archembeau found the pleasure of humility to be an unusual sensation. He knew he had become self-centered as he aged. Perhaps having to fight for his life had given him a new perspective. He was unsure. In any case, the smell of the bacon and eggs reminded him that he was terribly hungry.

Johan Easterly spoke up. "You must be famished after such a trying experience. Please sit down and join us." He waved to the kitchen cook, an Indian woman, and she began to put together a plate of food.

Father Demari said, "Please forgive me for not introducing you. Father Archembeau, this is our governor. Mr. Easterly is in charge of this place, and our kind host."

Archembeau, even in his sordid state, quickly summoned his political savvy. Addressing Easterly, he straightened his shirt and smiled.

"So happy to meet you, monsieur. I thank you for your kindness of the clothing, the food, and your hospitality. We are fortunate that you are in charge here, in the wilderness."

Easterly smiled back. He respected the man for giving his best attempt at diplomacy, despite his difficult circumstances. He was uncertain about him, and the other priest. "Father Archembeau, and Father Demari, if you will permit me to be direct... What are you doing here? You are not woodsmen. You are not hunting for furs, I assume. What is your intent?"

Water and wine were brought to the table for Archembeau, and a tin metal plate of eggs, toasted bread, and a slab of bacon was set down in front of him by the cook. He used the moment to gather his thoughts, by turning to her and taking her hand, and bowing slightly from his seated position. With his head down, he quickly raced through his thoughts and planned out his negotiation with the governor of the territory.

"Given our misfortune, Governor, I am sorry but I find myself in a...well, a state of confusion. Cardinal Richilieu sent a letter from Paris on a ship that left weeks ahead of our departure from Saint-Malo. He indicated that I was to be the leader of the church, here, in the New World. Furthermore, we would be in need of materials, men, land and money for the construction of the church here, in Quebec City. Myself and Father Demari are to lead this effort and work to grow it."

Easterly was not surprised. He had received the letter. He knew the church had decided to extend its reach to the New World. He lied to give himself time to work out what the best path would be.

"I will have to look back through my papers, I do not remember receiving a directive from the cardinal. I will happily house you and Father Demari here, until you can get established. The territory has not had a formal church presence, and we are sorely in need."

Renier Archembeau took his first bite of food in two days. He was an awkward eater in the best of circumstances, with his large nose and poor teeth. Now he brushed at the crumbs on his face with his stiff fingers, and sipped wine loudly from his cup while chewing the toasted wheat bread. It was the finest meal he had eaten in many years. Even if his poor teeth and stiff fingers required him to bite from the side of his mouth.

"Guillaume has told me of the unfortunate circumstances of your ship," Easterly went on. "I am concerned about the presence of a Swedish ship here in our waters. English ships have ceased their pirating of French fishing and trading vessels since our treaty from a couple of years ago. Dutch ships are still sailing here, but they do not pirate other vessels. It seems that Gustavus Adolphus had decided to expand his authority. I have heard word of the battles being fought in the north of Reinsland, and in the Holstein, between the Catholic and Protestant. It would be very distressing to see that war brought to these shores."

Sister Mary spoke up. "We had two members of the ship get lost, my young novitiate Jana and the first mate, Raul Monteaux. She was taken overboard, and he went in after her. They did not come back to the boat. Has there been any word of them?"

Easterly said, "I am sorry, Sister Mary, but I have heard nothing."

"They should have made it to shore," Guillaume said. "We were close to land. If there was ever a man who could survive it, it is Raul Montreaux. He is as good a sailor as I have ever seen, and a tough man."

"I am sorry for your loss, all of you. Your loss is our loss as well. That ship was filled with trade supplies for Quebec City. This is the frontier. We are always in short supply of everything." Easterly took a last sip of wine, and said, "I will search out some space for your church building. I will check into some local laborers with a man named Lucien Greely."

"Greely? I will remember the name. Thank you, Governor," Archembeau said between bites and sips.

Easterly stood to leave. "We have a cabin on the far end of the palisade. It has a door, but no lock, I am afraid. It has three rooms, and a large fireplace on the back wall. I helped to build it myself a few years back. You all are welcome to it. The roof will keep the rain out."

Guillaume said, "Has there been any sign of the men from *The Render*? Our captain stayed with the ship when we were stranded; a few dozen men were on that island with him. We will need a ship to go back there, to find them, and bring them back. Our ship was taken, but they may still be alive."

"I understand, but there has been no word... I have a fishing shallop docked here. She is stable and wide. Has a single sail; you could get there in a day or so. You can use it; the other men from your longboat were all wounded, though. You will need at least a couple of men to man it."

"I will sail back there this afternoon, sir. We have to know if they are alive. If so, we need to bring them back," Guillaume said.

Easterly paused and thought for a moment. "There is a fellow living on a fur trading ship that came in a few days back. I heard that he was picked up at sea? You may want to go talk to him. It is docked at the east end of the harbor, as we call it, which is just where we tie up the boats. It's called the *St. Longinus*, I believe."

# Chapter 14

# NANIBOSAD'S BEGINNING

The birchbark that made the wigwam's outer covering was waterproof, and Jana was thankful for that. The walk through the forest had been cold and muddy from a steady, drizzling rain. She was covered in scratches and mosquito bites. Sitting inside a warm room on a buffalo hide blanket, with her belly full, having cleaned up with Malian in the creek beside the Abenaki village, she began to feel somewhat normal for the first time since leaving the island in the longboat. The traditional Abenaki deerskin dress she wore was brown and hung down to her knees without clinging to her skin. It was surprisingly soft and supple, and decorated with blue and pink shells sewn into the seams in various patterns. Somebody had taken a long time to make this dress correctly. Malian traded for it when they arrived, using the pants she had taken from the ship. Though they were muddy, and smelled of seawater, the buttons and seams were a thing of curiosity to the Abenaki women. Malian had brushed her long hair with a bone toothed comb, getting the tangles out. Her hair was now pulled back and pony tailed in the way of the Abenaki women, even though it had some waves and curls. She felt much cleaner. Jana kept the shirt and the overcoat from the ship so that she could use it on the journey to Quebec City.

Better still were the moccasins. An elderly woman had traded with her, probably at Malian's request, shortly after they arrived. Her leather shoes with wooden soles were far less comfortable. Thinking about the amount of walking they were going to do, she was grateful for them.

Montreaux also traded for new clothing. He gave the snaphance pistols in the box that he had found on the ship. In exchange, he got a clean linsey-woolsey shirt, buckskin pants, proper moccasins, and a jacket. The Abenaki had been trading with English villagers and other tribes for close to twenty years. This resulted in advancement for their tribe with technology like clothing and metal for cooking, tools, and weapons. In addition, it resulted in the onset of illness that wiped out a full one third of their people. In the mid-1620s some of the Abenaki villages grew tired of the encroaching English settlements, and moved north and west, away from the technology, and away from the illness. The shirt that they gave to Mr. Montreaux was a trade item from those years. It was still in good condition here in the spring of 1632, but it had yellowed with repeated washes. He too was grateful for the kindness.

Unfortunately for the Abenaki, the move also brought them into greater conflict with the Iroquois Confederation. Now, they found their villages being raided, and their crops and animals being stolen.

Malian brushed aside the blanket that covered the hole at the front of the wigwam as she returned from tending Nanibosad. Jana and Montreaux could see she was anxious. They assumed this to be natural, given Nanibosad's condition.

"The elders want to speak with you now. Please come," she said.

They were a little surprised by this request. Montreaux presumed that they wanted to know about the ship. Jana was curious why the elders of the village would want to talk to her.

Malian led them through the center of the peaceful Abenaki village. Children were playing between the wigwams. Meat and fish were smoking over an open fire pit. They stared when they walked by, but they were strangers and different looking.

As they walked, Malian attempted to prepare them. "They will ask you questions about what happened to you. About your ship and how you both came to be here, in the forest with the Abenaki."

They followed Malian to a larger wigwam, a circular hut with a wood frame and an outer covering of birchbark. The inside of the wooden frame was draped with animal skins, and a central fire pit kept the chill and moisture out. The smoke in the fire pit was scented, and the room smelled of burnt pine and cooked meat.

An old man sat against the back wall. He was white-haired, slumped, and bent with age. He had a scarred face and was missing his left eye. He smiled at them as they entered. Jana could see that he was missing his upper teeth on his left side as well.

Three older women sat nearer the fire. The women were old as well, but not as old as the man. Maybe fifty, Jana thought. The middle woman, stern-looking and pretty, gestured for them to sit down across from them at the fire pit.

Malian said, "This is Montreaux and this is Jana. They were with us when the Iroquois attacked. He killed one of the Mohawk warriors in battle and tried to help us. Jana was taken by the Iroquois but escaped. We found them after. They are going to the fort of the Frenchmen at Kwenitekw (the long river). They have no supplies, no understanding of the forest. They need a guide to take them through the forest and safely to the fort."

Jana and Montreaux could understand none of this, as it was spoken in Abenaki. That sat in silence, watching the elders.

Malian said, "This is Ahowna, leader of our people." She gestured to the old scarred man.

After a long moment of silence, the old scarred chief spoke. "Nanibosad, Malian, and the others were brave to lead the Iroquois away from the village. Nanibosad is gravely wounded. The other men are injured, too."

Malian interpreted, speaking in French to Montreaux and Jana.

"I wish to know about the great ship. The cannons were loud enough to be heard even here, at our camp, far, far away. Where did it come from? Why did these men wish to harm you?"

Montreaux answered simply. "Those men are from the north, and they are pirates, raiders, like the Iroquois that raid the villages around them. They do the same to us. They did not want us alive to tell the men at the fort about the stealing of our ship. They wished to silence us."

Malian interpreted and the old man nodded. The three women sat silently.

He raised his finger in the air, pointing at them, and said, "What of the muskets and the gunpowder? Where are they now?"

Montreaux and Jana listened to Malian as she converted the words to French.

"The Iroquois took it from the ship, as far as we know. There were few muskets, as the ship was not for war, but for trading. The pirates took all of those things before they followed us."

The old man conferred with the women in whispers.

The scar-faced elder spoke. "In my lifetime, the English came. We traded with them at first, but we moved away from them. More of them came, and we moved farther west. Some of our villages went north, into the mountains. French traders came, and we traded with them, too. But we got few muskets. The Dutchmen came, and the Iroquois traded with them, and they got muskets. They started taking more land. So, we moved again. Then many of our people became ill and died, even though we didn't let the English into our village. Now you say there are more white men, from the north, raiders, come to take more. When does this stop?

How many more will come?"

Montreaux thought about what to say. "In the forest, Nanibosad asked me this question. I told him then as I tell you now, many more are coming. Many more. The Frenchmen are coming to trade. The English are coming here to live. And they will keep coming."

The scar-faced elder looked at Jana, apprehension showing on his face. "Is this true, what this man says?" he asked.

Jana nodded. "Yes, it is. There is constant war where I am from, and people will come to this place, to escape, and to live here, as they wish."

"What can we do then? How do the Abenaki survive?" The elder shook his head, gazing with his one good eye into the fire.

Jana was silent. She did not know the answer to that question. She looked at Monteaux, but he sat silently.

Finally, Montreaux said, "Run, hide, move away as you have done. It is what the Abenaki must do."

The elder shook his head. "It is all we have left, to give up our hunting grounds, our fields, our homes. Move on, rebuild, again. But every time we move, more people leave, the villages spread out, we grow weaker." Looking up from the fire, he said, "I can risk no one as your guide. We are few now. You will have to go on your own."

"So be it," Montreaux said. He touched Jana on the arm, and they began to rise.

The stern-looking woman spoke before they could rise. "Nanibosad was injured protecting you."

Malian looked down while she said the words in French.

The woman continued, "If he does not recover, you will owe the Abenaki for his life. And, Malian...if he takes his journey back to the beginning, you will need to go take your journey as well or go back to your own people."

Malian was shocked. She looked all of the elders in the eye. "You think this too? You all agree with this?" She stared accusingly at the other women.

The other two women sat silently, not making eye contact with Malian. They both shook their heads yes.

Malian looked at the elder man, staring into his one remaining eye. "You would do this to me, when the Abenaki need people! How could you allow this?"

"It is our way. You have no children. You are not Abenaki, you are Cayuga. Your husband is your keeper and links you to the People. You will join him on his journey, or you will leave and go back to your own people."

"What is it that they are saying?" Montreaux asked.

Jana put her hand on his arm.

Malian stood, her cheeks flushing red and angry. The old man looked into the fire, rather than at her face.

"You brought me here! You found me in the forest, you took me in. You saw that I was raised as an Abenaki! How could you do this?" Malian's accusation echoed around the wooden frame of the wigwam.

After a long moment of uncomfortable silence, he looked up at her. "You have no children. Soon, you will have no husband, and I will have no son. You will follow him or you will be Cayuga once again."

Tears began to flow down Malian's cheeks. The stress of Nanibosad's injuries, and this inconceivable betrayal, was overwhelming. She began to stagger backward as anxiety overtook her. Jana jumped to her feet and caught her before she could fall, and they turned and ran from the wigwam together.

Malian sobbed in Jana's arms, her entire body wracked with grief over the impending loss of her husband, and now of her adopted people.

They stopped between the wigwams and stood in the moonlight

under a maple tree, with leaves now fully formed as the spring crept toward summer.

She said in Abenaki, "It is so wrong. So wrong. Why do this? Why do this to me, now?"

Jana could not understand her, but knew that she was in need, so she held on.

"Just breathe in," she said to Malian. "He is not dead; when he is better, you two will live on, together." Jana held her in her arms and comforted her.

"We have tried to have children. It just has not happened yet. Now, he..." Malian struggled to finish the words.

"Let's go to him."

They walked through the village again, to Nanibosad and Malian's wigwam, where he lay inside. Entering through the doorway and crouching next to him, Malian reached out and touched his face in the fire light. He slept.

"He is warm. Has he slept long?" Malian asked the Abenaki woman watching him.

"A little while," she responded.

Jana stared at his ruggedly handsome face. He did not appear flushed, just asleep. The poultice on his chest was still leaking a little red blood.

Malian noticed. "It is time to change the poultice. Jana, pass those leaves to me."

She took them from Jana and she began to grind them up in a bowl with a wooden pestle.

"Is he drinking enough water?" Malian asked the Abenaki women.

"He drank a lot after he ate," she responded.

She mixed some ground powder from a clay container into the leaves and pumiced them into the bowl. She carefully peeled away the layers of the poultice on his chest, and Jana could see the ragged wound.

"How did you get the arrow out?" Jana asked.

"You cut off the shaft, then you use a heated long knife, like this one. You slide it in alongside the edge of the arrowhead and work it up and down until you can free the points on the sides of the arrowhead."

The bloody arrowhead was lying on the animal skin Nanibosad slept on.

"When it comes out, red blood is good. Clear is okay. White or green is very bad."

She picked up what looked like a strip of white cloth hanging on a rack by the fire and dropped it into the water boiling over the flames in a small iron kettle. "Then you pack it with this, the blue moss that grows on the underside of logs. Salt, and this seaweed, from the coastline. It grows in the shallows. Dry it out in the sun. You put it on in two layers, one wet, and one dry. The dry one you pack into the wound, like this."

Malian showed Jana how to pack the wound and secure the poultice. She took the wet leaf from the hot water and squeezed it gently. She took a dry one off the rack and packed the wound with the ground moss leaves and salt, packing it in place with a dry seaweed leaf, then folding the wet leaf over the top, which clung to his skin.

"Now, we wait to see," she said as she finished.

Her voice trembled. She turned and leaned back against the wood frame of the wigwam, resting her head against it.

The other woman got up and nodded, then left.

After a moment of closing her eyes and resting, Malian opened them and said to Jana, "You will need to pack your things for the journey. Take that blanket, there in the corner. We have another one. Roll all that you have up in it and tie it up with these."

Malian pulled some sinew strings from a skin pouch.

"You have done more for us than we could ever expect. You are the kindest person. I thank you, and I will pray for Nanibosad," Jana said.

"It is more than you understand. You have to take Montreaux and leave. If Nanibosad dies, they will see this as a life owed to the village. One of you would have to stay, to take his place."

Jana shook her head, confused by what she was saying. "They want you to leave, and one of us to stay? These customs make no sense to me... I cannot pretend to understand them. You have to protect yourself, Malian, you should not allow them to hurt you."

Malian raised her hands in resignation. "Go and prepare your belongings. Tell Montreaux, and leave at first light."

They hugged, and Jana went back to the wigwam she and Montreaux had been sleeping in.

He was already there, lying on a blanket, his boots removed. He was deep in thought when she came in through the small doorway. "We leave tomorrow then," he told her. "We will make the best of it. I spoke with the fellows who were with Nanibosad and Malian back at the cove. They told me which trail to take out of the village, which direction to head. They said there are mountains and some rivers. If we go northwest enough, we will come to a V-shaped river that flows south, then turns to the north. We can follow that up to the great inland sea, then walk the shoreline eastward until we eventually get to Quebec City. It will take many days."

"Nanibosad is sick from his wound...he may die," Jana said.

"It is a bad wound. It would have killed a lesser man already. But he is strong. He may pull through, yet."

"All of that talk back there, with the elders. They are going to make her leave if he dies," Jana said.

"It's pitiful," Montreaux responded. "I do not understand their ways, but they were not going to allow her to stay. I think the old man said she is Cayuga by birth."

"There is more. If he dies, they expect that one of us will stay, as a payment of a debt for his actions in saving us," Jana said.

Montreaux paused, thinking about that. "Well...we are not staying, neither one of us. We go at dawn, as soon as there is enough light to make our way."

"I will be ready."

"Cayuga...this is one of the five tribes of the Iroquois. Malian was born Iroquois. She was adopted by the Abenaki. This could be why they want her to leave..."

Despite being tired and comfortable in her clothes and near the warm fire, sleep came fitfully to Jana. She tossed and turned thinking about Malian and what would happen if Nanibosad died. Finally, she closed her eyes.

She awoke when it was still dark and did not remember falling asleep. Montreaux was gone from the wigwam. She gathered her few belongings by firelight and tied them up into a bundle that she could manage on her back. As the sun's first rays crept over the horizon, she stepped out of the doorway and shouldered her pack. It was a crisp and cool early morning. She inhaled deeply. The spring air smelled of pine needles and the stew pots cooking in the village. She heard voices whispering behind her and she turned to see who was coming in the dim early light.

It was Montreaux. He was walking in front of someone, dressed like a woodsman. He had found buckskin pants and wore a linsey-woolsey shirt under his dark blue navy duster coat. His pistols and a knife were pushed into his belt, and his wooden framed backpack was already shouldered.

Behind him was Malian. She was dressed for travel with buckskin pants under her deerskin dress. A backpack was on her back, and silent tears traced their way down her high cheekbones.

"Oh...Nani..." Jana whispered.

"Let's go," Montreaux said.

The three of them walked away from the Abenaki village on the trail to the north.

Lake Erie
Wendat Village
The Green Valley
Beaver Camp
The Crooked River

## Chapter 15

# INTO THE VALLEY

iotr's hands and arms looked like he had been working the forge. The skin and nails were covered with a grey soot from the repeated explosions of the gunpowder, and his veins traced lines through them like a river through a valley. Thames had set him to loading the muskets as he demonstrated shooting technique to the Huron warriors. Most of the village of nearly a thousand people stood outside the palisade walls, watching with curiosity. Thames had then used Piotr to demonstrate, showing proper hand position and how to not blow your own face off with the lit wick. He had Piotr demonstrate each step for loading. Over and over again, Piotr had loaded, aimed, and fired at the tree with a red cloth tacked onto the trunk. Step by step, he repeated the task. Sometimes, he even hit the cloth.

Now the Huron were taking their turns, and Piotr watched over as each one completed the same process he had. He stopped them and corrected them when they were doing something wrong, in the same way that Thames had. Two at a time, the warriors loaded and fired the muskets, then repeated it two more times.

Chogan, the son of the chief and the man who had smacked Piotr across the face, was the last warrior to give it a go. He did not ask for help, and he went through the steps of loading the weapon without difficulty. He shouldered it as if he had fired a musket many times.

Piotr assumed he had, or that he was a very quick learner. He closed the breech, cocked his musket, and fired it, making the red cloth jump on the tree trunk. His first shot, dead on the mark. Piotr stepped forward to hand him another lead ball, but Chogan waved him away. He reached into the animal hide pouch on his hip and pulled out a ball himself. Clearly, he had experience with these matters.

As he went through the loading process and rammed the shot home, the crowd began to cheer and chant. Slowly the hundreds of gathered Huron villagers began to chant his name, repeating it, over and over. He did not acknowledge their presence or their cheers. Chogan quietly and efficiently shouldered the musket. Aiming down the barrel, he squeezed the trigger. The musket barked and a smacking thumping sound came from the tree. The crowd yelled his name.

Thames tapped Piotr on the shoulder.

"Come on, we can be part of the show," he said, looking around at the crowd of people watching.

They walked down to the tree, and using his long knife, Thames cut the cloth free. He handed one side to Piotr, and they turned and held it up to the crowd. It was full of holes. The villagers cheered for the death of the red cloth. For them, it meant life. At least a fighting chance at life, for their homes, and their families.

They walked the forty yards or so back to where the group of shooters stood, and Thames handed the cloth to Chogan. "Good shooting! You look like you have done this before!"

Chogan accepted the cloth with a cruel smile. He held it up and looked through the holes at the sun sinking in the west. "It is a good weapon, but I have fired better." He looked at Thames as he said it.

"You have been trained?" Thames asked.

"I taught myself, on a musket I took from an Iroquois chief. He shot me with it, so I killed him, and took his gun for myself."

Chogan pulled back his loosely hanging deerskin shirt to reveal his muscled torso and a circular, star-shaped scar with a line extending out toward his left hip. It revealed an injury that would have killed most men, thought Piotr.

"With these guns, we are stronger."

Thames nodded. "There are more. Many more. We will trade them for beaver pelts. This will allow us to go back to France, sell the pelts, and bring you more things to trade. Blankets, iron pots, knives, tools. Many things that the Huron people need."

"We need muskets. You will bring more." Chogan spoke directly and with a slight edge in his voice. Just below threatening.

"Fair enough," Thames responded, a little dryly. He was already growing weary with this man's machismo.

Houdanaset stepped toward the group of men. His smile was an indication of his pleasure with the muskets. As he got closer, Thames went to his backpack and began to dig around. The Huron chief watched curiously. Thames pulled out a hunting knife, a long six-inch blade with a full tang handle and a metal guard. The handle was reinforced with carved walnut grips that were bolted on. The slightly curved, single-edged blade was not only sharp and pointed, but etched with acid that left behind an extraordinary pattern on the metal like the veins of a leaf held up to the sun. It was the finest looking hunting knife Piotr had ever seen.

Thames pulled out a leather sheath with a decorative rose in bloom burned into the shiny, hard outer leather. He pushed the knife back into the sheath and handed it over to Chief Houdanaset.

"Houdanaset, leader of the Huron, I give you this knife. This was made in Calais by the best bladesmith in all of France. This is our gift to you, to honor our friendship. We look forward to trading with you for many years to come."

Houdanaset took the blade from its sheath and inspected it closely. His old eyes grew wide when he saw the beautiful etching and intricately made handle. It was a spectacular knife, with beauty and utility. He held the blade up and looked deeper at the patterns in the etching, shaking his head with wonder. He rotated the blade in his palm, feeling the weight.

"The leader of our clan will carry this knife on their hip, from this day forward. It will be the knife of the Deer Clan. It has veins running through it, just as we do. They carry our blood and our blood lines going back to our fathers and grandfathers and beyond. So we will carry this knife to remember who we came from, and who our friends are, as we go forward in life."

The people standing nearby nodded and spoke their agreement in whispers to each other. Houdanaset had been a wise and careful leader.

"Come and sit by our fire, eat a meal, and rest until tomorrow," Houdaneset offered to Thames and Piotr, extending his arms toward the doors of the palisade walls.

They gathered their belongings and made their way into the village. Piotr had not been able to see much from the outside, other than the rooftops of the longhouses, and smoke rising up from their fires. As they entered, he saw that the village was even larger than it looked from the outside. The palisade had a walkway, a rampart, near the top of the wall so that a person could stand and see over, and shoot down oncoming invaders. Same idea as castle walls, Piotr thought. There was a central fire pit surrounded by stones and logs for seating. This had a large iron cooking pot on it that was steaming over the fire. Women and children were moving about freely, and a few dogs skulked around sniffing for food.

The longhouses themselves were larger and more impressive up close. He thought they could hold forty or fifty people in each one. He counted twenty-two buildings while setting his belongings down near the central fire pit.

Piotr noticed that many of the Huron were tall—taller than Thames, and certainly taller than Piotr. Many of the men wore an animal pelt on their shoulders, like a short cape over their back. They had jewelry of bone and porcelain hanging on their wrists and arms, and they decorated their clothing with shells and rocks. Many of the men carried tomahawks or steel axes, and all of the people, even most of the children, carried a knife of some sort on their waist.

Chogan was no taller than Piotr, but he commanded the respect of the Huron with ease. He was overly confident at all times, and Piotr saw that the men were always joking with him in an attempt to gain his favor. Thames noticed it too.

"Cocky little shit, is he not?" Thames whispered to Piotr at the fire pit.

"He reminds me of the Paquet brothers, all of their joking and bragging, the five of them rolled up into one person. He really knew how to shoot, though. I think he could give you a run for your money."

"He probably could, at that. I don't care. As long as he finds the beaver fur to bring to us. We can fill that ship and be on our way."

"Will you come back? If we do fill the ship, return to Saint-Malo, sell all the furs and make ourselves rich, will you come back to go to those far rocky mountains?"

"I will, if I can. Find a couple of like-minded travelers. Someone who knows the woods. And we would move fast, get out on the rivers and row our way west. Not for riches, or fur. Just to see it. Stand on them and look out at the world below. Then keep going. Find out what is after that."

Two middle-aged Huron women brought them carved bowls filled with whatever meat was stewing in the pot. Corn and squash and some beans that Piotr had never seen before were also floating in the stew. A filling and much needed dinner. Piotr and Thames thanked them for it, and tucked it away, using their knives like a fork and noisily drinking the rich broth right out of the bowl.

With much gratitude to the women, and many of the Huron gathered around the fire pit, they attempted to make their exit. Thames was hopeful to make a bedroll outside the palisade and be gone at sunrise. Houdanaset would not hear of it.

"Stay here, we will smoke a while and talk about the way of things."
Another offer not to be refused.

They sat around the fire pit and passed a pipe of tobacco between them, along with several other Huron men who had joined them. Chogan sat near his father and smoked the decorative pipe. He inhaled a lung full of smoke, then stood and walked across the circle. As he leaned down to hand the pipe to Piotr seated cross-legged on the ground, he exhaled through his nose, blowing out all of the blue and pungent smoke onto him.

Piotr was not sure if it was an insult, an accident, or possibly some sort of tradition that he did not understand. He didn't want to create offense, but the action caught him as funny, and he laughed aloud, looking directly at Chogan as he took the pipe. He surprised himself. He didn't laugh often, but this struck him in an odd way, and he could not contain it. A few of the gathered Huron laughed with him, in surprise or politeness.

He stood with the pipe and made an elegant attempt to inhale deeply, the way Chogan had. The pipe filled his lungs with smoke. He knew immediately that he had gone too deep, but he did not want to embarrass himself or Thames. He stood and walked across the circle, handing the pipe back to the seated Chogan, choking the thick smoke back into his throat. Before he could finish the hand-off, the smoke overwhelmed him and he coughed uncontrollably into Chogan's face and outstretched hands, blasting him with smoke and spittle. Now, all the Huron laughed aloud; some of them were belly laughing.

Thames's eyes went wide, and his hand instinctively dropped to the pommel of his knife, an uncertain expression on his face. Piotr covered his mouth and stepped back, a little dizzy from the strong tobacco.

To his credit, Chogan took it like a man, sitting stock still with spit dripping on his nose and chin, not smiling or changing his expression. Houdanaset, a smile creeping into his cheeks, reached over and gently took the pipe from Chogan's still hands. He turned to the group, inhaling elegantly as Piotr had done, then holding it in his lungs for a second and rearing his head back. He blasted out a sneeze as hard as he could, with smoke and snot flying across the group around the fire. The Huron men and women roared with laughter.

Thames and Piotr did not know what to make of the situation, but they both burst out laughing, joining the Huron in camaraderie.

The middle-aged warrior to Houdanaset's right stood and took the pipe from him, also mimicking the elegant inhale Piotr had used. He then turned around so his butt faced the fire and bent over, putting his head between his legs. He pushed out a massive loud fart while expelling all of the blue smoke, so that it looked like the smoke shot out of his ass. The people around the fire pit exploded with laughter at such foolishness. Even Chogan, rocking back on his seat with his head back, laughed at their collective joke. The brief tension that had arisen was shattered.

The Huron told stories late into the night around the fire, in French and their native Iroquois language, and they did not find their bedrolls until well after the moon had risen and shone deep into the night.

The morning found them bleary and tired. Thames and Piotr struggled from their bedrolls, having slept by the central fire pit in the Huron village. Just after dawn, there was already activity: dogs were barking, and cooking pots were emitting smells that drew Piotr's attention. His stomach rumbled as he pulled on his moccasins and his mouth tasted awful from the pipe smoking. Thames packed his backpack, rolling up the blanket he used as a bed as tight as he could. Piotr was working on the same when the two women who had given them the stew the night before walked over. They each carried a pouch filled with pemmican and a small wooden bowl filled with stewed corn and beans. After thanking them profusely, they each ate handfuls of the vegetables, with much gratitude, and washed it down with water from their bladder canteens. They put the pemmican in their backpacks.

Thames shouldered his backpack, then helped Piotr with his. "Let's be off, then."

Thames was in no waiting mood.

They walked to the opening of the palisade. The single young boy watching over the wall waved them out into the open field beyond. As they walked through the open entryway, they found Chogan standing there, waiting. "I will walk with you and we shall talk a bit," he said.

Thames nodded and they set off toward the river.

"I can get beaver pelts. I know where there are many, many beavers," Chogan said.

"That is what we want," Thames responded, curious why this conversation was happening.

"It is not that we just go and hunt the beaver. There are enemies, Iroquois and others, hunting them too. I want to know, are you honest about getting more muskets?"

"I am. We have more. We will meet you back here at the Wendat village. We will bring them, you have pelts, we will trade," Thames promised.

"We need the muskets before the summer ends. When the weather cools and the trails dry out, the Iroquois will come. They will attack the Wendat village demanding tribute. They will try to force us to abandon it and go farther west again. We will not leave again."

"I understand," Thames said.

"You will bring us more guns. The Huron will attack the Iroquois! We will push them back, force them to abandon their village. The People will be strong again."

Thames and Chogan shook hands in the frontier way, forearm to forearm. Thames agreed to provide weapons that would disrupt the social and political landscape of the region for years to come. Chogan was trying to obtain weapons to protect his home and to take the fight to his enemy. Piotr watched them carefully. There was no fondness between them, but they had a mutual interest. They could just as easily kill each other as work together.

As Chogan turned back to the village, Thames and Piotr headed south on the river trail. After a bit, Thames turned and said, "Let's pick up the pace."

They started off at a jog. Though Piotr was young and strong, carrying a backpack, a musket, ammunition, powder, his ax and his knife on his belt proved to be a heavy load. Thames kept the pace slow, and they made their way down the trail. Piotr could see the tracks from Eggard's cart in the dirt. After a mile or so, Piotr settled into the pace and just ran with Thames. He estimated that they were more than doubling the pace of the column. They would catch up to them in a day. Probably tomorrow, if they could run all day.

The sweat flowed from his brow and his shirt was wet with it all the way through when they stopped two hours later. Thames slowed to a walk, and they went alongside each other. When they were running, Thames had stayed in front.

"You kept up. I am impressed," Thames said.

"I will hardly be able to walk tomorrow. I have never run for that long in my life. Even running from the battlefield at Lutzen, I did not run for that long. I stopped and walked."

"We have ground to cover. The Iroquois call that the bear trot. They, and the Huron, can run all day, make camp, eat a handful of pemmican, and do it again, every day, for a week."

"I noticed they were all pretty much tall in the village back there. Long legs. I didn't see anyone wearing a backpack, either. Also, the musket gets heavier." He huffed and breathed heavily.

"You would rather be without one?" Thames raised an eyebrow.

"No. Not saying that." Piotr was tired, but he was not exhausted. He knew the difference.

"Let's keep at it, then." Thames broke into a loping jog.

Piotr had no choice, so he stepped into his pace and started running. His legs were tired, but his heart beat to a rhythm. They went for another hour or so, stopping as a red sun was setting in the western sky. Piotr had become acutely aware of his surroundings. He could hear crickets and wind rustling the leaves in the branches, just over the pounding in his heart and the breath roaring in his ear. They made camp in a clearing off the trail. No fire, just bedrolls. He fell asleep immediately.

In another day of bear trotting and walking they came upon the back of the column. The trail had left the river's path, turning south and west off of a tributary stream. Now the trail was under the canopy. The leafy green forest was so dense that he often could only see a few yards down the path as they ran. When they slowed to a walk, he could hear horses: the plodding footsteps thumping the ground, the jangle of reins, bridles, and packs strapped to saddles. As they drew closer, Thames looked over at him with a smile and pointed up the hill. They were very close.

"Hello the column!" Thames yelled.

"Halloo!" came the answering call. Sounded like Anton Paquet, thought Piotr.

As he and Thames walked up the hill to the rear of the column, they found Eggard standing by the mule and his two-wheeled wagon. Anton, Abel, Gerard, Mason, and Abraham Paquet were loaded up with packs and grinning from ear to ear. Abraham greeted them first. "Look at what a mess you two are! Is someone chasing you? Why have you run so hard?"

"They missed us so much!" Gerard said.

"You could not wait to get back to see us again! How thoughtful!" Abel said.

Thames wiped his sweating forehead on his sleeve, and said, "Missed you? No, no. We just figured you would get lost without us."

"Lost? We aren't lost! We are just wandering the forest in the New World. You know, taking a little walk in the woods," Abel said.

"It's all going to plan then, I see," Thames said.

"Well, we were planning on starving to death in the next few days, so we are right on schedule," said Mason.

Hugs and handshakes were shared, and the group got underway again. Thames made his way to the front and met up with Linville. Piotr hung back and walked with Eggard and Mule.

Eggard looked at him with a big smile. "It's good that you're back. Mule was getting tired of pulling this thing alone."

Piotr stepped in behind the cart and gave it a shove over a rock under the wheels.

For three days, they continued to follow the stream to the southwest. Finally, the hills began to grow smaller, the forest even greener and thicker. The stream itself shrunk to a narrow trickle, and the canoes were pulled and stashed in the forest.

On a sunny Sunday at mid-morning, Captain Linville called a halt as the trail wound down to a plateau with a small clearing in the trees. He asked them to gather as a group, and the men of the *St. Longinus* stood together on top of a hill, looking down from the grassy precipice into the green valley that lay before them. From there, they saw blue streams cutting through the background of the valley floor. Looking through his spyglass, Linville could see the marshland ponds stretching out across the valley. These were fed by a river flowing southward through the center of it all. He did not know what river it was, but it fed this green place, and the entire valley lived off of its water. It was the lifeblood of this fertile alluvial plain.

"This is it," he said, looking through the glass, while Thames, Flagger, and the rest of the men made their way up to the overlook. "Gentlemen, this is what we have come all this way for. Three thousand some-odd miles. This is the place, God be praised! This is where we make our future."

Linville took his hat off and wiped his eyes with it. Thames and Flagger looked out over the valley, nodding in agreement.

"We can camp there." Thames pointed down the valley a half mile or so. "At the base of that hill. From there, we can access the whole valley with the dugouts, via that stream, or we can go afoot to the outer reaches."

Abel was equally moved. "By God, it is a beautiful place. Have you seen such a thick forest? Green everywhere. We will not starve in this place. There will be game enough for us to eat." The Paquet brothers stood together, grinning at the group's good luck.

Eggard looked down at the valley and said, "This would be a fertile place to farm, you could grow all that you need here."

"If you could keep yourself alive. We are not alone here." Flagger pointed as he said it, to the distant south and west.

There in the sky was the telltale smoke of a campfire, drifting upward in the close to windless morning sky.

"The locals may not be too happy to see us," Mason said.

"They may not be too happy, and they are most likely not Huron," Thames pointed out. "We will cross that bridge when we come to it, I suppose. For now, we will set camp and hunt for food. Supplies are running low. We have much work to do, and thank God that we are all alive and fit enough for it."

Linville bowed his head and placed one hand over his heart, raising the other up in the air. The crew followed suit, removing their hats and bowing their heads.

He said his version of the Lord's Prayer aloud.

"Our father who art in heaven, let your name be sanctified. Let your kingdom come, let your will be done, on earth as it is in heaven. Give us each day our daily bread, forgive our trespass, as we forgive those who trespass against us. Do not submit us to temptation, but deliver us from evil. Today, we stand before your glory, at the table you have set. We thank thee for this blessing with gratitude and humble appreciation. Amen."

The group replied with a heartfelt "Amen."

A moment of silence followed as the men looked out at the incredible view. Slowly, laughter and a ripple of excitement ran through the group. Men patted each other on the back and began to shout.

Thames looked around at the sunlight. "All right, let's move! We are losing daylight, and we have work to do!" They gathered their wits and got back into a line.

The following few days brought backbreaking labor at a level that made the unloading at the dock in Quebec City seem gentle. At the base of the hill Thames had pointed at, they built their base camp. Rocks were found and placed, and trees were felled for the foundation of a small cabin. A wide lean-to was constructed from the branches of an oak that had recently fallen, so that some of the men could sleep under cover. Piotr was sent with the mule to carry some of the canoes from where they were stashed to the camp. The dugouts were so heavy, he thought it would have been easier to build new ones. Hunting parties were sent out. Thames came back with a large white tail doe that Eggard skinned and roasted on a rack above a central fire pit they built in front of the cabin they raised. It was enough to feed the group of men for a few days.

As the camp took shape, Eggard had Piotr gather mud and sand from the bank of the stream. Piotr and Mule brought carts filled with it back to the cabin, piling it up near the walls. Eggard mixed it with buckets of water and handfuls of grass, until he got the consistency he wanted. Then he and Piotr chinked in the gaps on the walls of the quickly rising cabin. With the rest of it, they filled out the walls of the wood-framed chimney. Using it to build a thick layer between the fire and the wooden frame, they mudded all the way up to the top. Eggard pronounced that it would do the job, and that they could use it to cook, once the mud dried out and hardened. After four days of working at it, the camp at the base of the hill began to take shape.

Eggard had Piotr take the two-wheeled cart and gather a large pile of sand from the bed of the stream. He then covered a five-foot-square section of the wagon bed with a two-inch-thick floor layer of mud. He built a two-foot-high half oval with a tunnel sticking out, on top of the floor layer. Then he and Piotr spread mud on top of it, using the sand as a mold. When the mud dried, they scooped out the sand inside, hollowing out a space. This created a mobile oven mounted on the wagon. Piotr never knew mud was so useful.

They started small fires in the oven and the chimney and kept them lit for a day to speed up the drying process. Now they had two ways to cook, in the cabin fireplace or in the mobile oven. Eggard was pleased with his handiwork, and he used the last of the flour, salt, yeast, and water to make a few dough balls. After they rose, he baked them in the mobile wagon oven, to see how it would work. He was pleased to see that it baked good bread, and the crew enjoyed a few pieces of bread for the first time in weeks.

"Feeding a group of this size is difficult," Eggard told Piotr. "They are always hungry. There is never going to be enough food. Unless we trap a lot of beaver."

"We eat the beaver?" It had not occurred to Piotr.

"Yes, we sell the pelts, but the meat will feed us for days."

"What does it taste like?" Piotr asked.

"Like a pond," Eggard said.

Flagger came to them, as they stood near the cabin walls. He had an armful of birchbark strips to be used as shingles for the roof of the cabin.

"We have run into a problem. We are out of nails." He said this with a smile below his thick beard. "I think it is time, Eggard."

"Shall we show him what we brought?" Eggard smiled as well. "Come on." He signaled with his head and walked behind the cabin wall.

On the ground was a canvas bag.

"Go ahead, Piotr, pick it up. It is for you," Eggard said in his accent.

Piotr looked at the two of them, curious what they were playing at, and bent to the bag. It was incredibly heavy and would not budge without great effort.

"Open it up," Flagger said.

He untied the string holding it together and pulled open the flaps. There were handles sticking out. Tools. He pulled out a forge hammer, then another small ball peen hammer, a set of tongs, and something else at the bottom. He dug down into the bag and there was an anvil.

"You carried an anvil...through these woods...down that trail?" He could not believe it.

"No," Eggard said. "You did. And Mule. It was on the wagon, behind the muskets, since we left Quebec City."

Piotr thought about all of the logs, holes, and mud he had pushed the back of the wagon through, over, and around. He shook his head and smiled ruefully.

"Marta's gift to you, since you fixed her onion. And the blacksmith was dead, anyway."

"There is more." Eggard pulled several lengths of spring steel from under the bag. Enough to make dozens and dozens of nails.

"We were all impressed with your skill, back at the public house. So, we thought that you could put them to use, out here, as needed. Now it is needed. We need you to make nails."

"I will need a forge," Piotr said.

"That is what all of this extra mud is for," Eggard said. "We will build it over there, at the bottom of the hill."

Piotr had noticed the Paquet brothers had been at work building a modified lean-to in the small clearing at the base of the hill. He had assumed they were building a space for themselves to sleep in. They weren't.

They had constructed a traditional looking roof angled from the ground, but they extended it with branches from a felled basswood. They braced it with posts set into the ground. It actually looked pretty sturdy, he thought. It was a big enough space for him to work in and still be out of the weather. It was a short walk to the stream, and still large enough to sleep in.

Flagger and Eggard grabbed the anvil and picked it up together, crab walking with it to the lean-to. Piotr followed with the bag of tools. Under the roof of branches there was a large stone with a flat surface, and they set the anvil on the stone. More impressively to Piotr were the small bellows and the chunks of coal stashed in the corner.

"You got the bellows, too."

"Yes, once the mud sets up, we should be able to have a forge.

Enough for you to make some nails, tools, whatever we might need," Flagger said.

Piotr was stunned. He had been given very little in his life. This was a gift of immense proportions. He felt a surge of pride in being valued by these men.

Eggard put a hand on his shoulder and said, "Each of us is blessed with gifts to give to others. You have this knowledge and skill. None of us do. It is for you to use, for the betterment of all of us."

Flagger looked over the place and said, "You have a roof to keep the sun off, and the rain out. Tell us what we need to do to set it up for you."

Together, they used the mud to build a small bowl-shaped forge on top of a stump, fitting the bellows into the side of it to feed air to the fire. They made a rough-hewn but sturdy worktable from split logs. Piotr set it in just the right position so he could go back and forth from the forge to the anvil. He found he had a real working space for smithing. When the mud had dried, they fired up the forge for the first time. The bellows blew air into the fire, and they heated a length of the spring steel to a reddish glow. He went about making enough nails needed to finish the cabin, and then many more. It was his job, and it was an important job.

That night he slept in the lean-to next to the heat of the forge. As he lay down to rest, he had a feeling of intense gratitude, and he was certain his father would have been proud of the work he had done.

*Chapter 16*

# THE CHURCH

Lucien Greely was happy. A rare occurrence in his life. He rarely had been given a gift, and one of this magnitude was precious. He wolfed down his morning pancake and oatmeal bowl with unusual relish. A man of his size required a large amount of food on a daily basis.

The cause of his joy on this fine morning was the gift of labor.

Father Renier Archembeau, and his red-haired helper Father Demari, had come to him at the behest of Johann Easterly, esteemed governor of the Quebec territory. They requested his services to help build a church. It was a gift that would keep on giving.

"Thank you for seeing us on such short notice. You will have to excuse my dawdling, Monsieur Greely. I am infirmed a bit at this time," Father Archembeau had said.

"Nonsense, Father, it is my pleasure to host you this day, here in the New World. You have come a long way, no?" Greely had developed a way with aristocratic manners in his hometown of Nantes. It served him well with royal pretenders, like this priest, and with the real thing, dukes and ladies and the lot. It also served him well with the lowlifes, thieves, prostitutes, and traders he dealt with on the docks.

He ushered them onto the porch and into the one-room cabin, pulling a chair back from the long table for the elderly priest. "So, how can I help the church today?" he asked.

"The governor has indicated that you can provide laborers? For construction? I have acquired a small plot, down past the dock, alongside the trail by the river. The church has sent me to establish a presence here in the New World. I am trying to do just that."

"A presence, Father? Do you mean the building of an actual church?" Greely thought of the churches he had seen in Nantes or Paris. The ornate carvings and glass work completed with unparalleled skill.

"Yes, an actual church building. A place of worship, here in Quebec City. The first of its kind."

"Father, my men, they are laborers. They are not artists. They don't have the ability to carve or lay the stained glass in such a way as is customary in Paris or Marseille."

"We are not looking for a cathedral, Monsieur. Greely. We are looking for a place to begin. A simple cabin, with a room for the sister, and perhaps some small additional rooms for myself and Father Demari. A central area for the church service. And a kitchen area, for us to prepare food. This is all we seek."

*Oh, is that all*, thought Greely. A simple four-room cabin, with a standalone kitchen. A palace, by comparison to most New World homes. In Quebec City, a lot of cabins were unfinished, missing walls, sections of roof, or fireplaces.

"I understand, this could take many days to build. When were you looking to start?"

"As soon as possible, of course." Archembeau smiled when he said it. Greely thought he looked like a bird, with his long nose and red cloak.

Father Demari said, "We can help, the father and I, we will pitch in. And Sister Mary is a right good cook, she will help as well."

"Well, perhaps we should build the kitchen first, eh?" Greely laughed, half joking. These pathetic novices were so green. He cared not at all about the building or how long it took. He just liked the location. It was on the river, across from the ships that were docked, sitting at anchor. Right in front of the *St. Longinus*. Thames, that bastard, his ship was floating right there. They would be coming back to load it up, right in front of his sons, laboring on the church walls. He would leave them a surprise to find there.

"I believe we can be of service. I can spare three men, most days. Some days will only be two. We can help out, and I assume we will collect a small fee for services? Correct?"

"The matter of payment is, I should say, more difficult, at this time," Archembeau explained. "You see, we lost all of our belongings except one trunk when we were stranded at sea...a blunder on behalf of our captain...so, our money, you see, is gone. The money given to us by the church for construction is, well, eh, missing."

"I heard about that, terrible luck. Well, if there is no payment..." Greely left that hanging in the air. Maybe he could extract some money from this ancient buzzard.

"We can pay you once weekly services start, installments, and I have written to Cardinal Richileu, in Paris, for more funds. Will that be satisfactory? For now." Archembeau and Demari looked at him expectantly.

"I understand...I do have a couple of locals, savages, that work for me from time to time. They could come, and my oldest son knows plenty about cabin building. He could manage their progress. I will have them meet you there on site, tomorrow morning? After breakfast? You can show them what you want at that time."

He fit it all together for them.

"That would be wonderful. We will come then to the spot where the first church will stand in the New World!" Archembeau stood with outstretched hands for a double handshake. Greely shook them, his massive paws enveloping the aged priest's weathered hands.

As they left, Lucien waved his eldest son, Remy, over to talk. Remy was the most competent of a fairly incompetent crew. Lucien put his arm around him conspiratorially, which he was always hesitant to do, given that Remy had chronically rotten breath.

"The cannon, are you able to move it?"

"Aye, it is on the palisade wall, at the corner. There are two there, and another on the other end."

"You are going to help build the first church in the New World. Congratulations. You'll be famous. Probably put your name in the scrolls for it. Use those two old Chippewa bastards we give booze and food."

Remy grinned sardonically at the joke, his poor teeth showing.

"More importantly, they are building right where that bastard that choked me has his ship anchored. You are going to keep tabs on them. And get far enough along that we will stash that cannon there, pointed right at that ship. When the time comes, they will get attacked, and shot to hell. We will take all they have and trade it with the next fur hunters that come along. Because more are coming, sure as sunrise, more are coming."

"I understand." Remy knew not to question directives.

"Good; get those two old Indians to sober up, they are working tomorrow, and for the next couple of months. Just make sure it is not finished before they have filled that ship with their furs."

"The cannon, though, if I move it, Easterly is gonna know..." Remy was always thinking.

"I will tell him I want it down there for protection. At least while you all are working. He will not question me." Lucien Greely was suspicious of almost everything, but his influence with the governor of the territory was rock solid. Of this, he had no doubt.

"All right, then, in the morning, you are off. Keep an eye out, and make sure I know what they are up to. We will hit them when the time is right. There won't be a wrestling match this time."

His cruel smile reappeared. That was how he looked when he was happy.

# Chapter 17

# MAY FLOWERS

The trail to the north of the Abenaki village was steep and led them into the green mountains. Thankfully, it was well worn and easy enough for them to see in the daytime, as none of them knew it well. Malian had taken the lead, being the one with the most knowledge of the forest. For the first two days they had walked and walked, stopping only to refill bladder canteens at streams, eat handfuls of pemmican, and sleep on the ground with no fire. They covered as much ground as possible. Montreaux and Malian were worried that the Abenaki would pursue, given their sudden departure from the village. But no one had come for them. Not yet, anyway. Bug-bitten again and dirty, after days and nights in the woods, Jana was thankful that they had been allowed to leave the village without incident.

Her companions were good people. She had grown to trust Montreaux and found him to be reliable and optimistic. Despite sleeping on the ground, cold at night with no fire, Montreaux awoke each morning smiling quietly as he chewed pemmican and drank from his canteen. He would not complain to them, even when she could see he was tired or uncomfortable. He was a strong man, not boastful or arrogant.

Malian's strength was immense. Not only was she incredibly strong on the trail, walking all day on a few handfuls of food; she continued to lead them, even though she was grieving. She would spontaneously cry silently from time to time. Jana cried for her, too, as they walked. She had seen what true and complete love looked like from her parents, and she had recognized it when they met Nanibosad and Malian by the old willow at the cove.

As they walked and the mosquitoes buzzed her ears, she thought back to the cove just a week or so ago. It seemed like forever. "Do you think they made it, in the longboat, to Quebec City?" she asked Montreaux in a whisper, as they walked on the trail in the green mountains.

Montreaux said quietly, "Guillaume is a good man. Excellent sailor, among the best I have ever had the pleasure of sailing with. If anyone could get them to port, he could."

"Sister Mary is so old. So is Father Archembeau. I worry about them; they cannot take so much strain…"

Montreaux walked in silence for a few steps. Then he said, "One thing about getting old…you have to be tough, to live that long. Who is tougher than Sister Mary? That woman has not one ounce of quit in her. I am sure she kept them going."

Jana and Montreaux walked along a bit farther. Finally, Malian signaled them to stop, and they dropped their packs on the trail to rest for a while.

"I have been meaning to say," Jana said, "I didn't see him, the man that grabbed me, in the water. If I had, maybe I could have pushed him away, or fought him off. Because I didn't, you went in after me…and now, you are here." She pointed around the forest. Even now, higher in elevation as they walked the steep trail, the tree canopy was over top of their heads.

"You need not feel sorry for being attacked. That warrior saw an opportunity, and he tried to take advantage of it. You gave him a reminder of why not to do that again." Montreaux dragged his hand across his face, like a claw, to remind Jana of the scratch marks she had left on the Iroquois. "I have been in worse predicaments. I survived them. You and I will survive this one, too." He pointed at Malian. "Besides, we have an excellent guide."

"She has been so strong."

"I have noticed. Like Sister Mary, she has grit." Montreaux was surprised as the admiring words came out of his mouth.

"I noticed that you noticed," Jana whispered.

Montreaux grimaced. He had always taken pride in his stoicism. Perhaps not so much, here.

On the afternoon of the third day, the trail turned to the west. They came across a mountain stream that had to be crossed. Malian waved them over to look at it before wading through. Jana thought about her other companions on this journey: mosquitoes and deer flies. They swarmed about constantly. Sometimes she covered her head with a cloth, even in the midday warmth, just to keep them off. Now, after so much walking, hunger was also a companion. The pemmican kept her going, but it was trail food, not a meal. The empty pit at the bottom of her stomach was beginning to affect her. She was feeling weaker.

In the clear stream water, she saw speckled trout. "There are fish here, look." Jana pointed.

"There are, here, and some here," Malian agreed. "This might be a good place to stop for a rest, and to gather food." She looked around the forest, seeing opportunities for food, while Jana and Montreaux saw trees and leaves.

"Can we risk a fire?" Montreaux asked.

"I think so. We are far enough away now." Malian inhaled deeply.

Montreaux stared at the stream for a moment, looking at the fish. "We have no nets, or line. How can we even catch them?"

"Nets? Line? No, no, that will not work," Malian said. "Follow me." She headed downstream a little way and found what she wanted. "Here, gather these rocks."

Malian waded into the stream and picked up a cannonball-sized rock, moving it next to another in the stream.

Montreaux and Jana joined her in the stream, picking up larger rocks and moving them down to where Malian indicated. She quietly built a small dam, tight enough that the larger fish could not get through but not so tight that the water stopped flowing. She then formed a small corral of rocks in a circle attached to the rock dam, leaving an opening for the fish to get in.

"This will do. Stay here, with this." She handed Montreaux a rock to cover the opening of the fish corral. "When the fish swim in, you close it off. Wait for us to drive them down."

Montreaux nodded, now understanding. They had built a fish trap.

Malian waved at Jana, and they walked back upstream on either side. "Find a stick, like this." She picked up a stick about six feet long, so Jana did the same. Once they were downstream about forty yards, Malian looked carefully into the water. There she saw several speckled and brown trout, big enough to eat. She nodded at Jana and gestured: they were to jump in. Jana thought of how foolish they must look, but the need to get food was desperate.

With a splash they jumped together into the near-waist-deep water, poking their sticks and creating a general ruckus that caused the fish to swim away in a panic. Then they walked together downstream, herding the fish in front of them as they went.

Montreaux stood on the rock dam, looking down into the water with the rock that would serve as the corral gate in his hands, poised to seal them in. Slowly, as the women walked closer, fish began to appear at the dam, darting back and forth. A few swam into the corral, seeking refuge from the noisy splashing. As the two women got closer still, more fish appeared, and began to splash and dart around.

Once they got to a few feet away, the women splashed their sticks and even more fish swam into the circular rock corral. Malian gave Montreaux a nod. He stepped into the stream and set the rock into place, closing off the corral of fish. He then stepped over the rocks into the circle and quickly jammed his hands down into the water, grabbing a speckled trout, and tossing it out onto the bank. His years at sea had taught him how to handle a fish. Hesitancy would not work. He bent to the task, grabbing several more and tossing them out onto the bank. Soon they had a flopping mess of fish in the grass. Malian and Jana climbed out of the stream and Malian pinned a trout down with her foot, then took her stick and gave it a short, sharp blow to the head. The fish immediately stiffened.

"Like this," she said.

Jana tried to step on one, missed, then got it pinned on her next try. She whacked it on the head and it stopped moving. They were all speckled and brown trout and one catfish. A few of the brown trouts were nearing two pounds and would be a meal by themselves.

Malian examined a speckled trout and pulled her knife, slitting it from just under its mouth to the underside of the tail, pulling it open with her fingers. She reached up into the body cavity and pulled out the intestines of the small fish, dropping them into the water inside the fish corral.

"Gut the rest and throw the insides into the trap," Malian told Jana. "I will get a fire going; we can camp here and rest for the day. We will eat and sleep and move out again in the morning."

Montreaux climbed out of the water and started to help her, opening them up expertly with his sharp knife and pulling out the guts with no difficulty. Jana was hesitant again, but did it successfully, dropping the guts into the water.

"I never really liked fish very much," she said, as she held the intestines of a trout between her fingers and dropped it into the water.

"You will feel different when we get them cooked." Montreaux slit another one open and gutted it in one swift pull. "Leave the catfish for me. It is too large to just gut, I will fillet it." He walked over and grabbed it behind the pectoral fins, so it could not spike him with its final spasms. Using the ground as a table, he cut in behind the gills and slid his knife along the vertebrae to the tail, pulling off the entire side of meat in a slab nearly a foot long and an inch and a half thick. He flipped it and did the same to the other side, laying the two slabs skin side down on the grass.

Malian came back as they finished. "Fire is going. I found some sticks to roast the fish with. Just push it through the mouth and out by the tail."

She climbed into the water and opened the corral gate by moving the rock, and also moved a large rock out of the dam. "We have to open it up so the fish can move again."

"Leave it better than you found it." Montreaux nodded.

They cooked the trout and the catfish fillets on the fire and ate as much as they could. Jana found that she liked the taste of the fish. Most anything tastes good when you are really hungry. She pulled on her overcoat, covered her face with her hood to keep the bugs out, and fell asleep as the sun went down. Exhaustion, combined with a full belly, the warmth of the fire, and the comfort of good companions, put her into a heavy sleep.

Piotr felt the thunder in the middle of the night. He actually could feel the ground vibrate with the power of the sound. He lay in his bedroll beneath the lean-to roof of the forge. The fire had gone out some time ago, but the clay stayed warm for hours afterward. He had taken to sleeping there, with his tools. Since he was at the base of the hill, he had dug a small trench around the outside of the lean-to, keeping the water from flowing in as it came down the hillside. So even though the vibrating thunder woke him, he was not concerned about rain. He would stay dry, back behind the forge, under the roof of the lean-to.

But the thunder didn't stop, and the horses began to whinny and snort in fear. It kept vibrating the ground. It was a long rolling thunder and seemed to keep echoing. Half asleep, he pushed himself up and tried to rub his eyes, but everything was shaking.

"What is happening…" he said to no one.

He heard the snapping and breaking of wood and then the shouts of the Paquet brothers and others. He stood up and walked outside, barefoot. There was no rain. This was not thunder. In the darkness he could see movement down by the stream at the bottom of the valley, where the canoes were kept. In the moonlight, it looked like a wave of brown and black was crashing through the lower part of the camp. He ran toward the sounds and realized the brown and black wave had fur. And hooves and horns.

He got closer and saw that it was a wood bison herd. They were stampeding through the stream and the camp. The canoes were in their path and were being trampled. He watched as the last of a few hundred of the massive animals rumbled through camp in the dark, the ground shaking as he stood on it. Thames ran past him, chasing after them. "Come on!" he shouted.

Piotr followed him, still barefoot, but at least dressed, as he had slept in his clothes. Thames was carrying his musket, and the wick had been lit. He must have had the foresight to light it after the herd woke him, knowing what it was. Piotr watched as the last of the bison began to plow into the stream, water and mud spraying as they churned and pushed their two thousand pounds of meat and bone through to the other side.

Thames caught up to the last one crossing and dropped to one knee, cocking the musket and bringing it to his shoulder in a single motion. He fired from fifteen feet into the side of a massive cow. The bark of the musket and flash of fire from the barrel caused the herd to startle and run even harder.

The bison cow he hit took no notice of the shot. She plowed through the stream as if nothing had happened.

Flagger ran past Piotr with a musket on a full sprint down the hill as well. He ran to Thames's side; Thames was already reloading. His wick was also lit, and he cocked and aimed down the barrel at the cow, now pulling itself out of the stream. His musket roared, the flame creating a flash of light in the night. This time the cow brayed out a scream of pain and staggered a couple of steps, then regained itself and began to follow the herd disappearing into the darkness of the valley.

Piotr caught up to them. Thames jumped up; he had reloaded and was up and running, following the bison cow. On the run, he turned and handed the musket to Piotr. "Take it!"

Piotr was not sure what was going on, but Thames jumped three fourths of the way across the stream, splashing into the water, and in two quick steps he was out on the bank. He turned to Piotr with arms out, still running. "Toss it!"

Piotr tossed it to him, trying to not spin it. Thames caught it on the run, chasing after the cow. Piotr followed, jumping into the creek, waist deep. He struggled for a few steps and scrambled out on the other side.

"Piotr, catch!"

He looked up as Flagger was ramming a ball home. He quickly tossed his musket at Piotr, who could barely see it in the dark coming toward him. He reached out and snatched it instinctively, trying to keep the barrel pointed away from himself. He groaned when he caught it, the weight and the hardness of the metal and wood stinging his hands. But he held on and took off running after Thames in the darkness.

Another blast and flash of fire light from Thames's musket barrel told him where to go. Thames had nearly caught the slowing cow and fired into her side. Still, she did not stop. With a grunt and blast of air from her nostrils, she kept up her gallop. Piotr ran behind him and saw that she finally was beginning to slow. He was able to run next to her. The cow saw him on her flank. Lowering her head and breaking stride, she lunged toward him, slicing upward with her horns to hook him. Piotr jumped away as the horn ripped through the air where he had just stood. Dancing backward, he half-cocked the musket as the cow stopped and turned to face him.

She lowered her head toward the ground, and Piotr saw blood drip from her flaring nostril in the moonlight. She took a step toward him as he cocked the gun all the way back to the firing position and brought it to his shoulder. The cow began her charge. Piotr looked down the barrel, putting the bead on the cow's head, squeezing the trigger. The pan flashed and the barrel spat flame, smoke, and the .58 caliber lead ball. It struck the beast just above the horns, smashing into her fur and flesh. At such close range, the ball carried tremendous energy and it buried deep, cutting through the mound of flesh and smashing into the spine just above the head.

The bison grunted and her head dropped, plowing into the ground. Her front legs followed, collapsing and driving her front end downward, but her back legs still had power. Driving the head down, they flipped her hind legs over her head, somersaulting onto her back, and sliding to a stop at Piotr's feet. The massive beast sprayed his bare feet with dirt and rocks.

Thames and Flagger arrived a second later, both panting heavily in the night air. The three of them stared at the massive bison for a few seconds as she lay splayed out with legs in the air.

"Well...teats up," Flagger said, matter-of-factly.

Thames clapped him on the shoulder and the three of them began to laugh, a little maniacally, as adrenaline rushed through their veins.

"We're gonna need Mule to drag it back to camp," Flagger said.

Piotr brought Mule back on a hitch line with a coil of rope over his shoulder. He had no idea how they could tie the massive bison up so that they could drag it.

Flagger and Thames had opened the cow from throat to anus, removing the intestines by scooping them out with their hands. Even in the dark moonlight, he could see that they were blooded up to their elbows. Flagger tied the rope around the horns and looped extra length around the front legs at the shoulder, and with Piotr leading Mule and the two of them pushing, they managed to drag it back to camp.

In the morning, Piotr came down from the forge, this time with moccasins on, to see the cow in the early morning light. It was even larger in daylight. Eggard was hard at work already, removing the hide.

"Good morning, Piotr. I see you are a great hunter, among all your other skills."

"It was dark and I pointed the musket and shot it. I was lucky, I easily could have been trampled and smashed," Piotr said.

"Our canoes were not so lucky." Eggard nodding at the side of the stream.

The canoes were scattered everywhere. A few of the dugouts were smashed into multiple pieces, with chunks lying scattered about.

"Go and take a look. Figure out what we have to rebuild," Eggard said.

Piotr walked over to survey the damage. It was devastating.

Some of the canoes were downstream with men out trapping. The ones that remained had been stored next to the stream, simply pulled out and left on shore near camp. The bison did not seem to care as they charged through them, stomping holes through the bottoms. He flipped one over. Several holes were obvious in the stern and right through the hull. At least five were ruined.

"These are mostly firewood," he shouted back to Eggard.

"Aye. We have much work to do. Come and help me finish with this animal."

Piotr worked with Eggard, removing the hide and quartering the bison. Even the quartered sections of meat weighed a couple of hundred pounds each. He brought Mule down to the bison and they worked through the morning hauling up the meat to the cabin. He and Eggard put together a triangular smoking hut of sticks and branches tied together with lashing. They cut dozens and dozens of strips of bison meat, salted them, and smoked them over the fire pit by hanging the strips under the walls of the hut. This would dry out the meat and preserve it for future use. There was enough meat to do this several times.

In the meantime, Eggard cut several steaks and set them to cooking over the fire pit on a lattice of sticks. They would have a large meal.

That afternoon Captain Linville returned, rowing upstream from trapping beaver with four of the men. He saw the shattered dugout canoes and the buffalo sizzling over the central fire pit and smoking in the smoke hut. He put two and two together.

Thames came down to meet him and exchanged the canoes with a new group of five men to go out with beaver traps. Linville's canoe was loaded down with pelts. They had had good success, and they had only gone downstream a mile or so from camp to ponds that were connected and fed by the stream.

"You have done well, eh," Thames said to Linville, greeting him and smiling.

"They are thick in there." Linville pointed downstream. "Last night?" He asked about the dugouts.

"Yes, in the middle of the night, a bison herd came through. Smashed the canoes. I ran out and tried to shoot one. Piotr and Flagger followed me and we chased it down, shot it twice more. Eventually Piotr got in position and put it down. We have food for several days," Thames explained.

Linville looked around at the camp and bison. "Well done then, lads. Avoiding starvation is always good. We were lucky that they didn't come directly through camp. They would have wiped out the place."

"Myself and a few others can take the canoes you brought back, but now we have a shortage. We will need to build a few more."

Linville pulled out his pipe and tobacco pouch and said, "I have been on boats my entire life, but I have never built one. Anybody know how?"

Eggard, still cooking steaks, turned and said, "Avoid hardwoods. They work fine, but they are very heavy. Spruce or chestnut work well for a dugout. Not as heavy to carry and they grow straight and long. There are chestnut trees up on the hill." He pointed to the hill rising above the valley, past Piotr's forge.

"You take a few men and be at it then, when you are done here. Thank you, Eggard, for your hard work, and your knowledge."

"Aye, Captain." Eggard flipped the bison steaks over. "In a minute or two, we will have all the steak you can eat. Gather everyone around, and we will be in for a treat."

They ate the bison together, pulling it off of the fire with knives and cutting it into long strips of chewy, delicious steak. Rarely in Piotr's life had he ever eaten so much. Lunch and dinner blurred together into one continuous meal, as he and Eggard kept butchering the massive bison cow. Men wandered in from their chores to pull a steak off the fire and eat it whole, only to come back an hour later and do it again.

In the early evening, they hung the last of the strips for smoking in the hut. Piotr's hands, arms and chest were splattered with blood. He had taken his shirt off early on, seeing that there was no way to do this job in a clean fashion. He went down to the stream, waded in and scrubbed with sand on his skin to get the dried blood off.

When he came back up to the central fire pit, Eggard had staked out the bison hide onto a few trees and was scraping it with his long knife, removing the fatty tissue under the hide, leaving the skin to dry out. Piotr joined him and they made quick work of it.

"You will keep the hide, Piotr. You can use it to make a blanket or a coat; you may need it come winter. It is warm in the summer here, but the winters are cold and snowy, like in Daneland."

"I thought we were leaving to head back across the sea, by fall. To sell the beaver fur. Make our money."

"Aye, that is the plan. You can use it on the boat, as it will be cold when we are on the sea. But trust me when I tell you, not all of these men will make that trip," Eggard said.

"What do you mean, not make the trip? Some of us may die?" Piotr asked.

Eggard was bent over, working the last bit of the hide. "That is possible, yes. But I am talking about something else." He stood up to his full height, bloody torso, hands, and arms. His dirty white linen tied to his bald head. "Piotr, back home, we worship God, yes, it is so...but we also worship men, the kings, the dukes, the rulers and landowners."

Piotr thought for a moment, and said, "Yes, but when we return, we will have money, if we can fill the ship...we will have money and can buy our own land, true?"

"You could maybe buy some land with what we get from our work. Some. In order to buy land, though, someone has to be willing to sell it. Why would the nobility want to sell it? And why would they sell it to us?"

Piotr realized Eggard was right, in that they were a different class. Even Captain Linville, a ship owner and successful, was not royalty. Nor was he connected to higher positions in the church or government. He had not thought all of this through.

"But look around at this valley, Piotr. This is the richest place I have ever seen...you could grow anything here. The soil is fertile, the water is pure. And there are no stone walls that divide it. This land is open...to those who would work for it."

"It is beautiful. That is for sure. I am not certain the Huron would be willing to let us stay and take the land from them. Or other tribes..."

Eggard interrupted him. "True, it is not free. Nothing is free. Anyone who would lay claim to this land will also claim the struggle that comes with it. But you would be free to struggle as you choose. Not as someone else, a noble, demands."

Piotr picked up his shirt. "It is a heady thought. To be free, to live in a place where you are the king of what you see...but, Eggard, you lived here, in the New World, with your woman. You were free. Yet you went back."

"I did. The place we lived was good, but not like this valley. And I made the choice on my own. And all of these men, they will make that choice for themselves. And no one will stop them."

Piotr nodded. He pulled more of the finished strips of meat off of the fire while silently thinking.

Eggard then planted one more thought in Piotr's mind. "If I were young, like you, I would find a good woman and live out my days here. I would never go back again. Even with the money. You will be rich here, richer than a king, in a valley like this."

Piotr chuckled. "The only women I have seen since we left Quebec City were the old Huron women who were good at cooking stew. This valley is rich, but I don't see a lot of women here."

"I suppose you're right. I will finish up here. In the morning, you and I will head up the hill and find a chestnut tree for the dugouts. Make sure the axes have a sharp edge before you go to sleep."

"Aye," Piotr said. He placed the last of the smoked meat strips in the bag Eggard had set out and made his way toward the forge and the ax heads.

Tall orange and yellow flowers grew alongside the trail in the patches where sunlight shone through the canopy to the forest floor. Jana stopped and picked one with orange petals. She sniffed it, then wove it through some buttonholes on her dress. The last several days on the trail had been hard. The trail was steep and rocky, and they grew wearier as they walked each day. Jana saw that Malian was growing pensive as the trail had taken them westward over the mountains.

Now, they were moving out of the steep, rocky portion into broader rolling hills. At times, when they were on the top of a hill, she could see glimpses out through the canopy. As far as her keen eyes could view, the forest continued, covered in a multitude of shades of green. The green was so thick that it looked like the landscape paintings she had seen in the monastery by master painters. There seemed to be no end to it. Just a rolling horizon that kept creeping away from them as they walked farther and farther westward.

Malian pointed out that being silent and unseen was more important than moving fast. She insisted that fires only be started as the sun was setting, and she woke before dawn to put them out. This kept their smoke from being seen from a distance.

When they stopped to rest, Montreaux attempted to ease her fears. "Malian, no one has followed. If the Abenaki were coming, they would have found us by now."

"It is not the Abenaki I fear. I know this place. I have been here before." Malian spoke in a whisper.

Montreaux listened.

"As a young child, I was on this trail. The trail is taking us through the southern part of the Oneida homeland. After that, we will pass through the Seneca lands."

Montreaux thought for a moment. "Seneca are Iroquois. So are Mohawk, and Cayuga, too. You were born in a Cayuga village?"

"Yes."

"So, if I understand it, the Iroquois are a group of tribes. Banded together, for protection? What are the other tribes again?"

Malian explained, holding her hand up with her fingers spread. "The five tribes. Mohawk guard the east, the Onandaga are in the center and keep the council fires for the confederacy. The Cayuga live on the north, above the finger lakes. The Oneida are in the south, we actually walked through their territory for the last several days."

Montreaux nodded. He realized that, as much as he valued Malian's expert guidance through the forest, he had underestimated both her knowledge and importance. Without her, he was certain they would have blundered into a passing band of warriors by now.

Montreaux asked, "So soon we will be in Seneca territory?"

Malian nodded and closed her eyes for a moment. "When I was a girl, a Seneca woman was mother to one of the families in our longhouse. I remember the stories she told, about the Seneca parents. They force their children to run long distances. They force them to survive with little food or water, out in the forest, alone. Often, they send young warriors to battle against the tribes in the west. It is how they achieve manhood. The other Iroquois tribes call them the Keepers of the Western Door. No tribes will attack the Iroquois from the west because they fear the Seneca."

Montreaux now understood why she was anxious. Jana, having been standing and watching the trail, sat on the ground, next to her. Malian noticed the orange flower.

"The flower...it is the flower moon, now. May. We call it the month when life returns. We..." her words trailed off. Malian lowered her head. She had no *we* anymore. No tribe. No family. No husband.

She had only the companionship of these foreigners she had come to know.

Malian wept silently. Jana reached out and took her into her arms. As she sobbed, she curled up into the hug, tears sliding down her cheeks.

Jana comforted her and held on. There was no poultice for this wound.

Montreaux simply waited. They had only made it this far because of the knowledge and skills of this woman. They needed her to survive. He rose and scouted around the trail, watching to make sure they were alone. Having seen the Iroquois warriors in action, he did not want to be found.

After a bit, Malian recovered and stood up. She and Jana gathered up their belongings.

Jana looked down the trail and said, "Let's keep going."

Malian shook her head to clear it, and inhaled sharply, her eyes red and cheeks flushed. Then she nodded and started off.

For several days, they marched along. Twice they heard groups of people coming, and they were able to scatter off the trail into the forest, hiding silently until the groups passed. Each time it had been native men, women, and children. Not war parties of young warriors. They were not looking for strangers, they were traveling. They were lucky.

Montreaux believed they were more than half of the way to Quebec City, but the westward direction of the trail had taken them farther into the New World than he had ever dreamed of going. As a sailor, it was not in his nature to want to walk these forested hillsides. He was hopeful that the trail would turn north soon, but he could only estimate where they were on the map he had memorized. It was a vague reference point for a man used to knowing his location by the stars.

It was the morning after they ate the last of the trout they had caught and smoked by the stream side when their luck ran out. Montreaux noticed it first. They arose, before dawn as usual, and gathered their belongings. Jana kicked dirt over the last of the coals, still barely glowing from the small fire from the night before, and shouldered her pack. Silently, they started down the trail, as they had every morning for twelve days.

It was the smallest of movements, but it was out of place. Just a few leaves on a branch, moving unnaturally, not with the wind, as if someone had bumped them. He reached to his belt and loosened his right-handed pistol while they walked. A few minutes later, he heard a rustle in the leaves behind them to his right. Almost imperceptible. So small it easily could have been a squirrel or a rabbit. But the hair on his neck and arms stood up, and he knew that it was no animal.

Montreaux in the back, Jana in the middle, and Malian leading had become their customary positions. He quietly caught up to Jana in a few strides and walked next to her for a few steps. Without leaning toward her, he whispered, "Mademoiselle, do not show surprise, but we are being followed. Please ease forward and tell Malion."

He walked with her a few steps, then slowed enough to let her get out in front of him. She caught up to Malian in a few steps and whispered words of warning. They kept walking, and Malian picked up the pace slightly so that they were walking fast for more than a hundred yards when Malian suddenly stopped. She turned to the north side of the trail, looking back and up the slope of the hillside.

Montreaux and Jana both stopped instinctively, to keep their spacing. Montreaux, standing next to a large ash, dropped to one knee, as if to tie his moccasins. He looked over his shoulder backward on the trail, but saw no one coming. He heard the spear, but never saw it, as the stone point thumped into the bark of the ash just above his head. The shaft of the lance vibrated as he stood up sharply, his eyes wide.

"Look OUT!" he shouted.

The Seneca warrior who threw it came from out of the bush about twenty yards away, charging with a yell and a knife in his right hand. Montreaux grabbed the shaft of the spear and yanked it from the tree, turning toward the man. He lunged, jabbing with the spear; the man nimbly danced to the side, deflecting the spear downward with his left hand and slashing the knife toward Montreaux's head, his eyes blazing. His step back to avoid the knife redirected the spear upward toward the warrior's midsection. Montreaux tried to drive it forward into his guts, but the warrior deftly grabbed the shaft with his free hand. Montreaux twisted it free of his grasp and thrust again, finding purchase in his right thigh, just above the knee. He felt the tip drive home.

The Seneca warrior screamed in pain and dropped the knife to the ground, grabbing the shaft of the spear with two hands. Montreaux released the spear and turned, running down the trail, following Jana and Malian. They had taken off at a full sprint to the west. He churned after them, his feet thumping the ground and heart thumping in his chest. He stole a glance over his shoulder and could see men coming down the slope toward the trail at a run. He did not have time to count them.

The first arrow passed over his left shoulder, well above his head. It zipped into the leaves, disappearing from sight. Another followed, sticking into a tree to his right as he went by as fast as he could go. He heard a thump, and felt the arrow hit. It lodged in the wooden frame on his backpack, sticking out awkwardly like a signal flag as he ran down the hill. He prayed he would be lucky as he ran on, trying to catch up with the two women, who were as fleet as the wind, he saw with wide-eyed amazement.

*The chase is on*, he thought as he ran, *and it will not end well. They will wear us down. Eventually. They can run in teams, with some on our heels, and others following at a slower pace, then trading places as the chase group grows weary.*

Jana and Malian could run well though. He looked at their long strides as they covered ground quickly, despite their backpacks and belongings. He made the decision that he would run till he couldn't anymore. Then he would stop and turn, with pistol and knife, and kill as many as he could, to buy them time.

The whoops and yells behind him told him they were coming. And they were many.

Piotr swung the ax for what felt like the thousandth strike into the chestnut tree. They found the downed tree on the back side of the hill above where the forge sat at the base. It had reached a century and a half and seventy-five feet of height in its time, but it had fallen after rot finally got into the core at the base. The branches themselves were four feet in diameter, thirty feet out from the trunk, and this was what they were after. The trunk was so thick, it was not feasible to use for a dugout. He and Eggard had selected the branches and removed them, working together on opposite sides, taking turns striking until they cleared it. The tree had fallen sometime earlier in the winter, so the wood was still fresh.

The chestnut tree grew straight and free of knots. The Paquet brothers worked with them, dragging the branches over to a clearing to keep whittling down at the center. They had selected three branches of about thirty feet and were working them down to hollow them out and round the front and rear so it would flow through the water. They would leave bench seats in, below the gunnel. A dugout canoe of this size could hold five men and a lot of fur. If they got them thin enough at the wall and base, the fairly light wood of the chestnut would still allow them to portage when necessary.

They chopped and hollowed out the logs. They used fire in the center and burned out the middle. They wet down the sides as it burned to keep it in the center. The smoldering logs provided them with heat while they slept and reduced the amount of chopping. On the morning of the second day, they had a rough-hewn version for each of the canoes, with the inside hollowed out, but the outside not yet shaped. Eggard felt it was better to haul them back to the camp and complete the final work there. They dragged them down, trailing behind Mule.

Captain Linville looked them over at camp. Thames, Flagger, and most of the men were out working the trap lines. Piotr looked at the stack of fur bales under the birchbark roof of a hastily erected storage shed.

"They are certainly big enough. Twice as long as the old dugouts. They will carry a lot of fur," Linville commented, smoking his pipe and thinking. "I am wondering about getting all of these bales of fur upriver on the Crooked River. I don't think we can build enough canoes to carry it all out, not in a single trip, anyway."

Eggard and Piotr thought about this. The Paquet brothers came over as well.

"If we have to leave some and make repeated trips…this will add weeks," Eggard said, removing his linen cap and rubbing his bald head.

"We could relay it," Abel said. "Haul it all up to the river. Move some of it down. Come back for more. Move the whole load one step at a time."

"It would be slow, but it saves us the risk of leaving any of it behind," Linville said.

Abraham walked around the unfinished dugout, eyeballing it. He held his hands up in the air, as if he were measuring a distance.

"What are you thinking, Abraham? Spit it out, you always go silent when you're thinking," said Anton.

"Barge," Abraham said.

"Ahhh, a barge...a river barge," Linville said, puffing on his pipe.

Anton said, "We take two dugouts. We could haul them over to the river, then build the barge on top of it there. Use those two as floats and put a platform across the top."

"Like a pontoon bridge. Abraham, can you build such a thing?" Linville asked.

"We need lots of nails. And lashings. We could do it, then."

The men turned toward Piotr simultaneously. "Do we have the nails?" Linville asked.

"Yes. I made dozens, they're in the box, by the forge," Piotr said.

"Good lad. All right then, that decides it. Leave this one here, we will finish it. Take Mule, and a horse. Haul the other two back up the trail to the Cuyahoga. Take what you need and build the barge there."

"It will take a few days, do you think?" Mason asked the others.

"A week is about right. Pack what you need."

Gerard acknowledged and the group scattered to gather their goods.

Piotr loaded his pack at the lean-to. He put in a change of clothes, what little pemmican he had left, and the smoked bison. He grabbed the box of nails he had made, and all of the sinew cords he had. He shouldered the wooden frame, musket in right hand, and started to walk up the hill. He paused after a few steps and turned back and gathered his war club, slipping it into its carrying position on the pack. It would not do to forget anything.

The group of seven men made their way back up the hill toward the downed chestnut tree and the hollowed out branches they had started turning into canoes. Anton paused, looking out over the valley and down toward the camp. As his eyes traced their way back up the hill in the midday sun, something flashed a reflection of the sun on the side of the hill, catching his eye. He stared, trying to make out what it was he saw through the canopy. After standing for a moment, he pointed. "Look at that big son of a bitch."

"What big son of a bitch?" Abel asked.

Anton pointed.

"That is big," Abel said, now seeing the rock under the canopy of leaves.

Abraham shielded his eyes from the sun, staring in the direction they were pointing. "Big," he agreed, nodding.

"You want to go have a look? I'm going to," Anton said and started off.

The other four Paquet brothers looked at each other. Gerard raised his hands in resignation and followed him across the side of the hill.

Abel said, "Tell us what you find, but don't be all day about it! We have a lot of work to do, you know!"

Gerard and Anton walked the side of the hill, one leg lower than the other, till they came to the large object that had flashed in the sun. It was a rock. Unlike any other rock they had seen, at least in the valley. It sat perched on the hillside, large and impressive.

"Phhheww, look at that," Anton said. He walked all the way around it, looking it over. "It sure doesn't look like the other rocks around here. Look at these shiny specks in it." He ran his hand over it, brushing some grey moss off the top.

"Anton, look at this." Gerard waved him over as he knelt down at the base of the rock. He began pulling moss and leaves away from the ground, exposing what was below.

Anton came over and knelt down as well, and they brushed away the plants and debris collected over thousands of years. When they saw it, they knew it. They both raised their heads, looking each other in the eye, with big grins growing on their astonished faces.

"Holy sh...can you believe it? Do you see this!" Anton shouted.

"Shhhhhh, don't be screaming out here!" Gerard cautioned. "Let's dig it out of there."

They scraped with their hands and knives to cut away soil and roots holding the three fossilized footprints of a Dromaeosaur in place next to the rock. Eventually, they dug under, and pulled them free from the ground they had occupied for thousands of years. The whole fossil was about as big as two dinner plates, and a couple of inches thick. It was heavy and solid, and they brushed away the dirt to look closer.

Anton put his hand into the deepest of the three footprints, splaying out his fingers to match those of the toothed bird that had stepped there, so many thousands of years earlier. "Talk about a big son of a bitch, you ever seen bird tracks like that?"

"Its feet were bigger than my hands...must have been as tall as we are...this is just like that footprint that the governor had, back in Quebec City. I'm thinking he may want this, too," Gerard said.

"Absolutely, he will. We are taking it with us and selling it to him for that museum back in Paris."

They gathered it up and Anton wrapped it in a linsey-woolsey shirt from his pack, tucking the heavy fossil away in his backpack. They would make a tidy sum.

As they walked away, happy and excited, neither of them noticed the movement of the large rock. It shifted, slightly, kicking up a little dust and dirt in the loosened soil of the hillside, sliding down into the hole the two men left behind.

## Chapter 18

# ENEMIES AND
# REUNIONS

Father Renier Archembeau did not come to work on the construction of the church. His view was that he was an administrator, a spiritual guide, of sorts. He was busy writing letters to the church in Paris, asking for supplies and support. Nearly everything had been lost. He had managed to keep his own missal, Order of the Mass, and a crucifix in his personal belongings. He found a candlemaker in the tents here at Quebec City, but had no money to pay him, for they were all living on the good will of Governor Easterly. At a minimum, he needed incense burners, a stole, cruets, a pyx, a patan, and a chalice. Not to mention the church building itself. He came to find out that there was no blacksmith in this place, as he had died. He composed three letters to Cardinal Richilieu and reworded them multiple times, but no ship was leaving to take the letters back, anyway. He spent his days writing and planning.

Guillaume and Sister Mary walked the dock to work on the church construction almost every morning together. He had grown to enjoy her company. Rowing together in the long trip after the loss of *The Render* had created a bond with the elderly nun. The entire journey, she had encouraged people, taken care of wounds, and held a steadfast belief in their safety, as granted by the Lord himself. She was devout, and she had not a shred of doubt in her mind when it came to her faith in God. Because of this, she did not fear death, nor would she stand by and allow suffering. Not when she could do something about it. Guillaume appreciated her for that.

On this beautiful summer morning in the New World, Father Demari joined them. His cherubic frame had leaned out since they had arrived just a few weeks earlier. He worked most every day with the two older Indians that Lucien Greely had provided on the construction of the church, and the labor, combined with his diet of meat, fish, and whatever greens he could find, was causing him to lose the fat he had carried since childhood. His mop of red hair stayed, though, and he had not found a way to cut it since they had left Saint-Malo, so it stuck out in odd curly angles, flopping when he walked.

Guillaume, Father Demari, and two of the crewmen from *The Render* had sailed Easterly's fishing boat back to Les Iles de la Madeleine. They circumnavigated it, even sailing up close to the shoreline at the beach, looking at the vegetation with a spyglass. Not only was the crew not there, neither was *The Render*. The ship had disappeared without a trace, leaving them to sail back in bewilderment. They were left to wonder where and how it could have happened.

"We should stop and see if there is anyone on that boat again today," Sister Mary said as they started down the gangplank toward the far western end of the dock. She had been bringing it up almost every day, since Governor Easterly said there was a fellow on the ship that had been shipwrecked and rescued.

"We have stopped by twice, Sister, no one was on it. You saw that I yelled up from the dock, but no one came. They are either not on it or they aren't interested in talking to us."

"It doesn't hurt to try again, you know. What does it cost?"

Sister Mary was always persistent. Guillaume admired that as well.

They came to the side of the *St. Longinus*, at the far end of the dock. No signs of life were evident on the deck as they were walking up. From the dock, it was hard to see onto the deck in any case. But Guillaume was a man of the sea, and he could see that the ship was being maintained. Not only was it tied off correctly and in proper trim, but someone was cleaning it. Everything above the waterline was clean and neat. It took very little time for a ship at anchor to begin to show signs of distress. Someone was wiping it down with seawater to keep the fungi from growing and rotting out the wood. He noted that someone was cleaning the sails, as a couple had been taken down and removed.

But no one appeared to be on it as they approached.

"Hello the ship!" he shouted out.

No response.

He shrugged and turned to walk to the church construction site when a voice shouted out. "Hello the dock!"

A small man with a large nose stuck his head over the side. He wore a blue sailor's cap with a white insignia. He looked down at the elderly nun and the seaman at her side.

"Good morning, monsieur and madame, what can I do for you?" he said in questionable French.

Sister Mary smiled up at him. "Good morning to you, as well. I'm Sister Mary Therese O'Boyle. My good man here is Guillaume...uh, Guillaume, it just occurred to me that I don't know your last name...ha! Anyway, we are wondering, you see, we were lost at sea when our ship ran aground. We were able to row to safety, after many tribulations. The governor, Mr. Easterly, he said that there was a man on this boat that had been lost at sea... I, well, we, were wondering if this man was someone we knew of, from our ship, uh, maybe?"

"Un momento."

The man disappeared. A moment later, a rope ladder flopped over the port side to the deck, and a man in a black naval coat and sailor's pants appeared at the side. Guillaume did not recognize him at first, as he made his way over the side gingerly. His hair was longer, his beard was unkempt, his clothes were a little too large, and when he stepped down on the dock, he stooped a bit. But when he turned and Guillaume saw his face, he could not mistake his captain.

"Gilbert? Captain Laurent? You are alive!" Guillaume clasped him by his narrow shoulders, looking into his face.

Gilbert Laurent did not recognize Guillaume for a second. He was recovering from his wounds, and the stress of having lost his ship and his fortune. His mind had necessarily gone into a protective mode, blanking on much of the recent trauma. Seeing Guillaume's face, his eyes flicked back and forth, scanning for recognition. After a long moment, it registered. Thoughts and images poured through his mind, overwhelming him with emotion, and tears wetted his eyes, tracing lines down his weathered cheeks.

"Guillaume, you are Guillaume!" the bent old man said. "You, you made it back...I thought you were all lost. I was shot, and..." He turned to Sister Mary. "Sister, you are here, alive! I thought all were gone...but here you..."

Sister Mary stepped forward and hugged Captain Gilbert Laurent. This defeated man did not resemble the man who was in charge of *The Render* when it left Saint-Malo. He needed help, and she would give it to him.

"It is true, we are alive, Captain Laurent. I am so glad to see you again," she said, holding him close, as he sobbed in her arms.

"Montreaux, is he alive? Raul, where is he..." Captain Laurent's voice trailed off as he looked in Sister Mary's eyes.

"We were attacked, you see, by a ship that chased us. It fired on us and he tried, tried to hide us, Mr. Montreaux did. He did his best to save us, but, the other longboat, it was hit. Those men died there. It was difficult, but Raul tried his best, Captain."

Guillaume put his hand on Captain Laurent's shoulder and said, "We will tell you all about it, Captain. We are glad to see you alive. Come, let us sit down and talk a while, maybe we can make sense of what has happened."

"Is he alive?"

"I think so, but I'm afraid I don't know. Come, let us tell you our story. We have much to share."

Guillaume, Sister Mary, and Captain Laurent started walking over to the church construction area, and Perdo watched from the deck of the *St. Longinus*. After a few seconds, he shrugged and climbed down the rope ladder to join them.

His thighs were burning with the effort, but he kept pushing. Piotr swore that the long dugouts had gotten stuck on every rock and downed tree or branch along the way, as Mule and the horse dragged them toward the river. Finally, after two full days of difficult travel, they had made it to the Cuyahoga River. He was tired, but a bit of rest would set him right. They set up camp just off the trail at the river's edge.

They gathered firewood from chunks of downed trees, and plenty of it was dry enough to use. Soon, a makeshift camp to work from while they built the barge was set. He and Eggard added a quickly made lean-to with long tree branches near the fire. Enough to sleep under and stay mostly dry, at least.

The next day, they got the barge under construction, dragging downed spruce trees to camp for the platform, and finishing off the dugouts, shaping them with axes and fire. It was backbreaking work, and Piotr could feel it in the soreness of his hands. He realized his hands and forearms were beginning to look like his father's had, muscled and veiny, after years of working the forge.

The Paquet brothers liked to talk while they worked. Enough to where Eggard could hardly stand it. They never really stopped talking, because as soon as one of them finished, another would start up. When there was a lull in the banter on the second day at the edge of the crooked river, Gerard and Anton showed off their fossilized footprints to the group.

"Have you ever seen anything like this?" asked Anton, unwrapping the linsey-woolsey shirt from around the fossil.

"Can you imagine a bird this size? Look, it is bigger than my hand!" Anton held up the fossil with his hand inside the print, demonstrating.

Piotr stuck his hand in, and it too was outsized by the fossil.

Eggard stuck his massive hand inside the footprint next, but his hand was too large and thick to fit. His palm filled the center space, and his splayed fingers, thick as sausages, covered the extended toes tipped by a pointed claw like nail imprint.

Gerard shook his head, looking at Eggard's massive hand, and said, "Hmm, it was tall, eh, but not so tall as you, behemoth."

"Maybe it wasn't tall, it just had big feet," Piotr said.

"No, no, no, it was tall. Very tall. Taller than you, mon ami." Anton was certain.

Mason jumped in and said, "Piotr is right, maybe it was just a regular chicken, with massive feet. So it could carry large things when it flew. Like a cat or something."

"Coconuts," Abraham said.

"Why would anyone want a footprint of a flying chicken that carried coconuts?" Eggard asked.

"It didn't carry coconuts. It was tall...a great deadly beast...this is a valuable thing! People want these, you know!" Anton insisted.

Successful at baiting him, Mason and Abraham quieted down for a minute, while Anton put the fossilized footprints away.

In the momentary quiet, Piotr heard a sound. He thought it was a scream, perhaps a bird, maybe an owl. It was faint, but the sound registered differently with his brain. He stood up and walked a few steps away from camp, toward the trail along the crooked river, to the east. He instinctively angled his head, straining to hear.

The brothers began to talk again. He turned back and held his hands up. "Something is coming."

The camp went quiet and he heard it again. It was a scream or yell of some kind. From a person. "Did you hear it?"

256

The men all broke into action simultaneously. Grabbing matchlock muskets and lighting the long wicks at the fire, the Paquet brothers put hatchets into their belts as well. Eggard picked up the large tree-felling ax, which was like a long hatchet in his large hands, and slipped another smaller trimming ax into his belt.

Piotr looked down at his belt; he had his knife and his small English ax. Abraham pulled his warclub from his backpack and tossed it to him. They all started walking toward the sound.

"Move quiet, stay off the trail," Anton said, taking point.

They fanned out behind him, moving through the underbrush quickly. Piotr moved quietly, as he had learned, with light feet, avoiding sticks and loose objects. They moved parallel to the trail along the river, watching. They peered through the trees looking for signs of movement or something that could have made that noise.

The trail followed the path of the Cuyahoga. The Huron call it the Crooked River. It moved to the east and downhill before them. As Piotr peered down the hill, he saw where runoff water from the surrounding area flowed across the trail. The water had eroded a shallow ditch too wide to jump without a running start. A few flat rocks lay in the bottom of the eroded channel, easy to use for stepping on. The path was little more than four feet wide as it came down the hill, opposite from where they stood. Trees were thinner on the hillside coming down to the river, and several had fallen down on the steep slope. Green bushes had become ground cover where sunlight got through. Piotr sensed that they could hide in the leaves on their side of the hill and still see what was coming down the path.

They crept forward in silence. The sound of feet thumping on the dirt of the trail and heavy breathing resonated. Anton raised his hand to silence and pause the group. Then he waved them up to take cover. He ducked behind an old downed tree, its roots sticking up in the air as it lay on its side. The group followed suit in an instant, ducking behind the log that Anton hid behind. Piotr crouched beside Eggard, and they peaked over the log to see what was coming. The brothers raised their muzzle loaders and took them from half-cock to full, ready to fire.

In a few seconds they saw what was making the noise.

A woman, running smoothly toward them, crested and started down the hill leading to the ditch. A dozen yards behind her was a second woman, running smoothly as well, and a moment later came a bearded white man with a large backpack. He was laboring and breathing heavily. An arrow stuck out of his backpack at an odd angle.

The first woman jumped over the ditch, turning to wait for her comrades. The second woman jumped over as well. The man stumbled to a stop before the ditch, unable to make it across with the heavy backpack. He shrugged out of his backpack, leaving it in the center of the trail. He jumped down onto the rocks and quickly climbed up the other side. The three of them, now on the same side of the ditch as the men from the *St. Longinus*, began to talk hurriedly.

"Why have you stopped? GO! Keep running, I will make a stand here, it will give you time to escape. Go now!" He spoke in French to the women, panting.

The two women did not run; they stared at each other and the man, breathing heavily. The black-haired woman, clearly an Indian, drew a stone tomahawk from her belt and said in French, "I have nowhere to go."

The other woman looked at her and the man, then drew a knife from her belt, turning to face whatever was following them.

"Jana! Go, please go! You can outrun them!" the bearded man pleaded in a whisper.

"I am not leaving either of you," the other woman, Jana, said.

The man sighed and shook his head, looking disgusted. "Get to cover, then. Hide and surprise them, kill as many as you can," he said resolutely.

He stepped off the trail and crouched behind a tree drawing his two long pistols from his belt. He cocked the first one and then the second, holding one in each hand. The two women crouched and hid behind bushes on the opposite side of the trail.

For a moment there was silence in the forest again, except for the sounds of birds and insects. Piotr looked down the trail and saw them, cresting the hill, starting down toward where the backpack was lying in the trail. Running in a single file line, nearly silent, Indian warriors. He quickly guessed that they numbered at least twenty. They could be Huron, he thought, but he knew they weren't. They were Iroquois.

The lead warrior came to a stop when he saw the backpack sitting in the trail, and the men behind him stopped as well. Piotr watched as they scanned the trees around the trail, looking for their prey, or perhaps suspecting a trap. He started back down the hill again, toward the backpack, at a walk. The others followed. His head was shaved, except for a central strip of long hair growing toward the back. He was tall and long-limbed, with ropy muscles down his arms and legs. He had green and white stripes painted on his left arm and shoulder.

From behind the log, Piotr looked down the hill at the bearded man with the long pistols. For some reason, perhaps he felt the gaze, he looked right back at Piotr, meeting his stare. The bearded man's eyes widened in surprise. He shook his head and blinked a few times, as if to clear his head. He quietly stood up and stepped around the tree onto the trail, drawing a bead with his right hand, and squeezing the trigger.

Jana crouched in the bushes next to the trail, hiding there with Malian. The handle of the knife in her hand was shaking but she did not feel fear. Her mind was strangely calm, and she was seeing everything with acute detail. She watched as Raul Montreaux breathed deeply behind the tree, gathering his strength. She could smell his breath; he was looking up the hill at something. Something that surprised him, as his eyes widened and then he blinked rapidly, shaking his head to clear it. She looked up the hill and saw a young man's head. He was peering over a log, back down the trail at their pursuers. He had longish, sandy brown hair, and was watching Montreaux intently, as if he were waiting for a signal.

Montreaux then stood up and turned toward the Seneca across the ditch, firing his right-hand pistol first. It went off with a flash and a bang, and a small cloud of white and gray poured forth from the barrel. The tall warrior snapped backward as the ball struck him in the shoulder; he staggered, then fell backward to the ground. Montreaux took aim with his left hand as the Seneca began to scatter in surprise. The pan flashed and the barrel erupted with smoke. He sent another ball at the Seneca, but in the haze of the smoke, Jana could not tell if he hit any of them. Suddenly a larger explosion of multiple muskets came from just up the hill.

The volley surprised and scattered the Seneca completely. They disappeared back into the trees, hiding behind whatever cover they could find.

"Reload."

She heard a one-word command in French from the hillside. Looking up from her hiding spot, she saw the young man and a large, bald man next to him through the cloud of smoke and leaves. The bald man was the one who had given the order.

An arrow zipped past her head, sticking into the ground between her and Montreaux. He holstered his right-handed pistol and drew his knife out. He flipped the other pistol around, so he was holding it by the barrel, like a club.

The Seneca began to reappear. As the smoke began to rise through the branches, she could see several of them working their way down the hillside toward their position, moving from cover to cover. They were not deterred by the surprise of the men behind the log on the hillside. They rightly made the determination that they still had a significant numeric advantage.

The first Seneca warrior to charge ran across the path from his hiding spot, jumped over the ditch, and landed just short of Montreaux with a tomahawk and knife in his hands. Montreaux came from around the tree, swinging the pistol like an ax at his head. The Indian deftly blocked it and thrust his knife toward Montreaux's throat. Montreaux parried it with his own knife, and the blades clanged together. The two men were locked for a moment, straining against each other, when the Seneca warrior stepped back and raised his foot, snap-kicking Montreaux in the chest, sending him sprawling onto his back on the trail. He stepped forward to deliver a killing blow to Montreaux as more Seneca came charging down the trail.

Malian came from his right silently, jumping out from the bush, swinging the stone tomahawk downward at his chest. He tried to block it, but the stone blade smashed into his forearm, biting into the flesh and crushing the bones below it with a cracking pop. He snarled in pain and whirled toward her, raising his knife in his left hand to stab her. Suddenly his knife went flying out of his hand as the young man charged down the hill from behind the log and smashed it with a long war club. Shocked and in pain, the Seneca froze for a second, but the sandy brown-haired young man did not. He followed his first strike with a second that smashed the stunned warrior in the chest, knocking him to his back, writhing in pain. Montreaux scrambled to his feet, sucking air in trying to catch his breath. Two more Seneca warriors clambered across the ditch, but they did not charge headlong into Malian and the young man with the club. They paused, squaring off just out of reach.

Jana stayed put, peering through the bush, out of sight, as Malian and the young man began to inch backward. Two more Seneca jumped across the ditch, joining the others, and they began to creep forward to engage. As they drew closer, Malian attacked with her stone tomahawk, swinging it overhead at the nearest one. He blocked it and grabbed her hand, pulling it down and twisting it so she spun toward him. He latched onto her throat with his other hand, dragging her backward toward the ditch. The young man jumped in swinging the club, but the other Seneca stepped in front blocking his advance. Malian gave a muffled scream of rage and snapped her teeth at his wrist, as she twisted to try and escape.

He was taking Malian.

As he backed toward the ditch with Malian struggling like a wildcat, Jana rose from her crouch under the bush and drove her knife into the warrior's right hip. She felt it hit home in his bones. She tried to pull it free, but it stuck. The Seneca warrior snapped his head back, snarling in pain, let go of Malian's throat and smashed Jana across the face with a backhanded fist.

Her head snapped back as his fist hit her eye socket, and she didn't feel herself falling and spinning backward to the ground under the bush. She blinked as sparkling light swarmed her field of vision. All of the sounds she heard became muffled. She looked up into the branches of the bush for what felt like half an hour but was only a few seconds. Suddenly, her vision cleared and she could hear screams of war and rage.

She looked up to see Malian had twisted free, biting the Seneca holding her on the wrist, freeing her hand with the stone tomahawk still in it. She had jumped backward away from him behind a protective shield of Montreaux and the young man with the club. The two Seneca engaged with the young man and Montreaux, swinging and thrusting knives and tomahawks. The other two warriors who had come across the ditch were closing in to strike the young man while he was occupied trying to swing his club at the warrior across from him.

The largest man she had ever seen charged down the hill from behind the log with an ax in each hand. He smashed the advancing Seneca warrior in the chest with a big ax in his right hand, cutting through meat and bone, crushing through his sternum, killing him before he hit the ground.

The other Seneca jumped back and away at the sight of the huge bald, bearded man. The giant man jerked the ax free from the chest of the warrior and turned to face them on the trail with Malian, Montreaux, and the young man.

As they backed away in confusion, a fusillade of three shots rang out, sending musket balls at the Seneca now coming down the hill. A cloud of smoke obscured everything as it was blasted down the hill toward her. Jana realized she could move now, and rolled to her feet, crouching as she ran through the bushes to get behind the men on the trail.

"Move! Up the hill!" someone shouted. She tried to run but stumbled and fell to her hands and knees.

Malian grabbed her clothes and pulled her to her feet. Arrows thumped into the trees and on the ground near her. Jana shook her head as she still was not seeing quite right. She felt something wet on her cheek as she used her hands to get to her feet and struggle up the hill. There were more men behind the log, coming up the hill, carrying muskets. One of them stopped and turned when he got to the trail, firing down the hill at the Seneca. Smoke was filling the trees now, obscuring the trail as they all ran up and away to the top of the hill.

When they got to the top, they didn't slow down. They ran as fast as they could.

One of the men said, "They're not gonna like this...us killing their friends. They will be coming after us."

"We have got to get back to camp, we can make a stand there."

Jana heard these men speak, but all of the words sounded like they were an echo across a big empty field. Still, she kept running, trying to keep up. Malian kept a hand on her, pulling her along as they went.

Finally, she saw a campfire smoking off the trail with her one good eye, and they all stumbled into the camp, scrambling for positions, reloading muskets and barricading hastily. Her stomach suddenly began to cramp and illness overwhelmed her. She staggered over to the back of the camp by a horse and a mule, retching silently as what little food was in her came out.

Malian came to her, bringing her closer to the others and helping her sit down near the small campfire. The large bald man brought a bladder canteen of water, and handed it to Jana, looking down at her face.

"She took quite a blow, but she will heal up fine," he said, kindly.

Montreaux borrowed powder and ball from Anton Paquet. He took the .58 caliber ball and shaved a bit of lead off with his knife so it would fit in his smaller chamber, then began reloading his long pistols.

As he gave him the powder and ball, Anton said, "You are one brave son of a bitch, sir, taking on a pack of Iroquois like that."

He said, "I had no choice. I thank you for your kindness, helping us like this. When I saw you behind the log there...I thought I was dreaming." He looked at Piotr.

Piotr said, "We heard a sound, a scream. We went down the trail to investigate and found the three of you coming toward us."

As he tapped down the ball in one of his long-barreled pistols, he said, "Raul Montreaux, first mate of the cargo ship *The Render*. This is Malian, and Jana."

"Piotr, Eggard, Anton, Abel, Gerard, Mason and Abraham." Heads nodded as muskets were reloaded.

Anton said, "So, just how is it you found yourself in the forest of the New World being chased by a group of angry Iroquois?"

"And why are they so angry with you?" asked Gerard.

"It's a long story...our ship stranded, we tried to row for shore in our longboat, and we got chased down by a pirating warship. Jana and I ended up separated from our group, and they rowed on without us, to Quebec City, hopefully. We found Malian, and she offered to lead us back through the forest trails. We were hoping to stay undiscovered, but we didn't. We ran into these fellows here, and they attacked. So, we ran. They stayed on us and I was about played out...then we ran into you, and we took our chance."

With that, a silence fell over the camp. Only the sounds of heavy breathing, insects, birds, and the wind moving through the leaves were heard. All remained still, watching, but no one came. Even the Paquet brothers were silent.

After a while, Eggard spoke. "They will wait till the sun is setting, for the shadows to get long, so they won't be seen until they are upon us."

"We need to set fires, over there, where they will be coming from," Abraham said.

"Take an ember, some kindling, head over and do it fast," Gerard agreed.

"I will go. I can still run fast, if need be," Abel said.

"Me too. I will go, I am faster than you, anyway, Abel," Mason said.

"It doesn't make sense to risk three men. Only one. I will go and light all three. Spread them out, so we can see who comes up the trail," Piotr said.

There was silence after he said it. He was right, but they did not know how close the Seneca were, or even if they were coming.

"I can take the bucket, filled with hot coals. Carry some logs and kindling. I can be fast."

Eggard thought about it. It made more sense than risking three men. "Go now, go and we will cover you from anyone on the trail or in the forest, before we lose the light of the day," he said.

Piotr grabbed the bucket and scooped some hot, glowing coals from the campfire into it with a stick. He grabbed a handful of dried grass and kindling, and some logs they had gathered and left next to camp. He gave Montreaux his matchlock musket to use, should it be needed. Jana sat up and watched with her good eye as he stepped out of the camp with an armload of logs to burn. Taking a last look around, he started off.

He ran awkwardly carrying the logs. He made it to a suitable spot and slid to a stop on his knees, brushing away debris. He set the grass and kindling out on the ground, stacking a few logs above it in a pyramid shape. He scraped a few red coals onto the dry grass, blowing gently. A small flame burst forth, catching the dry grass and spreading. Piotr gathered up the rest of the logs and kindling and started for the next spot to repeat the process, closer to the river. He felt rather than heard the footsteps coming from behind him and to his left. When he looked up, a Seneca warrior was silently charging him in a crouch, having snuck closer by using cover along the riverbed. He heard the explosion of a gunshot from the camp and a ball whizzed by in the air to his left, but it missed the incoming Seneca, who now was in a sprint directly at him with a long-handled club raised in the air.

He was caught in the process of setting down the remaining logs and kindling and instinctively judged he would not have time to complete that motion and pull out his knife or ax. So he didn't try to do that. He turned and, with a step and underhanded shove, threw the armload of logs at the charging man.

Already starting his swinging attack with his club, but unable to stop his advance in time, the warrior ran face first into the airborne firewood. His right-handed hold on the club was loosened, and it flew forward, smashing directly into Piotr's forehead, just above his eyes. Piotr's head snapped back and he stood, stunned for a split second, before toppling over backward onto the ground.

More Seneca began to charge forward, moving from cover to cover as they came toward the camp. Piotr realized he was in trouble, exposed on the ground, but he could not get his arms and legs to work. He looked back and saw blasts of smoke from the muskets at camp, but he did not hear them. He blinked and raised his hand to his face, feeling wetness, then looking at his hand. His fingers were covered in blood. Puffs of smoke were now exploding out of the tree line, as the Seneca began to fire their own muskets back at the camp. He rolled to his side, desperately trying to get his legs under him. He only heard a constant buzzing sound, as if a honeybee was flying inside his ear. The Seneca jumped from bushes to trees, trying to draw shots from the muskets, so that they could charge while the fur traders tried to reload.

The muskets from the camp had all fired, but Montreaux drew his long pistols and fired them one after the other at approaching Iroquois, giving Piotr a precious few seconds to restore his addled senses.

Piotr got to his knees, and then stood up shakily, fumbling to pull his ax from his belt. Unsteady on his feet, he turned to face the warrior who had run face first into the logs. He was now rising to his feet, a bit more steady than Piotr. The young Seneca warrior pulled a knife from his belt and began to advance on him.

Jana blinked to try and clear her vision. Her right eye was blurred, but she could see with her left that Piotr was fumbling to pull out his ax or knife. She screamed as she saw the Seneca warrior pull his knife and start toward him in a crouch, knife extended.

A musket shot rang out to her left, from up the trail along the river. The Seneca was struck in the ribs, falling to the ground just in front of Piotr. He rose up and then staggered sideways and fell again, flailing on the ground. Several more shots came from the trail, and whoops and screams. As Jana watched, another group of Indians began advancing on the Seneca.

"Huron. Those are Huron. Come on!" she heard someone say.

They rose up as one group and began to advance toward the Seneca in the trees. She heard them scream as they jumped over the makeshift barricade they had set. The Seneca in the trees whooped and yelled, but she could see them retreating, running back on the trail. The Huron screamed and yelled out taunts at them as they fled. The Seneca were unwilling to engage with the Huron now involved as well.

Piotr stood, a bit wobbly on his feet, but standing. His forehead had split right above his eyes, and was bleeding profusely down his face, as head wounds are prone to do. Jana and Malian got up and ran toward him, as the Huron and the men from camp all came to gather around, still pointing weapons at the trees where the Seneca had been.

Piotr looked blearily at his Huron rescuers, recognizing some of them from the target practice instruction he had completed with Thames at their camp. He blinked with blood tracing down across his nose and down his cheek. Chogan came forward from the group, raising his hand to Piotr's face, holding him by the chin to examine his wound.

"You see, I knew that one day you would be a great warrior! That is why I counted coup upon you! Now you will have a scar to show off."

Piotr smiled, eyes not quite focused. He said, "That...great shot, from there, you..."

"Did you not believe me when I told you? I am the best marksman of all the Huron, maybe of all the Frenchmen, too."

The group of fur traders and Huron smiled and breathed in the deep, cleansing air of victory. Clapping each other on the backs, shaking hands New World style by gripping forearms, and thanking the Huron for arriving when they did.

Piotr smiled awkwardly with his swollen face, grasping forearms with Chogan and nodded his thanks. His brain was struggling to form the words he wanted.

Anton Paquet said, "That's the first time I've seen firewood used in such a manner. Resourceful, eh! Too bad you didn't throw it a few steps earlier, maybe you wouldn't have taken a hammer to the face, eh!"

They laughed, together, relieved at being alive.

Chogan sent a few of his warriors to watch the trail and forest to see if the Seneca would return. He and his other Huron companions began to walk back toward camp with Abraham, Gerard, and Abel Paquet.

Jana and Malian approached, and Montreaux went to help Jana, who was also still a little unsteady on her feet. Blood still dripped down her swollen cheek from the cut that split open on her eye socket, running through her eyebrow. Her eye was swollen and turning purple now, distorting her face. She and Malian walked into the group, and she found herself standing next to Piotr.

"Well, you two make quite a pair, I must say. Faces all smashed up together like that," Eggard said. He put his large arms out and steadied Piotr in one and Jana in the other. "Come, let us get you looked after, and talk to our rescuers." The group made their way back to the campsite.

Anton asked, "Mr. Montreaux, I want to hear the full story of how you got here again. You say your ship stranded, eh? Where did this happen?"

"In the gulf." He nodded and gestured with his head. "Les Iles de la Madeleine. We were trying to hide out from a storm, a nor'easter, behind the islands. Our anchor broke loose and we stranded on the sand. The hull got sucked down into it, and that was it."

The Paquets and Eggard understood, remembering what they found on the island. Piotr found himself having a hard time keeping up with conversation, and realized his head was pounding. He sat back next to the campfire and rested. Jana laid down across from him, rolling to her left side, while Malian looked her wound over.

Gerard put his hand on Montreaux's shoulder. "We found the island you speak of. We stopped to look; there was a fire burning on the island, a big fire. We found what must have been your campsite. Do you know of what I speak?"

"You found it? Was anybody alive?" Montreaux asked.

"We found many bodies. We did find one man alive, but he was severely wounded. He had been shot. He was the captain of the stranded ship. Your ship. He said his name was Laurent, Gilbert Laurent. He sailed with us, back to Quebec City. He was still alive when we left to come here...for this."

Montreaux shook his head in despair. "Captain Laurent alive...the men. All dead. I knew it had all gone wrong. When the ship that attacked followed us. In our longboat. *The Render* was trailing it. They sent *The Render* after us. And it followed us, but it was being sailed by a Swedish crew, I think."

"Swedish. Here, now, too. Like everybody else. Trying to get a piece of the New World," Anton said.

"I don't know, but they were definitely pirating. They did not want us alive, that I know."

Eggard gathered smoked bison meat and added it to the stew pot over the campfire. "We can work all this out, but let us get these people fed, and thank God we are all alive," he said.

Montreaux was thinking. "I thank you all again for helping us. But I think we have made an enemy, with these Seneca."

Eggard nodded. "They know now we have allied with the Huron. That will give them cause to attack us. It also gives them a reason to think about that. Chogan and his men are no pushovers. We will need to be on our guard at all times. Even more so."

# Chapter 19

# SPRING RAINS

Each week Lucien Greely made the journey from his cabin near the ferry to the construction site of the first church in the New World. Along the way, he stopped in to check on local farmers, collecting "taxes" from the people who plowed their fields with one eye staring into the trees, watching for native savages.

Remy and the two elderly Chippewa men were following his directions perfectly, which was highly unusual. These directions were easily followed, though. Take your time. Dawdle. He did not want the church building finished before the fur traders came back with their goods. He wanted it all timed just right, so that their goods were on the dock, ready to be plucked. He figured the attack on the fur traders should be just before they got things loaded onto their ship. The cannon would be fired, to drive off the savages, but unfortunately, the ship would take terrible damage. And their goods would be diminished greatly.

He wondered if the old priest and his red-haired helper would put up a fuss, if they were around during the attack. He figured a donation to the church would keep that old buzzard from speaking up. If that weren't enough, he would simply disappear. Lucien Greely was not a man that you should cross.

Today, he walked down the dock with his heavy steps thudding on the wooden planks, announcing his arrival well before he got there. Much to his disappointment, he could see that the stones had been placed for the foundation of the church, and the first logs had been laid on them.

The outline of the building was in place and anchored already. *How in the hell had they got that far?* Remy, that dimwit, should know better.

Sister Mary saw him coming.

"Well, our benefactor is here... Mr. Greely, it is good to see you. Your son Remy has certainly been a lot of help to us. Though he is a careful worker, I must say."

He saw that the red-haired priest was there, working, and the two old Chippewa drunks. Remy was cutting a notch in a log on the opposite side of the lot where the church would eventually stand. Lucien recognized the old nun, but did not remember her name, just that she was bossy, and seemed to know everybody's business.

"Well, Sister, I have taught all my boys, in the business of building, leave nothing to chance," he replied with a homespun rural epithet to end her inquiry.

"Well, Mr. Greely, there is very little chance these walls will fall, I can say that with all honesty. They are the most carefully constructed cabin walls in the whole of the New World."

"Well, better built right than falling and leaking come winter time, eh, Sister?"

He was not going to be dragged into a discussion about the work when he was providing labor for free. Well, almost free. They would get paid for their work later.

He left the red-headed priest and the nun where they stood, striding through the future rooms of the church, stepping over the carefully laid logs. He looked up at the sky and shouted back at the old bag and the young priest. "It looks like the weather will be going to the dogs, anyway. I doubt you will get far today."

As he strode away over the future wall of the church, he could hear the old nun questioning his weather predicting skills with the young priest. He was not making friends with that one, he was certain.

Remy was engrossed with chopping the log to notch the ends and didn't notice him coming up from behind. He startled in mid-ax-swing when Lucien addressed him.

"Well, you dumbass, you are mucking this one up too, I see. Why the hell are you working so fast? You already got the walls laid out, for chrissakes! It will be up in no time at this rate!"

"You scared the hell out of me," Remy said, shaking his head. "I have to get the small room at the back done, so I can hide the cannon, you know."

Lucien looked over the framework of the building, outlined with logs lying on the ground. He was right about that. The back room would face the dock, right at the ship. They could open the door when the time came and blast the shit out of it. At least the smelly-breathed fool was thinking about the future, he had to give him that.

"I see that. Just remember, those bastards won't be back for a good while yet. Don't get so far along that the old hag and the red-headed virgin are moving into the place, with that buzzard of a priest writing his letters... Just get enough done. No more."

"I know what to do," Remy replied dryly.

Maybe he was growing a pair, finally.

Lucien turned and headed off without another word. He looked out at the ship at the dock, waiting to be loaded. He saw a bent old man and a short fellow wiping down the sides of the ship. They seemed to be taking good care of it, he thought bitterly. But his cruel, happy smile returned to his face as he felt the first drops of rain. He gave a wave at the old nun and pointed at the sky, shaking his head as he walked away.

The work on the river barge left Piotr with a pounding headache. He had a particularly hard time swinging the ax. The thud of the blade into the wood traveled up through the handle, into his arms, right to his forehead. A knot the size a tin cup had formed on his forehead, like a horn trying to sprout from his skull. A cut where the skin had split was trying to close over the swollen knot, but the swelling was keeping the two sides of the wound from mending. Eggard thought they could not even stitch it, because the swelling was too severe. So, it wept a clear and red fluid and drained down the bridge of his nose. It was like he was crying tears of blood much of the time. He looked horrible, but he felt worse.

Chogan and his Huron warriors had stayed for a day and a half after the conflict with the Seneca, keeping watch with the rest of the men. Then they had left, scouting farther on down the trail, where the Seneca had last been seen. He really did not care about what Chogan or the Huron thought. He also didn't care about the Paquet brothers or Eggard ribbing him about his head wound. But having to look two women in the face, especially young and attractive women, was hard to do. He couldn't help but notice that when they talked to him their eyes wandered north from his eyes, staring at the massive lump on his forehead, and the leaking wound dripping down his face.

Jana's face was healing faster than his. Her eye socket and cheekbone were still purple, black, and blue, but the cut that ran through her eyebrow had closed on its own. Her young skin was supple enough to allow it to close, despite the swelling. In another few days, she would only have some discoloration on her skin. Piotr thought that she had remarkable eyes. They glowed with a greenish blue joy when she accomplished something. She was quiet in her confidence, silently smiling at her own success. She ate only her fair share and did more than an equal amount of work. He also noticed that she was a quick learner. Each of the Paquet brothers had found a reason to teach her some important skill related to river barge building.

Even under these trying circumstances, Malian was stunningly beautiful. But none of the Paquet brothers seemed to take an interest in her in the same way as they did Jana. It wasn't that she was a savage. It was that she seemed to be attached to Montreaux. She deferred to him, she sat with him to eat, she counseled with him on all matters. And he deferred to her. Always thanking her politely for each of her kindnesses, like bringing him food or a bladder canteen of water. In many ways, they behaved like a couple, but Piotr noticed that they did not sleep in the same bedroll, but next to each other. The three of them took a position on the opposite side of the campfire from him each night.

He was surprised, as he sat down by the fire after having packed up for departure back to the camp in the green valley the next day, when Malian and Jana came to him and insisted he go to the river with them.

"Piotr, I wish to see that wound cleaned," Malian said.

Jana reached down and grasped him by the forearm, pulling him to his feet. He looked at them dubiously, not wanting the help or attention, but also not wanting to say no. He left with them, walking through the scrub plants and grass to the river.

He heard the Paquets behind him making fun, and his cheeks reddened, which made his forehead hurt again.

"Yes, Piotr, come to the river and take a bath with us, while you're down there!"

"Come on Piotr, we are going to clean you up."

"Clean you all over."

"We'll take care of you good, Piotr!"

He wasn't sure which one was saying what, and he did not look back at them.

Jana and Malian had no such compunction, both turning their heads and glaring until silence overcame them, for a moment.

At the river, Malian told Piotr to take off his shirt, and she produced a clean poultice from her bag, wetting it in the waters of the Cuyahoga.

"We have to clean his head and body, especially his hair and his hands, so when he touches it, it won't get dirty," she instructed Jana.

Jana didn't hesitate, even though Piotr did, and she began to pull his shirt up over his head. He stopped her and stepped back, easing the shirt up, over his swollen forehead. She took it and wetted it in the river, scrubbing out some of the dark spots and then setting it on a rock to dry. She then laid him back in the water and began scrubbing him everywhere. She used sand to rub him down, knocking off all of the big chunks, at least. She had him lie back over her knee and dipped his head back in the water, washing out his now-long sandy brown hair. For a moment, he found himself relaxing, and closed his eyes as she removed the dirt and debris from his scalp.

Surprisingly to himself, he cared little about taking his shirt off. He was certain they had both seen men in far worse positions than this, and were only being nice in attempting to help him. When they led him out, Malian showed Jana how to clean the wound with her knife, carefully scraping away dead and loose skin. With the poultice tied around his head, he slept soundly that night, for the first time since the Seneca had cracked him.

The next morning the group started out early for the return trip to camp. The river barge was so heavy they didn't try to take it out of the water. Instead, the Paquets, Montreaux, and Malian moved it to an island in the middle of the bend of the river. They pulled it up as far as they could, tying it off to a large river birch that had sprouted a few decades earlier, its expanding roots causing the island to grow.

Their return trip to the main camp was easier, with no massive dug-outs to drag behind Mule and the horse. Muskets and a backpack allowed them to travel light, with the axes and other tools on the pack animals. They made good time, arriving in a day and three-fourths, just as the sunset was beginning at the camp. Linville and Flagger greeted them as they made their way down the hill past the forge and Piotr's lean-to. They were surprised by the addition of the three strangers.

"Welcome back, gentlemen! I see that our numbers have grown? It seems you have a story," Captain Linville said.

Eggard greeted him with a handshake. "We do, Captain, we do. It was not all wine and roses."

The Paquet brothers went to work unloading the horse and Mule and depositing their gear at the cabin.

"Is there any food?" Anton asked as he walked by toward the cabin.

Flagger waved to him and the rest. "We have suffered since Eggard's departure with you, but we have food enough in the large pot, some beaver, and Thames shot a deer. We also found a stash of ramps growing near camp. Eggard, you would be proud, I made a stew with all of it together and some salt and kitchen pepper." Flagger said this with a proud smile from under his beard.

Linville noticed Piotr's head, and looked Jana over, as well. He noticed the black and blue under her eye, and the cut still healing on her eye socket. Piotr's wound was more obvious with the poultice tied around his head.

Linville said, "I assume you two didn't do this to each other?"

"No, sir, we had a run-in with some Iroquois. Seneca, to be exact," Piotr said.

"Well, you're still standing, so it must have gone okay. Come, all of you, get some supper before they eat it all. And it looks like rain is coming." He pointed up at the darkening skies.

Eggard said, "Thank you, Flagger, for making the stew. Captain, this is Jana, Malian, and Raul Montreaux."

Linville looked carefully at Montreaux's face. "I believe I know you, sir."

"Saint-Malo," Raul Montreaux extended his hand, "we have met in Saint-Malo. Raul Montreaux. You are the captain of the *St. Longinus.* Captain...Linville?"

"Yes, I am. What happened that got you all the way out here?"

"That is quite a story, Captain. One I can hardly believe myself. I had the good fortune of meeting these two fine women, without whom I would not be alive." He looked at the two of them with genuine gratitude.

"Come then, let's get you all fed and you can tell us your story."

The group headed to the cabin and Flagger passed out bowls of his meat stew. A hot meal under a roof was greatly appreciated by all, especially the three newcomers. Outside, the wind picked up, and dark clouds began to roll in. The rain came down in fits and starts as they sat eating, and it gathered strength as the sun fell below the horizon. By nightfall, a steady rain was falling, soaking everything to the bone. Piotr had left his backpack under the lean-to and was hoping it stayed dry. The angle of the rain and wind was such that the rain would blow into the forge. It would be soaked and difficult to light tonight. A wet night with no heat from the fire was not appealing. Sleeping undercover in the cabin was looking like the better option. With the three newcomers, he assumed it would be a crowded room, but that did not bother him at all. The group talked through the evening, well into the darkness of the night. The stories of how everyone came to be in this lush green valley were told. Having a new person to talk with was a rare treat in the forest, and both sides enjoyed the conversation.

As he'd said, Montreaux knew of Captain Linville and Thames from Saint-Malo. In turn, they knew who he was; his reputation as a quality first mate was common knowledge among the seafaring folk in the port. Montreaux, his memory sparked by the conversation, recalled having sailed on a fishing vessel with Thames when he was a young man. He remembered him as a competent young sailor and deckhand.

The rain stayed steady with occasional claps of thunder and flashes of lightning. Jana and Malian sat quietly in the corner. Grateful for the warmth of the fire and the hot food, it was not long before eyes grew weary in the darkness of the night. Having lived outdoors since their departure from the Abenaki village, Jana actually felt strange trying to sleep under a roof. Linville and Flagger offered up the cabin for them to sleep in, but they insisted that everyone be undercover on a night such as this. They all spread out bedrolls and collapsed into sleep, dry and warm, despite the storm outside.

The valley was lush and green with the heart of spring having passed and the warmth of summer. It had been a very wet spring early on but had been unusually dry for a couple of weeks. As was often the case, a dry spell leads to rain. This rain fell heavy and got heavier as the night went on. Long rolling blasts of thunder echoed down on the valley with flashes of lightning spraying the sky from time to time. Flagger was the only one who heard it, because he was the only one awake. He sat outside the cabin under the roof overhang, on a pile of firewood stacked against the wall near the front door, watching the rain, his long legs stretched out on the logs as he reclined against them. He took the time to smoke his long-stemmed clay pipe, enjoying the little bit of tobacco left in his pouch. He figured he'd stay up for a few hours, just to be watchful. Though it was unlikely that anyone would be out on a night like this.

The thunder and lightning were enough to get him to occasionally turn his head and stare out across the camp. The flashes lit up the area, allowing him to see in the dark, if only for a moment. After a bit, he sagged back into the logs, relaxing like they were a rocking chair. He could feel drowsiness taking hold of his mind, and he closed his eyes for a moment. They snapped open when the lightning blasted overhead and thunder rolled across the valley shaking the very ground.

Strangely, he felt as if the shaking of the ground continued, unabated. Then he heard a snapping and popping sound that was not rain, thunder, or the crack of lightning in the sky. It was followed by a rumble and more snapping and popping, but he could not place its location.

He jumped to his feet, looking around the camp, unsure of what was happening. A tree splintered and crash to the ground up the hill. He ran the few steps to the corner of the cabin and looked out into the rain, trying to use a flash of lightning to see what was making the noise. He froze when he saw it, unsure how to react. His clay pipe fell from his open lips, past his thick beard, to the ground.

The meteor that formed the rock fell from the sky. It was superheated by the friction of the molecules rubbing against the gases in the atmosphere. By the time it struck the ground, it was a combination of molten and solid rock. It exploded with the impact on the Earth's surface. The explosion was so strong that it scattered the innards of the meteor back into the sky, spewing them in all directions for more than two thousand miles. Bits of it came raining down far away from the impact.

The chunk of of it that formed the rock on the hillside in the green valley weighed one hundred and fifty-eight pounds when it was propelled skyward away from the impact crater. It shed pieces of itself while flying through the air in molten drops, spraying them across the countryside. When it came to earth in a muddy swamp it was superheated, and it plunged down into the soft ground, baking the mud that folded around it into rock. In just seconds that material hardened under the pressure and heat. For years it sat there, smoking and steaming, and finally cooling, underground. Its journey across the surface of the earth began and then lasted millions of years, finally bringing it to rest on the hillside of this lush green valley. Now, the spring rainstorm softened the ground, and the rock began the last leg of its journey.

It started gradually, sliding a few millimeters in the wet mud, then stopping again. As the dirt gave way, it slid downward a few feet, thumping against the trunk of a spruce tree. The tree strained, holding the weight for a few seconds before splintering with a cracking pop, and the rock slid right through the stump, roots, and mud. The hillside steepened and the rock nosed down and rolled over itself, and all eighteen tons began to tumble. It smashed through an immature stand of maple trees and rhododendron bushes and blew right through the side of an oak that had shaded them. This caused the oak to fall sideways on the hill with a loud crash, shaking the earth as the rock gained momentum. It tumbled and bounced now, gathering speed, and annihilating everything in its path.

The hill steepened even more and, for a moment, the rock was airborne, traveling some thirty feet before the hill flattened and it thudded on the ground, shaking and rumbling. It rolled toward the base of the hill and began to slow on the flattening surface as it approached the camp of fur traders, seamen, and lost souls sleeping in the cabin.

In the dark and the rain, Flagger squinted in stunned amazement as the rock came down the hill and took its last tumble, then crashed to a stop. It landed on the anvil that sat next to Piotr's forge. The crashing impact made a loud ringing metallic clang as the rock drove itself onto the hardened iron point of the anvil. The rock split open with the impact, nearly breaking itself into two pieces, and came to rest on top of it. Bits of wood, dirt, leaves, and moss were sprayed in all directions on its path, outlining the trail of destruction it left, until coming to rest a mere forty feet from the corner of the cabin where he stood.

It had happened so fast, in the rain and the thunder, that Flagger did not even process the need to run. He walked toward it, not caring about getting wet, his eyes wide open in the darkness and rain. Halfway between the cabin and the now-split rock, he stopped and turned, staring at the cabin of sleeping people, calculating the trajectory. If the rock had kept coming down the hill...he rubbed his wet beard as he got closer, shaking his head in disbelief.

He pushed on it with his hand, checking the stability. It was not moving anywhere. It had cracked open like an egg when striking the anvil and came to its final resting place.

He looked back at the cabin, still shaking his head, and said aloud to nobody, "In all my days..."

His eyes went skyward, and his hands made the sign of the cross.

As the sun rose, so did the occupants of the camp. The rain had stopped, leaving everything wet and chilly in the early morning air. They stood in a circle around Piotr's lean-to, with surprised, bemused, and somewhat disbelieving expressions. All were there, except Flagger, who slept soundly on the logs stacked outside the cabin, his clay pipe in his left hand. He had been up till nearly dawn, too shocked and surprised to fall back asleep.

It was obvious in the morning light from the trail of destruction coming down the hill that, had the rock not been stopped where it split on the anvil, it would have continued into the cabin. The cabin where they all slept peacefully, dry, and warm during the storm.

Heads were shaken in disbelief at their good fortune. Together, they whispered and shouted, laughed and wondered, how such a thing could happen?

Slowly, the group began to drift off to take care of the necessary morning tasks of running a camp. Finally, Piotr was left standing with Linville, Eggard, Montreaux, Malian, and Jana.

Linville said, "Mr. Montreaux, I was going to suggest that you and the ladies stay, if that is your intent, and we would add on to Piotr's lean-to. Possibly turn it into a second cabin. Now, I am not so sure. We will need to move that rock out of there, maybe even finish breaking it into two pieces."

Montreaux said, "Thank you, Captain. With your permission, we have talked, and we will stay on for some time. At least until we can get an escorted passage to Quebec City. The forest can be a dangerous place, we have learned...but rest assured, we will pull our own weight."

"I am not the least bit concerned about that. Our workload is not small. We need to hunt to keep the camp fed, and you look the part. We need help with drying and processing the fur. The list of things to get done does not get any smaller."

"I am no hand as a hunter, I am a sailor and fisherman by trade, but I will do my best. Malian, though, is an expert. She kept us alive on the trail." Montreaux gestured to her.

"We need all the help we can get, we appreciate it," Linville said.

Eggard said, "Piotr and I will help you with building more shelter. And we can all use the cabin when it rains. Provided it is not raining large rocks down on us."

Piotr stepped closer to the rock, seeing something shiny on the side of it. It was pyrite. This made him curious. He had seen enough rocks in his father's shop that had gold embedded in them. Separating the rock from the gold was difficult, but fool's gold was frequently present in rocks that had actual gold in them.

He got down on his knee and peered into the split in the rock. He thought he saw something shiny, but it was too dark for him to get a clear enough view. He went to the forge, placing some sticks, and looked around for some wood to add to it.

Jana asked, "Do you need an ember?"

"Yes, please, I want to get the forge lit and use a torch to get a look at what is up in that rock."

Jana went down the hill to the central campfire.

Linville peered into the crack. "I cannot make out what is inside there. Maybe we could hook up Mule, and the horses, see if we can pull it backward off of the anvil?"

"I think we could do it with them pulling. We have lifted houses with'em, don't know why we can't pull this thing off. I will get the ropes," Eggard said.

Jana came back, carrying a piece of pine bark with an ember glowing in the center. She had some dried moss as well, and soon had it lit. She and Piotr stoked the forge, building the fire. Piotr showed her the bellows, and she fed air into the fire to make it grow. Piotr wrapped a stick of pine in a strip of oilcloth and dipped it into the flames. It lit quickly, and he knelt down with it to put light into the crack in the massive rock.

Squinting and peering into the opening, trying to see around the anvil wedged into the crack and the flickering light from the torch, he got a glimpse of what he had thought might be there. It was shiny, with yellow and brown shades, fingering out through the core of the massive boulder; the center of the stone was crusted and splintered with it. A large vein of gold embedded in the center of the rock itself.

He sat back and stared at the crack, blinking, as he tried to process all that he had just learned. He had seen gold every day working in his father's shop. He had watched as his father extracted it from stone and molded it into ingots, as well as amazing pieces of jewelry. These pieces were always small. The largest stone with gold in it that he had seen was the size of a small hat. This was the size of a cooking pot. If what he saw was real...the value of it could be massive.

He turned toward Captain Linville. "You should look at this."

"What do you see?"

"I'm not certain, but it is shiny. Take a look and see if you see it as well."

Linville crouched down, peering into the space with the torch, squinting against the smoke. He caught a glimpse of a shiny, sparkling reflection of the torch's firelight.

"Piotr, is that..."

"I do not know for certain."

"It's gold?"

"That is what it looks like when it is raw, still in the rock. I watched my father extract it from rock many times in his shop."

Eggard arrived with Mule and some rope.

"Tie it on, see if we can roll it back off the anvil."

They got it tied off with some effort, anchoring the ropes to the edges of the rock. Despite his considerable strength, Mule was unable to budge it. Eggard called up the Paquet brothers and Flagger, along with Montreaux, Jana, and Malian. Linville and Piotr pushed on the opposite side. They strained; still the rock would not budge. They spent half the day at it, with no movement at all. Sweating as the sun rose to the middle of the sky, the group grew weary, and were close to giving up.

"Piotr, are you sure this is worth it? We are wasting a day," Anton asked.

"It will be more than worth it if what I saw inside there is real."

Linville, holding his lower back with his right hand, and sweating in the sun, said, "We will give it one more go."

"Hello the camp!"

A shout came from the stream. They all looked down the hill to see Thames and the rest of the men, returning in the dugouts and birchbark canoes, laden with pelts.

"My god! Look at those canoes, they are going to sink under the weight of all the fur!" Abel said.

As a group, they ran down to greet them. The canoes were overladen with the weight of the beaver pelts. Only half the men were returned with this group.

Flagger, having risen from his sleep on the logs, asked, "The men, where are the men?"

"We had so many furs, we couldn't fit. Some are walking back, trapping for another day then walking here in the morning. They will carry the furs on their backs. We went down another mile or so from where you were, Captain, and found a chain of ponds extending many miles to the west. There are dozens in every pond. Too many to count. We have only just gotten started," Thames answered excitedly.

Linville nodded approvingly. "Well done, then. Any other troubles? Savages?"

"We have been watched from the forest by a few sets of eyes. I can tell you that. But none have approached."

Flagger grabbed the front of a dugout and began pulling it ashore. "We have had our share of excitement around here, too. Let's get these unloaded!"

Shouts of excitement sprang up from the men. A few jumped into the stream to pull the canoes ashore and unload the haul of beaver pelts. Thames came up the hill to Linville, shaking hands.

"Welcome back and well done! We have something to show you."

After the canoes were unloaded, and a midday meal consumed, the whole group were now holding onto various ropes, which were attached to Mule and a packhorse. They were all ready to pull, waiting on Linville's signal.

"Steady now, altogether! Go!" he shouted.

The ropes snapped taut with tension. Thames, Flagger, Piotr and others on one, and Montreaux, Eggard, and the rest of the men on the other. Malian and Jana managed the horse and Mule. Linville and the Paquet brothers were pushing down on long poles of spruce jammed under the two halves of rock, trying to lever it loose. Linville watched carefully and saw some movement in the massive boulder. It was working.

"Keep pulling!"

The rock slowly moved backward away from the hanging roof of the lean-to. The anvil was stuck in the crack and rose up off the stump with the movement.

"Harder!" Linville exhorted the group.

They redoubled their efforts and the rock rolled backward more, then suddenly split into two pieces, falling open with the core exposed to the sun for the first time in two hundred million years. The ropes all lost their tension and the people pulling on them lost their footing, falling to the ground. Rising up from the grass on the hillside, they all stopped and stared at what they saw inside the rock.

Yellow and brown, grainy and fingering out in all directions, clearly defined against the deep dark gray of the granite, was raw gold, shining in the sun. The group fell silent, staring at the beauty of the rock.

Malian looked around at the faces of the Frenchmen. The look in their eyes was not something she had seen before. They were staring at the rock the way men do when they lust. When they covet what has never been theirs. She was taken aback, and uncomfortable. She saw that even Jana stared at the rock too, as if it were magical and held some kind of hypnotic power. In her confusion, she looked to Montreaux, to see his face.

He too was staring, but his eyes broke away from looking at the shiny yellow rock and met hers. His eyes crinkled at the corners as he smiled.

Linville was the first to speak.

"It seems our luck is in, gentlemen. Mon dieu, our luck is really in."

The camp of men, women, horses, and a mule collectively roared with excitement.

The Paquet brothers ran up to stare at the broken pieces of rock, touching it and dancing around with excitement. Thames and Flagger ran their hands over the shiny, hard rock and shook their heads in disbelief. Eggard took off his dirty linen cap and rubbed it on the rock surface, to see the effect. Some of the more yellow gold glinted a little brighter in the sun. He spat on his cap and rubbed it harder on the stone.

Piotr stared at it for a moment, then looked at Jana. She met his gaze, and this time her eyes did not drift upward to the knot on his forehead. He walked over to the forge and his tools and pulled out the chisel. It was not very big, he thought. *I may have to make a bigger one.* He pulled out the sledge and balanced it in his hands. It would do.

Jana stood on the other side of the forge, and asked him, "Have you ever seen anything like this?"

He nodded. "I have. My father was a goldsmith. I have seen dozens of rocks with raw gold in them, but never anything so big. I am not sure how I am going to get it out of the rock."

"This is your job?"

"I am the smithy, at least here, in the wilderness. It will be my job. No one else here has any idea how to do it."

"Can you do this alone?" Jana asked.

"It will be easier with help. Truthfully, I am not certain about how to go about it entirely. I was young and I never finished training, but I will do my best, I suppose."

"I will help you. If you wish. My father was a window maker and I often helped him in his shop. He taught me to be a good assistant."

Piotr nodded his head and blushed a little, which caused his forehead to throb.

"I will take all the help you can give."

That evening, the company sat around the central campfire. A few pieces of venison were roasting on the sticks serving as rotisserie spit. The mood of the group was high and excited. Not only were the beaver pelts stacking up fast, the incredible find of gold inside the rock had set the group's collective imaginations on fire. Whispers and secret conversations were constant. These men seeking their fortune were now certain they had found it. After they had eaten and settled down a bit, Captain Linville stood and addressed the men of the *St. Longinus*. He began with his story.

"Where I grew up, in the town of Grigny, no one had any money. We were all poor. Not just my family, mind you, I mean everybody. We lived only an hour's walk from Paris, but no one ever went there. It was as if it were another world. We were not skilled tradesmen, we were laborers, working for other people. My father worked every day, every single day, till he dropped dead. My mother never stopped trying to make things better for us, and she too worked until she dropped dead from it."

He looked around to measure the audience. The men had stopped milling about, gathering in a group, listening.

"When my wife died, she had never known riches. I had some luck early delivering cargo after I bought the *St. Longinus*, mostly barrels of salted fish and molasses, but all of the money was going to pay for the boat, or the next journey. I spent everything I made just to keep working. My wife never got to experience actual wealth. She worked every day of our life together, until she too, died from it."

The audience nodded. They had known and respected this man. Many had worked on his ship for a long time. In that time, he had never spoken of his past, except to a select few. This was the most they had ever learned about his life outside of the ship.

"My son and daughter, they have never known the security of not having to work for food money. Many of you know my son, an apprentice shipbuilder in Saint-Malo, and my daughter, who married a bookmaker in Paris. She is probably the richest Linville ever, and she lives week to week with her husband and my grandchildren."

He raised his hands outward to the group, as if he were holding up the words.

"And I have been very lucky. Very lucky. Most men that start working on fishing boats as a kid, they never get to own a ship. They get to work their fingers to the bone, with rope burns and blisters, until they die at sea. I know how lucky I have been. I am grateful for it." He paused for a long moment.

Anton Paquet shouted, "Lucky again, Captain, all of us, lucky again!"

"We are, Anton, we are. But why? Why us? Why are we so lucky? Do we deserve it? I don't know, I don't know. But I have learned that hard work brings good luck. And this crew has worked hard, and hardly complained. Nary a word, even when food supplies have run low. We made it across the sea together, we have made the trek to this valley together. We have had tremendous success. And, with our Pelletier leading us, we are finding the furs!"

He pointed at Thames, and cheers rang out.

"Now, a different kind of luck has followed our hard work. Luck like I have never seen. And it may play out well for all of us. It may, but it probably will not."

A long pause, then their faces grew more somber, curious, and confused.

"I have not had my own wealth, but I have known men who had

wealth, real wealth, so much wealth that they did not have to worry about food anymore. They did not have to worry about the cost of the roof over their heads or doing business. Many of those men had so much that they couldn't spend it...but none of them were happy. They were lucky, but not happy."

Gerard Paquet said, "Not to disagree, Captain, but I would rather have the money than not. We all have been poor, poor enough to starve. A little security seems good to me."

"And I as well, Gerard. Security is a good thing. No disagreement there," Linville acknowledged. Most of the men were probably thinking the same thing. "You will have your security, because we will have money. Piotr is going to crack that rock and dig out the veins of gold on the inside, and we are going to carry it all back with us."

"Aye, Piotr, aye!" someone shouted.

The men followed with a collective, "Aye."

Linville continued, "The gold, and the furs. We will sell it all and divvy up the money. To make it clear...we had an agreement with the fur, when you signed on with the ship. That agreement stands. For the fur. For the gold, I had no hand in finding it, Flagger saw it first, and Piotr will have to dig it out, and each crewman will get an equal share. Equal."

The crew of the *St. Longinus* cheered together, clapping and shouting. Several men slapped Piotr on the back, causing him to blush, which made his forehead hurt.

Several men made comments.

"Each man gets the same amount. Seems righteous and fair."

"What will be, will be the same for all."

Piotr was standing and watching. He was certain that they did not realize the difficulty of getting the gold from the rock. He was also certain that they did not understand purity. It might not be all that valuable if the gold was not pure. He did not know how to find out the purity of the gold in the rock. Therefore, he could not know its value. That would have to wait until they got back to civilization. Probably not Quebec City, but Saint-Malo, or even Paris.

Eggard had been listening to the whole speech attentively. He stood up, his great height making the group take notice. "We have three new-comers in camp, three people who have joined our merry crew of fur traders and knights-errant. I believe they have as much right to the discovery inside the rock as any of us."

Jana and Malian recoiled in fear, from their seat on the ground near the fire. Jana's eyes opened wide, and she pulled her knees up toward her chest. Most men would be furious about sharing any of their wealth with a woman, let alone something so valuable. Montreaux stood up and stepped toward Eggard, extending his hand in friendship. "We cannot, gentlemen, in good faith, accept Eggard's offer. We are imposing upon your good will enough, by simply being here with you in the forest."

"Yes, you can...accept our offer...I mean, and you will," Thames said as he walked out of the circle of men and shook Montreaux's hand as well. "You have done just as much as anybody in regard to that big rock. You three were here when it fell. Many of us were not even back in camp yet. We were still in the forest on canoes. Now the fur, yes, we have taken that risk. But the rock? I see no difference between us in regard to that."

Linville looked the group over in the firelight. "Any objections?"

No hand was raised. Jana and Malian, surrounded by rough men, but rough men who had just gifted them something of considerable value, were unsure of how to respond. They sat quietly watching with wide eyes.

Linville smiled broadly and raised his arms up in the air. "Well then, gentlemen, let us finish our work. Then we will find our way back with these furs and rocks of gold! For the first time, in my life anyway, we will really be rich. And we will have one hell of a story to tell when we see Saint-Malo again, eh?"

The crew rousingly shouted their agreement, stood, and began to scatter and mill about, chatting before attending to the camp chores of the evening.

Linville and Thames made their way over to Piotr through the men. "I see you got a scratch. Was it well earned, at least?" Thames asked.

"It was hard earned," Piotr said.

Thames grabbed him by the shoulders and looked at the poultice on his forehead that was getting dirtier and dirtier as the day went on.

"You sure that is all that happened?" Thames was looking over at Jana and Malian and shaking his head. "You, Eggard, and the Paquet brothers go into the wilderness to build a boat and come out with two women? Hell of a story."

"I cannot explain it."

"Can you do what you need to do," Thames cast a sideways glance at Jana, "to the rock, I mean."

Piotr blushed a little, never having done anything with a girl, and said, "I think so. It will take time. Several days, maybe weeks."

Linville said, "Get to it then. We will have Jana be your helper. Montreaux and Malian will go about hunting and food gathering for the crew. We will all be hungry again in a couple of days, unless we improve our stocks. They can be useful and help Eggard with that."

So, Piotr thought, a plan had been set. Putting it in motion would be harder than anyone knew. It was going to be a large amount of work, but he wasn't afraid of work. He had to admit, though, he was a little afraid of what would happen if it didn't work out.

## Chapter 20

# THE TRAIL BACK

The ringing of the sledge on the steel became a familiar sound in the green valley, and the French fur trappers often looked up the hill appreciatively while working by the stream. They saw Piotr and Jana banging away at the rock, sweating in the mid-day sun. He showed her how to follow the vein of iron pyrite and to free up the gold-infused rocks hidden underneath. She was a quick study.

The granite was unusually hard and resistant for some reason, and he and Jana had chipped away at the core of it to try and free the gold. They were using a thin vein of quartz that ran through the granite to wedge open the core, and split off chunks as he found them. The steel chisel was about an inch and a half shorter now than when they started three weeks ago, and he had repaired the tip a few times in the forge.

Piotr's hands had gone from stiff and sore after the first few days to so stiff he could hardly un-grip the sledge. He would wake up with his fingers curled, as if they were holding the handle in his sleep. He had to consciously try and straighten them out. Over the three weeks his hands and arms grew stronger, but he still soaked them in the cold stream water each evening, holding them under at Jana's urging. She was also still checking on the lump on his forehead. As the swelling went down, the wound had finally closed and was no longer weeping fluid down his face. He was left with a black and blue bruise on his forehead, with a slender, healing cut through the center of it. Malian told him it would leave a scar. Thames and Anton Paquet told him he looked better with it.

Piotr watched Jana as she worked. She was lucky, in that her black eye had subsided to just a slight blue bruise under the eyelid. Even that was fading. Piotr found that he was pleased when he looked at her. He noticed every detail about her. How hard she worked. How she solved problems rapidly, faster than he could. He didn't consciously think these things, bur rather felt them somewhere in the deep center of his chest. The thoughts that did push their way to the front of his mind he restrained. He had been taught by his parents and the church that these were not acceptable.

Besides, she was a year older than him, and he was not a person of importance.

They had enlarged the lean-to and extended walls on the sides so the prevailing wind and periodic rains couldn't get in. Jana, Malian, and Mr. Montreaux had taken up some of the space, and the heat of the forge kept them warm in the night or when it rained. They spent their days helping with the trapping and skinning of beaver, or hunting.

Between Malian and Eggard, the camp was getting more food sources, other than meat. With Montreaux, the three of them had gone downstream, coming back with a stringer filled with more than a dozen large catfish. The camp ate grilled and stewed fish for a few days.

Piotr found Malian and Montreaux to be good company in the evening. Most nights, they sat around the forge, coals still glowing as the sun went down, and Montreaux told them stories of his time at sea. Malian continued to educate the other three about the ways of the forest.

During the daytime, Piotr and Jana kept carving, cutting out pieces of stone filled with the vein of gold. Once they had a growing pile of palm-sized rocks, they realized they needed a way to carry them. Jana offered to make a basket. She had learned to weave baskets from her mother. They would collect the long pieces of shaved wood from her father's window making shop. He was always making frames of different shapes and sizes, using a heavy spokeshave to shape the wood. She was taught to not waste anything.

Here in the valley, she did not have wood strips, so she used the reeds growing by the stream. She cut them at the base and split them into two halves with her knife, stripping them vertically from the stem. Then she weaved the pieces in the way her mother taught her, so that the walls would support the center, and the center would support the walls. She realized the heaviness of the rocks would burst through the reeds, so she reinforced the walls and the bottom with green spruce branches. Now the basket sat, filled most of the way to the top with various sized rocks, each one with a vein of shiny yellow and crusty brown metal.

As the days passed and their work together filled their time, Jana began to talk. She talked about her family, her childhood, and finally, about how she got to this green valley in the New World.

"My mother was from Saint-Morant. My father was from Wurzburg. They met when he came to her town when he was at the end of his indentured service to a window maker. They were selling their windows to the duchy, and she was working in the castle as a handmaid. She left her job and went with him, against her parents' wishes, when she was sixteen years old. He was a few years older and finished out his servitude, so they moved to Bremen and he started his own shop. I was born there, in Bremen."

Piotr listened. She used her hands when she was excited about what she was telling. Despite the difficulty in her life, she was not sad and did not seem to feel sorry for herself. She told him how her father had disappeared at the hands of the Swedish soldiers, and how her mother had sent her to a Catholic convent, to protect her. She told him about *The Render* and the longboat, the large ship that fired upon them, and the dead men on the ship. She told him how Raul and Malian had helped her. She told him about Nanibosad. Finally, she told him about running in the forest from the Iroquois. He shook his head in amazement, and his thoughts about her deepened and became a constant buzz in the back of his mind.

As they worked in the sun, she asked him to tell his story.

At first he was reluctant. He thought about what he could tell her.

It occurred to him that here in the valley there was no risk of someone knowing his secrets. But if they ever went back, not to Saint-Malo, but all the way back. Back to Zlotoryja...there would be a risk for anyone who knew.

Why would he go back there with her? He wondered why he had even thought that.

After eating a supper of catfish with the crew around the central campfire, as the sun went down, they returned to their lean-to and sat back with the heat of the forge warming the shelter. He decided to stop ruminating and tell her. Malian and Raul Montreaux sat on the buffalo hide. Might as well just tell the truth, he decided.

"I am the son of a goldsmith. Gold and copper. There is not enough gold just to be a goldsmith in Zlotoryja. Copper is what puts food on the table, my dad would say."

Piotr was surprised by the power in the memory of his father's voice. Tears came to his eyes, and his voice thickened and wavered a bit as he remembered the sound.

"I had only a couple of years of actual training. I was almost fifteen when the call to war came. The Lutherans were invading in the north. My father was often asked to make decorative pieces for the armory of the duchy, so they knew him, and they knew his reputation as a skilled smithy. He was also part of the town militia. When the call to arms came for the men of our town, he was given the honor of leading the men into this battle."

Piotr gripped the tongs and flipped the chisel over in the red coals, heating both sides of the edge.

Before he could start his story up again, Thames and Captain Linville came to check on their progress with the rock. Piotr poked the chisel and shifted the tip in the hot forge with the tongs. Might as well heat it up and restore the tip while they were resting.

"How goes it?" Linville asked.

Piotr gestured to the basket, filled most of the way. "Getting there."

Thames knelt by the basket and picked up a fist-sized rock, gleaming in light of the forge. He rotated it in his hand, like he was inspecting an apple. "How much is there?"

"Still more. I think I have most of it, but the more we dig out, the more we find."

He paused, seeing the look in Thames's eye as he gazed at the stone. "We don't know what it's worth, you know," he said.

Linville turned his head and asked, "What do you mean?"

"Purity. The value is in the purity. We don't know that. We won't know until we get it back. All the way to a goldsmith in Saint-Malo, or somewhere. I cannot melt down the rocks. That requires an expertise I never got to learn. It's worth a lot, but we don't really know how much it is, until we get to someone who can value it."

"That is what we'll do, then. Quietly. When we return to Saint-Malo...maybe we wait and take it all the way to Paris. Not a lot of goldsmiths in a fishing town like Saint-Malo, anyway," Linville said.

"We will have money from the sale of the furs. We can take our time, find the right person, keep it a secret," Thames said.

Jana said, "We have been speaking of secrets. Piotr was telling us his secret."

Thames and Captain Linville stopped and exchanged glances. They then stepped over near the heat of the forge and sat down to listen.

Piotr looked ruefully at the group. He hated being the center of attention.

"Well, I was saying, the Duke of Brettenberg came to the shop that evening, late. Unaccompanied. No men with him, which, I knew right away, something was up. He had a suit of armor with him for repairs, he said. He asked for my father to help. I was still up but my dad and mom were asleep, so I woke him. He came out and they talked in the shop. My dad had me sit over in the corner and wait. So, I did not hear their conversation, but my dad looked at me several times as they talked. I thought I had done something wrong."

Thames and Linville listened silently, as did Malian and Montreaux. Jana quietly continued weaving reeds together for the next basket while she listened.

"The son of the duke, whose name was Piotr, too, was sixteen."

"The age of manhood," Linville said.

"But the duke didn't want him going off to war. He was a small fellow, about my size, bright yellow hair. The duke wanted the armor modified to fit me. Helmet and all. Because he wanted me to go in his stead. No one was supposed to know, of course, because the accusation of cowardice would be bad for the duke and duchess and their son. My father's job was to protect me, keep me away from the fighting. Then afterward, we would be paid for our conspiracy. And our silence."

"But your father was killed…" Thames said.

"He was. He was injured when a mounted knight charged through our ranks. He took a lance through the stomach," Piotr said, mechanically. He didn't want to tear up. He tried to keep the memories at bay, but the more he spoke, the more details came back to him. The image of his father once again came back to his mind. Lying on the ground with blood pouring from the wound, the mounted warrior unable to pull the lance free, because it went through his father and stuck in the ground, pinning him there. His father grunting in pain with both hands on the lance.

After a pause, Piotr continued. "When the mounted knights get through the pikemen, then you can get overrun. We were being routed. I charged at the man on the horse and struck him with my club, unseating him. But his horse bolted and knocked me over, and when I tried to stand, he swung his sword at me. I tried to duck away, but it caught the top of the helmet and tore it off of my head. I struck him before he could recover from the swing, in the head, and he went down. Our men fell upon him and killed him."

They listened quietly, patiently waiting for him to continue.

"As our lines broke down, everyone was yelling and running. I pulled my father to his feet, and tried to move, but we only made it a little way. I set him down by a tree, and he was bleeding, bleeding everywhere. He told me to put my helmet on. I tried to tell him that it got knocked off... but he, he couldn't understand. All of the men from the village that were still left alive recognized that I was not Piotr of Brettenberg, but Piotr Nowak. Son of the smithy."

"So, you were found out," Captain Linville said.

"I was. My father rallied them. He grabbed me by the shoulders and said to stay here, by the tree. No matter what, stay behind. He stood up and led a charge of all of our village men back into the melee of oncoming soldiers. I followed, behind their line. I saw the helmet, on the grass with a gash in the top from the mounted knight's sword, so I ran over and put it on. I looked up and the men of my village, led by my father, ran straight into musket and cannon fire as they charged up the ridge. They were slaughtered, all of them."

Piotr's voice quavered at the last words.

"And he led them to it."

Thames and Linville stared at Piotr. Montreaux as well. These men had seen war and a battlefield. They understood what had happened.

Thames said, "Your father led the townsmen into the slaughter to protect you, knowing they would die."

"Yes."

A long silence followed. Thames shook his head and blew out the air in his lungs in a sigh.

Captain Linville finally asked, "Why do you fear returning then, Piotr? If your townsfolk died...so, who was left to tell?"

Piotr closed his eyes, thinking back to the pain of that difficult day and the weeks that followed it.

"I walked back to the village, alone, intending to go home to my mother, but was intercepted by the soldiers of the duke and taken to the castle in the duchy. The duke said he was happy that I was alive, but he wanted me to leave as quickly as I could. I took off the armor and left it with them, and I went back to my mother and the shop. I told her what happened, but she had already heard; she thought I was dead and was just thankful I was alive. We went to sleep, grieving the loss of my father and the men of the village. The next day, the duke addressed the town square and blamed the defeat and the loss of the village men on my father's poor judgment. His son, dressed in the armor that I had worn, testified that he had witnessed my father mistakenly lead them into charge of certain death."

"Dirty bastards. Nobility...always dirty bastards," Thames said.

"The people in the village were so angry they attacked my mother in the street, striking her and threatening to hang her. She made it back to the house and told me I had to leave, to hide in the forest. So, I ran. I slept in the forest. I snuck back into town in the morning, hoping to talk to my mother. The duke sent soldiers, they took my mother back to the castle, and they stole everything in our home and in my father's shop. My mother was yelling and tried to stop them. But they said it was a fine, a penalty to pay the families of the men who died at Lutzen, from my father's mistakes."

"And so, you could not stay," Eggard said.

"I had nowhere to stay, and nowhere to go. I wandered, stealing food from gardens and garbage piles. I went west to France, toward Paris. Then north, I ended up on the dock in Saint-Malo, asking you for a job."

"A job that I'm glad that I gave," Captain Linville said.

"And I'm glad he did too. You have become a good crewman and a good friend," Thames said.

Malian and Jana hugged Piotr. It was strange to him, having lived with this secret for so long, to tell another person. He teared up, but he would not allow himself to give in to his emotions and did not crumble into a blubbery mess. He was stoic, but he was relieved with the telling of it.

"Piotr, I am glad to know your story. I thank you for telling it. Your bravery has been appreciated." Linville put his hand on Piotr's shoulder and shook his hand, gripping forearm to forearm. "We came to check on your progress for a reason. We have collected about all of the beaver fur that this valley will yield. It is getting close to the time to move on."

"Back to the ship," Thames added.

Piotr looked at the rock. "I think there is not much left, but we keep finding more." He remembered the chisel in the forge and pulled it out with the tongs. The tip glowed red in the evening light. He took it to the recovered anvil and started tapping out the rough edges.

"We are going to start to pack up tomorrow. It may take a few days to get all of the fur to the barge."

"I understand," Piotr said, wiping his eyes with the back of his hand.

Thames and Linville waved their goodbyes and thanked the three newcomers for their contribution to the cause. Piotr looked at Jana; they had to pick up the pace and be done with it in a day. She looked back in his eyes, and he knew that she understood, without any more talking.

The next morning a new reason for urgency took over the camp. Piotr was chiseling out the last of the vein of gold, bent down and tapping on the chisel, when he realized someone was watching him. He stopped and stood up, looking around. Chogan raised his hand in greeting; he and his men were almost invisible through the leafy screen of trees. Piotr blinked a couple of times to make sure he wasn't seeing things, then waved back at the future Huron chief.

Thames and Eggard had spied the Huron and came walking up the hill and the two groups met near the lean-to.

"Welcome, friend! It is good to see you again," Thames said.

"Are you hungry? We have some meat in the pot," Eggard offered.

"Messieurs, we have no time for food or talking. We have come to ask for your help, again, and to warn you. The Iroquois are on the march again. A scout came back to the village three days ago. Seneca and Oneida warriors attacked a Leni Lenape village southeast of here. They are on the warpath. It's likely they are moving this way, to attack the Huron village. They come early this year, raiding, collecting tribute. We need more muskets. We need them now."

Thames said, "I understand. We have more guns on the ship, but not here. Piotr, may I?"

He walked to the lean-to and grabbed Piotr's musket. He handed it to Chogan. Eggard handed his musket to one of Chogan's men.

"Take these. We were preparing to leave soon. We will leave today and come to the Huron village. We can stand with the Huron there, if need be." Thames and Eggard shook hands with Chogan, and they left the camp in a single file jog.

Thames looked at Piotr, and said, "Looks like we leave today. No more time left. We can't get caught flat-footed out here by hundreds of Iroquois warriors."

"Aye," Piotr agreed, rubbing the scar on his forehead.

That afternoon they had Mule hitched to the cart. The tools, the anvil, the bellows and two baskets were stacked under the tarp. Thames and Linville led the way up the trail, back to the barge stashed on the Cuyahoga River. Piotr and Eggard were once again at the back of the line of men on the trail. He was glad that Montreaux, Malian and Jana were back near the cart while they walked. The trail was smoother with footprints, but it still seemed the cart hit every log or rock and needed to be pushed along. They all helped, and Thames set a faster pace. In addition, Montreaux, with his brace of pistols, was a welcome sight.

Each horse and each man were loaded with bales of beaver fur as they walked. Montreaux, Jana, and Malian each carried one on their back as well. They slept that night with no campfires, eating only smoked meat from their packs.

In two days' time they had made it to the Cuyahoga, the Crooked River as the Huron called it, and recovered the barge from the island where they had left it beached. The next morning at dawn, they were walking north on the trail Piotr and Thames had run down when trying to catch up to the crew. Heading back to the Huron village, the loaded barge floated alongside them, poled along by Captain Linville and the Paquet brothers. They were hopeful the Huron had more furs to add.

With the furs loaded onto the barge, the men were moving faster. Piotr, Jana, Montreaux, Malian, and Eggard had stayed on the trail, still following along with Mule and the cart. Soon, the barge got into the current, and moved faster than the men and horses on the ground. By mid-day, it had drifted well ahead of the rest of the crew. The barge could continue being poled all night on the river, traveling in one day what would take the walking men two. Thames and Flagger waved at Captain Linville, telling him to go. No reason for the furs to travel as slowly as the men.

Linville shouted, "We will wait for you at the village of the Huron. We will get their furs loaded, and then we can all get back to the *St. Longinus* as wealthy men!"

Piotr and Eggard heard this from the back of the line. Piotr saw him standing on the back of the rough-hewn barge in his black boots and long coat and gave a wave as well. He watched as the barge rode the current around a curve in the river ahead of them. It disappeared into the leaves and branches.

The trail was smoother and more well-worn along the Cuyahoga, so Mule was able to move without as much help over logs and rocks and such. Having given up his musket to Chogan's men, Eggard had taken the broad ax out and carried it on his shoulder while they walked. Just before sunset, they camped on the shore with only a single fire for cooking. Thames insisted the fire be farther away from the river, screened from view at night by the leaves. This limited the food they could eat and caused general weariness and increased frustration among the men. Thames did not care. Speed, and staying hidden, were more important than comfort now. He desperately hoped that they would not encounter the Iroquois on the trail.

As the sun reached the tops of the trees on its downward path, the sound of musket fire in the distance echoed downstream toward them. Gray and white smoke began rising above the tree line. At first it was a few shots, then it became a full fusillade. Thames shuddered at the sound, fearing the worst. Immediately he told everyone to get the wicks lit on their matchlocks.

"We are moving fast now." He led the way up the trail at a fast trot with matchlock in hand, pointed toward the musket fire sounds. The line of men and horses followed, and the trot became a flat-out run as they could hear screaming and war whoops through the trees. Due to the leaves and curve of the trail, they couldn't tell what they were running into. Piotr pushed the cart as Eggard led Mule at a fast trot. Jana and Malian strained to see what was upriver.

They followed the trail around the curve of the river, and Thames slowed the line as the sounds of musket fire told them they were getting close.

Suddenly they got far enough downstream to see through the leafy branches. The barge was taking musket fire from the opposite shoreline. Lead balls were hitting the barge, and a few Iroquois warriors were in the water, trying to cross where the river was shallow, and get at the barge. Shots were being fired from the barge as well by kneeling Paquet brothers, directed back at the approaching warriors. Twenty or thirty Iroquois were firing from hidden positions in the tall reeds along the shore. The barge was getting pummeled.

Thames made a fast choice and whispered orders to the men. "Form a line along here." He pointed to a downed tree alongside the trail some thirty yards ahead. "We will fire a volley at them from there."

It was a shot of more than a hundred yards with very little chance of hitting anything. His hope was that a show of force would drive them off.

For the group of Piotr, Malian, Jana, Montreaux, and Eggard back with horses and Mule, he whispered, "When we fire our volley, use the smoke as cover and take the horses, get up the trail past all of this and get back in the tree line, keep going to the Huron on the shore. Tell them we are here. We are going to hit the Iroquois when they make their charge across the river."

"Aye," Eggard responded. Piotr just nodded.

"Mr. Montreaux, Malian, Jana, stay with them, if you please, keep your pistols at the ready."

"Aye, good luck," Montreaux said, nodding and drawing out his right-handed pistol.

Piotr threw his backpack onto the cart, grabbing his club in his right hand, and the bridle of Mule in the other. He watched as Jana, Malian, and Montreaux each grabbed the reins of a horse and crouched down, waiting to run. Montreaux took the point position.

Mule tossed his head and grunted, curling his lips back and licking the bit in his mouth. The horses were all nervous at the sound of musket fire and the smell of smoke.

Eggard patted Mule and said, "Easy now, old friend."

Piotr saw that the barge was not moving forward in the current. The river was blocked with fallen trees that had been dragged across from shore to shore. The barge had sailed into the branches, jamming itself up and coming to a stop. This was a trap.

Piotr blinked at what he saw next.

There was a body floating face down in the water behind the barge. He couldn't see a face, but he could see a black overcoat and boots.

"No..."

Whoops and screams began to build from the Iroquois hidden in the shoreline. Piotr could still not see them, other than some rustling in the reeds and branches on that side of the river, but he could hear them. Then a fusillade of shots poured forth from the reeds, hammering the barge, and pouring smoke onto the water of the Cuyahoga. The screams turned to splashing as they came charging out from the reeds and branches, tomahawks and knives in their hands. As they lunged toward the barge, stuck in the shallow water, the crewmen of the *St. Longinus* fired from their position upstream, and the noise of twenty muskets barking stopped the Iroquois in their tracks. The shots zipped and splashed around them. They jumped back, turning in the shallow water and lunging back to the shore for cover.

"Reload!" Thames shouted.

As smoke from the volley filled the air, Montreaux surged forward with two horses reined in his left hand and his pistol in his right. Malian and Jana followed, each leading a horse and running after Montreaux. Eggard pulled on Mule's bridle and they started forward, though much slower than the women and Montreaux, as Mule was pulling the heavy cart. Piotr pushed as hard as he could on the cart. As they ran down the trail, the gap grew wider between the three in front and Eggard and Piotr in the back. As they got past the cloud of smoke blasted out from the crewmen's fusillade, the Iroquois began to realize that a slow-moving target was on the opposite shore.

Piotr heard the crack and the zipping buzz of a musket ball as it flew over his head. Another one smashed into a log lying near his feet, kicking up wood and mud into the air. Mule simply could not go faster, and the other three were now way out in front, running along the trail.

More shots began to come his way. One plowed into the corner of the cart, splintering a furrow in the wood. Piotr guessed that they must present a ridiculous and tempting target, with the enormous Eggard leading Mule and him pushing from behind. The cart was bouncing hard on the uneven trail and sporadic shots were still humming and zipping at him or past him, but Mule followed the trail. In what felt like an hour, but was actually about thirty seconds, they made it past the open area. Eggard, Mule, and Piotr caught up to the other three and got off the trail, into the leafy cover of the forest. The shots from the Iroquois stopped coming their way as they were out of view.

Piotr and Eggard were out of breath after the quick sprint, but Piotr peeked back through the leaves and branches at the barge. Two Iroquois warriors lay in pools of blood on the trail just past where the barge was stuck. They must have been the ones who dammed up the river. They had been shot through the torso.

The men on the barge had fought back.

Montreaux handed the reins of his horses to Malian and pulled up the tarp, searching desperately through the cart.

"What do you need?" Piotr asked.

"A rope, a long rope!"

He found a coiled rope, then turned and ran from the cover of the trees toward the barge. He tied a loop while he was running, stepped out onto the muddy shore, and threw a perfect toss onto the branches of the log holding the barge in place. A musket ball sizzled the air as it zipped past his thigh, smacking into the shore and spraying him with muddy water. Seeing what he was trying, Malian gathered up one of the horses and backed him up so he could be available for the rope. Montreaux came running back, tossing the rope to her.

She caught it and looped it through the harness. She slapped the horse on the rear, and it surged forward.

The rope went taut but the tree in the water was not moving. Jana, Piotr, and Eggard ran over and pulled on the rope with Montreaux joining them. The tree began to move; they pulled until the blockade of branches broke apart. The back of the barge started to turn with the current, and then broke loose from the branches. It began to drift down river once again.

Piotr could see movement on the other side of the river as the Iroquois trap was defeated. They began to leave the reeds and follow the barge, running through the tree line along the opposite shore. They stopped shooting at the barge while they were moving in the trees, at least.

Anton and Abel Paquet reached down into the water and grabbed the man with the black coat and boots, pulling him up onto the barge. They were crying and shouting. Anton waved his fists in frustration at the Iroquois on the other shoreline. Gerard stood on the barge platform and reloaded his musket as he stared at the man lying on the deck. Mason pressed his hands to the man's forehead as the barge continued down the river. Piotr knew the man on the deck was dead. As the barge went past, he saw a man on the back with a long birch pole, guiding the raft. It was Abraham Paquet.

Captain Linville was lying dead on the deck.

Thames, Flagger, and the rest of the crew came running up the path, staring at the barge, muskets loaded and pointing downstream.

"Who was down? On the barge? Who was it?" Thames shouted.

"The captain," Piotr said, his voice breaking.

"Are you sure? Piotr, are you certain?"

Piotr nodded, looking down at the muddy ground.

Thames closed his eyes and inhaled sharply. He rubbed his eyes, then ran his hands through his long black hair while he held his face to the sky, eyes closed. Flagger stared down at the trail in silence.

Then he gave orders. "We have no time for grief. There are some cliffs on the opposite shore. That may slow them down. We can catch up to the barge and get it to the Huron village. We have to go."

Thames shook his head but put his hand on Flagger's shoulder.

"He is right. Mr. Montreaux, all of you, thank you for freeing the barge. We are going to go after it and try and keep them off. Get to the Huron village."

"Godspeed," Montreaux said.

Thames, Flagger, and the men set off at a fast trot after the barge.

Eggard took Mule by the bridle, and they started their way down the trail, Piotr pushing on the cart when needed. Malian, Jana, and Montreaux, leading the horses, moved out behind the cart. Thames, Flagger, and the men running in front quickly distanced themselves from the horses and the cart.

Piotr could see the barge moving downstream and the line of men jogging up the trail. He could no longer see movement on the opposite shoreline, but he was sure that they were still there, running along with the barge, waiting for their chance.

He kept pushing the cart, helping Mule through the muddy spots, as they came to a straighter portion of the river. Intermittent gunshots caused him to look up and see that a running battle was coming from both sides of the river. Blasts of gray and white smoke would come forth from the tree lines, and musket balls whistled across the river. Meanwhile, men were running along both sides, going from cover to cover. The marksmanship from the Iroquois was good enough to kill anyone who ventured out in the open. The fur traders ran from cover to cover, firing back when they saw a blast of smoke or movement in the leaves.

The barge sat in the middle, slowly floating through the smoky haze with bullets zipping back and forth. The Paquets fired at the occasional movement or when they saw smoke come out from between leaves. Abraham crouched, hidden on the port side of the barge, using the birch pole to keep them moving and trying to get the barge closer to the western shoreline, nearer the men of the *St. Longinus*.

Piotr shouted to Eggard, "The Iroquois will not give up. They want the furs. Chogan said they are trading with the Dutch."

"They will if they lose a man or two. Unlike generals, they value the lives of their warriors. We have already shown them we have teeth."

This sporadic running battle continued as the barge made its way northward on the current of the Cuyahoga.

Finally, about a mile or so short of the stopping point for the Huron village, the Seneca and Oneida warriors stopped. The east side of the river suddenly went quiet, and Piotr could see no more movement in the tree line. The men slowed to a walk, staying behind cover, and keeping their musket wicks lit and pointed at the shoreline on the opposite shore. As the group of pack animals and people worked their way up the trail toward the village, Piotr and the others looked out across the river, scanning to see if anyone was pointing a musket at them.

"Look!" Jana said, pointing across the river.

Piotr strained to see what her keen eyes had found. A tall man stepped forward from behind the leafy screen into an opening. Piotr could see him now as well. His head was shaved on both sides, and an earring hung from his right ear with a long feather. He held a trade musket pointed at the ground, and he was bare-chested. There were green and white stripes of paint on his chest and cheekbones. He was showing his face to them on purpose. Piotr knew this was a different way to count coup, to show that he has no fear. He was signaling that he intended to see them again. The big warrior made eye contact with Piotr, and he held his stare from across the river. Piotr stopped pushing on the cart and stared back across the river for a long few seconds. Then the man turned away and disappeared back into the trees. Piotr realized that a challenge had been made. He wondered when that challenge would have to be accepted.

"Eggard, they have stopped pursuing us," Montreaux said.

"Yes, they are probably planning on attacking the Huron and they do not want to give away their numbers."

"Will they come back?" Jana asked.

"They will. But the Huron village is strong. Walled off and guarded. We need to get there as fast as possible," Eggard said.

Thames came running back down the trail toward them. "The others are up at the barge. You need to go fast. If the Iroquois are part of a larger force, they will hit us again."

"They will come at dawn, just as the sun rises," Malian said.

Thames turned and looked at her. She had hardly spoken since meeting them a month ago; he wasn't sure what to make of her. Her experience and wisdom were evident, and he sensed this information should not be ignored.

He nodded to her, accepting her expertise. "Then we have to get to the Huron village and get behind their palisade before then."

The group double timed up the trail and caught up with the barge and the crewmen. The Paquet brothers were ashore, standing in a watchful arch, guns pointed out toward where the Iroquois had last been, with the rest of the crewmen in deep discussion. Piotr saw the body of Captain James Linville laid out on the front of the barge. With his eyes closed, he looked like he could be asleep, Piotr thought. The bloodstains and hole in his shirt told a different story.

He felt sick to his stomach, suddenly, as when his father had died. There was no way to care for the body while they fled. Lacking any other ideas, the Paquet brothers had wrapped him up in a blanket and carried him to the cart, placing him on top of the tarp. His hat was missing, and his narrow, rather aristocratic face was at peace, eyes closed. His skin had turned ivory white, his cheeks having lost their pink hue.

Flagger pulled him aside, his eyes wet at the corners. He spoke in a whisper. "Just keep the cart moving. I'm joining the men on the barge. If you run into trouble, get into the tree line, you understand?"

"Yes."

Flagger put his hand on the body of Captain Linville, then walked off with his head down.

Piotr walked behind the cart, staring at the body of his captain. He had known all along that they could all die, for the risk on a venture such as this was so great. But he had not thought of it in that way. He had simply been running away from his problems when he stumbled into this opportunity. Then this man, this crew, had taken him in and he had earned a position among them. There was pride in this.

Now, losing Captain Linville felt like losing his father again. For a while, despair and confusion overwhelmed his thoughts, causing his mind to race in multiple directions at once. He looked at Jana as she led two horses, walking on the trail in front of him. She cried silently as she led the pack horse. He blinked away tears, rubbing his eyes with the back of his right hand while pushing the cart with his left.

Piotr pushed on in the mud, following Mule with heavy feet, and hard thoughts in his mind.

## Chapter 21

# THE BATTLE AT
# THE PALISADE

They left Captain Linville's body on the cart hidden in the trees, wrapped up tightly in the blanket. There was no time for a burial. Out of practicality, the Paquets took his pistols, Anton and Abraham each sliding one into their belts. They gave Piotr his pipe, his tobacco pouch, and his metal pick. Piotr placed the items in his pack silently, unsure of what he would ever do with them.

Piotr stood on the rampart next to Flagger, peeking over the wall as the pre-dawn light came creeping over the horizon in beautiful red and yellow streaks. The Huron village was just beginning to bathe in it, and insects were beginning their daily drone. They came from the east as Malian had predicted, using the sun's rays to blind the eyes of the defenders on the wall. Malian had seen it before from the Abenaki village. The Iroquois intended to breach the palisade wall made of tree trunks. Once they got inside, they would demand tribute from the Huron. If it was not given in the form of food, slaves, and goods, then it would be taken, and the Huron village would cease to exist.

The palisade wall stood twelve feet high, and the rampart that the men stood on allowed them to crouch below the top of the wall, and then stand up and fire over it. The Huron had cleared trees for nearly a hundred yards around the wall, using those trees to build it. It was made like a latticework, with trunks and sticks woven together for strength.

Now, crouched behind the wall with the wicks of their muskets lit, the men of the *St. Longinus* had plenty of space to pick their targets, even with an unfavorable sun. With the death of their captain in their minds, they had vengeance in their hearts.

As the red and yellow rays crested the horizon, the Iroquois charged across the open field. They ran silently with muskets, bows, and spears in hand, and they ran fast. When they had covered half the space a collective roar came tearing from their throats. The people they attacked always cowered when they heard this sound. For many, it was the last voice they would ever hear. They were the dominant fighting force in the region and were only growing stronger.

Thames waited until the last possible second, letting the charging warriors get to within easy range. Then he gave the order.

"Fire!"

The men of the *St. Longinus* stood and shouldered their weapons, pointing them over the wall, and let loose. The thunderous blast from the fort stunned the charging Iroquois, stopping them in their tracks. More than twenty of them fell, dead or seriously wounded. Many of the Iroquois dropped to one knee and returned fire. The musket fire created a smoke cloud that obscured visibility. This normally would have made selecting targets more difficult, but for the men behind the wall, it simply obscured much of the morning sun's rays. Piotr stood and fired, then ducked back down behind the wall. He felt musket balls and arrows thump into the wall.

As the Frenchmen reloaded, Chogan and his men stood up and fired a second volley into the confused Iroquois, killing several more, stalling their charge completely. Several Iroquois warriors dropped to one knee and began to return fire or reload their muskets. Now they were exposed on the battlefield. Some of them began to advance through the smoke, but they were having a hard time seeing targets. The warriors who got closer to the wall exposed themselves even more and were hewn down with arrows from the Huron. Some sporadic single shots blasted from the palisade, and more Iroquois warriors dropped, bleeding and writhing on the ground. More than thirty of their men were down, and they had not reached the wall. Their war chief, the tall man with the shaved sides of his head who had stared at Piotr from across the river, called out a retreat, and the Iroquois ran back into the tree line.

Cheers went up along the wall, but Thames shouted, "Stop braying! They'll be back!"

The men went quiet and quickly reloaded.

"Hold your fire. Keep your eyes open!" Flagger added, walking up and down the line of men on the rampart peeking over the wall.

The tall muscular Seneca war chief was stunned. They had never faced the withering barrage of musket fire that occurred in a set piece battle. They had always overwhelmed their enemies with the speed of their attack, and the fact that they were superior in individual combat to nearly everyone they faced. He regretted the failed attack on the barge, and now realized his attack had given warning to the Huron. Worse, the men behind the wall were the men who had fired at them on the river. They had allied with his enemy. His mind raced as he developed a new strategy.

Behind the wall, Piotr reloaded, pouring powder down the barrel, then ramming the patch and ball home. He had obtained another musket from the cart. His hands were shaking. Flagger looked him over while he reloaded.

"You all right?"

Piotr nodded. "A little worked up."

"Hmm...it's a good thing. I don't think we get out of this without bleeding."

Piotr nodded again and said, "Aye."

"Keep your wits," Flagger said. He ran off with long strides to check on the few crewmen standing on the back side of the Huron palisade. Huron warriors with bows manned the back of the village wall, for the most part, but Thames felt it wise to place a few muskets back there as well.

Jana and Malian stood under the rampart with the old and the young men of the village. They were armed with knives and small axes. The Huron warriors looked at them strangely, wondering what two women, one of them white, were doing here with the warriors. The Huron women were in the longhouses, standing at the door with knives and axes at the ready, protecting the children.

The entrance of the palisade did not face out to the pathway leading to the village the way gates did in a castle in Europe. Instead, the wall circled around the village and the tail end wrapped around the head, as if drawing the beginning of a spiral. There were no gates that could be closed, and certainly no moat, to protect the defenders. The entryway was simply two sections of the wall that ran parallel to each other for about thirty feet on the open end of the spiral. The Huron stacked lodge poles, baskets, branches and any other loose objects they could find from wall to wall to create a barricade for the oncoming attackers. On the rampart, they had stacked stones to throw, and containers of water in case the Iroquois set fire to the wall. It reminded Raul Montreaux of the defenses he had seen in the streets of old French towns.

He climbed on top of the small barricade and stood with his pistols drawn, peeking around the corner of the front entrance. An arrow flying so fast through the air he could only see it as a blur thumped into the wall next to his head, vibrating to a stop at impact. He jerked his head back from the corner. The second attack began.

The Seneca chief had devised his strategy. Several wounded men were lying on the ground near the entrance. Using hand signals, he had signed to them from the tree line. He asked them if they could still fight, and they all said yes, even though a couple of them were clearly incapacitated. They had laid down and remained still for several minutes, long enough that the men looking out from the ramparts believed these men were dead. Moving very slowly, they laid on their sides in the grass and reloaded their muskets with as little motion as they could manage.

316

Shots rang out from the north side of the palisade, where the tree line was closest to the wall. Several Iroquois were attacking from that side. Thames shouted out for a few men to follow him and jumped down from the rampart. Running across the circular village, they climbed up the rampart on the other side. Flagger joined them. They took aim over the wall and Thames was about to tell them to fire, as the Iroquois were beginning their charge at this part of the wall. He realized something was different. They were charging into musket range, then dancing and running sideways.

"Hold! Wait," Thames shouted.

The Iroquois grew more brazen, running even closer before turning and sprinting back out of range, moving individually instead of in a mass charge. Thames wondered what was going on.

His cheek on the stock of his musket as he drew a bead on a distant Iroquois target, Flagger said, "They are trying to get us to waste our lead."

They heard a war cry coming from the entryway to the village and some shots were fired. Thames and Flagger looked at each other. Flagger turned and jumped down off the rampart, running back across the village toward the entryway barricade.

Thames screamed as he ran, "Stay here, hold your fire till you have a good target, then let them have it!"

He then turned and followed Flagger on a dead run.

Screaming war cries suddenly echoed from the tree line in the east, charging out of the forest and firing at the wall, more than two hundred Seneca burst from the trees. The men on the rampart took aim and eased their hammers back to full cock.

Simultaneously, seven "dead" Seneca warriors sprang to their feet in the grass near the palisade, made a sprint for the entryway, and began scrambling over the barricade. The remaining hundred warriors charged from the wood line, screaming and creating as much noise as possible. They came with fierce intent.

Chogan had realized the attempt at distraction and came running toward the entryway to the village as well. He yelled as he ran past Piotr on the rampart.

"Piotr!"

Piotr turned away from the wall and jumped down to the ground to follow him. He hit a little harder than expected and stumbled forward, rolling to the ground. Thankfully, his musket didn't fire and blow off his face. He scrambled to his feet with his musket in his right hand. Jana and Malian, standing under the rampart, stared for a second, then Jana tossed him his war club. He caught it in his left hand and headed out after Chogan at a sprint.

The wounded Seneca were over the barricade and jumped down, landing on their feet. Their appearance was so fierce, it would have startled the hardest veteran. Painted and bleeding from wounds, they advanced with murderous intent.

Raul Montreaux waited for them.

He stood with his pistols drawn, facing the barricade. When the first warrior jumped over, landing lightly on his feet with a knife and tomahawk in each hand, Raul calmly eared back the hammer and shot him in the face. The man's head snapped back, and he stood for a moment with the top of his head blown open. His eyes blinked, then he collapsed in a meaty heap to the ground. Mason Paquet was on the rampart at the end of the entryway, and he leaned over the wall and fired straight down into the next warrior coming over the barricade, killing him instantly. As he tried to duck back behind the wall, the third Seneca over the barricade shot him in the throat with his musket. Mason fell backward off the rampart, dead before he hit the ground. Montreaux fired with his left-handed pistol into the side of the warrior who shot Mason, causing him to grunt and drop to a knee. Montreaux dropped the pistol in his right hand and pulled his knife as the other four wounded Seneca scrambled over the barricade into the village entryway.

Two of the warriors went for Montreaux and two began to rip the barricade down.

Montreaux was not going to yield ground, because letting them gain entry in the village was not a possibility. He didn't intend to die standing in the doorway, so he advanced toward the Seneca. Suddenly a blur passed him from behind at full speed and smashed into the Seneca with a screaming war cry. Chogan, despite his short stature, was incredibly fast. His flying tackle drove the lead warrior to the ground with Chogan landing on top of him and smashing his skull with a tomahawk.

The other warrior hesitated in attacking Montreaux now, surprised by the ferocity of Chogan's attack. Montreaux used the moment and thrust his knife at the warrior's stomach. The warrior saw it and parried it with his tomahawk, dancing sideways to avoid the next thrust. Chogan leapt off of the downed Seneca and closed on the warrior in a fast rush from the ground. The two men toppled over to the ground, rolling and grappling, trying to gain an advantage. The other two warriors stopped dismantling the barricade and charged Montreaux together. Piotr rounded the corner of the wall on a run, and the two warriors halted, then squared off with him and Montreaux, feinting and moving just out of reach.

The men on the wall and in the field were all firing now, arrows and musket balls flying. A few of the crewmen were hit standing on the rampart, and several Seneca were hit charging across the grass. They had quickly learned not to gather together, and they attacked the wall from many places at once. As they got close enough, two of the warriors locked their hands together and launched a third warrior upward over the wall. Some of these men landed on the rampart and began slashing and stabbing the Huron or crewmen there. Several went over, missing the rampart and landing on the ground inside the wall. Some of them came up firing arrows or swinging tomahawks at the Huron warriors waiting under the rampart. Others were stunned by an incorrect landing and were quickly dispatched by the Huron warriors raining blows upon them.

Malian and Jana stood waiting under the rampart, knives in their left hands. Malian held her stone tomahawk in her right. Jana had taken an ax from one of the crewmen and held it in hers. A tall Oneida warrior landed on the rampart above them, quickly slashing the crewmen standing there and jumping down to the ground. Landing right in front of them, they attacked him together. He blocked their initial swings with a long-handled club, and brought his knife to bear, slashing at Malian's throat with a left-handed thrust. She ducked under it and fell backward as she lost her balance, dropping her stone tomahawk. Jana slashed her knife across his thigh before he could move away, and it bit through his leggings and breechcloth, laying open a long wound. He threw his head back and snarled in pain and tried to stab her with his knife, but Malian regained her balance and grabbed his knife arm, locking her arms around it and twisting it to his side. Jana drove her knife into his exposed chest below the breastbone. It sank in, all the way to the handle. The warrior roared in pain, but the strength went out of him as he tried to step back. Jana pulled the knife free, leaving an open wound that spewed out droplets of blood.

Piotr did not have time to stop and shoulder the musket, so he dropped it as he spun away from the Seneca warrior in the entryway. The warrior fired his musket from the hip, and the blast of smoke and bits of patch stung the skin on his shoulder and neck, but the ball whistled past his ear, missing him. Piotr swung his club up with his left hand, knocking the musket barrel away, and brought the club back down with two hands at the warrior's head. He raised the musket to block Piotr's swing, but the metal-studded war club splintered the stock of the Seneca's musket, smashing downward and crushing his collarbone. The warrior crumpled backward to the ground, stunned by the blow.

Eggard, from his spot on the northern part of the wall, realized the thrust of the attack was at the entryway. He tapped Abraham on the shoulder, pointing at the entryway. He could see Piotr, Chogan, and Montreaux in pitched hand-to-hand fighting.

"We have to help them!" he yelled.

Eggard handed his loaded musket to Abraham, then jumped down off the wall, grabbing the broad ax as he ran toward the gate.

In the entryway, Montreaux and the other Iroquois closed in on each other, parrying and thrusting. Montreaux used his long-barreled pistol as a club and blocked a knife thrust, but a blow from the tomahawk on his wrist caused his hand to go immediately numb and limp, and he dropped his knife. The warrior closed and tried to chop downward with his tomahawk. A hand and knife blade came across Montreaux's field of vision, stabbing the warrior in the neck to the hilt. Chogan had found the advantage with the warrior on the ground, killing him with a thrust, and charged to aid Montreuax, attacking from the side with deadly efficiency. He twisted the heavy-bladed knife free, opening a ragged wound in the man's throat. The Seneca fell to a knee, bleeding out, then collapsing.

Piotr, Chogan, and Montreaux turned to face the entryway, as more Seneca and Oneida began to charge into the partially dismantled barricade. Flagger, Thames, and Eggard all arrived at the entryway and saw the dozens of Iroquois funneling into the walls of the entryway.

Piotr took a quick glance at Eggard, his large hands gripping the broad ax, then turned his eyes toward the approaching savages, his spirits buoyed by the large man's presence. Several defenders standing on the ramparts realized what the Iroquois were doing and began to fire into the group running into the gate. Smoke from their powder filled the air between the walls, making it hard to see. The Seneca and Oneida warriors entered the fray, only to see the line of men awaiting them, shoulder to shoulder, through the smoke.

Both sides paused for a moment, taking stock of what stood before them. Then they clashed...slashing, shooting, chopping, and screaming.

An arrow took Flagger in the shoulder, causing him to grunt and fall back. Jana and Malian came running from where they had been under the rampart and caught him as he staggered back from the group. Malian broke the shaft off at the skin, and he turned and rejoined the fray. Thames fired his musket into the charging Iroquois, hitting a man in the chest and knocking him back. Side by side, Eggard and Piotr swung their ax and club. The space around them opened as the Iroquois did not want to get near them. This caused them to bunch up as they climbed the barricade, stumbling over each other into the blades and axes of the other defenders in the entryway.

The tall Seneca war chief, head shaved and painted with green and white stripes, smashed through the barricade and rushed into the melee. With a long-handled metal tomahawk in one hand and a knife in the other, he charged ahead to Piotr's right. Thames met his charge, blocking his tomahawk swing with his empty musket and chopping it downward to block a thrust of the knife. The tall Seneca hooked the musket with his tomahawk and jerked it away from Thames's hands. Thames let it go, snap kicking the man in his stomach and pulling his French ax with the upward-curved head and his knife at the same time. They clashed and parried, blades and ax heads clicking as each tried to gain an opening.

Chogan closed with a fury from the side of an opponent, blocking his ax and shoving him into the arc of Piotr's swing, which smashed his upraised arm, breaking the bones and causing him to fall back away from the fight with his arm hanging limp. The Seneca war chief's slashing thrust of his knife clanked off Thames's blade and slid across his chest, opening a cut through his deerskin shirt. Thames jumped back as the war chief raised his tomahawk to strike. Chogan turned and dove headlong into the war chief with reckless abandon, knocking him sideways into the wall, and grasping his raised wrist. Piotr and Eggard swung wildly, keeping the other Seneca and Oneida from rushing to the aid of their war chief. Thames recovered, striking him in the head with the butt of his ax and grabbing his free hand, wrenching away the knife. Together they pulled him away from the line of his men, dragging him into the village where Huron warriors jumped on him. Chogan ordered the men to keep him there. Dripping blood down his chest, Thames and Chogan turned back to the fight.

The loss of their leader paused the Iroquois. They began to step back away from the barricade. More Huron ran along the rampart to the entryway to the fort, firing arrows at them. The Paquet brothers dispatched an Oneida on the rampart.

Abraham pointed at the entryway and said, "Shoot them, over there!"

Abel, Anton, and Gerard turned away from the wall, took aim, and fired over the heads of the men into the Iroquois in the entryway between the walls. The Iroquois charge broke, turning and fleeing the fort, back to the tree line with arrows and sporadic musket fire chasing after them.

Slowly a ragged, tired cheer rose from the defenders of the Huron village. Thames did not stop this one. They were retreating, and they were defeated. More than fifty Iroquois lay dead in the grassy field around the palisade, and a few more inside or in the entryway. Several Huron and Frenchmen had been killed, including Mason Paquet. Dozens were wounded. Their victory, though, meant survival for the Huron village, the men of the *St. Longinus*, and the wayward travelers that had joined them.

The smell of burnt gunpowder and coppery blood wafted through the village. For half an hour, nobody in the Huron village moved much. Tired, smoke still lingering near the ground, they were exhausted with the shock and chemical surge in their veins. Many men vomited; several just sat down where they were and put their heads in their hands for a few minutes.

Eventually, the needs of the living took precedence, and people began to work. The dead were moved to suitable locations. Mason and the other crewmen who had died were taken to be buried with Captain Linville. Malian and Jana tended to wounds. The arrow in Flagger's shoulder, the slash on Thames's chest, and a dozen others. Jana removed the arrow, as Malian had shown her. Fearing corruption of the wound, she then heated a knife blade till it was orange and inserted it into the hole, cauterizing the wound. Flagger grunted in pain, but stoically did not move. Malian made a poultice of dandelion and burdock root, combining it with wood ash from the fire. She put the sticky paste on Thames's chest and Flagger's shoulder.

The Seneca and Oneida dragged their wounded away, those who could walk, as they disappeared back into the tree line. Houdanaset, chief of the Huron, sent men to follow, just in case they came back. Chogan and his men looted the bodies of the dead Iroquois, taking weapons left on the ground, and giving the coup de grace to any who were immobilized but still alive. They recovered a few more matchlock muskets, and some black powder and shot, as well as knives, axes, and bows. Scalps were not taken, and bodies were not mutilated. The captured war chief of the Seneca, whose name was Ghonka as they came to find out, was tied standing to a stake near the center fire pit in the village. He was given water and food by Huron women and treated respectfully. Piotr wondered what his fate would be.

"He will be tortured, for days, till he dies. They will not let him go, and they will not let him live," Thames said.

Piotr shook his head. "Horrible way to die."

Thames and Flagger sat drinking water from bladder canteens, having had their wounds patched, and nodded in agreement.

"It is...they see it as a source of pride. That man will see it as a test of his courage; the Huron will be grateful to him for resisting. The stronger he is, the more powerful they become. In the end, though, he will succumb."

Piotr did not want to think about that, but Thames wanted information from the tall Seneca. He asked Piotr if he knew any English or

Dutch. Piotr did not. Flagger was able to speak some English, and they went and talked to the Seneca while he stood, tied to a lodgepole stuck in the ground. Piotr watched as they questioned him. Piotr shook his head in disbelief, because it looked like a few men having a civil conversation. They were trying to kill each other a few minutes ago.

Ghonka, fierce-looking with wide cheekbones and warpaint still on his face, stood tied to the stake. He answered their questions. He was even polite. Piotr was certain that he would kill them all if he could get free of his ropes. His politeness was covering his hatred for those around him. He maintained an air of superiority at all times, and clearly disdained the Huron. The way his eyes burned, Piotr thought, he had transferred some of that hatred to the Frenchmen.

The Huron joined the crew of the *St. Longinus* and helped reload the barge. The Frenchmen had unloaded it, fearing it would be taken by the Seneca and Oneida, before they attacked. Everything had been brought inside the Huron palisade. Now, they reloaded it with their fur from the green valley, and the added furs the Huron would trade in exchange for more muskets. Flagger and Thames, his shirt still slashed open and blood-stained across the chest, were busy marking and calculating totals in a small book that Thames kept in his pocket.

The Huron women were incredibly fast and efficient. They made the trip from the river back to the confines of their village palisade, repeatedly carrying fur bales and talking. The Huron men either joined in the labor or kept watch across the Crooked River, lest the Iroquois return. The women wore deerskin shirts painted with purple and yellow designs, and their hair pulled into a ponytail or braided.

Houdanaset, chief of the Huron, came to their barge to speak to Thames in French.

"The Wendat thank you. I thank you. Your sacrifice for the village will be remembered. Stay with us and feast tonight. Celebrate the defeat of our enemy."

Thames smiled and shook forearms warmly, but this offer would be refused.

"We thank you for providing us shelter in your village. We are lucky to have friends such as you. We have to return to our ship. We must get the muskets that you are promised, in exchange for this bounty of fur."

Houdanaset understood, and he wanted the additional muskets. "It is good that we can trade together. I will send my son and a few men to walk with you and bring back the muskets."

They shook hands with promises of more trade when they saw each other again. Chogan and his men walked out ahead of the line of crewmen, scouting the trail ahead.

The bodies of Captain Linville, Mason, and the crewmen who had died in the fight were carried to the mouth of the Cuyahoga, where it fed into the great lake. Piotr joined in the digging of graves in the sandy soil. His hands and feet moved slowly, and everything felt extra heavy. Piotr cared not about the gold or the furs, the riches. Burying Captain Linville felt like losing his home once again. They were leaderless, and he did not know how they would continue.

The crew took to their knees over the graves to pray. Flagger led the prayer, his beard flapping with the breaths of air expelled as he spoke.

"We give back to you, o God, them that you gave to us. Their stay here has come to an end. Your son taught us that life is eternal, and that love does not die. These men came to this place with an open mind and an open heart. They accepted the risk of the journey without fear. They journey to you now, also without fear, for they come to your open arms and the place you have prepared for them. We offer them to you now, in your name, Lord. We ask that you take them in and accept them in mercy."

Flagger covered his face with his hand for a moment, gasping. Then he closed his eyes and rubbed his shoulder with his good arm.

Graves were filled, and the crew of the *St. Longinus* stood around for a long while after Flagger said the prayer, uncertain what to do next.

326

There was silence for a few minutes. Then a murmur began to take hold. The Paquet brothers knelt together.

"Our brother is gone. Our captain is gone. How are we going to sail the ship back with no captain?" Anton asked.

"How can we even get the furs sold? Captain Linville had all of the connections," Abel said.

"Captain Linville owned the boat. Mason would have been the first to know that if we sailed into Saint-Malo with no captain and no boat owner, there would be an investigation from the constabulary," Gerard said.

Abraham nodded. "Jail. We could end up in a Paris jail."

Thames raised his hands above his head to draw their attention. "Quiet down, quiet, all of you... We have lots of things to worry about now, but we can only go one step at a time. First thing, we get back to the ship. We make for Quebec City as fast as we can. With an eye on the trail for the Iroquois."

Thames looked at each man, his eyes circling through the group. He was not a big talker, but he knew that these men needed someone to follow now.

He chose his words carefully.

"Captain Linville spoke of finally being a rich man. He wanted all of us to be rich. Well, these men all died as rich men! Because of what we found, and the work we've done. Right now, we stand here as wealthy men, in possession of a fortune. We will find our way back to Saint-Malo, but we have to keep our wits about us. Stick together, do our jobs. There is no other path."

Eggard stood up. He pulled Piotr up to his feet as well; a tear tracked through the dirt on his leathery cheek and ran down to his beard.

"Of course, Thames is right. All of these questions will be answered in time. We have to face the future together, with courage. I have stood with you, men of the *St. Longinus,* and our new friends," he gestured to Montreaux, Malian, and Jana, "shoulder to shoulder. We will stand together again, as we finish this journey. All the way back to Saint-Malo."

"Aye. Stand together."

A collective reply came from the men as they rose from their knees and began to gather their belongings for the trail ahead. Soon the line was in order, with Thames and Flagger at the front. The Huron scouts went on ahead, and the men began their slow, steady steps away from the Huron village and the green valley that lay beyond it.

Eggard clucked at Mule to get going, and Piotr looked back over his shoulder as they left the gravesite behind. The cattails at the river's edge were swaying with the wind, and small tufts from their seed pods drifted on the breeze. The crude crosses stood on the sandy bank, sticking up like saplings. He blinked away tears, as they walked on the trail back to Quebec City.

## Chapter 22

# MASS AND MAST

Flagger had the worst of it. His right arm was nearly useless now. Jana and Malian had got the arrowhead out quickly, but the hole in his shoulder was deep and he was struggling to regain his strength. Piotr watched as Flagger struggled with daily tasks. Being on the trail with pack animals required the use of two good arms. He flinched and grimaced, but never said a word of complaint. Eggard said that he didn't know how to complain.

He could no longer handle a musket, so Anton gave him Captain Linville's ornate snaphance pistol in exchange for his matchlock musket. Flagger wore it in his belt, on the left side, so he could pull it with his left hand if need be. It was quite a gift, as a pistol of this kind was worth almost a year's income for the average sailor. After two days of walking, Thames had enough of watching him struggle and sent men to stop the fur barge. Flagger took a spot on it, so he could rest. Malian rigged up a sling for him with an old shirt.

Jana took over for him in the line, leading a packhorse loaded down with supplies. She got in line with Piotr and Eggard, near the back of the column. It seemed natural for Montreaux and Malian to take up spots back there as well. When the column stopped to camp at night, the men tended to group with who was near them when they walked. Three campfires would be lit each evening, and they would prepare food over each. Eggard would start their fire and get their dinner cooking, then go to the other two campfires and make sure they had what they needed. Or, at least, what was available. They had eaten a lot of beaver meat and were down to the end of it, and the buffalo strips were entirely gone. Malian, Montreaux, and Eggard fished in the evenings with some success, but this served only to supplement what meat was left. They also hunted with Chogan and his men in the evenings, and gathered from the forest what they could, sometimes returning with an occasional rabbit, but not enough to feed everyone. They were nearing exhaustion of all food stores. Fortunately, they did not have too many more days on the trail before they would be back in Quebec City.

Piotr noticed that Eggard, Malian, and Montreaux were talking together frequently. He could see that a friendship had developed. Eggard was closer in age to Montreaux, and they had a lot in common, having grown up on the sea. Malian was more attached to Montreaux than ever and seemed to enjoy Eggard's company.

He realized that he and Jana were now spending almost all of the days walking together. He liked having her there, listening to her talk, and wondering about her. At night, when he lay down on his buffalo hide, he struggled to sleep, thoughts of her in his head. They seemed to agree on most things. But he was unsure of himself and did not know how to pursue her, or even if he should. After all, he was a nobody. A lost soul. A wanderer with no position in the world. *Maybe*, he thought, *maybe after we return with the furs and the gold. Maybe then.*

Jana found herself leading her packhorse, always getting in line in front of Piotr and his mule. She had thoughts that did not align with returning to be a nun. As the days of working together on the rock, and now walking the trail back to civilization passed, she made a decision. She set her mind to that outcome.

There were two things that kept both Piotr and Jana from acting on their thoughts: hunger, and the difficulty of the trail. They had no time to be scatterbrained on completing all of the tasks that were needed to keep the men moving. Thoughts about the future and the past had to be set aside, as they dealt with the present.

In time, the trail led them back to the river that fed the great falls. The barge and the canoes could not be used any further, as the water flowed so fast, they would be unable to escape the current and be swept over the falls. Decisions had to be made. Thames, having become the de facto leader, asked for input around the campfire.

"We could build wagons, out of the barge," Anton offered.

"Wheels, we have no time to make wheels," Abel said.

"We are pretty much out of food. We could use a day to hunt and gather," Eggard said.

Flagger joined in the conversation. His arm was out of the sling after several days on the trail, but it was still stiff and sore when he tried to use it. It moved slowly, but it moved. "Even if every man carries a large pack of fur, we would be leaving half of it behind. The horses are overloaded already."

Thames said, "It's either two trips, or we make use of travois. Build one for every two men and have them share the load. Or we cache half of the fur and make a trip back."

They started construction of several travois and planned a day of stopping. Hunters were sent out in search of food, and everyone else went to work with lashings and branches. Piotr and Jana found themselves alone together, tending to the animals. As the crewmen set about building, Eggard walked up to Piotr. "After you are done here, you should gather what food you can along the shore of the river. Clams, cockles. Whatever you can find, as I showed you."

"Aye, I can go after I water Mule."

Eggard said, "I, or we?" He looked at Jana unloading the packhorse. Piotr blushed a little.

"Just stay watchful. Do not be...preoccupied," Eggard said, smiling under the dirty white linen tied around his head.

"Well, I won't do anything you wouldn't do," Piotr said.

Together, he and Jana made their way along the riverbank, looking into the sandy shoreline areas. They walked upstream away from camp where the river narrowed and flowed even faster toward the falls.

Eventually Piotr found some sandy stretches that had the telltale tiny holes in the sand. He showed Jana how to dig up the clams with a knife. They were different looking from the ones he and Eggard had found, but similar in size. Piotr found himself talking more than ever before with her. In an hour or so, they had mostly filled a burlap sack that he wore over his shoulder. Piotr bent down and dug out a deep clam, then looked up to see Jana standing next to him with clams in her hands. She smelled of fresh river water and pine needles. He sheathed the knife as he stood up. For the first time, they stood and looked at each other eye to eye. She stepped even closer to place the clams in the bag. Her hands naturally went to his shoulders, and he found his arms wrapping around her waist as if they had a mind of their own. He pulled her close, and they kissed on the shoreline of the fast-flowing river that led to the great falls.

Neither one of them heard the footsteps. Lucien Greely moved almost silently. His long-barreled wheellock pistol had a thick pommel that was meant to be used as a club when needed, and an ornate, hand-carved trigger mechanism. He used it, and it made an audible click as he thumbed it back into the firing position.

Piotr froze, the sound of the trigger echoing into his mind, fogged with sensations he was feeling for the first time.

"Hello again, boy," Greely said.

His thick voice registered in Piotr's brain. His eyes opened wide and he separated from Jana. He was stunned by what confronted them in the form of this hateful man.

"You put a knife to my son's throat. Did you think that would go unanswered?"

"I…I was protecting my people. It was you who threatened us. You had your beef with Thames, and you lost."

"I didnae lose, boy. I was simply waiting for you all to collect the fur for us."

Piotr slowly stepped sideways away from Jana, trying to separate her from the threat. She sensed his intent and moved slowly away. As she stepped sideways, her right hand went to her belt and felt her knife handle in its sheath.

Piotr looked at Greely's eyes. He saw the hateful, callous glare. This man would have no remorse.

"We found the fur. We found more than you can imagine. We can make you and your sons rich men. But you have to let us go. We have to get back to Quebec City to cash in the fur. We can pay you then."

The sardonic smile on Lucien Greely's face told Piotr that Greely was enjoying the confrontation. He was reveling in Piotr's attempt to wiggle out of it. They would have to fight now. He felt for purchase with his moccasins in the sand. Then he made his lunge for the long barrel of the pistol.

Greely was fast, incredibly fast for a man so large. He stepped back and sideways, causing Piotr's lunge to come up short. He brushed away Piotr's grasping hands and smashed him in the chest with the heavy pommel. Piotr fell straight to the ground. The cold, wet sand hitting his face kept him slightly aware. He struggled to all fours, his face just above the fast-moving water at the shore's edge. The world was spinning and he could not get his breath. He had never felt such a heavy blow and thought that his sternum or ribs were probably broken.

Jana drew her knife and lunged at the large man, but Lucien grabbed her by the throat with his meaty fist, holding her up so that her feet were suspended above the sandy shore. He slammed the gun barrel down on her wrist and she dropped the knife. She felt his hand closing around her windpipe.

She fought back, scratching and tearing at his face. He simply extended his long arm and she could not reach him. She reached out at him with her moccasined feet, kicking at his groin, and made solid contact. He grunted in pain; then, dropping the pistol and nearly doubling over, he threw her to the sand. He stood up after a second and grabbed her roughly by her arm, slapping her twice across the face.

"You little bitch!" he screamed.

He spun her around roughly and pushed her down so she was facing away from him on all fours. Then he grabbed her by the back of the neck with one hand, pushing her face down into the sand. His other hand latched onto her backside, thick fingers grabbing her deerskin dress.

Piotr shook his head to clear it and stood to face Greely. His hand found his ax at his belt. He pulled it as he rose to his feet, turning on wobbly legs to attack.

"You won't stay down, eh'"' Greely said, looking at Piotr.

He picked Jana up by her dress and threw her into the current of the fast-moving river. The water hit her with so much force that she was taken downstream in an instant.

Piotr stumbled forward, swinging the ax at Lucien Greely. Greely stepped back and slapped downward with his large hand, knocking it to the ground easily. He grabbed Piotr by the shirt and smashed him across the face with a backhanded fist. Then he spied his pistol on the sand and bent to reach down for it while holding Piotr out with his left hand.

Piotr's head was spinning, he could barely maintain his feet, but his hand went to his belt and found the knife Eggard had given him in the hold of the *St. Longinus* during the storm.

Greely grabbed the pistol, trying to thumb back the hammer with one hand and shoot this impudent bastard in the face. His hand had gotten wet and sandy. He let Piotr's shirt go and used two hands to cock the hammer back. He pointed the gun up at Piotr's face.

Piotr barely stood on shaking legs and his vision had gone blurry, but he pulled the knife from its sheath. He couldn't get his hand to grip it correctly, so he held it backward, with the blade laying downward along his forearm.

Greely pulled the trigger as Piotr's legs gave way. The shot zipped over his head, skipping across the river. A cloud of smoke swirled around the two of them. Piotr's ears rang from the gunshot.

Screaming at his own incompetence, Greely grabbed Piotr by the shirt, steadying him so he could club him to death. He did not see the knife in Piotr's right hand.

He reared back with the pistol to smash his head in. Piotr awkwardly drove the knife into his ample gut, just above Greely's right hip. The thrust had been weak, but the knife was sharp and the blade went home.

Greely grunted in pain, then he shoved Piotr backward into the river with one hand. He knew better than to pull the knife out, so he covered it with his hand and staggered backward toward his horse, leaking blood out onto the sandy soil.

Piotr hit the water flat on his back, his head still reeling. He floated spread-eagled to the surface, the swift current taking him downstream. His only thought was to stay on the surface of the cold water. His body followed Jana downstream toward the great falls.

Jana was fighting to swim toward the shore, but the current was so strong she was being swept down river. She tried to dig her heels into the bottom, but just bounced along and spun. She stole a look back as she fought the current and saw Piotr hit the water after being thrown by the large man. She saw him float to the surface on his back, unmoving.

She frantically redoubled her effort, finally finding purchase with her foot on a large rock under the surface that slowed her enough to get her hands on it. She was able to crouch on it and stop her progress. She saw Piotr coming toward her in the fast current. He wasn't swimming, just floating. Her mind exploded with the fear that he was dead. She waited for the split second that he came near and pushed off the rock toward him, grabbing desperately to get hold on him. She got a firm hold on his shirt and held on while the heavy current pulled them faster and faster.

He woke from his daze to grab onto her in the water, blinking and sputtering, trying to right himself. She kicked her legs hard and rolled over the top of him, positioning herself closer to the shore, kicking and reaching for the overhanging branches with her outstretched hand. Several times she made a grab for them, touching them in the rapid current. Piotr weakly thrashed in an effort to swim toward the shore. She planted her legs down in the neck-deep water, her feet scraping rocks and sticks on the bottom, and pushed them closer to shore. With a last burst of kicks she reached again and grabbed a branch in the entirety of her fist.

She willed herself to hold onto Piotr and the branch, despite her arms being stretched by the current into an iron cross. She pulled on the branch, moving them closer to the shore. A foot on the silty bottom and a step toward shore brought them even closer.

A large, meaty hand grabbed her by the wrist holding the branch. With incredible strength, it pulled her closer to shore against the current. She held Piotr close, dragging him in with her.

Then more hands grabbed her, and the large hand reached out and grabbed Piotr by his buckskin shirt, pulling them both from waist-deep water. Jana found herself coughing and spitting out river water. Someone pulled her up to her feet, taking her back away from the river's edge.

The large hand she had seen was Eggard's. Piotr was being carted by Eggard and Montreaux. She was being held by Malian. She closed her eyes and tried to keep awake, but dizziness was taking hold.

"Breathe. Just breathe Jana, in and out. Just breathe with me."

She heard Malian's voice, but she was blinking as her vision was fuzzy. Slowly she came back to her senses. Piotr was behind her on the ground. Montreaux and Eggard were talking to him as well, trying to get him fully awake. Piotr finally shook his head and rolled to his side, coughing. He saw Jana on the ground and scrambled free of the hold of Montreaux and Eggard, reaching to her, taking her in his arms.

"Jana," he said, weakly.

Jana hugged him back. Finally, she said, "Who was...?"

"Greely. It was Lucien Greely," Piotr said.

Thames was beside himself. The camp had heard the gunshot from Greely's pistol reverberate from upstream. Chogan and his men had spotted them in the river, and Eggard, Montreaux and Malian had sprinted downstream until they got ahead of them and pulled them in.

After hearing of it, Thames and Chogan went upstream to where they thought they were when attacked. They found Piotr's English ax and brought it back. Greely had ridden a horse eastward on the trail away from the scene of the attack. He was leaking a lot of blood for the first hundred yards or so. They lost the trail in the fading light and came back to camp.

"I should have killed him. Back when I had the chance," Thames said.

"You had no cause at the time," Eggard responded.

Piotr was still shaken and was sitting by the fire, drying out, next to Jana. "I may have. I felt the knife go in."

Chogan shook his head. "We found a blood trail. A lot of blood, but he was riding fast. He's hurt. He is not dead."

Eggard waited until everyone had their say. After listening carefully as Piotr and Jana told their tale, it was obvious they were shaken. "You were lucky," he said. "He is an evil man. He attacked you because he feels joy in the suffering of others. He wanted you to suffer, so he could gloat. That is all he really has in the world. If he were a good man, a man with cause, he would have killed you quickly. To be done with it."

Thames said, "When we find him, we will not need to gloat, and we will be quick about it."

In the morning, Piotr and Jana took their spots at the back of the column. Jana had the better of it. She looked back repeatedly as Piotr went through spells of periodic dizziness from the pain in his ribs. Still, they kept up. Piotr used two hands to push the cart. This helped to keep him steady.

They came to the great falls. Even in his current state, Piotr could not help but stare in amazement at the amount of water going over them. He shuddered to think what it would have been like to go over those falls and fall to the rocks below. No one could survive that fall.

They continued downstream to the lake the Huron called Ontario. Following the southern shore, they walked eastward with their load of fur and baskets of gold rocks. In five days, they had made it to the end of the lake and downstream along the river that flowed past Quebec City and out to the Gulf of St. Lawrence. They had made it to the ferry landing. Thames kept the entire group back on the trail as he and Flagger approached cautiously. Piotr, his head having cleared; the four remaining Paquet brothers; and Eggard crept through the woods, flanking the landing area with muskets pointed.

Flagger and Thames found no one there. The ferry was still tied to the crossing rope. There was no one in the cabin on the other side that they could see. There was no one operating the ferry. It was moored on the opposite shoreline.

Thames and Flagger examined the area, unsure if this was a trap, or simply that no one was available to man it. Before they could counsel with anyone, they heard a small splash. Anton Paquet was in the river, swimming across toward the ferry.

He and Piotr had crept along the shoreline quietly and had watched carefully for a few minutes. No one was in the Greely's cabin. No smoke from the chimney, no movement or indication of any one being there.

"I will go across, you cover me." Anton handed Piotr his musket and shrugged out of his backpack.

"I should go, Anton, you are a better shot. You cover me," Piotr said.

"Your ribs are mush. And I'm a better swimmer, anyway," Anton said, stepping into the river's edge. He stopped and turned around.

"If anything happens to me...you make sure Abel and Gerard give those footprints to Easterly."

"Aye, I will," Piotr said.

Anton pushed out from the bank, swimming well with a sidestroke, staying as quiet as possible. The current was moving him downstream quickly, but he looked strong enough in the water. Piotr kept his musket cocked and pointed across the river, scanning for anything. Anton's musket was next to him, leaning against a tree. Nothing showed itself on the other side of the river, other than some branches moving with the wind.

Anton reached the ferry, his head bobbing in the water. He looked around for a bit, then pulled himself up onto the raft. Shaking the water off, he untied the tether and began pulling the ferry across the river on the towline. Still no movement on the other side.

They moved a small group across. As they came ashore, they searched Greely's cabin. The cabin was empty and cleared out. All of the blankets, food, anything of value, was gone. They remained on guard with men spread out and muskets trained on the surrounding tree line. Several crossings later, the entire crew was standing on the river trail of the northern shore. With daylight left, Thames ordered them all up the trail for the last leg of the journey back to Quebec City.

Guillaume had never seen Sister Mary so excited. She busily set up the few pieces of furniture they had. The cabin and the church of logs were nearing their completion. A roof was in place on the living quarters and partially in place on the church itself. Enough of it was done so that most of the church was covered. Father Archembeau had declared that the first celebration of mass would occur on the upcoming Sunday.

Sister Mary, Father Demari, and Guillaume had worked hard at building the church. They had drawn Captain Laurent into the work, and, as his health improved, he and Perdo had contributed to the construction. Strangely, the two of them had not shown up today, nor had Remy Greely.

As things progressed and the building began to take shape, Father Archembeau had even taken part in some of the physical labor, although his effort was short-lived. Still, he wrote letters, and scrounged through the camp, getting the contributions necessary to conduct a mass. The locals were beginning to talk behind his back. They learned that when he showed up, they would be offering more than a piece of meat from the stew pot.

The small back room that would be used for storage was closed up. Lucien Greely had said to leave it, as he wanted to keep some of his things there during the construction. None of them had looked in to see what they were. After all, Greely was giving them the gift of labor from his son and the two Chippewa men. His privacy should be respected.

They climbed the last hill toward the outlying edge of Quebec City. No more than a mile to go. The summer sun was now still high on the horizon, burning orange and red even though they were into the evening. Tomorrow would be a good day, Piotr thought. A good day to load the ship. He was excited to see the ship and the city of logs and tents, as were all the men. A ripple of energy came through the column, as all of them could see the end of this part of the long journey.

Thames was leading the column when he stopped and raised his arm. The men stood still for a second, a few of the horses shuffling their feet anxiously. Piotr scanned the forest, looking deep into the shadows under the canopy as far as he could. He saw nothing, but Mule threw his head up and snorted. He didn't like the smell of something.

"Can you see?" he asked Jana.

She moved to the edge of the trail looking up the hill toward Thames and Linville at the front. She could not tell what the holdup was.

Montreaux gave Malian the reins of the horse he was leading and pulled out his snaphance pistols. Something felt wrong.

Piotr shrugged out of his backpack and pulled his war club free. Eggard looked at him and pulled the two-handed ax out as well.

"I'm going to go up and take a look," Flagger said, pulling out his pistol. He shrugged his shoulder and stretched his arm, then started up the line of men toward the front.

Thames had stopped because there was a person standing on the trail at the top of the hill. Sort of. The person was tied to a stake driven into the center of the trail. Thames could see that whoever it was, they were sagging against the ropes that tied them. He could not tell who it was, because there was a burlap sack over the person's head.

Flagger quick-stepped it back down the line, his right arm hanging, but holding onto the pistol. They huddled about Flagger to find out what was going on.

"They got Perdo tied to a stake, I think. He may be dead already. They look to be trying to set up an ambush on us. Thames stopped us rather than charging ahead, or I think we would be dead already. Don't know how many are up there, but they got the high ground. Chogan, you and your men go into the tree line and see if you can get on their flank. Mr. Montreaux, Eggard, ladies, bring the horses up and we will have you set up off the trail with the travois. You all stay there, protect the fur."

Flagger delivered all of that in a single breath. He looked at his injured arm in disgust. "Piotr, go with Chogan and his men. I am of no use."

Eggard lit the wick of his musket with coals from a cooking pot tied to the wagon. He looked Piotr in the eyes. "Be smart. They will be watching from off the trail."

"Aye."

Piotr stepped off the trail into the bush with Chogan and the Huron men. He looked back over his shoulder. Jana was staring at him. He stared back for a moment.

She silently mouthed the words "be safe." He nodded and followed Chogan into the trees.

Lucien Greely was sweating, and it was not a warm evening. The sweat created a light sheen over his forehead, and his skin tone was not the normal ruddy pink that he had developed as a large man who drinks too much. Instead it was ashen and grey. His cheeks were slightly sunken in. He felt the fever coming over him a day or so after that little bastard had stuck him. How he had let that happen was beyond him. He was getting soft. He should have caved his skull in, but he had wanted to take his time with it. He had pulled the knife out after he had gotten away down the trail and sealed the wound with a hot ember. It hurt quite a lot. Then these fevers started, and he was getting a shooting pain in his side.

Sick or not, he had work to do. Work that gave him a reason to smile.

He had his sons set up the ambush on the trail. He recruited a few of the local farmers who paid for his protection. He also put the two Chippewa men on the flank, so they could shoot anybody who tried to flank them. Those bastards had to come up the hill, and they would find their little friend, along with his partner who took care of the ship. Then they would face musket fire as they charged. He figured most of them would be killed initially, then he and his sons would take the rest. They would take all of that beaver fur and sell it to the next fur trading ship that came to Quebec City.

He looked at his sons, lined up, hiding behind the logs, muskets pointing down the trail. Disappointing, each one of them.

"Let's kill these sons of bitches," he said to no one in particular.

Thames watched from the trail as Lucien Greely stood up from cover behind a downed log and walked out to the center of the trail. He pulled the burlap sack off the head of Perdo, who was tied to the stake. Perdo was alive. Greely pulled his knife from his hip and put it under the chin of the little Italian man who had piloted the *St. Longinus* from Saint-Malo to Quebec City.

Thames raised his hands in the air in front of him. He kept walking up the hill, getting closer to Greely and Perdo. "Greely, I am the one you have the argument with. This man has done nothing to you. Let us settle this, you and I."

"Woodsman, I don't care what you want. You put a knife to my throat. That was your first mistake. Now you and your men are going to pay for it."

Greely's son, the man Piotr had held a knife to on this same trail just a few months ago, came out from behind the log pushing Captain Gilbert Laurent in front of him. His hands were tied behind his back.

Remy pushed him with a knife to his throat and said, "Where is he? The one who held a knife to my throat. Where is he? Where is that bastard who done that?"

Greely looked at his son. This was not exactly to plan, but for once, he was showing some guts. "Remy, uh, this is not the plan. You get back to the…"

"I WANT THAT SON OF A BITCH! Or these two here are going to die now!" Remy shouted with an air of authority that Lucien Greely had never seen before from his son.

In the woods, the two Chippewa men watching the flank were silent, looking at the forest while everything was going on to their left. They saw the Huron warriors and the white man coming up the hill. They were drunk, as they had gotten a jug from Remy for their work at the church. They didn't really want to be here, and they still had more left in the jug. One picked up the jug and gestured with his head. The other man stood up and waved to Chogan. Chogan waved back.

Piotr watched as the two Chippewa men just got up from behind the log where they hid and walked away silently into the forest. They carried their muskets and a jug of whisky. Piotr exchanged a look with Chogan, and they let them go. They crept closer.

Flagger walked closer up the trail behind Thames and pulled his pistol from his belt. "Enough of this..."

He walked toward Greely, raising the pistol as he stepped closer.

"Stop. This man will die. And we will burn your ship down to the waterline!" Greely shouted.

This stopped Flagger where he stood. He held the gun out, aiming down the barrel with his good arm, but he stopped advancing.

Piotr and Chogan crept closer, now completely flanking the men on the trail. Chogan signaled with his hand, and his men fanned out so that they could each take a target. Despite their position, this was still a long shot through the branches and leaves. Piotr and Chogan shouldered their rifles and eased them back to full cock.

On the trail, the Paquet brothers and several crewmen started creeping closer with their muskets, fanning out to both sides of the trail.

Chogan looked at Piotr, his cheek on the rifle stock, and gave a small nod. Both of them sighted down the barrels and squeezed the triggers.

Chogan's shot hit Remy in the neck. It splintered through his spinal column and sprayed out the back where his skull and neck joined. He lurched sideways and fell into Lucien Greely, nearly decapitated.

Piotr's ball hit Lucien Greely in the right shoulder, breaking his humerus just below the shoulder joint and cracking into a dozen pieces that stuck in the bone or blew out the back of his arm through his tricep. His arm dropped the knife he held and he stared down at his son, dead on the ground. He stood for a second in shock, then he turned and ran back up the trail with blood streaming from his arm.

"Shoot them!" he yelled as he ran past his remaining sons and the locals who had been coerced into helping him.

Several of the farmers he had recruited turned and ran into the forest, not willing to be part of a full-on gun battle. His remaining sons fired down the hill.

Thames took a musket ball in his left calf and spun to the ground, grabbing at the wound. Flagger fired the pistol and felt two balls pass through his coat, but he remained unhit. Anton Paquet fired up the hill, striking one of the ambushers in the shoulder. A shot struck him in the toe, blowing a hole in the end of his boot.

Smoke now clogged the trail. Chogan's men fired into the ambushers from their flanked position, killing two of the locals and sending the rest into a panic. They turned and ran into the woods, abandoning the fight. The Huron warriors screamed and charged from the flank, drawing knives and tomahawks in a full sprint. Piotr dropped his musket and picked up his club, running at full speed behind the Huron. Flagger and Eggard and the rest of the men of the *St. Longinus* charged up the hill firing. Eggard charged at full speed with his ax in two hands. They had to break the ambush before they could reload.

With their allies fleeing, the Greely brothers were now badly outnumbered. One turned and ran at a dead sprint, leaving the rest behind. High ground or not, the remaining Greelys did not have time to reload. The charging crewmen, Chogan and his Huron warriors, and Piotr gave no quarter. Jumping over the logs they hid behind, swinging blades, axes, and clubs, they dispatched the rest of the Greelys without mercy or forgiveness.

Thames hobbled up with his leg bleeding, and he and Flagger untied Perdo. They pulled the cloth gag from his mouth while Eggard cut the ropes binding Captain Laurent.

Captain Gilbert Laurent looked at them all wide-eyed for a split second, then jumped to his feet and ran at a dead sprint up the hill, following behind the running Lucien Greely as fast as he could.

Perdo spat the gag out of his mouth and screamed, "The SHIP!"

Lucien Greely knew his life was ending. He saw the amount of blood pouring from the wound on his arm. He knew he would probably not last long. He did not care. He only cared about destroying the thing that would hurt those who had hurt him.

His rage fueled his stride and he ran with purpose, his massive, powerful legs churning. He was sweating hard and breathing so heavy that he could feel his lungs burning. It did not matter, he told himself. Get to the cannon. Kill the ship.

He burst from the trees over the trail to the planks of the dock, then stumbled, skidding to his knees painfully. He tried to push himself up but only had one good arm.

Sister Mary Therese O'Boyle saw him bleeding and trying to rise to his feet, and she immediately came running to help. "Mr. Greely, my goodness, you're hurt, those shots! Let me..."

She turned to look for help as she ran to him, and saw Father Archembeau and Father Demari walking toward them on the far end of the dock. "Help! Help! Mr. Greely is hurt."

Archembeau and Demari looked up in surprise, then hurried toward the elderly nun and the bleeding man. Greely roared and rose to his feet, as Sister Mary tried to take him by the hand. He roughly shoved her to the side, knocking her to the wood of the dock. He charged forward, running to get to the unfinished church.

Demari and Archembeau were taken aback. Father Archembeau stood in confusion, and Father Demari started forward, walking into the path of the charging man. Greely's backhand knocked the young priest off his feet. He simply ran right over the old priest, stomping him into the planks of the dock as he ran by.

Behind him, Captain Laurent was gaining ground. Flagger was leading the crewmen as they followed Captain Laurent.

Greely grabbed a lit lantern hanging on a pole on the dock as he made it to the cabin door. He kicked it open and saw the prize he coveted.

The cannon was loaded and primed. It just needed to be aimed. And lit. He set the lantern down, cursing his wounded arm, and grabbed the cannon with one meaty fist, pulling it from the room and aiming it at the *St. Longinus*, right at the waterline. He picked up the lantern and smashed it into the cabin wall, spraying oil, all of it bursting into flame in the tiny room. He bent down and picked up the candle with his one good hand, and his face twisted into a delighted, evil grin one last time. The wick was still lit.

He put the flame to the primer on the cannon.

As the powder lit, Gilbert Laurent dove headfirst into the barrel of the cannon, knocking it upward off of the intended target. The sixteen-pound ball exploded out of the cannon's mouth and raced through the air, smashing directly into the center mast of the *St. Longinus*. It broke into two pieces halfway through the wooden shaft before exiting out the other side, splintering the mast a few feet off the deck. The rigging held the mast up for a split second, then it tumbled downward onto the dock like a falling oak. The tangled mess of ropes, splintered wood, and crow's nest all came down, crashing into the dock with a thud.

Greely turned, his vision blurring. He heard the cannon go off but was having a hard time maintaining his balance. He tripped and fell backward into the flames that now engulfed the room and were spreading to the rest of the wooden building. His shirt and pants caught fire, and the pain roused him to move. He turned to get away, disoriented and stumbling, and ran into the doorway of the church. Nearly blind and in horrible pain, he fell in a crash against the far wall, where the flames from his clothes licked the wood and spread anew.

# Chapter 23

# THE INHERENT RISK

The church burned to the ground. The fire spread so fast it was impossible to put it out in time, even if they could have organized a bucket brigade. Lucien Greely's remains were found a few days later as they sifted through the building for usable nails. His corpse was unrecognizable.

The *St. Longinus* was still afloat. Though Captain Gilbert Laurent had lost his ship, *The Render*, his heroic action saved the *St. Longinus*.

The ship's mast, however, was in ruins. It was severed a few feet above the deck. The rope and riggings were tangled into a complicated bird's nest of knots.

They set up camp in the field next to the burned church. Flagger and Thames gathered everyone around a stump they had used to fuel a central campfire. Carefully maneuvering his sore arm, Flagger spoke first.

"Good news. The boat didn't sink. And we can untangle the ropes, but the central mast is unsalvageable. We have to rebuild it. This will take weeks, if not months. I doubt it's possible that we can get out before winter arrives. As we have been told, winter comes early to this place."

Thames, still hobbling about with a rag tied around his calf, said, "The governor... he owes an explanation, and then some."

"That he does," Flagger said.

"Has anybody ever replaced a mast?"

Eggard said, "I have repaired one. We used iron bands, wrapped them around and nailed it all back together. It held up well enough."

Thames nodded and then looked around. No one else volunteered any further information.

Montreaux, Malian, and Jana sat at the fire next to Piotr. Jana asked, "Could you use a mast from another boat?"

Thames smiled patiently at her. "We could, but there are no ships here, with a mast for us."

Montreaux and Jana looked at each other. "We know where there is a ship. With a mast it will never use," she said.

All eyes turned to her.

"*The Render*. We left it on a beach in a cove, by a big willow tree," she said.

Montreaux added, "She tells the truth. *The Render* was in one piece, but she is beached for good this time. The mast, sails, and rigging you could use."

They all took a pause and thought about it. Several heads turned to look at the dock with the broken mast laying across it, the collapsed rigging and tangled ropes stretched across the deck of the *St. Longinus*.

Abraham Paquet broke the silence. "It could work, you know. We get the broken mast out. Sail out of here with the two short masts and a partial rigging..."

Gerard Paquet added, "We should be able to at least get four small sails rigged."

Others began to nod. It was possible.

Thames said, "It will be risky, we will be fat and slow, loaded down with fur...and more...there's storms, English ships. Hell, that Swedish ship could still be out there somewhere."

"Necessity is the mother of invention. An old Greek philosopher said that, I believe," Eggard said.

He picked up a jug of whisky at his feet and, after taking a pull, passed it over to Flagger. Flagger took a swig and passed it on. "I saved this for a special occasion," Eggard added.

Piotr said, "You carried that jug all the way down the trail and back again?"

Eggard, Flagger, and Thames grinned.

"Nope." Eggard said.

Piotr smiled ruefully. "I am...a rube."

Thames stood up. "Even if we find *The Render*, and then fix the mast, we still have to get across the sea back to Saint-Malo." He addressed the issue everyone knew but did not speak. "And, we have no one to captain the ship. I have sailed on oceans all my life, but I am no captain. Linville, God bless him, knew the sea like the back of his hand. He knew how to sail a ship, by God...without him, well, I have my doubts."

The group sat glumly. They had not properly grieved for their dead. There had been no time. The loss of their leader left a hole in their hearts, but it also left a hole in their thinking. Linville was the final arbiter, the decision maker, and the organizer. He had balanced the risk and reward for the group. Now they had no real leader. Everyone respected Flagger, and the same could be said for Thames. They even feared him a little. But they had all followed Linville.

Ghonka slept with his back against the pole with one eye open. His hands were tied to it, behind his back. His eye spied the small ax that was left in the firewood. The Seneca war chief had survived for eight days now. His back, arms, and chest were covered in cuts and welts from the beatings. His face had a shallow open cut across the cheekbone and forehead. His nose was broken and dried blood coated his nostrils. It was painfully swollen, twisting up his features. Each day, they untied him and made him run the gauntlet. Two rows of people armed with switches and sticks. He ran through the middle as they struck him and yelled at him. He had done it without complaint, only dodging the larger blows from people with heavier sticks.

They kept him fed and gave him plenty of water. The young boy who brought him his food had grown less and less afraid of him. When he asked the boy to untie his feet so he could sleep better, the boy refused. He asked again, each night, just so he could get a little sleep. The boy refused again. On this night, he asked if he would just loosen them a little. The boy agreed to that and loosened the knot on the lashings so that he could move his feet a little. Then he left to go to sleep.

He waited, dozing against the pole, until deep in the night. The moon was at a quarter, and it was very dark. Perfect. Each night, he had been working the lodge pole back and forth, loosening it a little at a time. Tonight, he grabbed it with his hands tied behind his back and brought his loosely tied feet under him in a deep squat. He stood up while holding onto the pole, pulling it straight up out of the ground. He did not grunt with the strain because he could not afford to make any sound. He shuffled backward, carrying the pole behind his back, and fell as silently as he could to the ground. He shimmied and wormed until his bound hands were free of it. He crawled to the firewood pile and pulled the small ax free. He flipped it over so the blade was up, holding it on the ground between his feet. He sawed back and forth until the rope that had tied his hands for eight days was cut. He did the same for his bound feet.

Flexing his fingers, he took the ax and silently made his way through the village to the palisade entrance. He walked slowly and stood tall. In the dark, he looked just like any tall Huron warrior walking in the scant moonlight. He silently waited for the young man guarding the entrance to turn and walk away. Normally, he would have buried the ax in the back of his head, but he did not trust himself in his depleted condition.

The guard moved away from the entryway, walking down along the palisade wall. Ghonka waited a moment, making sure not to make a sound. Looking back over his shoulder, his twisted features curled into a snarl and his eyes blazed with hate for the Huron. They had defeated his warriors and tortured him, making him suffer for days. He would take his revenge against them, and those who allied with them. He turned and ran through the entryway, disappearing in the darkness outside the palisade wall.

The crew set to work removing tangled ropes and the broken mast. Their future was uncertain, but this work had to be done. It was difficult labor, but they were used to difficult things. The dock became busy with activity, while happy reunions and sad goodbyes were taking place.

Piotr and Thames helped Chogan and his men load the travois with muskets, lead, wicks, patches, and powder. They tied them down with cordage, and gripped their forearms to say goodbye. They gave Chogan and his men one of the pack horses as well, stacked high with muskets. Chogan held on to the forearm handshake a little longer, looking Piotr in the eye.

"You could come back with us, if you want. Come live with the Huron. You and that woman," he glanced at Jana, "raise your children to be strong!"

Piotr smiled and said, "That actually sounds pretty good..."

Thames grinned and clapped Piotr on the back. "He has work to do with us, before he can go off with the woman."

Chogan smiled. "What work could be more important?" He laughed, shaking Piotr's arm. "I think we will see each other again someday, brave Piotr. Live well."

They waved as they walked off, travois full of muskets in tow.

Piotr understood that he was doing what he needed to do for his people. He had made the journey, befriended them, and fought with them, all to protect his people. *He is an impressive man*, Piotr thought. *Even if he is cocky*.

The reunion for the remaining crew of *The Render* was more than emotional. They gathered on the dock near the *St. Longinus* later in the day. Raul Montreaux and Gilbert Laurent hugged and kissed each other on each cheek as long-lost friends, each amazed to see the other alive again. They were joined by Guillaume, Sister Mary, and the two priests, bruised and banged up by their encounter with the charging Lucien Greely, but all back on their feet.

Sister Mary grabbed Jana in a warm hug. She was so excited to see her alive she broke into tears.

"When you were pulled into the water, I was so stunned," she said through gasping sobs that Jana felt through her hair, "I thought you were gone. Taken from us. Then Mr. Montreaux went in right after you…and then he didn't come back…we heard him shout and tell us to go. How did you ever survive, and make your way?"

Jana hugged her deeply in return.

"So many times, I thought we would never return, or even live." She felt hot tears escape the corners of her eyes and trace down her cheeks. "If not for Mr. Montreaux, and Malian, I would never have returned."

Malian stood quietly and patiently off to the side of the group. Jana broke the hug long enough to wave her over, and Sister Mary's full-body hug greeted her with no pretense or hesitation.

"I have you to thank!" Sister Mary said as she hugged Malian, more tears flowing.

Sister Mary said, after finally releasing Malian, "Mr. Montreaux, I am happy to tell you that the men of the *St. Longinus* have agreed to take anyone who sailed on *The Render* back to Saint-Malo. They said that Captain Gilbert saved the ship, and that none of us would have to pay a passage fee on the *St. Longinus* ever."

"Thank you, Sister Mary. I have news...Gilbert...in that regard. I am not going back to Saint-Malo," Raul said to Captain Laurent.

Sister Mary looked at him and then turned her eyes to Jana.

"I am happy for you, Mr. Montreaux. You deserve happiness. When you dove in the water, that took courage. You have decided to end her commitment to the church, then?"

Montreaux looked confused for a moment, then handed the answer off.

"Uh...Jana is an incredible young lady, Sister, she can speak for herself."

Jana blushed lightly, her cheekbones glowing. "I, um, have made a decision to go back to Saint-Malo, and then back to home. I, we, have some matters to address. I will be going back on the *St. Longinus.*"

Sister Mary looked around, now confused herself. Then she spotted Piotr walking up the dock to help with the mast. "Oh! So it's that young buck with the shaggy brown hair, then. He seems a good lad."

"I think he is."

"It is no small thing, to end your novitiate. Are you sure, Jana?"

"No, I am not sure about anything, anymore. But I think this is where I am supposed to go. So many times we came close to danger, and somehow God brought us back to this place. I believe my place is going to be with that young man."

"So, why are you staying?" Father Demari asked Montreaux.

"Malian," Montreaux said.

Malian smiled and Montreaux took her arm.

"Ah...I see, pleasure to meet you, mademoiselle!" Demari said. He and Father Archembeau exchanged a look. Then Father Demari said, "I can tell you all now, I will be staying here in the New World as well. I will be restarting our efforts here, with support from Sister Mary. Once Father Archembeau gets back to Paris, he will inform them of our efforts here. This place, it needs a good nun, and a good priest!"

Sister Mary added, "And we have a church to rebuild!"

Father Archembeau said, "I will be on that ship, mast or no mast. I have letters to deliver, explaining what has happened here to Cardinal Richilieu."

Gilbert Laurent took Montreaux's hand and said, "I will inform the trading company of your incredible courage, Raul, regarding *The Render*. I will see to it that you are cleared of any wrongdoing in the records."

Montreaux shook his hand. "Captain, no one did anything wrong. Every decision was a good one...I am staying, simply because I have a reason to stay."

"You do, Mr. Montreaux. Yes you do," said Captain Gilbert Laurent.

The group of lost souls now reunited talked for a good while longer on the dock, each explaining their story to the others as they tried to make sense of all that had happened to them. Eventually, the need to prepare for their parting overcame the desire to see each other again.

Malian and Jana stepped away from the group as they gathered Jana's supplies for the journey on the *St. Longinus*.

Jana said, "Montreaux is a good man. A truly good man. I wish nothing but joy for you and him. Where will you two go?"

"Eggard has told us of a village to the northwest. He lived there years ago. There are other people, like us, living together. We are going to build our own cabin there, together. It's far away from the Iroquois, far north of their territory. Raul and I, both of us have no one else. But we can have each other."

"You can and you will, Malian. Thank you for saving us, thank you so much."

They hugged as sisters.

Montreaux also spoke with Thames and Flagger about the matter, letting them know that he would not be going back on the *St. Longinus*.

Thames understood, with one reservation. "She is a beautiful and brave woman, Mr. Montreaux, and I wish you the best. I am concerned, though, that our only link to the location of *The Render* is a young woman with no real seagoing experience."

"You will be fine with Jana guiding you, but I think I have another way to help solve your problem," Montreaux said.

"We are open to any solutions at this point."

Montreaux waved Guillaume over and introduced him. "Jana knows the cove where *The Render* sits. Guillaume piloted the longboat from the cove to Quebec City. In the dark. With the two priests as oarsmen. He knows the miles of coastline between here and that ship, and he has as much experience at sea as I do. Captain, he would be an excellent mate on any vessel. He and I have sailed together on many voyages, and I trust him as a brother."

They shook hands, and Thames asked one question. "Is there any chance you have replaced a mast?"

"No, sir, but I was a shipbuilder before I was a sailor. I have worked on them. I know it's not an easy task, but it can be done," Guillaume replied.

"Well, you are welcome aboard, Guillaume."

The loading of the ship continued as they removed the tangled ropes and the broken mast. Piotr and Eggard carried the gold-infused rocks in their baskets, with a blanket draped over them, to store in the hold. Thames pulled a few of the gold rocks out and gave them to Montreaux and Malian.

"An equal share, for both of you," he said. "I only ask, please wait until we are well away before you reveal this to anyone here. I wish to leave without incident."

They nodded, and Montreaux said, "We understand." He placed the rocks in a pouch, and handed them to Malian, who placed them in her backpack as they headed out of the hold.

Flagger saw the exchange as he walked down the steps of the hold. His arm still hung from his side; he had regained some movement, but not the full use of it.

He said, "I will be taking my share as well, old friend."

Thames turned, deeply surprised. "Flagger, I...we have so much fur to sell...we will finally have money! Real money. You will be able to do whatever you want back in Saint-Malo."

Flagger smiled under his thick beard. "I can do what I want here. It's a new world. This place...it has a new order of things. It's on you, not who you are or who your father was. And, with my arm...I can't do the work. I will be a liability." He shrugged his shoulders and the stiffness in the arm was evident.

"Flagger, we need you...you have more knowledge than…" Thames realized he was reacting incorrectly. Flagger had the right to make his own decision, as did every person on the ship. He had made it, and it should be respected. He looked down at the deck and breathed a heavy sigh. "What will you do?"

"I will be staying on with Marta. She has asked me to join her in her ventures. Seems there will be a new ferry operation opening up soon."

Thames's eyes moistened, and he offered his hand to shake. "I wish you well, my friend. You are the best seafaring man I have sailed with. You answered every call." He gave Flagger his share of the gold and added some extra to cover his share of the fur sales.

Flagger said, "You know, the answer to the problem of a lack of a captain has been staring us in the face. Captain Laurent, from *The Render*. Make him your captain for the return journey. He knows his own ship, so his knowledge for the mast rebuild will be priceless. He has years of experience at sea, as a successful captain. He needs the money. Give him an equal share, same as everybody else. Well worth it if he gets you back to Saint-Malo. And, Montreaux says he is a good captain, which is good enough for me."

"It had occurred to me, sort of, that this could be the right move. I was thinking about asking you to become captain...but, this might work."

They shook hands as coworkers, and as friends. They both knew what his departure meant.

"Listen, you take the pack horses. Give Mule to Montreaux and Malian....and there is one last job I need you for..." Thames said. He pulled out one of his pistols. "Let's go pay Governor Easterly a visit."

"I'm with you."

Thames headed up the stairs and looked back when Flagger stayed where he was, staring into the darkness of the hold. He understood and went up to the deck.

Flagger stared into the grain of the wood in the hold. The old planks were hard as stone. He put his hand on the wood of the main beam, worn smooth over the years. The weight of the loss of Captain Linville was heavy in his heart. He could feel his presence in the hold of the ship, and spoke to him one last time.

"Well, Captain, she is still set to sail, broken mast and all. You put together a fine crew this time, sir. A fine crew. Best I ever sailed with. They will finish the job for you. I wish that you could see that... I wish you could hear the bells when they arrive at Saint-Malo one last time. When the crowds gather at the dock for a ship come home. When the journey ends. You would have been proud of 'em."

He stood a moment longer, then left the hold for the last time.

Their boots and moccasins thumped on the planks of the stairs as they approached the governor's quarters. Thames, Flagger, the Paquet brothers, Piotr, and Eggard walked purposefully. They were all armed to the teeth, carrying knives, pistols, axes, muskets, and one unusual club. Thames beat the door with his open palm, but no one answered. He stepped back to kick the door, but his leg was sore, and he hesitated.

"Allow me," Eggard said. He stepped to the door and kicked it with his massive boot. The wooden latch burst open, splintering into a thousand pieces. The group entered, but the office was empty. They looked about the room; everything was in order, but no one had been here for at least a couple of days. The Paquet brothers were the most sorely disappointed, as they were carrying the fossilized footprint to sell. There were four bottles of whisky on the desk, and a letter, written by Easterly in a flourishing script. Anton picked it up and gave it a once-over.

"What's it say?" Flagger asked.

"It seems he knew we were coming..." He straightened the paper and held it up to the light of the window.

"Dear Captain Linville," Anton paused and sighed, "I regret not being here in person. My duties have called me away. I heard about what happened to the *St. Longinus*, and to poor old Greely. I suppose he had it coming, given what he had done. Rest assured, there will likely be no official investigation from the governor's office. Please accept my token of appreciation. These four whisky bottles are from Scotland, and they are all considered to be that land's finest production. Please take them with my regards, your friend, Governor Johann Easterly."

"He is a clever bugger," Abraham said.

The Paquets began scrounging through the office, opening cupboard doors, and looking into shelves. Most were empty. Gerard opened a cabinet in the corner of the room, and in it were two fine-looking wheellock pistols. They were ornate, inlaid with silver and copper. Patches, balls, and powder, and extra springs were stored with them. He pulled them out, setting them on the desk by the letter. Anton pulled open the desk drawer and found a quill and ink.

"I suppose he would want to trade these anyways."

He bent to the task of writing on the back of the letter left by Easterly. It was slow and awkward, but he finished and signed it with a flourish.

"What did you write?" asked Abel.

Anton dug through his backpack and dropped the heavy fossilized footprints onto the desk with a thud. Then he gathered the ornate pistols, shot, balls, patches and flint into his pack.

"I told him he paid for it."

They gathered the whisky bottles and headed out the door with a broken latch.

The *St. Longinus* pushed off with Perdo at the helm, and two short masts rigged as best they could to give them access to the wind. The small Italian pilot expertly worked them away from the dock into the current. They left with a new captain, the uncertainty of finding *The Render*, and still having to replace the central mast. As Captain Linville once said, every journey has its risk and reward.

Piotr and Jana stood in the sunshine and blue sky, waving to the people gathered on the dock. Several locals had come to watch them go. Montreaux and Malian waved back. Flagger and Marta waved, too. As they got farther into the river, Marta grabbed Flagger's bad arm and held it up in the air, waving it for him.

Piotr yelled out, "Take care of Mule!"

Montreaux and Malian yelled back, "We will!"

Eggard stood next to Piotr and Jana. He waved back at the people on the dock as the boat drifted farther out, then turned and leaned down toward Piotr. "I thought you would stay, young one. I thought you would stay here and build your life."

Piotr and Jana looked at each other. He took her hand in his. "We have to go back, Eggard. To Saint-Malo, and all the rest of the way. We have to find out what is left for us."

Anton Paquet joined them on the deck in the sun. "Saint-Malo, you say? We may not even make it out of the St. Lawrence...we have no proper sails, we have to find a lost ship, just to use the salvaged parts, and then we have to sail across the sea!"

Anton grinned and they smiled, joining him. Piotr now understood why Anton and his brothers were always laughing. Together, they watched from the deck of the *St. Longinus* as the people waving on the dock grew smaller in the distance, and the currents carried them toward their future.

# TO BE CONTINUED IN...

# ONE HOUSE

HAVING FOUND EACH OTHER in the New World, Piotr and Jana return to the Old World in search of the remnants of the lives they left behind. They arrive with the hopefulness of youth, but are met with the reality of being simple Commoners in a land designed for the Nobility. Together they will fight to build their own place in the world and create a future that will last for generations.

Follow Piotr and Jana's story in *One House*,
to be released worldwide in the winter of 2022.

# AUTHOR'S NOTE

The loss of the American Chestnut Tree in North America is probably the greatest ecological disaster to strike any forest in the world. It is estimated that four billion chestnut trees occupied the eastern woodland forest in North America. Their long, knot-free wood provided the structure for homes, barns, fences, and furniture in early America and pre-America. Their nuts provided food for wildlife and people for centuries. They were the dominant tree species in the eastern forest ecosystem well into the mid-1800s.

With the introduction of the chestnut blight, they were gone in forty years. They have managed to avoid extinction by sending up stump sprouts that grow twenty or thirty feet high then succumb to the blight and die.

The American Chestnut Foundation is working to restore these trees to the forest. You can find out more about their mission at acf.org.

# ACKNOWLEDGMENTS

This book is a work of fiction but a labor of love. The following people gave their energy and time in support of the creation of this book. Their support, feedback, and opinions were incredibly helpful.

Dr. Deborah Gordish
Jamie Chmielewski
Jack Chmielewski
Grace Chmielewski
Mary Chmielewski
John Stock, Esq.
Heather Stock, illustrations
Christine Naylor
Emily Hitchcock
Devin Ortega
Lisa Page

The creation of this novel was a great journey of learning and growing. I thank each of these people for their patience and faith.

# ABOUT THE AUTHOR

 JIM REDWOOD grew up in Delaware County, Ohio. He spent the summer days of his youth running through the forest and farm fields surrounding his family home. He has an undergraduate degree in Education from Bowling Green State University and a Master's degree in Special Education from Ashland University. His career as a teacher focused on teaching reading and writing to students with dyslexia and dysgraphia. His knowledge in the field of literacy, and a fondness for storytelling, led to an irresistible urge to write and the development of his first novel, *Two Ships*. When he is not writing, a walk in the woods is still his favorite escape.

Connect with Jim at his website: JamesRedwoodAuthor.com.

CPSIA information can be obtained
at www.ICGtesting.com
Printed in the USA
LVHW032156181221
706127LV00001B/43